THE UNENDING WAR

BY

IAN WOOD

Hi Rhys

I hope you enjoy reading this as much as I enjoyed writing it.

Cheers

[signature]

03/03/2023

1

DEDICATION

This novel is dedicated to

KOBE

My friend

ACKNOWLEDGEMENTS

I would like to give special thanks to my father, Dr Ritchie Wood, who read the first draft and proof read the final draft. He made many invaluable suggestions. Ilona Fenton read an early draft and made a correction.

My further thanks to Dr Ritchie Wood who also drew the map and diagram.

Thanks also to Mike Collins of Freakhouse Graphics for the cover art.

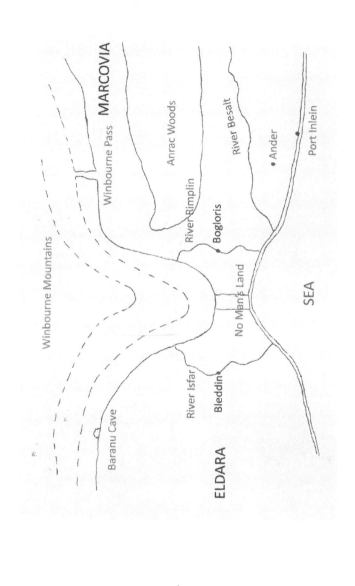

CHAPTER 1

The Assessor sat in the peasant hut, tapping his delicately manicured fingers on his knee.

'Crying won't help. You need to look at me. Do you know who I am?'

The peasant woman looked up, bleary eyed. 'You are an Assessor.'

'I am the Assessor, the only one, I will assess your baby. There is nothing you can do.'

The sobbing peasant woman buried her head back into her hands. Who had betrayed her, who had told them? After all, her baby was so young, only three months old. It was bound to happen, but the people in the village were her friends, or so she had thought, and it had happened far too soon.

'Look at me!'

Again, she looked up.

'Do your baby's hands glow with blue light?'

'I don't know.'

'How can you not know? It's your baby, it's a simple question. Do you want your baby removed because you are an unfit mother?'

5

'You will remove him, anyway,' she conceded.

'So he does have glowing hands, why else would we remove him?'

'I don't know.'

The Assessor turned to one of his guards and told him to book a room as it was now obvious they were going to spend the night here. Ander wasn't a bad village, a break from the major cities, a pleasant enough way to spend the night, he supposed.

He looked out of the window. 'Do you know what makes me such a good Assessor?'

'No,' she replied.

'Pain.'

'Pain?' she asked.

'Yes, pain. I know how to inflict pain. I am very good at it. Pain reveals all. It helps me to assess.'

He turned to the other guard. 'Markus, take her away. She won't co-operate. Leave me alone with the baby.'

Markus started to move towards her.

'No,' she screamed, 'I'll tell you anything.'

'Not anything. The truth.'

'I can show you.'

'Go ahead.'

She turned to her baby.

'Make grass,' she said. 'You like grass.'

The baby looked at her with those big adoring eyes that only a baby can have for his mother and started to move his hands. They moved together rather awkwardly. Slowly, a blue glow shone between them. The baby moved his hands, the blue glow becoming larger. He gurgled and jerked his body.

Images of blue magical grass hung over his crib. He gurgled happily as his pudgy hands moved between them, moving them softly as if in a gentle breeze.

'Bloody Hell!' said Markus.

'Markus. Shut up and get outside,' said the Assessor.

Markus walked sheepishly out of the peasant hut.

'May I apologise for my Guard's outburst,' said the Assessor. 'It was most unseemly. Now, where were we?'

The baby continued to gurgle, playing with the blue grass, moving his hands clumsily through the blades.

'That's very good.'

'He likes grass,' said his mother.

'You do realise that we need him.'

'Yes, it is the way of the world.'

'We all must make sacrifices for the war. Tell me,' the Assessor said slowly, deliberately, carefully, 'um, does he always listen to what you say?'

'Oh no!' she laughed, a tear in her eye. 'He is only a baby, they are very naughty, you know.'

The Assessor laughed. 'How old are you?'

'I am sixteen.'

'And his father?'

She hesitated. 'I'm not sure.'

'All right, that's all right. I don't suppose you know where his father is now?'

'No, he travels.'

'A soldier?'

'A travelling salesman. He doesn't even know that he has a son.'

'That's all right.' The Assessor was thinking. The father's out of the way, that's convenient. He stood up and looked out of the hovel's window. Brown paper, torn at the edges, was used for panes instead of glass. What to do, what to do? He looked out across the fields, the corn ripening through the brown haze, swinging in the wind. It might even be idyllic, if it weren't for the misshapen peasant hovels dotting the landscape. He had to have the baby, it was going to happen, but the mother, it was unprecedented, but hey, how did precedents start, they had to start somewhere, but this was a one off, unique, he couldn't mess it up. First, he had to try and work out exactly what was going on.

He walked over to the baby. 'Make grass, you like grass,' he said, as kindly as he could.

Nothing. He repeated the request. Nothing.

The peasant woman laughed. 'He won't listen to you. I'm his mother.'

So, it was like that, was it? A plan began to form in his mind, to hell with precedent.

'I want you to bring your baby with you to the Inn tonight. You can stay the night with us. I have some thinking to do and then well, I'll make you a proposition.'

'What proposition?'

'I have to think first, then the proposition will follow.'

'But why at the Inn? I live here.'

'Think of it as a holiday.'

'A holiday? I live here.'

Not for much longer, he thought. If I get my way and I usually do, the only time you'll see this godforsaken village again is if you are on a bloody holiday.

'It'll feel like a holiday. It'll be fun.'

'The Inn?' The Assessor obviously knew very little about fun or the Inn, probably both.

'Look. Just come with us.'

'Do I have a choice?'

The Assessor had had enough. He was not used to bargaining with peasants. Actually, he was not used to bargaining at all. Even the King took him seriously and he needed time to think.

'Right. You have a choice young lady. You can walk peacefully with your baby to the Inn and enjoy your holiday or we'll drag you there, tie you up and you won't enjoy anything. Understand?'

'OK. I'll come.'

'Good. I knew you'd see sense.'

She stooped down and picked up her baby who gurgled quietly, oblivious to the fact that adults were talking about him, determining his future. No doubt they'll tell him all about it one day, how they had talked, the Assessor thinking, why they'd done this great thing and offered him this wonderful opportunity, as adults do to adolescents when they're trying to convince themselves that all their decisions were made with the child's best interests in mind.

But, that was for another day, a day of talking around a log fire. Today, they just walked, silently, picking up Markus who had been guarding the door. They walked down the dusty road towards the Inn. The Assessor, imperious in his ermine robes, Markus clanging along in chain mail armour, the peasant woman carrying her baby close to her breast. Peasant eyes peered around corners and curtains at them. No doubt, one pair of eyes showed signs of guilt ameliorated by the silver coins received for informing the authorities of the baby with the blue glowing hands, who liked grass.

They continued down the dirt track until they came to the Inn, a wooden building which was easily singled out in the village as possessing the unique property of having two stories and a series of symmetrically arranged windows. There was no sign illustrating two headed Kings or horseshoes; they were unnecessary.

The other guard, Andrius, was waiting by the entrance. 'Sire, I have booked us two rooms,' he looked at the peasant woman, 'um, will that be enough?'

The woman looked questioningly at the Assessor. 'Don't worry,' he said reassuringly, 'you will be quite safe with me. One child for a woman of your years is quite enough.' She looked relieved. 'Andrius, just make sure there are two separate beds for me and the woman, you two can make do as you see fit.'

Andrius walked off with a peculiar grin on his face and Markus started to follow him.

'Wait!' ordered the Assessor. The two guards accustomed as they were to taking orders waited just inside the doorway.

12

'Andrius, you, the woman and the baby will go and see the rooms. The mother and child will go inside and you will stand outside. Do you understand?'

'Why, of course, Sire.'

'Andrius, you will make sure that they are safe. Is that clear?'

'Of course, Sire.'

'Well, that's it. Off you go.'

Andrius led away the peasant woman with her baby. He wasn't quite sure what to say, so he said something silly and called her Ma'am. She was rather shocked by this and was not too sure what a Ma'am was but it sounded important. Apparently, he was going to help her if she needed anything. It went unsaid that 'All I want is to go home with my baby' didn't count as anything so she decided that the best course of action was to say nothing, sit in her room and play with her baby.

The Assessor turned to Markus who was somewhat bewildered and wanted to desperately know what he had done wrong. 'You will come with me to the bar. I need to run some ideas by you.'

Now the exam for being a guard was not particularly hard, it was actually rather easy given that there wasn't one. Well, not for ideas, anyway. It was more a case of looking tough, following orders and being good at hitting people. Markus, broad shouldered, six foot four inches tall and with large fists powered by bulging muscles was rather good at this. The whole idea thing had never been tested but he rather suspected the reason he passed the taking orders part rather well was because he hadn't many ideas of his own interfering with what his masters wanted him to do. He did know that when other guards complained he didn't really know what they were actually on about.

Now, this Assessor character seemed to be one of those folk people called intelligent. Markus had been in similar situations like this before and he had a tried and trusted tactic – agree with anything that was said. He had never been in trouble for agreeing with suggestions, however little he understood them.

So he agreed to go to the bar.

While the Inn never needed a sign, the bar definitely did. It looked as if someone had randomly nailed a large piece of wood across one sidewall of the lobby. No one was there. The whole mystery was only solved by the sign nailed at an angle on the wall saying 'BAR'.

The Assessor sighed, desperately hoping they served anything other than mead as he hit the bell. The receptionist walked across the room and smiled sweetly.

'Yes, Sir. Can I get you anything?'

The Assessor looked around and could see no beverages in sight.

'What do you have?'

14

'Mead.'

'Anything else?'

'No Sir, I'm afraid not.'

'Oh, dear me!'

'It's very popular. All the locals like it.'

'I can tell. They're obviously all in here,' he said sarcastically.

'I'm sorry. Monday is our quietest night.'

'Of course it is. Right, Markus, what'll you have?'

Even Markus didn't have to hesitate for this question. 'Mead, Sir.' He desperately hoped and doubted that every other question would be this easy.

'Right, two bottles of your finest mead. Well, I suppose that's a ridiculous request, you only have one type, don't you?'

'I'm sorry Sir, does it come in different types?'

'I don't know and I doubt I'll find out here. Just give us two bottles and some privacy.'

She wondered off and came back with the two bottles and two glasses. The Assessor threw some money in her general direction, felt he was being rude, so he said 'Thank you.' He waited for her to go back to the Reception. Why shouldn't she, there were so many people here at the Bar?

'Markus, you are probably wondering why I am talking to you about this idea of mine.'

'Yes, Sir.' That was definitely easy to agree with.

'I have a difficult decision to make and it would help me to discuss it with someone. Now ordinarily, I would find someone else, but you are all that is available.'

'There is Andrius, Sir.'

The Assessor looked at him grimly. Markus immediately realised his mistake, he hadn't agreed and now there was the grim stare.

'Fine, fine, that is irrelevant. Now, you shouted out at the baby.'

'Yes, Sir.'

'What were you thinking?'

Markus looked at his feet for inspiration and found none.

'Come on man, you're not in trouble, why did you shout out 'Bloody Hell!''

'I was surprised by the grass, Sir.'

'The grass?'

'Yes, Sir.'

There was a pause. The Assessor thought if this idiot says he was surprised that the grass was blue instead of green he was going to hit him. The Assessor took a gulp of mead. It was beginning to be clear if Markus had two brain cells to rub together they were separated by the vast chasm of emptiness inside his skull and their chances of finding one another were being further reduced by the mead.

The Assessor calmed. He realised if he could make this simpleton understand his reasoning anyone could and that was the important thing. The King needed to understand.

'Don't worry. What was it about the grass?'

'Well, it was blue,' the Assessor was glad he had calmed down, 'but that is to be expected with magic. Magic is blue.'

'And why was that surprising,' the Assessor asked.

'It was grass. All the other babies we have assessed can't make grass, they can't make anything, just a bit of a blue glow.'

'Excellent. What else?'

Markus was at a loss.

'The mother, Markus, the mother.'

'Yes, yes, he listened to his mother.'

'Isn't that remarkable?'

'Well, she is his mother and he does disobey her, she said so, children are like that.'

'Children, Markus, children. Is that a child or a baby?'

'A baby.' Markus looked into the distance. Maybe the distance was more inspirational than his shoes or maybe his two brain cells collided in an avalanche of understanding.

'Bloody Hell! The baby understood her! How can that be possible?'

'Exactly,' the Assessor slapped his thigh 'and, moreover, the baby understands no one else. That is why I am bringing the mother with us. This could be the most powerful mage we have ever encountered and we need his mother to help us teach him.'

'That's why she's with us!'

'Exactly.'

They returned to their drinks and sat silently, happy. The Assessor contented that if he could make this Dunce understand, the King and His Court wouldn't be a problem. Marcus, delighted he had negotiated the complex corridors of ideas with some success. It gave him confidence.

'Sir, could I ask you a question?'

'If you wish.'

'You said you would hurt her baby to see if he was capable of magic. Would you have done that?'

'Yes, but mothers usually back down as you saw.'

'But, Sir, would you have done it?'

'Of course,' the Assessor smiled, 'I'd have pinched the baby lightly on the arm, that is all.'

19

'Oh, thank you, Sir.'

'Markus,' the Assessor paused and looked up at him, 'I do my duty, but I try not to be a cruel man.'

'Thank you, Sir. It's an honour to serve you.'

'Well, thank you, Markus. Shall we retire?'

'What? Stop working? We are too young.'

The Assessor laughed. 'I meant go to bed.'

'Oh, yes, Sir. See you in the morning.'

The Assessor went to the room where the woman sat on the edge of her bed with her baby. She was smoothing his brow and singing the simple peasant song her own mother had taught her.

The Assessor sat on his bed and looked into the woman's large brown eyes. He noticed for the first time that she had long, flowing, somewhat curly, jet black hair.

'I am here to offer you a choice.'

'I have had no choices so far.'

'That is true. You know the rules. Everyone does. The baby comes with us and you know there is nothing else that can be done. The Kingdom desperately needs mages. It is wartime and it is your duty to give him to us. He will be well fed, educated and looked after. That is his future. He will become a magic wielder, perhaps a great magic wielder, his destiny is to become a mage.'

'What then is this choice that lies before me?'

'It concerns you and your future. You can stay here with your friends and live out your life in this village.'

She looked away and then at the floor. 'Some choice. Someone betrayed me and my son.'

'True and it is likely you will never find out whom. Now, your second option. You can come with us.'

'What? I am just a peasant woman. What could you want with me? You want my son. No woman is a mage.'

'Well, the whole woman thing is a bit complex, but we won't worry about that. The thing is, he listens to you. You talk to him. If you come with us, you must help us to make him become the most powerful mage possible. Do you agree?'

'What choice do I have?'

'You have a choice.'

'A choice between a peasant's life without her son and living with a traitor who smiles at me and calls me friend or go with my son.'

'That is correct.'

'I will come with you.'

'And you agree to help us with your son?'

'Yes.'

'And you will be obedient?'

'Yes.'

'Good. Time to sleep.'

The Assessor took off his cloak leaving his shirt and trousers on for reasons of modesty, got into bed and slept, content in his decision. If this baby was already so powerful, what would the adult become he wondered as he drifted into sleep?

In the morning, he put on his cloak and went downstairs with the mother and baby. Markus and Andrius were waiting, Markus a little bleary eyed. The four of them, the peasant woman clasping her baby, walked out of the Inn towards the coach with its four horses.

The guards sat on the raised seat at the front while the Assessor helped the woman into the coach. On the Assessor's orders, the guards slapped the horses with the reins and they started to move.

'Oh, I never asked,' the Assessor said, 'what is your name?'

'Belinda'

'Nice, and your child?'

'Morovius.'

They rode on.

Belinda picked up her courage. 'May I ask your name?'

'Certainly. They call me the Assessor.'

CHAPTER 2

They rode out from Ander, bumping along the dirt track, the coach wheels following faithfully in furrows that had already been carved out of the dirt by countless wheels before them. Belinda bounced along in her seat, cradling Morovius as best she could. Her baby seemed unconcerned, cuddling up to his mother's breast as he was accustomed.

'Not that comfortable, is it?' asked the Assessor.

'I thought a coach would be luxury. Is this how the rich travel?'

'Yes,' he laughed, 'if you think this is uncomfortable, you should try riding a horse.'

'Is that worse?'

'Well, it's OK as long as you like chaffed legs and a sore backside.'

'I think I'll stick with the coach.'

They carried on. Belinda looked out of the window. The various crops on peasant smallholdings passed them by. Beet, corn, rapeseed, fallow land, there it all was. The basis of the agriculture of the Kingdom. The fruit of the labour of poor peasantry on which the entire edifice of the Kingdom, its knights, nobility, magic users and states of office, rested. Peasants working tirelessly in fields, hoping only to survive until next season, fearing the winter and all its cold horrors. The occasional cow or sheep wandered in its paddock, a sign of wealth amongst the peasantry.

Eventually, they reached the River Besalt and the bridge necessary for its crossing.

'What is it?' Belinda asked.

'What is what?' asked the Assessor.

'All that water. I have never seen so much water.'

'It's the River Besalt. You should see the sea.'

'What is that?'

'The sea is salt water as far as the eye can see. This is freshwater. It flows into the sea. There are rivers all over the land.'

'Really!'

'Oh, yes. It's a sight to behold.'

The coach rumbled on, Belinda day dreaming about a place where water stretched on and on without end. They passed a series of villages which were only distinguishable by their differing crops. The River Besalt stuck in her memory, all that water rushing onwards, crashing against rocks, hemmed in by the banks on either side. It was strange how sometimes in Ander they hungered for water and yet relatively close by it gushed forth on its way to the sea.

They stopped twice at Inns, making the best of the meagre accommodation on offer, the Assessor acting the perfect gentleman and leaving the peasant woman unharrassed. Morovius appeared to remain in good humour, oblivious of what was going on around him.

Eventually, they saw the walls of the city of Bogloris in the distance. Belinda was as surprised as she had expected. After all, everyone had heard of Bogloris, the largest city in the Kingdom of Marcovia. The home of the King and His Court.

'That's it, isn't it?' she asked.

'What is?' the Assessor replied.

'Bogloris. It's where the King lives.'

'The King and thousands of other people. The Court, the merchants, artisans and people like me.'

'Is it big?'

He laughed. 'Well, compared to Ander it's huge, but then I suppose most things are. Its streets are narrow though, everything is on top of everything else, all crammed in together. I think the King's Palace and the park are the only places where there is much room.'

They approached the drawbridge.

'Allow the Assessor entry,' shouted Andrius. They waited as the cogs were slowly activated, the drawbridge slowly descending across the moat. The coach slowly moved forward.

Belinda had never seen so many people, they were everywhere. Bustling, jostling, trying desperately to get somewhere and never seeming to arrive. Men shouted in the streets at no one in particular. Other men stood over stalls shouting something about their wares that no one could possibly understand. Little children ran, dodging around the adults.

Yet, somehow the coach continued down the narrow cobbled streets without hurting anyone. It was chaos, no doubt about that, but there seemed an indefinable purpose to everything. At last the coach came to a stop next to a huge gated residence. Inside these gates there were gardens, the only greenery Belinda had seen in Bogloris.

Unbidden, the guards opened the gates and the coach moved into the Palace grounds. It went in a semi-circle up to the front of the Palace.

'Wait here', the Assessor ordered Belinda. He descended and asked Marcus to accompany him and for Andrius to make sure the woman and her baby were unharmed.

27

The Assessor and Markus climbed the steps up into the Palace. They marched through the long familiar corridors to the Court, ignoring the various dignified paintings which adorned the walls.

The huge doors to the Court slowly opened.

'The Assessor,' announced the town crier.

The Assessor wondered why he always needed to be announced. He was the only Assessor in the Kingdom of Marcovia, it was his only title and he had been doing the job for years. Who the hell else could he possibly be?

He walked into the centre of the Court, Markus remaining on the circumference of the huge room with the other guards.

'Your Majesty,' he said.

'Yes, Assessor, I hope you had a successful trip,' said King Almein.

'I found one candidate in the village Ander.'

'Only one on your whole journey? That's not up to your usual standards.'

'One can only find what is there, Your Majesty.'

'You brought him back?'

'Well,' for the first time, as far as he could recall, the Assessor hesitated. 'Yes, Your Majesty. He is incredibly accomplished.'

'and….?' Asked the King, sensing his servant's unusual hesitation.

'There is a small matter.'

'A small matter! You bring a small matter before a King? Surely I have clerks for that.' Queen Elbeth, sitting at his side on her throne, tuttered.

'Ah, well, not so small. A little break in precedence.'

'A small matter that is a little break in precedence fit for the attention of a King. I am intrigued.'

'So am I,' said Archmage Marinus. 'Particularly if it concerns one of my potential pupils.' Marinus puffed himself up to his full importance. He was a rarity in the Kingdom – an old mage. He was one of the very few mages who had survived the periodic and predictable battles of the war unscathed. Now he headed the School and oversaw all mage training.

The Assessor paused. This would need all his skills. 'The baby I found has impressive potential and tremendous power.'

29

'Power indeed.' said Marinus. 'Does he throw fireballs?' The Court laughed.

The Assessor continued undeterred. 'As Your Majesty knows normally a baby's hands merely glow. This baby can make things magically.'

'What kind of things?' asked the King.

'Well, he can make grass.'

'Grass!' laughed Archmage Marinus, 'so now we can win plenty of battles with grass.'

'Your Majesty,' continued the Assessor, 'the thing is in my twenty years of assessing I have never encountered a baby who can make anything of any sort. This baby can make grass and perhaps other shapes and objects. I have never seen such power in one so young.'

There was a moment of silence. The Assessor hoped that allowing time for this to sink in would enable the Court to be prepared for his small matter which broke precedence.

Amran, the Chief Exchequer, had been sitting quietly next to the King as was his entitlement. He knew he was valued as an advisor for his ability to ask pertinent questions. It was his turn to speak, the confusion had gone on long enough, now was the time for the Assessor to come clean.

'None of this breaks precedence. Despite the Archmage's cynicism, it would appear we have a mage of some potential. Now spit it out, what precedence have you broken?'

The Assessor looked around. He had to argue his case before King Almein, Queen Elbeth and the Chief Exchequer Amran. Archmage Marinus would oppose him regardless. If he could convince the first three, the assembled knights, Lords and assorted nobility would follow. He commenced.

'The usual magical baby merely has blue hands. This baby's brilliance does not just extend to making magic grass. His mother talks to him. Not so remarkable you might think, mothers talk to their babies. The thing is that this baby understands what she says. Realise, this is only a baby, a few months old and he understands the spoken word. He can follow instructions on how to do magic. The snag is the baby only understands his mother.'

'What have you done?' asked the Archmage, his face reddening.

This was it. There was no turning back. The Assessor rubbed two sweaty hands together.

'I have brought his mother to Bogloris to help in his training.'

There was a collective gasp in the Court. Lords and knights muttered to one another. Queen Elbeth tuttered. King Almein stared ahead, straight at the Assessor saying nothing. Chief Exchequer Amran smiled, he always knew the Assessor was a strange one.

Archmage Marinus stood up, red faced, sputtering. 'This is a complete outrage. You've done it this time. No woman is to be allowed near magic – this is unconditional.'

'So far the conventional has not won the war.' The Assessor was relieved by the Exchequer's words. There was hope.

The Assessor continued. 'This baby's great potential needs to be nurtured. Only his mother can do this by simply telling him what to do. What harm can she cause? She is just a peasant from Ander. Belinda knows nothing and was shocked just to see the River Besalt, she can do no harm. On the other hand, as his mother, she can assist her baby to become the greatest mage we have ever had. Never have I seen a baby with such power and all this will be lost without her. The baby understands no one else, only his mother.'

'Great power, he says,' Archmage Marinus replied, 'all the baby can make is grass. Are we going to win the war with grass? Are we going to slow down the charging warriors of the enemy with a pile of grass? I need to see a fireball.'

The Assessor blanched. He hadn't seen this coming. He was used to getting his way through the power of reason. Surely, the fact that the baby could make magical grass and listen to his mother was enough. Now, he needed a demonstration, matters were out of his control, there was no argument left.

'That would appear to be reasonable,' adjudicated the Chief Exchequer. 'If the baby can show potential to be useful in battle, the mother can stay. Otherwise, she goes back to Ander and we keep the baby.'

'So we are agreed,' said King Almein. The Court murmured approvingly and there was a nodding of heads.

The Assessor started to sweat. Grass was one thing, but a fireball? He needed all the help he could get. 'Asking a baby to draw upon the power of the land through a stone floor is too much. He should be laid in earth so that he can utilise the earth's magic.'

King Almein agreed and ordered a guard to bring in some earth. The Assessor started to walk away to get Belinda and her baby. He managed to walk alongside the guard. 'Make sure there's plenty of blue jains in the earth,' he told him. The guard nodded. Hopefully, the jains would help the baby in this new task.

The Assessor and Markus walked back through the corridors to the coach which was still waiting outside. 'Wait here Markus,' the Assessor ordered, as he entered the coach. Belinda, holding Morovius, looked at him expectantly.

'Right, the thing is Belinda, there has been a slight complication. King Almein is quite happy for you to stay here in Bogloris with your baby but there is one condition.'

'A condition? What condition could I possibly fulfil?'

'Not you, Morovius. I don't really know how to put this but as you know we are at war. All they want is to see Morovius throw a fireball. Hey, it hasn't got to be very big, think you can tell him to do it?'

'I don't know. I have noticed little flecks of fire on his fingers, but I tell him to stop. Fire is dangerous.'

The Assessor jumped up in excitement, hitting his head on the coach's ceiling. 'Ow! That's awesome! He's a fire mage, not defensive. Right, he's going to be put in some earth with plenty of jains.'

'What are jains?'

'Jains. Well, they are those blue flecks and crystals throughout the land. It's what gives magic users their power.'

'Oh, I see. I just thought they were pretty.'

'Well, I suppose they are, but they are a lot more than just pretty. Now, Morovius will be placed in earth containing plenty of jains. You must ask him to concentrate, build up energy. Let him go a little blue, don't worry, that is perfectly normal. Then tell him to shoot off the biggest fireball possible.'

'Isn't that dangerous?'

'He'll be lying down. Tell him to shoot up.'

'I don't know. It seems wrong somehow.'

'Belinda. Listen to me. It's quite simple. He shoots a fireball and you stay here with your son in Bogloris. He does not shoot a fireball and he stays in Bogloris and you go back to Ander alone. You have no choice. They need to see a fire mage.'

Belinda nodded, everything was happening so fast. She had left Ander and now she could be going back. All these people running around, the huge palace in front of her, the powerful Assessor, horses everywhere and now she had to manage this test. She had no choice.

'All right.'

'Please try to stay calm. I shall be alongside you all the way.' The Assessor smiled in what he hoped was a comforting manner – he failed. Belinda followed him nervously, clutching Morovius close to her.

She had never seen such long corridors and all those paintings! The Inn at Ander had one painting of a horse. These corridors were full of people, men and women's faces, some of children, some families and she wondered who they were.

'Don't worry. They're all dead. Only dead people are displayed in corridors.'

Belinda wondered why you had to be dead in order to make it into the corridors.

'Who were they?'

'Just old Kings, Queens and their families.'

'Just'. He said it as if it were nothing to be a King or maybe he didn't care about the dead. He didn't appear a superstitious man.

At last they reached the Court.

'The Assessor and....' the town crier was at a loss.

'Belinda and Morovius,' the Assessor whispered.

'Belinda and Morovius,' went up the cry.

Belinda stumbled, still clutching her baby. She was deathly pale. All those important people in long flowing robes, covered in gold and jewellery. She could not imagine that such wealth existed. And the Court itself! How could one room be so large? She looked up, the ceiling was way above her culminating in a painted dome.

'Please be calm, my dear,' said the Assessor. He was pointing at the wheelbarrow full of earth. It glistened with the jains within it. Quietly he thanked the guard alongside for such a bountiful load.

'Put your baby in the dirt,' the Assessor told Belinda.

'But all those jains. I have never seen so many. Will they hurt him, you said they have magic.'

'Oh no,' laughed the Assessor. 'They will give him power. Magic users draw upon jains for their power.'

She placed Morovius carefully in the dirt filled wheelbarrow in the centre of the Court. All eyes were upon her.

'Your Majesty wanted a fireball?' asked the Assessor.

'Well, the Archmage wants one,' said the King.

Morovius started to change his hue to a slight bluish tinge. 'See how he absorbs the power,' the Assessor quietly told Belinda. 'Tell him to absorb more.'

'Feel the jains, Morovius, fill yourself with their power,' Belinda told her baby.

The Court stared at the baby who started to glow with the power of jain. He laughed and moved his hands back and forth, jerking his head. The Court was totally silent, quietly the Archmage stood up.

'Tell him to think of a ball between his hands,' said the Assessor.

'Make a ball, Morovius, between your hands.'

The baby started to move his hands. Blades of grass appeared.

'Not grass, a ball,' said the Assessor.

'A ball, Morovius, a round ball.'

The baby looked at his mother with those big blue eyes. He gurgled and kicked his feet. Slowly, magically, a shape began to be produced between his hands. It was round.

The Assessor wiped the sweat from his brow. 'Tell him to make the ball into fire.'

Belinda looked questioningly, afraid.

'Just do it or you go back to that damn village.'

'Morovius, make the round thing into fire.'

The baby stared at the blue ball between his hands appearing to concentrate. His mother had told him, it must be right. Tiny wisps of smoke came off the blue ball and it started to change colour, pink streaks, then red flickers, spreading across the ball until it was a mass of yellow and red flame, all contained within the ball.

'Shoot it,' ordered the Assessor.

'Where?' screamed Belinda.

'Up into the ceiling.'

'Morovius, shoot it upwards.'

The baby laughed, moved his hand backwards and then made an 'oo' sound. He jerked. The fireball shot out of his hands at tremendous speed up into the ceiling and smashed through the dome, up into the sky until it exhausted its energy and dissipated.

Amongst the gasps and murmurs a loud 'Bloody Hell!' could be heard. Luckily for Markus who as a guard was not allowed to speak in Court, everyone was so surprised they did not notice who shouted.

They stopped looking up and covered themselves as best they could fearful of the expected falling debris. The Assessor grabbed Belinda and threw her over her baby and himself on top.

They needn't have worried. The fireball had reduced the dome to dust and smoke, leaving a perfect hole in the top of the Court's ceiling.

King Almein quietly brushed dust from his shoulders.

'Archmage Marinus.'

'Yes, Your Majesty.'

'You'll pay for repairs.'

'But Your Majesty....'

'No buts. The Assessor was happy with grass. I'd have been happy with grass. Lots of grass. You asked for a fireball, you pay.'

'Yes, Your Majesty.'

'And the peasant woman, Your Majesty?' asked the Assessor.

'She stays,' decided the King. 'Ladies and Gentlemen of the Court. The Assessor appears to have discovered a fire mage of great power. One, moreover, who listens to his mother. I have always approved of children who listen to their parents.'

CHAPTER 3

'Well, it's been quite an adventure,' said the Assessor as he accompanied Belinda and Morovius to the wet-nurse quarters. Marcus ambled alongside, his large gait easily keeping up. He was relieved no one had noticed, or at least hadn't said anything, about his outburst in the Court.

When they reached a series of huts fenced off from the rest of the city, the Assessor took them to Belinda's new dwelling. He opened the door for her and asked Marcus to stay outside.

The hut consisted of two rooms, a living room and a bedroom. The Assessor explained that the large building in the middle of the complex was the shared dining room and toilet facilities. There was a gong in the morning to wake everyone up and it sounded twice more to announce lunch and dinner. Finally, a gong sounded at night for lights out.

'But, the important thing I must tell you is about your son. He is the key to you living here. You must help the mage teachers to develop his skills. The fireball is all well and good, in fact it was extraordinary, but there is a great deal more to being a fire mage than that.

'There are fire arrows and the whole issue of direction. Direction is crucial. We don't want our mages shooting down our own warriors. It's all about concentration. Look, you should be fine. Morovius appears to enjoy magic, so he should be a good pupil.

'Now I must go. I know what it's like. When someone introduces you to somewhere you think they will be around to help and befriend you or at least provide some guidance. I shall not. I just assess.

My role in your life and your son's life has come to an end. I must be on my travels. Don't worry, you will be well cared for.'

'Thank you.'

'Thank me? For taking you and your son away from your home?'

'I think a different Assessor would just have taken my son. You brought me and advised me on what I had to do in Court. Thank you.'

'You're welcome. I was just doing my job.'

And with that the Assessor departed, leaving mother and child together for whatever fate would throw in their direction. He walked with Marcus away from the camp.

'Marcus, a question.'

'Yes, Sir.' More questions, he hated these, you couldn't just agree with a question.

'Do you know who shouted out 'Bloody Hell' in the Court?'

'Well…'

'Do you know, Marcus?'

'It was me, Sir.'

The Assessor laughed. 'I like your honesty. Do me and yourself a favour.'

'What is that, Sir?'

'In future be honest with me. I'll make sure you are comfortable, but be careful what you say to others. Most importantly, say nothing about me.'

'Yes, Sir.'

'Do you understand?'

'Yes, Sir. I'll be honest with you, careful with others and nothing about you to anyone.'

'Excellent! You have been with me on a few journeys helping me to assess. Have you enjoyed them?'

'Yes, Sir, it is an honour to serve you.'

'If you wish you may accompany me on all my journeys.'

'Yes, Sir. Thank you, Sir.'

'You are welcome.'

They walked away from the complex to continue on their journey to find new babies and infants who showed magical abilities and could be of some service to the Kingdom of Marcovia.

Meanwhile, Belinda sat in what she supposed was the living room with Morovius still clutched to her. What had happened? She knew she would be betrayed by someone in the village, but so soon! She thought she had no enemies. Maybe she didn't, but silver and gold have a power all of their own. But, and it was a crucial but, she hadn't lost her son. She'd lost everything else, but maybe she would gain something in the big city. The streets certainly weren't paved with gold but there could well be more opportunities here than in a little village.

She suddenly realised that she was hungry, very hungry. The Assessor had told her that there was a dining room, but when could she go? She suddenly missed him. She had only met the Assessor yesterday but already he seemed like a friend, well what was a friend, no doubt one of her 'friends' had betrayed her?

But at least the wait was over. They had to come for Morovius at some point and it could have been worse, a lot worse. The Assessor could have been a profoundly cruel and crude man who had just taken her son. It was almost a relief that the inevitable had happened and it was far better than she could have hoped, she was still with Morovius. Belinda decided that the only person she could really call a friend, the only person she could really trust and love was with her right now, her son, Morovius.

44

'Together we will be all right. I shall never let you down. I shall serve you with everything I have. You are the key to my life.'

As if on cue in approval, a loud gong sounded. She walked out of her hut. Other women were doing the same, like bees called forth from their hive. She followed them and then realised they were going to that building, the one the Assessor had said was the dining area. Good, food at last, she needed it, most importantly she needed it to keep Morovius well nourished. She made her way to the dining area.

She looked across the yard noticing the jains which glistened in the late evening Sun. So they weren't just pretty after all. They were the key to everything and the source of the real power in this land. She reached the dining area with her baby and walked in with the other women.

She took an empty seat and looked around. Some of the women were with children and some without. She had heard of this wet-nursing, raising and feeding someone else's child for money. Apparently rich women did not love their children and paid for another to complete the chore of dealing with their naughtiness. Well, she wasn't rich and she was different. Belinda was a peasant and always would be. She saw some of the women get up, forming a queue with a plate in their hands and decided to join them.

They formed an orderly procession, each receiving some dollops of food from the kitchen staff. It was not particularly appetising, but healthy enough. After all, the powers that be needed their mages in waiting to be healthy babies.

45

She finished and made no attempt to join in the general chatter which filled the air. Somehow, she didn't think the fact she was with her own son would be greatly appreciated. She quietly made her way back to her hut. She was exhausted from everything that had happened and suckled Morovius before going to bed.

A gong awoke her, no doubt breakfast and she repeated her quiet ceremony of last evening before going back to her hut. What was she going to do, just play with Morovius all day? A knock at the door answered her question. It was a mage, probably in his mid-twenties with long blond hair, blue eyes and clothed in a flowing sequinned robe.

'I've been asked to help you train your son. Is that all right with you?'

She remembered the Assessor's advice about obedience.

'Certainly, Sir. It would be an honour.'

'Thank you. Shall we go?'

They went outside where a guard waited with a wheelbarrow glistening with jains. The mage who said his name was Berin, led them into an adjoining patch of grass. He called it the Green, but it was only about ten feet square. Belinda presumed it was still called the Green, because once, before Bogloris had become a city, peasants had congregated to discuss local matters. Anyway, that was why they called their patch of land the Green in Ander. This little patch and the name appeared to be all that was left of an agricultural peasantry in Bogloris.

'Right, guard, put that wheelbarrow in the centre of the Green. That's it, now away. Belinda, can you put your baby in the wheelbarrow?'

'Of course.'

'This I have to see. A baby who can wield magic'

'You weren't in Court?'

'Ah, unfortunately, I'm always there for the boring stuff like taxes. If any arguments break out, fights or babies casting fireballs through domes, I'm busy doing something dynamic like paperwork.'

'Paperwork is dynamic?' Belinda looked confused.

Berin laughed. 'It was a joke.'

'Oh, I see.'

Berin relaxed. Archmage Marinus's concerns about a woman being near magic were totally misplaced. This peasant woman clearly didn't have a clue. Belinda, indeed! She should have been called 'Couldn'tbedimmer', but he was going to make sure.

'You know your son's going a bit blueish.'

'Yes. The Assessor told me it's the jains.'

'That's right. Anything like that ever happen to you? It's important to be honest.'

'Of course,' Berin looked worried, 'I am always honest. I know nothing about magic.'

'You have never gone a bit blue or maybe even a little black, perhaps.'

'Black. Goodness me, no. Anyway, magic is blue isn't it? That's the colour it always goes.'

Berin smiled with relief. 'No black then?'

'No.'

'You've never seen black anywhere, with your son or with yourself?'

'No, never.'

48

It was obvious that there was no area for concern at all and he could proceed to try to develop Morovius into a powerful weapon for the King's army.

'All right then Belinda, he's gone blue enough, lots of power there.'

'Will he be hurt?'

'No, look at him. Little guy looks happy enough.'

Sure enough, Morovius was laughing and waving his arms and legs about in a haphazard fashion.

'Can he make a fireball?' Berin asked.

'Well, he did yesterday.'

'Wait, he's only a baby and we have plenty of time. We need him to cooperate. What does he like to do?'

'Grass. He likes grass.'

'Grass it is then. Right, over to you. I want you to talk to him.'

There was no need, Morovius was already making grass, a bush of it between his hands.

'All right, no need to talk to him about that.' Berin said. 'Tell him to put blue grass all over the Green.'

'Morovius, put the blue grass all over the green grass you see.'

Morovius made one of his baby jerks, a gurgle, blew a saliva bubble, it burst, he went 'Oo' jerked away and there it was. The entire Green was covered in blue grass.

'Fantastic! That's great.' Berin was smiling broadly. 'Bet the Archmage wished he'd asked for that in the Court.'

'He wants to play in the grass.'

'How can you tell?'

'I can tell, I am his mother.'

Morovius was put in the blue grass which now adorned the Green. Berin wasn't too sure if he was playing, didn't babies just kind of move their limbs around and smile regardless? He wasn't exactly an expert in child psychology. What he was more interested in was how long the grass would last.

Time elapsed, he checked ten minutes by the central clock and the grass was only just beginning to fade. Whatever it was that linked a magic user to the jains, this baby had it and had it in abundance.

'That's fine for today,' Berin told Belinda. 'I'll see you tomorrow. Oh, and Belinda.'

'Yes, Sir?'

'Tomorrow, he can show me his fireball.'

Berin set off for the main tower in Bogloris, the head-quarters of the mages. He walked up to the fourth floor and entered through the largest doors in the building. Archmage Marinus sat behind his large oak desk against the far wall. Marinus stood up and walked towards the large windows to his left overlooking the courtyard.

'Well?' Marinus enquired.

'She seems harmless enough.'

'Seems?'

'Look, she's just a bewildered peasant woman who is devoted to her son. She knows we can send her back to Ander whenever we like, so she is totally obedient. Besides, she appears pleasant enough.'

'But a woman near magic – it's an abomination.'

'Look, she can talk to her son, that's the important thing.'

'What is this son like?'

'He likes grass.'

'So I've been told.'

'In my opinion, he has incredible potential.'

'I just wish we didn't have to rely on a woman,' said Marinus.

'She is totally harmless. I asked her outright about magic, even if it was coloured black, she knew nothing. We are just dealing with a pliable, subservient peasant woman who to be honest, is quite ignorant.'

'Maybe, maybe....'

'Marinus, have you ever asked yourself whether you might have an issue with women?'

'I needn't ask, don't like the buggers.'

Berin laughed. 'Come now, they're just people.'

'Maybe, but devious, always planning, never straight forward like a man, never know what they're thinking.'

'Well, you have never met Belinda. She is too stupid to plan anything and is as straight forward as any man.'

'Fine, fine. I have witnessed the son. Power beyond belief.'

'Quite extraordinary.'

'Quite, Berin. Keep an eye on them. You are to be his main teacher, train him up well. Who knows, he could just end up winning us this war.'

'You never know.'

'You never know,' agreed Marinus.

The next morning, Berin, Belinda and Morovius set off again for the Green. Berin decided to dispense with the guard, after all, who would dare attack him, an experienced fire mage in the middle of Bogloris? Berin pushed the wheelbarrow, his long blonde hair wafting in the breeze. Belinda clasped Morovius to her breast.

They arrived at the Green and Belinda placed Morovius in the wheelbarrow as she was bidden.

'Right,' said Berin. 'Let's see this fireball.'

'How does he do it?' she asked.

'Well, he did it before.'

'I have forgotten what I told him.'

'How did you do it in Court?'

'The Assessor told me what to say.'

Berin laughed. This simple woman was no threat at all.

'Right. Just repeat to Morovius what I say.'

'All right.'

Berin went through the magic procedure again with Belinda, just as the Assessor had done in the Court. Feel the power of the jains, concentrate on a ball shape between your hands, make that shape into fire, shoot the fireball up into the sky.

Morovius gurgled, laughed and jerked his fireball up into the air, smoke smouldering in its path.

'No wonder someone swore in Court, that's great. How's Morovius doing?'

Morovius lay there, moving his limbs, blowing one of his spit bubbles.

'He's playing,' Belinda said.

'Good. I don't remember much as a child but I do know I hated boredom. As long as he doesn't become bored, that's the important thing.'

'He'll stop playing if he becomes bored and go to sleep.'

'Now, we can't have that, can we? Let's see, cutchie, cutchie coo.' Berin tickled Morovius under the chin.

'What are you doing?' asked Belinda.

'Not exactly sure,' answered Berin. 'He's obviously not a cutchie coo baby. Let's try something else.' Berin took an arrow from within his robes.

'Let's see if he can make an arrow shape.'

'How does he do that?'

'Do you remember how he made the fireball?'

'A little.'

Berin smiled indulgently.

'No problem, tell him to feel the power of the jains.'

She did as bidden.

'Now tell him to form this arrow shape between his hands.'

'Morovius, look at that stick.'

Morovius looked at the arrow.

'Make that shape, Morovius.'

Morovius simply made some grass.

'No, Morovius, that shape, please.'

Morovius made more grass.

They kept trying for another twenty minutes to encourage Morovius to make an arrow shape. The Green ended up being full of blue magical grass.

'I'm sorry, he likes grass,' Belinda said worriedly. 'Will we have to go back to the village now that he has failed?'

Berin laughed again. He was beginning to warm towards this peasant woman.

'Don't worry. Look, other babies are just rewarded for showing a little blue between their hands. Morovius is far ahead of everyone else at this age. It's magic my dear. It takes practice, a lot of practice.'

So they continued to practice, every day unless Berin was busy with paper work or something equally as exciting when another mage would call by. Usually, they would achieve far less success than Berin.

Time rolled by and Morovius continued to learn and develop his magical abilities. His fireballs became a little larger and he could make a single arrow. He also mastered some of the basics of direction. Eventually, he reached the age of four and was ready to join the other children in school.

CHAPTER 4

The night before the big day when Morovius was to go to school for the first time, Belinda decided to sit him down for a serious chat.

'Now, Morovius, you know that we have not met many of the other children and women.'

'Yes, Mum.'

'Well, the reason for that is jealousy. Now, I don't know this for sure but I think if the other boys find out that I am your mother, they will be jealous of you.'

'Why, Mum?'

'You see, the women with them are not their mothers. I was allowed to come here with you because you are special. All the other boys were taken away from their mothers.'

Morovius's eyes became wider and wider. He never knew this and stared intently at his mother. 'But why would anyone take them away from their mother?' he asked.

'It's just the way that they do things here in Bogloris. They take the little boys when they are babies who have magic away from their mothers and bring them here. They give them to other women called wet nurses. Have you heard the other boys calling the women 'Auntie'.'

'Yes.'

'That is because the women are not their mothers.'

'It makes no sense!'

'Well, I am sure they have their reasons.'

'But, why did you come?'

'You could understand me when I spoke to you, even when you were a little baby.'

'Can't all babies understand their mothers?'

'No, only you could do it. So, I came here to help with your training.'

'Is that how I met Berin?'

'Yes, that is the reason.'

'Woo!' It was all a lot to understand.

'Listen to me Morovius. You must listen. Do not tell the other boys that I am your mother. I think they will be jealous of you and you will not make any friends. The other boys will want what you have and as they cannot get it, could well end up hating you.'

'Hating me?'

'Yes. Please just don't talk about me.'

'All right Mum. I'll be quiet.'

'That's a good boy.'

They sat looking at each other for a short time.

'Mum, I'm tired.'

'Yes, it's time for your bed. You have a big day ahead of you tomorrow.'

Morovius went into the bedroom and went to bed, his head spinning. All those women, none of them mothers, what about the boys' real mothers...he dozed off to sleep.

The next morning, he set off with his mother to the school. It lay just outside the camp and he felt nervous as he was led by Belinda through the gates. He couldn't remember leaving the compound before.

The school was an imposing building, obviously old, and had seen numerous extensions throughout the centuries, each reflecting the architecture of the period. There was one architectural tradition that had remained intact – gargoyles. The tops of the walls were covered in gargoyles as if the designers were terrified that the gutters would overflow with rainwater. They peered down in warning at the new pupils converging on the school, their childhood days were over.

As Mother and son approached the building, they could see clearly hammered into the brass plate above the main gates the legend, 'Any use of magic against a fellow pupil will result in immediate expulsion – No exceptions.'

Belinda read the inscription and turned to Morovius.

'Morovius, you must not use magic in the school.'

'All right.'

She was confused. Wasn't this a school for magic users, why couldn't they use magic here? It made no sense.

They were walking up the steps into the school when a rather official looking mage, with splashes of grey hair, approached Belinda, his robes moving slightly in the breeze.

'Hello, are you Belinda?'

'Yes, I am. Is something wrong?' she asked, staring at him with unsure eyes, her black hair flowing.

'No, not at all. It's just a precaution. I must take you to see the Archmage.'

'Oh, you must be mistaken.'

'Your son is Morovius, is he not?'

'Yes, he is.'

'Then I am not mistaken.'

The teacher, who introduced himself as Novus, led Belinda and Morovius up the stairs into a large office. Archmage Marinus was sitting behind his desk.

'Thank you Novus. You may stay as this concerns you as his first teacher. Belinda, please sit down.'

Belinda, taking Morovius by the hand, sat down with her son next to her, his small frame squashed into the chair.

'I just need to have a quick word.' said Archmage Marinus. 'Don't worry, it's just a precaution.'

'I see. We are not in trouble?'

'Not yet,' Marinus waited for his words to sink in, 'and you will remain out of trouble if you listen to me. Did you read the sign above the main gates to the school?'

'Yes.'

'What did it say?'

'Not to cast magic in school.'

Marinus laughed. This woman was obviously as stupid as Berin had said. 'No, that would be silly in a magic school.'

'Oh.'

'No, the sign says not to use magic against another pupil. Do you understand now?'

'I think so.'

'Repeat what I said, then.'

'They can use magic, but not against one another.'

'Excellent, that's it. You see this is a military school, we are at war. Things can be rough. If pupils started fireballing each other no one would be left. Do you understand?'

'Yes. The pupils cannot use magic against one another.'

'That's right. Now, your son is powerful, very powerful. If he is hit or bullied, insulted or whatever, he can hit back, he can kick, he can bite, he can do anything physical, but he cannot use his magic. If he does, he will be expelled immediately, there are no exceptions, no circumstances in which this rule does not apply. Now, explain this to your son, clearly, so that he understands.'

Belinda proceeded to explain it all to Morovius as carefully as she could. Her son said he understood.

'Good, good,' Marinus said. 'Novus, take Morovius to your class. Belinda, you may go home.'

Belinda kissed Morovius on the cheek, told him to be a good boy and walked away. Novus led Morovius down the steps and through a long corridor, passing classrooms, hearing the muffled deep voices of various teachers. Sometimes, a high pitched voice could be heard, no doubt a pupil attempting to answer a question. Eventually, Novus opened the door to Form One. Three rows of double desks greeted them, occupied by a medley of young faces, arms usually resting on the table top in front of them.

'There's a space Morovius,' said Novus pointing at the middle of the classroom. 'You can sit there.'

Morovius did as he was told. The boy sat next to him said 'My name is Flavin, what is your name?'

'Morovius.'

'What an odd name.'

'What about Flavin?'

'That's also odd.'

They both laughed.

'Quiet now,' ordered Novus, 'does anyone know why you're here?'

Nervous silence.

'Come now. You will want to be in on my good side and boys who answer questions get on my good side.'

Every boy put up his hand.

'Yes, you in the front row. What is your name?'

'Magins.'

'Magins, you will call me Sir. So you say 'Magins, Sir.' All right?'

'All right.'

'Magins, say 'All right, Sir.''

'All right, Sir.'

'That's better. Now, what is the answer?'

'To what?'

'Say 'Sir.''

'Sir.'

'Now, the answer.'

'What answer?'

'Magins. Hold out your hand.'

Magins held out his hand expecting a sweet. Novus quickly took out a ruler and brought it down with force against Magins' outstretched hand.

'Anyone else want to be clever? Magins if you don't stop crying I'll hit you again, just harder. Stop it. You can see the healer afterwards. Now, Lesson One. You will call me 'Sir'.'

Silence.

'What do you all say?'

Silence.

'After me, say 'Yes, Sir.' Say it.'

'Yes, Sir.' They spoke in the unison that comes easily to the very young.

'Good. Now who knows why you are here?'

Silence and not one raised hand, a silence broken only by sobs from Magins.

'Magins, I am serious. If you do not shut up, I'll hit you again.'

'Yes, Sir,' said Magins.

'Excellent. You replied correctly. Well done. You see boys, it is easy. Call me 'Sir', do your best to answer my questions and you are in my good books. Get in my bad books and I hit you. Do you understand?'

'Yes, Sir,' they all shouted.

'Very good. Now, why are you here? You don't have to be right, just do your best.'

Silence, even from Magus.

'Right, you are now all getting into my bad books. Do you know what that means?'

'No, Sir.'

'I shall hit everyone of you. Now, who wants to be a hero and stop you all from being hit?'

Morovius slowly put up his hand.

'Yes?' Novus asked.

'To learn to be careful, Sir.'

Novus laughed. 'Well, almost Morovius...'

'Yes.'

'Say, 'Yes, Sir' or I'll hit you.'

'Yes, Sir.'

'Morovius, you have stopped me from hitting the whole class. Class, Morovius is almost right, you are here to learn. Not to be careful, but about other things. Anyone like to guess what you are here to learn? Just try your best and you shall be in my good books.'

Three hands raised. Various answers were offered and were greeted by Novus with encouragement. Corrections were made, boys were reminded to call him 'Sir', but it went well, other boys offering answers, only two boys were hit, one twice for crying too much.

It transpired they were there to learn. Apparently this is important in schools. Fun was not important, nor were games. They were to learn how to read and write, about numbers and most importantly, about magic. They had shown magical potential as babies and that was why they were fortunate enough to come to this school.

'But none of you have guessed the most important thing.'

They were tired and could no longer think, too much was being asked too quickly.

'War, you are here to learn about fighting and war. Now, you never ever use magic against another boy in the school, do you understand?'

'Yes, Sir,' was the chorus.

'But, fighting, you are allowed to fight. You will learn to fight and you will learn about war. This is why you are here because we are at war with Eldara. The Eldarans are evil and it is our job as Marcovians to battle against them. Do you understand?'

'Yes, Sir.'

A bell rang out.

'That's break time. You can now all go out into the courtyard. The boys who have been hit can come with me and we shall see the healer. When the bell rings again, you come back into class. Do you understand?'

'Yes, Sir.'

Morovius walked with Flavin and the other boys into the courtyard. Magins and the other offenders went with Novus to the healer who had a little office at the end of the corridor.

Magins and his partners in crime walked into the healer's office with Novus.

'Another of your walking wounded, hey Novus.'

'Yes, Boronus, they seem to have sore hands.'

'I wonder how that happened.'

'The usual, the usual.'

'I'm sure they deserved it.'

'Come here, boy,' Boronus said to Magins.

Magins walked over. Boronus rolled his hands together, the familiar blue glow developing and made a pushing motion towards Magins' hand. The red marks, bruising and slight cut slowly changed colour back to the normal reddish pink. The cut began to heal.

'There you are, good as new,' Boronus said.

Magins stared open eyed at the healer. 'Thank you, Sir.'

'Oh, Magins,' said Novus. 'Get used to the healer. I am sure you will be seeing a lot more of him. Now, go to the courtyard and play with the other boys.'

Magins made his way down the corridor. Meanwhile Morovius and his newfound friend Flavin were beginning the philosophical discussions typical of young boys.

'Does your willy get smaller in the cold?' Flavin asked Morovius.

'What?' blushed Morovius.

'Your willy, you know, that thing between your legs, does it get smaller in the cold?'

'I suppose so.'

'Well, mine does. I think it happens to everyone or something is wrong with me.'

'Don't worry, it happens to me as well.'

'Fine, then it's OK or we are both ill.'

'I feel all right.'

'Good, so do I.'

Morovius and Flavin continued their deep discussion until the bell sounded and it was time for them to go back to class. They could not help but continue their fascinating discussion, furthering their analysis by attempting to determine the size in warm weather, now that the effects of cold and hot weather had been decided.

Novus had had enough.

'Morovius and Flavin, front of the class, please.'

'Yes, Sir.'

'Come now. Hurry up, there's no point walking slowly and pouting.' The two boys walked quickly up to the front of the class.

'Morovius, you have achieved two firsts. You were the first to answer a question and now you will be the first to bend over. Are you listening to me, bend over.'

Morovius bent over while Novus went to the cupboard. He brought out his pride and joy, the slender and highly flexible length of birch wood he called the Tenderiser.

He proceeded to cane Morovius three quick, sharp whips to the buttocks. The tears rose up automatically in Morovius's chest and smashed into his eyes, forcing their way down his cheeks in huge sobs.

'Flavin, you're next. Hurry up or I'll hit you six times instead of three.'

Flavin bent over and took his three of the best with the inevitable pain and tears.

'Oh, do be quiet you two. You'll see the healer at the end of class. I can't have you two together. Morovius, you will sit on the far left hand side at the front, Flavin in the far right at the back. Now, move.'

The boys moved around and Morovius and Flavin sat as best they could in their allocated positions. Morovius dared a glance at the boy next to him, it was Magins. He doubted very much if Magins would be as good a friend as Flavin.

The lesson droned on, Morovius oblivious to the words, they were just sounds washing over him in his humiliation. Eventually, thankfully, the lesson ended and he and Flavin could go to the healer to have their wounds soothed under Boronus's hands.

The two boys made their way home, looking forward to seeing each other at dinner time. Morovius daren't tell his mother the truth about the day at school, but just said it was a little boring but not too bad. She assured him it would get more interesting.

Time passed. Morovius and Flavin's friendship deepened and they were always together. The two friends decided between themselves the boys they liked and those that they did not. They definitely didn't like Magins who seemed to be in trouble more often even than they were and seemed to have his name written in blood in Novus's bad books. The two young mages enjoyed practising magic together, Morovius attempting to help Flavin as best he could.

Every afternoon the class would go to the large field just outside Bogloris which had been assigned for magic practice to allotted classes between 12 noon and 5 o'clock. The field was large enough that bolts were dissipated by the time they reached its outer edges. Outside this time, it was used by anyone as pasture for livestock. However, for five hours you had better make sure your livestock were elsewhere as different classes would be practising all kinds of magic. The odd sheep that straggled over the field out of hours was soon to become fireballed mutton for dinner. Obstacles were placed at various intervals and fire mages and necromancers would attempt to swerve their bolts around them to hit scarecrows behind. Stone walls haphazardly dotted the landscape. Mages would attempt to loop bolts over them simulating how they would eventually fire bolts over melee fighters into the enemy magic walls. Defence mages would put up shields in front of them and fire mages and necromancers would fire bolts at the shields, testing both the shields and strength of the bolts.

Warriors were usually assigned their own section where they would practice against one another. They wore padding and used inferior, although still heavy wooden swords, which would hopefully not cause too much damage. The magic warriors would draw upon the power of the jains and charge each other with shield bashes and attempt to find openings with the swords. Novus and the non-combatants would analyse the fights, everyone learning from strengths and weaknesses. Healers would stand watching, hoping that the warriors' enthusiasm would get the better of them and some good blows would be struck and require their services. Usually, however, the healers would practice on rats which were plentiful in Bogloris and had been captured the night before. Novus would injure them in various increasingly imaginative ways and the healers would try to restore them.

75

Morovius and Flavin were both fire mages, although Morovius was far more advanced. Morovius attempted as best he could to develop Flavin's skills, how to concentrate, to visualise an arrow in your mind and to work with the jains to mold raw blue magic into the desired object. Morovius worked hard on his directional skills, swerving magic arrows around obstacles, a skill that was at this time totally beyond his classmates.

Lessons were usually boring, but they picked up writing and mathematical skills as children tend to do, despite poor quality teaching. Some lessons were interesting, particularly if they were about magic.

'So tell me, what type of magic users are there?' asked Novus.

Almost the entire class raised their hands. 'Morovius. Name one type.'

'Fire mage, Sir.'

'Yes, I imagined you'd get that one, being a fire mage yourself. Ah now, Magins, I wonder which one you will know?'

'A healer.'

'Sure, not a healer yourself, but you have been to see Boronus often enough.'

The class laughed. 'Anyone else?' He pointed to a boy called Orken.

'A warrior, Sir.'

'Quite right, but we have knights and peasants. Why are you, as a warrior, a type of magic user?'

'I can use the jains to increase the power of my attacks, Sir. I can attack without even touching another person, just the wind from my attacks can do damage. I can increase my speed and can develop great reflexes.'

'and most importantly?'

'and most importantly, Sir, one day, I shall ride an Anrac.'

'Well done. That's correct, Anracs. You have all seen the paintings. Anracs will only allow a warrior magic user to ride them. We do not know why but everyone else either has to use a horse, a donkey or walk.'

Pupils laughed.

'The Anrac, some say, is a magic horse who has been blessed by the jains but no one knows for sure. It would explain why only a magical warrior who is in communion with the jains can ride one. Anracs originate from horses, but are four times the size, two horns made of such strong bone curling from either side of its forehead that they could well be stone, huge thick legs to propel them at enormous speed; these magnificent beasts are the proud steeds of the magic warrior.'

'Right you are,' Novus continued, 'two more to go. You, Necarius, time to speak.'

'A necromancer, Sir,' said Necarius.

'Yes, quite right, the odd one out as we shall see. What made you a necromancer, Necarius?'

'Sir, I almost died when I was born.'

'Excellent, a near death experience when very young connects the necromancer to the netherworld. He never quite regains the land of the living, the power of the jains keeping him linked to the other side.'

The pupils all turned around to look at Necarius who sat alone at the back of the class. It was true, he rarely spoke, had no friends, no one could really remember him laughing, at least not properly and he was extremely pale, beyond that which is natural.

'That's enough, one more. Come, I don't want to ask Magins again. I couldn't stand it if he gets into my good books.'

Only Magins's hand remained raised.

'All right Magins, go ahead.'

'A defensive mage, Sir.'

'Quite right and you know this because…'

'I am one, Sir.'

'Worst luck for the rest of you. Apparently, the idea is and I find this hard to believe, but a defensive mage is generous of spirit. He does not harness the power of the jains to help himself or for destruction, but to aid his friends. He can form shields for warriors, he can make a fireball harmless, he can deflect arrows and bolts.

'Now the necromancer is the odd one out, as he is connected to the netherworld, but the other mages are all connected to the land and the four elements, earth, air, fire and water. The warrior is earth, grounded, solid, immovable as a mountain. The fire mage is obviously fire, wielding his damaging attacks. The healer is water, water being the life form of blood, the healer enables us to regain our water balance for health. The defensive mage is air. He molds air in his defences and can stop arrows and fireballs.'

The pupils all listened in awe. They knew little fragments of these theories but no one had put them all together like this before. For once he had not needed the threat of pain to ensure his pupils' attention.

The gong sounded. 'That's it for today, boys. Good listening, you are all in my good books.' A cheer went up.

79

'I shall see you tomorrow.'

They walked out of the classroom, Morovius and Flavin together as usual.

'Would you like to come to my place?' Morovius asked.

'Sure,' said Flavin. They went to Morovius's new place, new because he and Belinda had moved to a hut with two bedrooms as Morovius was now old enough to warrant his privacy.

As usual, they started to theorise about the world. The topic this evening was what is under a house? For some reason, this fascinated the pair. It was all a mystery, they had never seen underneath a house, what could be there, who knows?

'There's only one way to find out,' stated Flavin. 'We'll have to dig underneath.'

'Is that safe?' asked Morovius.

'Perfectly. We are fire mages. Nothing can hurt us.'

'That makes sense,' agreed Morovius.

They used sticks to start digging at the side of the hut. The ground was quite soft because the hut was new. They passed down below the thick wooden floor and could just peer down beneath it.

'Let's go down there,' said Flavin.

'Sounds like a good idea,' agreed Morovius.

They continued digging, admiring how many jains you could see as you went deeper.

'Awesome,' Flavin decided, 'we'll be really powerful down there.'

'Yeah, it's going to be our secret hiding place. No one will ever find us.'

'Not even Novus. We can hide here and he'll never hit us again.'

'Great,' Morovius agreed.

They dug with their sticks until there was enough room for one person. Flavin went down under the house.

'What's it like?' Morovius wanted to know.

'Very comfortable. Could do with a blanket on the ground.'

'We'll get one. No problem.'

'Yeah, we can steal one.'

Flavin came out and they continued digging until there was enough room for two. Down the two boys went, delighted with the fruits of their hard work.

'This is well comfy,' said Morovius. 'With some sweets we could live down here for a long time.'

'I'm a little squashed.'

'We can dig out some more later and put some pictures on the wall.'

'We could make a fire.'

'Well, we are fire mages, after all,' Morovius said.

'Morovius, where are you?' called Belinda.

'I am over here, Mum,' said Morovius.

'Where? I can't see you.'

'Over here.'

'Keep talking, Morovius.'

'OK, Mum.'

Belinda looked around and saw the mound of earth beside the hut. They can't have! Her heart began to beat fast and perspiration broke out on her brow. Those two will do anything. She needed help, but no time, the hole could collapse, what could she do, she had to get them out of there.

As much as she wanted to shout and scream, she knew it would be counter-productive. Keep calm, keep calm! Well, at least try to pretend to be calm.

'Morovius, Are you under the hut?'

'Yes, Mum,' Morovius replied, oblivious to any wrong doing or danger.

'Now listen to me, please. Are you all right?'

'Sure.'

'Is Flavin with you?'

'Yes, he is here.'

'Hello Flavin'

'Hiya.'

'Right, now you two. I want you to do something. Please come out of the hole very carefully. We can all go and get some sweets from the shop.'

Two heads appeared from the hole. 'Sweets?' they asked.

'Yes, sweets.'

'What kind of sweets?'

'Whichever ones you want.'

'What, the hard ones with the red stripes?' asked Flavin.

'Yes, now please come out carefully so we can all go together and get some sweets.'

'Awesome,' Morovius said.

The two boys quickly scrambled out of the hole, sweets on their minds, they knew the hole was a brilliant idea.

Belinda grabbed Morovius and hugged him hard.

'What's wrong?' he asked.

Belinda was close to tears. 'Listen to me you two. What you did was very dangerous. Please don't go digging again.'

'Why?' Morovius was mystified.

'The earth could have collapsed and you would have been stuck down there.'

'But, we are fire mages.'

'Trapped in there, the fire would just have hurt you, it would have had nowhere to go. No one would have known you were down there. It was very dangerous.'

Flavin and Morovius looked at one another and at the hole.

'But miners dig big holes,' Flavin said.

'Yes, but the dwarves only do it when they are adult and they use all sorts of strong wood to keep their tunnels safe. Even then, it is very dangerous and despite their mines being very carefully planned, some of them still die. Digging underground is a very dangerous, skilful thing to do.'

Morovius and Flavin looked at her carefully, she seemed very serious and thoughts whirled inside their little brains.

'I don't want to be a miner,' decided Flavin.

'Yeah, I am glad we are fire mages,' agreed Morovius.

Belinda laughed, delayed tears rolling down her cheeks. They all went to the local shop and she bought them some sweets, the hard ones with the red stripes. Belinda left the two to enjoy their sweets after they promised to both go straight home when they were finished.

'Tell me,' asked Flavin, 'why do you call your Auntie 'Mum'.'

'Well...' Morovius stumbled on his words, remembering his mother's advice.

'You can tell me, I'm your best friend. Best friends don't keep secrets from one another.'

'Well, she is actually my mother.'

Flavin sat bolt upright, startled.

'How can that be? None of us know our mothers, only the Aunties.'

'It happened when I was a baby.'

'We were all taken when we were babies, before we can remember.'

'I have been told that when I was a baby I could only understand my mother, so the Assessor decided that she should come with me to help with my training.'

'Wow, that's tremendous. You are so lucky!'

'Flavin please don't tell anyone else. I have only told you because you are my best friend.'

Flavin swore to tell no one.

Flavin walked home slowly, his brow furrowed in thought.

CHAPTER 5

Flavin continued home, thoughtful. Why didn't he have his own mother? Why should Morovius have his mother? She seemed so nice. It had been naughty to dig under the house. An Aunty would have hit him, Novus would have thrashed them but Morovius's mother just gave him a hug and bought them sweets – the hard ones with the red stripes. Where was his own mother? Did she even think about him? Life was so unfair.

At dinner, Flavin was quiet, pre-occupied. His Auntie wanted to know if everything was all right and initially Flavin maintained that it was, but eventually he succumbed. He had to tell someone, it was consuming him, the thoughts in his mind were a prison for the obsession from which he desperately wanted to be free.

'The thing is Auntie...'

'Yes, Flavin.'

'Well, you are not my mother.'

'We have been through this before, Flavin. It is the way things work. No boy who has magical abilities is with his mother.'

'You're wrong.'

'No, I'm right. I have been doing this job for a long time.'

The word 'job' shot through Flavin like a bolt. He started to cry.

'You're wrong, I tell you. There is one boy who has his mother. We all have Aunties and he has his mother. It's not right, it's not fair.' Flavin stood up, tears racing down his face, food uneaten and ran into his room.

Flavin's Auntie waited a few minutes for his most immediate emotions to ebb and walked carefully into his bedroom. Flavin was lying face down on his bed, sobbing. His Aunty sat next to him and put her hand on his shoulder.

'How do you know this Flavin?'

'I know, that's how!'

'Who told you?'

Flavin was torn. Should he betray his friend, but people had to know? Maybe, if people knew one boy was with his mother, others would be allowed to know who their mothers were, could even be allowed to see them. Maybe, he could see his own mother.

'Morovius.'

'Is it true, maybe Morovius is fantasising?'

'He calls her Mum and she doesn't stop him.'

'I see.'

It was his Aunty's turn to be thoughtful. She had always wondered why Belinda was so aloof, as if she was special, why she was never one of them. Of course she wasn't, she was a mother. Meanwhile, to pay for food for their families, the Aunties had to nurse and care for boys who had nothing to do with them. Flavin was right. Life was very unfair, indeed.

That evening, Belinda sat with Morovius as usual at dinner. She noticed some of the women were looking at her. The glances were furtive, but they were noticeable to someone with a keen eye. Something was going on.

'Morovius, anything happen in school today?'

'We practised fireballs.'

'That go OK?'

'Mine was the biggest and I was the only one who could get any direction.'

'Very good. Anything else?'

'No, Mum.'

That couldn't be it; Morovius had been the most advanced mage in the class from day one. Nothing unusual then and why should the women care? Belinda considered her own actions, she could think of nothing out of the ordinary. She would keep an eye out for anything different, some clue as to what was going on.

The next day at school, Flavin continued to be thoughtful. He talked a little to Morovius in the courtyard, about the sweet with the red stripes, nothing serious. Then he walked off and had a chat with Orken, the warrior whose dream it was to ride an Anrac. He also noticed Magins chatting away, to a warrior called Banshin, unfettered by Novus and his threats. Banshin was even bigger than Orken, indeed the biggest in the class. Maybe, that's how matters developed, mages needed a warrior by their side.

Certainly, Banshin would need Magins for his shielding abilities. A warrior's normal physical shield was not enough in battle. Further, in school they couldn't use magic against each other and so warriors were good allies for mages. Morovius started to think about the upcoming parade.

Suddenly, a bolt shot through Morovius, delivering him from his reverie. Flavin couldn't be telling Orken about Mum! He wouldn't do such a thing, he was his best friend and he had been sworn to secrecy. It was Morovius's turn to be thoughtful and worried.

In class, Morovius had a brief opportunity to talk to Magins sitting alongside him.

91

'You're good friends with Banshin, aren't you?'

'Sure, and you with Flavin.'

'Yes.'

'You all right, Morovius?'

'I'm not sure. I think so.'

'Well, if you ever need to talk, give me a shout. I'll probably do most of the talking but you never know, you might catch me going through a quiet patch, depressed or something.'

'Quiet in the front,' Novus shouted.

The two boys were grateful they weren't hit.

The next day there was an atmosphere in the classroom. Even Novus noticed.

'What is up with you boys today? If you don't start concentrating, I shall start hitting. Are you thinking about something? I know the parade is coming up but you still need to concentrate in class. Come now, are you guys thinking of something?'

Silence.

'Right, speak up. What's on your minds?'

Candera, who was the only healer in this class, put up his hand.

'Candera, what is it?'

'Well, I don't know about the others, but I've been thinking about women, Sir.'

'Women?'

'Yes. Why are there no girls in the class? Why are all magic users men? Are women too stupid, Sir?'

Novus knew this day would come. It always did in every class. Only once in his time as a teacher did he have to prompt a class to ask about women.

'OK, boys, what have you heard so far?'

Flavin put up his hand. 'We don't know our mothers, Sir.'

Flavin and Orken stared at Morovius who started to go red.

'All mothers are the same, boys. You don't need inferior peasants filling your heads with nonsense. You are lucky to have escaped the peasantry. What I want to know is what have you heard about women and magic? That was Candera's question and a very good question it is.'

Banshin, the warrior who was Magins's friend, put up his hand. 'I have heard the older boys talk about a Banshee. Is she a woman, Sir?'

'Well done, Banshin. Keep your ears open and you learn some things. Yes, once there were Banshees, all of them women. Black magic, not blue. Undisciplined, unpredictable, utterly devastating. They attacked friend and foe alike and were just pure destruction. You will learn more as you progress, but for now all you need know is that the Banshees are long gone, they're just a legend and they will never re-emerge. No woman will ever be trained in magic again. Even the Eldarans know this. For all their evil stupidity, even they know it is suicide to deploy Banshees. Only men can direct their aggression properly in battle, women are too wild, too emotional, too destructive.'

'What about our Aunties, Sir,' Flavin wanted to know.

'Your Aunties have been carefully selected to give you the best care for your development. Now class, settle down. The lesson will soon be over and after your break you can practice your magic.'

The class settled and Morovius returned to his normal colour. Orken and Flavin kept on glancing at him from the back of the class. Eventually, it was time for break. Morovius was relieved, he could feel Flavin and Orken's eyes burrowing into his neck.

He went to a quiet part of the courtyard, behind the sheds to be alone. It had to be, Flavin must have betrayed him to Orken. Just get through the day.

But, it was not to be. Flavin and Orken walked up to him, side by side, comrades in arms.

'Oi, you!' Orken shouted.

'What is it?' Morovius asked.

'I've been told you're a Mummy's boy. You need her to look after you, protect you, make sure you're all right. Can't be a normal boy, like us.'

'Leave my mother out of it.' Morovius was red faced, his hands forming fists.

'No chance.'

Orken's fist quickly shot up into Morovius's stomach, he crumpled and Flavin kicked him in the face. Morovius felt a tooth crack and tasted blood. The two boys randomly kicked him a few times. Luckily, because these blows were not well placed, they caused only bruising and pain.

'That's what we do to Mummy's boys around here, you need to toughen up. Come on, Flavin, you don't need to be around Mummy's boy any longer.'

The gong sounded, the boys went back to class. Morovius was understandably late as he could only walk slowly.

'What the hell happened to you?' Novus asked.

'I was hit for being a Mummy's boy, Sir.'

'Was any magic used?'

'No, Sir.'

'Oh, well, boys will be boys. Next time try to fight harder. We need to see Boronus, get you fixed up. The rest of you, I expect you to be quiet.'

Novus picked up Morovius and took him out of the classroom. As they left, the whispering started.

'Why is he a Mummy's boy?'

'His own mother?'

'Really?'

'Why?'

'Just because he could understand her!'

'It's wrong.'

And most frequently, 'It's unfair.'

Magins for once did not join in the chatter. He stayed quiet, thoughtful. He couldn't understand what Morovius had done wrong. His good luck didn't hurt anyone else. He decided that it was best not to get involved. The whole thing was just messy.

Novus carried Morovius into Boronus's office.

'Not me, I can assure you.' he told Boronus.

'What happened?'

'The boys have found out about his mother.'

'Ah, I see, unfortunate.'

'But inevitable.'

'Yes, Novus, you get back to the class. I'll try and talk to Morovius.'

Novus left and Boronus started to conjure up his healing spell.

'Just lie there quietly lad and I'll sort you out. You'll be as good as new.'

He cast his spell and decided to cast a second just to make sure. At least it would convince Morovius that he was genuinely attempting to help.

'Now listen. The teachers can't intervene as long as magic isn't used. This is a military school, we can't go around butting into every fight, we'd be doing nothing else. Now, you need to do two things. Firstly, fight back. You must get a few blows in. If in doubt, hit first. Your motto has to be retaliate first. That'll earn you some respect. Secondly, you have to make friends, allies. It's all about allies. You are an exceptionally fine mage. You should be able to use that to gain credibility and make some friends.'

'My best friend is one of the boys who did this to me, Sir.'

'Then it's time for new friends.'

Morovius walked back to the classroom. Flavin had caused this, he had betrayed his promise, betrayed their friendship. He had done this, he was the one who always came up with stupid plans, he almost got them killed under the house. That had been his idea.

Morovius walked into the classroom and ran straight to the back of the class. As Flavin stood up Morovius hit him as hard as he could in the face. A satisfying shot of blood burst from Flavin's nose.

Orken stood up to avenge his new friend.

'Orken, the rest of you, sit down,' shouted Novus. 'Morovius back to your seat. I'm not sure what's going on, I don't want to know, I don't care, but I'm sure Flavin got what he deserved. Flavin, you can sit there bleeding until the gong and then you can see Boronus.

'Flavin, I shall not tell you again. Shut up and stop crying. If you do not, I shall hit you and I hit a damn sight harder than Morovius.'

The class quietened. Occasionally, a pupil would steal a glance at Morovius. Eventually, the day came to an end. Flavin went to see Boronus and the other boys went home.

Matters were uneasy but quiet for a week. Eventually, they were on their usual magic practice ground. Morovius was working on sending two different fire arrows in different directions. The concentration needed was intense. Sweat broke out on his brow. Other boys looked on.

'No wonder he's so good. He has his mother to help him.'

'My Auntie beats me. I bet his mother doesn't beat him.'

'Flavin said she gives him sweets when he is naughty.'

'I never get sweets.'

The day came to an end and Novus walked off. Orken and four other boys approached Morovius, Flavin encouraging them from a distance. As soon as they were in range, Morovius hit Orken with an uppercut to the jaw. Orken stumbled but the other three rushed in, kicking, hitting and biting any part of Morovius they could see through the mass of bodies.

The other boys looked on. Magins told Banshin not to get involved. Eventually, Candera approached the fight.

'That's enough now. I think he's learnt his lesson.'

'He'll never learn,' said Flavin who had approached the melee when it was safe.

'Look, it's enough.'

The boys walked away leaving a battered Morovius lying on the ground moaning. Blood soaked the ground, Morovius's clothes were torn and there was a huge welt was on his back.

'Just lie there. I'll fetch Boronus.'

Boronus came rushing down with Candera and ran across to the gang that had kicked Morovius. He could hear their mantra from a distance - 'Mummy's boy,' 'It's unfair'.

'That's enough,' Boronus shouted.

The boys dispersed laughing and patting each other on the back. Morovius was curled up in a ball. Boronus started the chant of healing, the familiar blue magic forming its curling cloud between his hands.

'You'll be fine, lad. I've told you, you must make friends.'

Morovius groaned in response waiting for the familiar wave of healing to course through his body. It was good to feel the welcome knitting together of bones, the renewed formation of his teeth and for the blood to move freely through his veins and arteries.

When he was able, he sat up and said, 'I'm trying, Sir. I argue that it's not my fault, that I can't even remember that far back.'

'Try not being so good at magic.'

'Then Novus will hit me, Sir.'

Boronus could think of no response, so he tousled Morovius's hair and walked off. Candera still stood there.

'Probably not a good idea to help me,' Morovius said.

'I had no choice. I am a healer.'

'Thank you.'

Candera nodded and walked off. Morovius walked in the opposite direction. Candera was in enough trouble, there was no point in further endangering him regardless of how badly he needed a friend.

When Morovius arrived home, he could no longer hide the fact that something was seriously wrong in school. His battered clothes and emotions betrayed him.

'What happened to you?' Belinda demanded.

'I made a mistake.'

'What did you do?'

'I told Flavin you were my mother.'

'Damn, I thought something was up. The way the women look at us during mealtimes and you being so quiet. Are the other boys jealous?'

'Not only jealousy, they are beating me up.'

Morovius proceeded to tell his mother what had been happening, the beatings, the name calling, how Flavin had turned into his biggest enemy and enlisted the support of his new friend, the warrior, Orken. The rules, how there was nothing the teachers could do, only give advice like fight back and make allies.

Belinda was at a loss. Perhaps, she should have made some allies herself amongst the Aunties, she felt she had let Morovius down. Now, all she could think of doing was to approach Berin for help. He was a mage himself, he had been through the school, he would know what to do.

Early next morning, Belinda went to see Berin. It was the first time she had been to the mages' tower. The tall, thin building, reached up into the sky, small windows everywhere, each denoting a single mage's study. She had expected the building to be adorned with fancy engravings, weird statues and gargoyles but it was simply plain. The mages needed to show no sign of their power.

She was allowed to see Berin and explained as best she could Morovius's dilemma.

'Well, boys will be boys. I took my share of beatings at that school and Boronus is an accomplished healer.'

'Can he bring the dead back to life.'

'Of course not, but it can't be that bad.'

'Look, no other boy has ever had to face the jealousy of being with his own mother. Morovius has what they all want and will never have. Please, Berin, I implore you, please talk to Novus. That is all that I ask.'

Berin looked at Belinda carefully. Never before had he heard it expressed so clearly the predicament of magic users. For the first time he was considering a magic user's development. How had it affected them, never knowing their families in a society based on inheritance? What would it be like to know your own mother?

Maybe this peasant woman wasn't so stupid. No, it was probably just a mother's instinct, after all, she was talking about motherhood and little boys. It was the only thing she knew.

'Please stop begging, I can't take it. I'll talk to Novus but I can promise nothing. Novus is a hard nut to crack and I don't have any nut cracking tools.'

Belinda thanked Berin and left, her hands clenched, her shoulders knotted. Berin made his way to the school and waited for break time, Morovius was a decent enough lad, maybe he did deserve a break.

When it was break time he went into the classroom. 'Hi, Novus,' he said.

'Hi there, Berin. How you doing?'

'Fine, fine.'

'Still consumed by the mundane?'

'You know me. Nothing exciting happens when I'm around.'

'Right, why are you here or have you just come for a social visit.'

Berin proceeded to tell Novus about Belinda's visit.

'Well, boys will be boys,' Novus said.

'The thing is no boy has ever had to face the pressure of being with his mother before. You know, jealousy from the other boys and all that.'

'What? Are mothers that important?'

Berin laughed. 'Are you so old you cannot remember your childhood? Remember when we saw some of the nobles with their parents for the first time.'

'You have a point.' Novus conceded.

'Well, the other boys have that shoved in their faces every day. What makes the situation worse, is that Morovius is by far the most accomplished magic user in the class.'

'Yes, we could have a problem. I'll discuss it with Marinus.'

'Thank you. Just remember. Boronus can't heal the dead.'

Berin walked off, satisfied he had done his best, whilst Novus went to see Marinus, to break the bad news that they had a problem.

Novus and Marinus went through the normal 'Boys will be boys' conversation and made their attempt at understanding how the other boys were feeling. Little did they know that they were basing their psychological analysis on a peasant woman's insight.

'Let me think on it,' Marinus decided. 'The parade is tomorrow, maybe that'll take the lads' minds off things.'

The boys were incredibly excited to see the procession. It was an annual event but this was the first one they were old enough to observe. Obviously, only the professional soldiers would be on display as the peasants were left on the land to continue their backbreaking labour upon which the entire Kingdom of Marcovia rested.

The boys heard the preliminary speech from Novus. How privileged they felt to watch the flower of Marcovia walk through the streets of Bogloris. How valiant and brave their troops were in their unswerving duty to defend the Kingdom against the savage and cruel Eldarans. One day, if worthy, they would join their ranks and crowds would be cheering them onwards.

The boys were allowed to stand at the front of the crowd so that they could see the procession. Novus and Marinus stood on either side of them. They were not on the parade as they were both too old to fight and were now valuable as teachers.

King Almein and Queen Elbeth headed the precession. The Queen acknowledging the cheers of the crowd with a quiet wave of the hand, the King staring into the distance determining the future of his Kingdom. Alongside the King was his most trusted advisor, Chief Exchequer, Amran.

A respectable distance behind them came the landed gentry, the Lords, knights and landowners upon whom the King's authority rested. The gentry rode their mighty horses, thick set animals that could support a knight and his chain mail armour. They had their visors up so that the crowd could recognise them, Sir this and Sir that, their tales of strategy and courage on the battlefield were well known.

Behind them came the small number of mercenaries that the Kingdom could afford. At this time it was just the crossbowmen, carrying their implements of death with pride. Yet, despite all these distractions, a pupil would throw the occasional hate filled glance at Morovius who was dismally quiet.

There was a pause, dramatic in its intensity. This was what the boys and indeed everyone had been waiting for. The magic users were coming. The sound of the magic warriors became noticeable, their Anracs stamping out their chaotic rhythm.

'Here they come!' shouted Banshin anticipating his heroes.

And come they did. Mighty warriors in chain, legs astride their Anracs whose monstrous legs stamped out the tempo as the mighty beasts moved forward. Broadswords jangled against the warriors' legs, huge shields tied to the Anracs' sides. Those magnificent beasts, the pride of any warrior, the curled horns, spiralling forwards, daring anyone to risk impalement.

'Anracs, Anracs,' Banshin cried, 'I've never seen an Anrac.'

Orken was quiet, just stealing occasional glances at Morovius, occasionally whispering to Flavin.

Then came the healers, resplendent in their robes. Candera stared, open mouthed, he was not alone, here were his comrades. Men who served others, without whom most of these warriors would be dead. The healer, the necessary accompaniment to any warrior.

The defensive mages followed. Magins noticed with pride as one of them, breaching the silence of his comrades, whispered something to his fellow mage. You could be chatty and be a defensive mage! Novus was full of crap. Magins cheered his lungs out.

A hush fell on the crowd, polite clapping. Necarius clapped appropriately. The necromancers walked past, some with staffs to help them along, their bodies bent out of shape by contact with the Netherworld that no healer could cure. They were pale, deathly pale. One looked and nodded at Necarius; necromancers knew who their friends were.

A pause. Here they were. The crème de la crème of any army. The destructive power necessary for any war. Those who could destroy with a twitch of a hand – the fire mages. Wizened men, deep in thought of the death they had wielded, the destruction they would wrought against any foe. Everything else was really a side show, support for the most destructive of any conflict, those that can inflict the most damage and be truly deadly.

Morovius remained quiet. So was Flavin who glanced occasionally at him.

The parade passed by. Marinus approached Novus.

'The boys didn't even forget their conflict at their first parade.'

'I noticed as well,' agreed Novus.

'I did not pay for a new dome, just so that he could die without even seeing the battle field. Is he as powerful as everyone says?'

'Yes, if not more so.'

'Right, you have to stop the bullying. At best they will break his spirit and we can't have that.'

'I shall have to use violence.'

'You always do, Novus, you always do.'

CHAPTER 6

It wasn't long coming. The next day, at magic practice, the distraction continued. Magins, ironically, was the only one really concentrating. Novus had told him he was ready to practice permeable defences. His standard magical shields protected his allies but made it impossible for his allies to attack as the shield absorbed all attacks from friend and foe alike.

By concentrating and giving his barrier a greenish hue, allies could penetrate the barrier with full force but there were down sides. A little of their enemy's attacks could seep through and the greenish hue betrayed the type of defence he was using. The enemy would thus be encouraged to attack such a shield in the knowledge that at least some of their attacks would penetrate. Much work had been done by different mages to overcome these defects but to no avail.

But Magins was the only one working hard. No one else was perspiring with effort. Rather, it was all rather half-hearted apart from the glances and the whispers.

'I don't really get it. Fights should be honourable, one on one or at least a little fair. They're just ganging up on Morovius,' Banshin told Magins.

Magins took a temporary break from his tasks. 'Well, I think it's wrong as well but as I said before, we shouldn't get involved.'

Candera was training to heal a wounded rat whose tail had been chopped off by Novus and was not doing well. What would happen now he wondered? He had aided Morovius once, would they forget

111

how he had helped a Mummy's boy? What could be done? In for a penny, in for a pound, as they say.

Flavin was doing his best to stir things up. 'It's time for him to go. Mummy's boy is a blight on us all. If word gets out, everyone will laugh at us. We have to show the teachers that it's not fair and they will never do anything like this again.'

'It's just that he goes for me every time,' complained Orken.

'You're a warrior, he's only a mage who cannot use magic. There's nothing to be scared of.'

'That's why you always hold back, is it?'

Flavin stared at him, for once at a loss for words.

Another boy piped up. 'Come on, we are all in this together. We need to be united, but I do think that Orken has a point. Flavin, you do need to be more involved.'

Flavin had no alternative but to agree.

The lesson was over and the gang began their approach to Morovius, all eight of them. Some made sidelong glances at Candera. He would be next, they thought. Not as bad a thrashing as Morovius, but enough to ensure he would never break ranks with the class again.

Morovius saw the group and was surprised and pleased to see Flavin amongst them. His enemy, the one who was responsible for all of this, he had seen him talk, winding up the others. Little cowardly shit, always hanging back, letting others do his dirty work for him. Morovius wouldn't have been surprised to learn that the others had cajoled Flavin into taking a forward position.

Morovius ran towards them and hit Flavin with an uppercut to the chin. A crack filled the air. That was Flavin dealt with, seven to go. He kicked out, a mistake, Orken grabbed his leg and down Morovius went. The seven jumped him and now it was just a matter of time. This would be his last fight, they'd make sure of that. No more 'Mummy's boy', no more disharmony, they would restore peace in the class.

Novus started to run towards the group but stopped when he saw Candera running in the same direction. Candera knew he would be next and at least now they were distracted. He could get one good blow in before they noticed him. He hoped Morovius was not too injured to be of any use.

He kicked one of the boys from behind between the legs. The boy crumpled. The six turned on Candera, shocked.

'You've gone too far now.'

'You're just like him.'

'Mummy's boy.'

'Pine for your Mummy, do you?'

They circled Candera. He shot a glance at Morovius, but he was too injured to help, his right arm at an odd angle, blood pouring from his nose. Candera put up his fists.

'You are just bullies, you can't even fight one on one,' he shouted.

Banshin turned to Magins. 'He's right. We can't let this happen.'

'Shit, I knew we'd get involved. You've read too many of those bloody chivalrous novels.'

'I'm a warrior. The warrior code.'

'Great. Where's the princess?'

'We do have a Mummy's boy.'

'Enough, let's go. Banshin, pummel!'

Candera took a swing which was easily dodged. He looked at the oncoming Banshin and Magins. A mistake, it alerted the six attackers to the new threat. They quickly went for Candera, who blocked and dodged as best he could. It was to good effect. Banshin and Magins arrived, Banshin facing up to Orken, warrior to warrior, the other five against Magins and Candera.

Orken threw a punch which Banshin blocked and pushed away, opening a gap. He took full advantage and smashed Orken in the face as hard as he could. Orken stumbled and Banshin took the opportunity to help his friend. He kicked an attacker in the stomach and left Magins to finish him off.

Orken rushed Banshin and they rolled over, getting in short jabs when an arm felt free. They continued rolling and both saw a lone rock at the same time. Orken wriggled free and went for the rock but he was still a little stunned from Banshin's blow and was too slow. Banshin got to the rock first and hit it with force against the side of Orken's head. Orken collapsed.

Banshin ran to the group. He had to survey the scene quickly. Morovius was a mess, Candera was down but might get up, there were three attackers left, Magins was on his feet but was bloodied and looked groggy.

With a mighty roar he jumped on an attacker's back and brought both his hands together with great force against his foe's ears. Two to go, he liked the odds. He threw four punches and knocked them down, they were no match for him. The boys collapsed and Banshin ran to Morovius.

Novus watched the whole thing from a distance. Looks like the boys have sorted it out amongst themselves as he had always hoped, but Morovius didn't look good. He ran off to enlist Boronus's aid.

Meanwhile, Banshin was kneeling by Morovius's side and was increasingly worried. There was blood everywhere and it wasn't only his arm that was at an odd angle. They really had gone for him, were they actually trying to kill him?

'Candera, you have to heal him,' said Banshin.

'I can't. I can't use magic on a pupil. I'll be expelled.'

'He's going to die, I tell you.'

Magins got up. 'Look Candera. We'll say we forced you. Besides, he'll probably still have injuries after you do your bit, maybe the teachers won't notice.'

Candera did not know what to do. Someone seriously needed his help, isn't that what healers are for but wouldn't he go into the peasantry upon his expulsion from the school? Tilling fields, toiling non-stop and for what? To give his produce to Lords or pay rent on the land so that the nobility could live like gods? But, could he live with himself if Morovius died?

Morovius was in a terrible state, the odd groan was all Candera could hear. Morovius had broken bones and who knows what was going on internally. If Candera went for Boronus himself, it might take too long.

'Stand back,' he said. He didn't know why, his healing would succeed or fail regardless of where people stood, but it seemed the right thing to say. Banshin and Magins complied.

116

Candera started to mold the blue magic ball between his hands, light and dark blue strands flickered in the sunlight. He made the ball as large as he could and imbued it with as much power as possible, the dark blue tinge growing stronger. Then a sudden push of his hands and he shot it into Morovius.

Morovius would be able to remember very little. A tingling in his arm, a feeling of warmth which moved around and throughout his body. His knee made a definite click, he remembered that. He was aware he was lying on the ground. He opened his eyes.

Candera, Banshin and Magins were looking down at him. He looked around and saw his attackers lying and sitting around, moaning.

'Did I win?' Morovius asked.

'You sure did pal. Quite a fighter, you should have been a warrior,' Magins said.

'Wow, what are you three doing here?'

'We helped. Just a little,' said Banshin.

'Candera deserves all the praise,' said Magins. 'He healed you.'

'He can't do that. It's against the rules.'

'Well, he can and he did.'

Tears rose up in Morovius's eyes. He hadn't won at all, eight guys, he couldn't do that and Candera had broken the cardinal rule. He couldn't believe it.

'I don't know what to say.'

'Say nothing,' said Magins. He paused, thinking, 'or you could get us some sweets – the hard ones with the red stripes.'

They all laughed.

'You can all have as many sweets as you like.' Morovius was crying. The pain, the isolation, it wasn't his fault, they would all be with their mothers if he had his way and now these wonderful, incredible boys had helped him. Candera even risked being expelled. Morovius was still badly wounded, but he knew with a little more healing, he would be all right.

'Candera, whatever happens, I'll always try and help you.'

'Ah, well, a couple of sweets will be fine.'

Novus came back with Boronus.

'Well, I must say Morovius, you look quite well for a boy who has been beaten senseless, I can't notice that many injuries,' said Novus.

No one said a word, just a shuffling of feet and anxious glances at the ground. Boronus started to heal the boys and finish healing Morovius.

'Come now, what happened?' asked Novus.

'I healed him, Sir,' said Candera simply.

'Really? You used magic?'

'Yes, Sir.'

'Sir, he had to,' Magins came to his defence, 'we threatened him and Morovius was severely injured. The fight was over so we didn't gain an advantage.'

'So, Candera, you are a coward who can be threatened, are you?' asked Novus.

'No, Sir. I did it of my own free will.'

'I see, just as you were the first to go to Morovius's aid?'

'I suppose so, Sir.'

'Fine. I'll see you all in my office.'

Flavin took his opportunity to speak, now that his jaw was healed.

'Sir, Sir, Candera was not the only one using magic, so was Banshin.'

'No, I wasn't, Sir. He's a liar, Sir!' exclaimed Banshin.

'Enough Banshin. Continue Flavin. How do you know this?'

'He beat up so many people, Sir.'

'Did you see him use the jains, conjure up blue magic between his hands'

'Yes, Sir.'

'Are you absolutely sure? You are making a very serious allegation.'

'Yes, Sir, I am sure. I saw him conjure up blue magic and use the power of the jains.'

Banshin was stamping furiously, tears of anger welling up in his eyes. Flavin was not just a coward, he was a liar too!

'Right, all to my study. Now.'

'Yes, Sir,' they replied.

The boys stood outside the study. The air was crackling with nerves. Banshin and Candera pondered expulsion and what it would mean. Back to the peasantry they supposed. Ah, well, peasants could do with some healing and a strong lad was always appreciated.

Novus emerged. 'First, I want to see Morovius, Candera, Banshin and Magins.'

The four walked into his study.

'First things first. Banshin did you use magic?'

'No, Sir.'

'He definitely didn't, Sir. I was alongside him,' said Magins.

'Boys, I saw the fight. I know he didn't.'

Shoulders relaxed and Novus could hear deep intakes of breath.

'Now, Candera, you definitely used magic.'

'Yes, Sir.'

'Recite the most important school rule, Candera.'

'No pupil shall use magic against another pupil. The penalty is expulsion – no exceptions, Sir.'

'Well, not perfect but good enough. Repeat the first sentence.'

'No pupil shall use magic against another pupil, Sir.'

' 'Against' Candera, 'against'.'

The boys looked hopefully at Novus.

'Did you use magic 'against' Morovius?'

'No, Sir.'

'Did you enable Morovius to fight.'

'No, Sir. The fight was already over.'

'So, you did not use magic against another pupil, either directly or indirectly. You broke no rule.'

'Brilliant, Sir.'

'Now, I don't want you healing other pupils unless it's an emergency like today. However, a healer's role is difficult. All you want to do in battle is attack but you stand there vulnerable, healing. Deciding who to heal first, showing compassion under careful judgement. You did that, well done. Have a sweet.'

Candera burst into tears. 'Thank you, Sir.'

'Right, now Magins. What was your role in all of this?'

'Minor, Sir. Candera went first and Banshin wanted to help. I just went along with things.'

'Is this true, Banshin?'

'No, Sir. Magins has always felt badly about the way Morovius has been treated.'

'No, Sir,' said Magins. 'It was Candera who felt badly, I just joined in.'

Novus laughed. 'Be quiet. Nevertheless, you both did the right thing. Have a sweet.'

'Morovius.'

'Yes, Sir.'

'How are you feeling?'

'Me, Sir?'

'Yes, who do you think I'm talking to, the cat?'

'There isn't a cat in the room, Sir.'

'Oh, dear me, this is woeful. Are you OK?'

'Yes, Sir. I am bewildered. I am grateful. I am relieved. I am,' Morovius sought for an appropriate word, 'happy.'

'Good. Now lads, it is events like these that forge friendships and friendships are crucial in war. Look after each other. Tomorrow, I expect you to sit next to each other in class. No nonsense mind, or I'll hit you.'

'Yes, Sir. Thank you, Sir.'

'You may go.'

They walked out, Novus behind them. 'Right, the rest of you, come in. Flavin I shall see you last.'

'You lot, just stand there and shut up. In an army violence happens. You were beaten. Accept it. You were bullies and you were beaten. Learn from it. You have allowed jealousy to rule you, this must end now. Is that clear?'

'Yes, Sir.'

'Now clear off. I want to hear no more about this 'Mummy's boy' nonsense. We all have our individual lives. Some parts of it are better than others, some worse. Stop looking at what someone else has. Be grateful for what you have.'

'Yes, Sir.'

'Now, get out. Oh, and tell Flavin to come in.'

Flavin walked into Novus's office.

'Now, Flavin, you said that Banshin used magic.'

'Yes, Sir.'

'Is that right?'

'Yes, Sir.'

'Think carefully, Flavin. Did you see Banshin's hands glowing blue, using the power of the jains?'

'Yes, Sir. I did.'

'You are a damn liar, Flavin. I saw Banshin fighting. He used no magic,' Novus shouted.

'But, Sir…'

'No buts. This is your last chance. Now, did Banshin use magic? Did you see his hands glow blue with the power of the jains?'

'No, Sir,' Flavin said quietly.

'Speak up boy.'

'No, Sir.'

'So you lied?'

'Yes, Sir.'

'and you only admitted it when I said I saw the fight.'

'Yes, Sir.'

'You tried to get another pupil expelled on the basis of a lie. You're in for it Flavin. Bend over.'

Novus took out his cane and hit Flavin twelve times as hard as he could. The Tenderiser went whistling through the air, high pitched in its melody of pain. Flavin was crying but Novus still continued to hit him hard enough for blood to appear through his pants.

'Wait there. Boronus will heal you.'

Novus walked out and saw Morovius, Banshin, Magins and Candera huddled in talk at the end of the corridor. He walked off in the opposite direction.

'I can't tell you guys,' Morovius said, 'how much I appreciate what you did. And you, Candera, you risked everything to help me.'

'Oh, I risked nothing. I didn't use magic against anyone.'

'But you didn't know that. I'm really grateful.'

'Warriors are men of honour,' affirmed Banshin. 'We can't sit idly by and watch bullying.'

'Banshin, I swear, one of these days, I'm going to get those chivalrous novels you read and shove 'em up your arse,' Magins said.

They all laughed.

'At least I read,' said Banshin.

'True, I hate reading,' said Morovius. 'Real magic doesn't require reading.'

'and novels are a total waste of time,' added Magins, 'they tell you a load of crap about stuff that never even happened.'

'How would you two know? You hardly read anything,' said Banshin.

Morovius pondered this for a while. 'Do you think it would help to read?'

'Don't know,' answered Magins. 'As Banshin said, I don't do too much of the ol' reading myself. Hey, Banshin keep reading. One of us has to do it. You might find something useful in there one day. Who knows, eventually we might have to save a maiden.'

'Necromancers,' said Candera.

'What?'

'They have to read. Strange occult books. They need them to evoke their daemons and stuff. I've seen Necarius reading many times.'

'Necarius, interesting. Maybe we should recruit him. Tell him to read loads of crap and tell us of anything useful,' suggested Magins.

'Recruit him into what?' asked Candera.

'Our group.'

'We have a group?'

'I think we have a group now,' said Morovius. 'I feel like I belong with you guys. Let's be friends.'

'I'm already friends with this book devouring oaf,' said Magins pointing at Banshin.

'Well, we're almost there,' said Morovius. 'Let's go and find ourselves a necromancer.'

'You sure?' asked Magins. 'Necromancers are a right weird lot and they don't come much weirder than Necarius.'

'Of course, another reader is what we need,' said Morovius. 'I really don't want to do any of that reading myself and Magins and Candera are pretty useless in that department. All Banshin reads is crappy novels. We need someone who reads proper shit, he can tell us stuff and we don't have to read then.'

'There is also the fact that it makes sense in another way. A balanced party has a fire mage, a healer, a warrior, a defensive mage and a necromancer,' said Banshin.

'Another idea from those damn stupid novels, I expect,' said Magins.

'Well,' Morovius said, 'it does make sense.'

'I agree,' said Candera.

'See, you do get good ideas from those books,' said Banshin.

The four walked off to the compound to find Necarius. They knocked on his hut and his Auntie answered the door.

'Yes?'

'Can we speak to Necarius?' asked Morovius.

'No violence. I have heard that you lot are violent.'

'No violence, we want to be friends.'

'Friends? With Necarius?'

'Sure, why not,' piped up Magins, 'he's a lively enough lad.'

'You taking the piss?'

'No Auntie, he is quite the lively one in class.'

'Really?'

'Oh, yeah,' Morovius supported Magins's lie. 'He chats away like a good 'un. That's why we like him.'

'OK. Necarius,' his Auntie shouted, doubt in her voice, 'your friends are here to see you.'

'I have no friends.'

'We want to be friends,' shouted Magins.

'Why?'

'To make a balanced group for adventuring,' said the romantic Banshin.

'Shut up, Banshin,' said Magins. 'He'll really think we're taking the piss now. Seriously,' he started shouting again, 'we need someone who reads.'

'I read.'

'Great, we don't. We need you.'

Necarius walked up slowly. 'So you want to use me?'

'Well, in a way,' conceded Magins 'and we want a balanced group.'

'It's a balanced group now, is it?' asked Banshin. 'I thought those novels were full of shit!'

'Look,' said Morovius, 'we haven't got a good reason, we just want you to hang out with us.'

'I don't know.'

'I'll get you some sweets.'

'The yellow soft ones?'

They looked at him in surprise. Necromancers had to be different.

'Sure,' said Magins. 'Why not?'

'OK, I'll come along. Aunty, I'm going out for sweets.'

'All right.'

'You want me to read?'

'Yes,' said Morovius. 'Not a big fan of the reading thing myself.'

'All right. Give me sweets and I'll read and tell you about it.'

'I'll read as well,' said Banshin.

'Crappy novels, I expect,' said Magins.

'Better than you, you hardly read anything,' said Banshin. 'At least me and Necarius read.'

'I don't talk much though,' said Necarius.

'Fine, fine. Magins talks enough for three people,' Banshin assured him.

'True,' Candera agreed.

'I would defend myself but I can't because you'll accuse me of talking too much and I don't want that. I'm not falling into your trap,' said Magins.

They all laughed, even Necarius, a little. The newfound friends walked off to purchase some sweets – the soft yellow ones. They sat down on a slight rise near the Green, mouths full of sweet lemon sherbet, silent except for the odd slurping noise.

It had begun.

CHAPTER 7

The years passed and they had the good fortune of putting Novus behind them. He was replaced with Turinus, who was capable, it was believed, of teaching more advanced battle tactics. His introductory message was simple. He didn't hit as often as Novus, because by now the boys were better behaved, but he hit harder, a damn sight harder. Out of the frying pan, as it were.

School, of course, was school. Boring as hell. Endless lessons, the point of which no one was really sure. Even Necarius started to wonder what was the point of all this reading. The only good thing about it was at least they weren't peasants. That really would have been a grind.

But, it wasn't all boring. This was a magic school, after all. Afternoons were spent practising magic. Exciting, exhilarating magic. But even this had its frustrations. The concentration needed was immense and the fatigue that inevitably followed was a drag. Then there were the failures, the repeated failures. Indeed, a new aspect to a spell, such as a new direction, inevitably meant failure for some time before the skill was even barely functioning, let alone mastered.

It was particularly hard for Necarius, being a necromancer, the hardest of all the crafts because you were not just training yourself, you were trying to delve into another dimension. It didn't help that his reading was of little value to the others and they had to rely on Banshin to do most of their homework. Necarius practised as best he could and read every book he could find on the subject of evocation. Eventually, it reached the point when even Magins recognised something was amiss. He took his opportunity one day as the friends left school together.

'Necarius,' he said, 'are you upset or something? I'm not sure as you aren't that lively at the best of times but you don't seem your normal depressed self.'

'It's nothing.'

'Come on, Necarius,' said Candera, 'I'm a healer, I can tell these things.'

'Well I can't evoke. All I can do is cast blue bolts that don't have a patch on the fireballs of fire mages.'

'Of course you can evoke,' said Morovius. 'You're a necromancer.'

'Ever seen me evoke?'

'No, come to think of it, I haven't.'

'That's because I can't.'

There was silence all around. They thought of their magic sessions, Morovius as always was the most advanced and could now direct two separate arrows simultaneously. Banshin was developing his magic speed and power, damaged animals were being healed by Candera and even Magins had begun to develop the permeable greenish shield of protection. He had managed, albeit only for a few minutes, to form a moving bubble of protection around Banshin. Meanwhile, all Necarius had produced was the normal blue bolts that was the necromancer's sole solitary spell.

'Maybe you should read more.'

'Shut up Magins,' said Morovius, 'he reads all the time. Maybe we could help.'

'Like a conduit,' said Banshin.

'What's that?' asked Magins.

'Well, in my reading, you can act as a conduit for another magic user, enhancing his magic. Indeed, some people are natural conduits who have an affinity to enhance another person's magical ability.'

'Yeah, I remember something like that,' agreed Magins.

'Really?' asked Candera.

'Where did you read that?' Morovius wanted to know.

'Ah, well, never really. I just kinda made it up to sound clever,' said Magins.

'All right, all right. Now, Banshin, how do we do this conduit thing? How do we help Necarius?' asked Morovius.

'Well, I'm not sure. The books aren't clear. We just sorta fill him up with magic.'

'Perhaps,' Candera suggested, 'I could just heal him and Magins could shield him.'

'Yeah and Morovius can fireball him and Banshin can hit him,' Magins said.

'OK, Morovius and Banshin will have to stay out of it.'

So, the friends decided to try and perform a ritual that night. First they had to go back to class where the subject was about no man's land where the battle between Eldara and Marcovia took place. As they progressed in their studies so the emphasis had shifted more onto warfare itself, the history, the strategies and tactics and now the arena of the great battles themselves – no man's land, which lay ten miles to the West of Bogloris.

'Settle down class,' said Turinus. Morovius looked up at the imposing figure. Turinus was six feet four and broad. He was lucky there were Anracs as it is unlikely any horse would have built up speed with him in his armour. His hair and complexion were dark. Oddly enough, he didn't have a deep booming voice but all a man of his presence needed was to be heard. A magic warrior who had specialised in battle tactics and history, he was ideal to teach his classes about the war. He was also the ideal man to dish out any punishment if it were needed.

The topic today was no man's land, where the jains were so plentiful no grass could grow. An area where, lost in the past, the armies of Eldara and Marcovia had fought themselves to a standstill. A stalemate which had continued ever after as periodically the two armies would battle it out in an unending war. The only satisfaction to be gained was inflicting casualties on the other side and reducing its numbers.

A war of attrition to which no side had an answer. Sentry posts lined both sides of the ten mile border of no man's land, hemmed in on the South by the sea and in the North by the Windborne mountains of the dwarves. The sentries could run on fast steeds and provide warning if they saw any enemy movement. Besides, the time and effort needed to raise an army was such that the other side could not fail to notice. The sentries would soon inform the authorities of a large massing of troops. Both sides had the same problem. Neither economy was advanced enough to support a large professional army. Both relied on peasant soldiers who needed to be recruited and called up for each campaign before returning to farm the land. Besides, the constant battles kept reducing the numbers of trained soldiers and magic users. So the laborious mobilisation, taking months, was bound to be noticed by the other side.

No man's land was the topic of discussion today. They had fair notice, who had done the reading?

Turinus turned to the class.

'So, who knows anything about no man's land?'

Every hand shot up with the exception of the necromancers. It was a useful tactic. Be the first to answer with the only knowledge you had and you could daydream happily for the rest of the class.

'I see, even you Morovius, it must be a special day. Go on, Morovius, tell us the depth of your knowledge.'

'The jains have more power in no man's land, Sir.'

'Wrong, wrong, wrong. Morovius can't even get it right when he is the first to answer. Anyone like to correct Morovius.?'

All the hands went down.

'What about you neccies? Come on, you know. Necarius, tell us, this is your chance to embarrass your friend.'

'I don't know, Sir.'

'You do know, you know damn well what the answer is. Are you telling me this is the only assignment you haven't studied for? Tell me the answer or I'll hit you.'

'There is a higher concentration of jains in no man's land meaning that magic power is greater there, Sir.'

'Correct. Jains are jains, they can't be more or less powerful. The jains aren't more powerful in no man's land, they are just more plentiful there. That is also why we have no sea battles. If jains are in the sea, they are too deep to be of much value. If conventional soldiers fought at sea, they would merely deplete each others' ranks. By the time the victorious navy got to land, the magic users would be waiting and would annihilate them.

'But no man's land is different. Loads of jains means loads of power. You have something to look forward to. You can feel the power as you approach no man's land. It surges through you, ripples coming from your stomach up to your head, giddy with power. It is the best feeling in the world.

'It is thought that is how the impasse between us and the Eldarans first happened. We were on the retreat and had lost half our illustrious Empire to the invaders. We hit no man's land and with the increased power, we were able to mount a glorious defensive front. Ever since we have been trying to re-unite our homeland.

'Now does anyone else know the other main reason for the stalemate between us and the Eldarans?'

Banshin put up his hand.

'Yes, Banshin.'

'Magic only lasts three hours, Sir.'

'Wrong, wrong, wrong. Anyone else care to answer?'

No one did.

'The jains never become exhausted and neither does magic. Rather, magic users tire after three hours of constant magic usage. We have been trying to find a way around this but simply cannot. It's like our attempts to find a permeable magic shield which will not have a greenish tinge warning the enemy that they can partially penetrate. Such a breakthrough would be decisive but so far no one has succeeded in solving the problem. It seems as if the human body, even of the most adept mages, is only designed to cast magic for three hours. After that, exhaustion sets in.

'In a typical battle, the depleted conventional armies then take over and the stalemate continues. Even the conventional armies are very tired by now and their reduced numbers cannot win the day.'

'Yes, Candera, you have a question?'

'Why not hold back some of your conventional army in reserve to be deployed later in the battle, Sir?'

'Good question. The thing is that if you did that to any significant degree in the conventional stage of the battle you would be too reduced in numbers at the beginning and would suffer heavy losses.'

Florin put up his hand.

'Yes?' asked Turinus.

'So no one wins at all, Sir?'

'Sure, there are winners and losers in most battles. One side can enter another's land on victory and pillage a little, but no one has yet won decisively enough to actually go into the other Kingdom and re-unite the two lands. This would require a most conclusive victory and the ability to lay siege to the capital city. You would need almost your entire army to subjugate the enemy's land.

'You must remember, the Eldarans have forgotten that they are invaders and that Eldara is a part of Marcovia. They would initially resist our attempt at re-unification.'

The lesson continued. As usual, in the afternoon they went into the field for magic practice. Necarius practised his blue bolts while the others indulged in the more exciting magic arts. Turinus walked over.

'Don't worry, just practice your pentagrams and keep at your studies in the dark magic of Goetia. Necromancy is the hardest of all magic, you'll evoke one day.'

'Thank you, Sir.' Necarius continued practising. Maybe this conduit thing would do the job. He certainly hoped so. You never know, with his friends' help he might eventually evoke. As long as Morovius didn't think that a fireball was the answer he should be all right.

That evening, the five sat together in Necarius's bedroom. Morovius smiled, he wondered what his role in all of this would be, certainly fireballing his friend wouldn't help. He looked at Necarius's ring. The letters spelt out the name 'Coronzon', the Lord of the Daemons, whose permission was needed to evoke. They all sat around the table made of sweet laurel wood. On the sides of the table were yellow letters in a strange alphabet Morovius didn't understand. Necarius had told him the letters spelt out the names of the seven Kings and seven Princes of the Netherworld.

The table itself had been painted a brilliant yellow, blue and red in a seemingly haphazard but hypnotic design. There was a black pentagram in the centre. Its five points had symbols for the elements and spirit. A bowl of earth, incense for air, a bowl of water and a lit candle for fire. For spirit at the top of the pentagram, Necarius had painted an ouroboros, the ancient design of a snake eating its tail, the circle of perfection, calling to the daemon realm.

In the centre of the pentagram, there was a rectangle, made up of three blocks by four, each containing a letter in demonic script. In the centre of the rectangle was Necarius's scrying crystal in the shape of an egg. Necarius said it had materialised magically out of nothing in one of his sessions about six months ago – a gift from the Netherworld. Surely, if he could receive a gift from the Daemons he must be close to evoking.

'You sure this damn daemon will be contained in the centre of your pentagram,' Magins wanted to know.

'I'm not even sure it will work and I will be able to evoke at all. Right, let's do this conduit thing and Morovius and Banshin, don't do a thing, please.'

Candera, Necarius and Magins had brought in piles of earth glistening with jains so that they could stand in it, hopefully increasing their power. Candera started to heal Necarius while Magins put a

144

permeable greenish shield in front of him. Hopefully, Candera's healing could penetrate and imbue Necarius with increased magic.

Necarius, filled with healing and protected by the shield, concentrated on the scrying crystal. He generated blue magic between his hands and with a jerk, shot it at the crystal. He could see a desert in the crystal, it was as clear to him as if it was a painting but there was movement, spirals of sand curling off the dunes, caressed by the wind.

Suddenly, he felt himself in the desert and out of the room. He looked around. There were the four Watchtowers he had read so much about, huge towers made of obsidian. Where was Coronzon? He had to be about as guardian of the keys. Without Coronzon giving him a key, the Watchtowers would be totally inaccessible and his journey would be wasted.

He looked around and could see a horned head above a rise in the sand. He walked over. There sitting in the sand was the huge figure of Coronzon. He had to be at least seven feet tall, broad shouldered and with those characteristic cloven feet. Necarius sat next to him.

'You have come for your key.'

'Yes,' replied Necarius, feeling strangely cold but certain this was his chance.

'You may only choose one or rather it will choose you. That will be your only chance, you can never come here again once the key has been chosen. Perhaps you would like to wait for another opportunity.'

'I am ready.'

'Your decision is accepted. Now choose a key or rather let a key choose you. There are four keys, one for each Watchtower.'

Coronzon opened a pouch within which lay the four keys. One seemed to glisten in the hot desert sun. Necarius chose that one.

'That is the key to the Watchtower in the East. Within that Tower you will find twelve keys for twelve separate paths. Therein lies your daemon.'

'Thank you.'

Necarius walked to the East and approached the Watchtower. The key seemed heavy in his hand. It was large, at least a foot long and inscribed with complex symbols. He inserted the key into the massive door wondering how he could find the strength to open it. It opened of its own accord.

He walked into a large hallway. There were the twelve doors, each he presumed leading to the pathway that Coronzon had described. On the floor in front of each door lay a key. One glistened, beckoning. Necarius was drawn towards it. He inserted the key into the door which spontaneously swung open. He started to walk down the path when all of a sudden there was a load bang and he was covered in smoke. Eldritch flames of yellow, blue and red shot out from the floor.

There was another loud bang and suddenly he was back in his bedroom. He tried to stare again at his scrying crystal but couldn't see it as the centre of his desk was filled with dense smoke about three feet high towering above them. He looked around at his friends.

'Well, you managed to evoke a lot of smoke,' said Magins.

'Never mind, you can always try again,' said Candera.

Had he failed? Where was his daemon? Coronzon had said he could never go back to the Watchtowers again. Was this the end? Had Coronzon tricked him? Was he condemned to only being able to shoot blue bolts at his enemies?

''Allo.'

It was a strange high pitched voice.

'Who said that?' asked Morovius.

'Me, you fool. Can't see for all this damn smoke. Be good chaps and blow it away. I can't take much more of this. Bad for the lungs, well, I haven't lungs, but if I did the smoke would be bad news, I tell you.'

'Is that a daemon?' asked Candera.

'Just blow,' ordered Banshin.

The five friends blew as hard as they could but it was difficult. The smoke was thick and appeared reluctant to move.

'Blow harder you fools,' said the squeaky voice. 'I haven't got all day. Well, I have, not much else to do, I could think of something but I can't be bothered.'

They carried on blowing and managed to clear the top of the smoke. They blew and blew and blew. Still nothing. It was most perplexing. Eventually, when there was about nine inches of smoke left, a little grey head jumped up and waved at them, dropping back down into the smoke.

'Hiya guys, keep blowing. You know you can do it.'

Red faced, they kept blowing. The scrying crystal was gone. In its place was a small imp, about six inches tall, with a head disproportionately large for its tiny body. He had thin arms and legs, a fat belly and was a rather boring, nondescript grey colour.

'Is that it? That's your bloody daemon?' exclaimed Magins.

'Sorry, Necarius. Maybe you can try again,' suggested Banshin.

'What? You're disappointed! I'll have your bloody hamstrings.' The daemon jumped up into the air and opened his mouth revealing a series of sharp pointed teeth.

148

Necarius laughed. 'Imagine that, jumping around a battlefield, hamstringing the enemy.'

'Good things, small packages and all that sort of thing,' said Morovius.

'Good thing it's contained in the pentagram,' said Magins. The thought of being hamstrung seemed quite unappealing. 'We'll have to make sure it's tame before we let it loose.'

'Don't you oppress me sunshine,' said the imp and jumped up onto Necarius's shoulder. Magins started, concerned.

Necarius had a tear in his eye. 'I love him,' he said.

'Hey, has he a name?' asked Candera.

'You can call me Holy One, Lord of the Most High,' said the imp.

'Really?' asked Morovius.

'Only joking. My name is Enraefem.'

'Hi Enraefem,' they all said.

'Hiya, and Necarius if you don't like me, blame Magins. I wanted to be with you guys so I could see Magins. Bit of repartee, bit of chatter, that's what I like.'

Magins looked relieved. The chances of being hamstrung were appearing to recede.

'Anyway, I'm your daemon, whether you like it or not. I jump around, hamstringing away, I'm awesome.'

'But not very big,' said Magins.

'Why are people obsessed with size. You're like poorly paid prostitutes. Don't worry, I pack a punch and speed, nothing as fast as me, look.'

Enraefem did three jumps with incredible alacrity around the bedroom and landed back on Necarius's shoulder. Necarius stroked him. The imp purred.

'Well, let's leave these two lovebirds together,' said Morovius. 'I'm sure they have a lot to talk about.' He was concerned that Necarius was about to cry.

'Thank you, guys. I really appreciate the help,' said Necarius.

'You're welcome,' they murmured and quietly left.

They closed the bedroom door and started to leave the hut. They could hear Necarius sobbing.

CHAPTER 8

Turinus paced up and down the classroom, his huge frame periodically blocking out light from the windows. By now Turinus had developed an understanding with the class. They all realised that the noble ambition of the entire class listening carefully, asking intelligent questions and making sage contributions was futile. Even listening for extended periods was not really viable. There had even been occasions when a necromancer had been observed looking out of a window presumably contemplating the beauty of trees or something.

A mutually beneficial unwritten law had been established. Turinus had a code and then you'd better listen or he'd hit you. Turinus gave the code this morning.

'Listen up you lot, not just the neccies, the entire class.'

They started to listen, for the benefit of their health if for no other reason.

'This is important and not just for the warriors but for all of you.'

They were really listening now. Turinus had not only given the code, he had reinforced it.

'As you know, I am not overly fond of giving compliments. Waste of time, just gives people big heads, never had a compliment myself and I'm doing well. I'm a hard bastard, everyone knows I'm a hard bastard and that's fine. If I'd have had compliments, I might have turned into a weak girl's blouse and what would be the point in that.'

The class laughed.

'Right, but I am going to give you guys a compliment. You're not doing too badly. That's it, saviour the moment.'

More laughter.

'Even you damn neccies have managed to summon and I'd swear there was an hour a week ago when Magins managed to keep his mouth shut.'

Magins put up his hand.

'No, Magins, shut up, you have nothing useful to say. I have. As I said, you guys aren't doing too badly but there is one big step to go.

'Warriors and Anracs.'

A sharp intake of breath. Anracs. Had the time come?

'You warriors need Anracs. Without one you are incomplete. You are like Magins without a tongue or a neccie without a daemon, even if it is one of those little hamstringing bastards. You need an Anrac. The time has come.

153

'Now, I'm not having the whole lot of you going into the Anrac Woods, letting off fire bolts and causing mayhem. Form into small groups. Each group should have one and only one warrior with between four and six other people in support. I know some of you have already formed such groups. You call yourselves friends or something. Even some of you neccies have some of these so-called friends.

'Right. Now you can talk. Form into groups. We're off to tame Anracs.'

The boys started to talk and those who had already formed groups, like Morovius and his friends, were deep in conversation. Flavin naturally went with Orken and they went to recruit a healer and whoever else would join them. Eventually, all the boys had formed into groups and were ready. Turinus named each group after the warrior and allotted days in the following weeks when he would accompany them into Anrac Woods.

He explained the basics to the class and it all seemed highly exhilarating. Essentially, an Anrac needed to be forced to respect a warrior. A non-warrior had no chance, however great his magic, but even for a warrior it was hard to tame these proud beasts. Anracs respected one thing – force. It was necessary for each warrior to fight and force an Anrac into submission. As you can imagine this was no easy task and death was always a possibility, for the warrior and also the Anrac. That is why each warrior needed a supporting team.

Banshin's group was assigned two days the following week. Hopefully, matters could be settled in a day but it was unlikely. They determined to set out early one morning for the trek to Anrac Woods which lay to the North-East of Bogloris.

154

Banshin could barely contain his excitement, an Anrac, the crowning glory of any magic warrior. The preparations were equally exciting. He would at last gain his full regalia of warrior equipment. His chain mail, a broadsword and the great shield. The broadsword was another defining feature of a magic warrior. Normally wielded two handed, the magic warrior when drawing upon the power of the jains, was strong enough to wield it one-handed at speed. Banshin, like the other warriors, had practised this extensively and this coupled with his shield for defensive and shield bash properties made him formidable. The warriors began to question why a support team was needed, the typical hubris of youth. Turinus made it clear to them in no uncertain terms, that without a support team, the warrior faced certain death trying to face up to an Anrac. The class was amazed. A warrior was already formidable, how powerful was an Anrac?

At last, the time came for Banshin's group to make the trek to Anrac Woods. Turinus was on his own Anrac, while Banshin, Morovius, Necarius, Candera and Magins were on simple horses. Luckily for Banshin, his armour and weaponry were on Turinus's Anrac. As was typical of any magic user, he could only invoke the magic of the jains for three hours before exhaustion set in. If he had carried his own equipment to the Woods he would, as he put it, been totally knackered and no good even for rabbit fighting.

The trip was quite uneventful, after all, they were moving away from enemy territory and through peasant land of little strategic value. The boys were bemused by the attention they received. Peasants here rarely saw magic users, let alone a warrior on an Anrac. The young peasant boys were particularly fascinated and amassed on the roads to satisfy their curiosity. Here were the fabled warriors who kept their Kingdom safe from the evil Eldarans. Few could believe how large Turinus was and his Anrac was quite superb. The curled horns alone were a sight to behold. There were murmurs that despite the Anrac's huge size, it, like its warrior owner, was capable of great speed. The youngsters lapped up the admiration and remembered how overawed they had felt observing the annual parade when they were little boys.

At last, they could see the dense thickness of the Anrac Woods. As it was the height of summer, it did not look too foreboding and sunlight glistened through the trees to welcome them into the depths of the Wood. Nevertheless, as Turinus told them, they needed their wits about them. Anracs had a tendency to herd and if they felt threatened, there was no hope of the party escaping the Woods alive. Then, there were the normal everyday dangers of a wood, the wolves and getting lost. However, Turinus came on these trips every year and knew his way around and wolves were not stupid enough to mess with magic users. As Turinus put it, Necarius, even your little bastard of a hamstringing fiend could deal with some overgrown dogs.

Turinus explained their tactics. Handling a pack of Anracs was impossible but one did wonder off alone from time to time. Then Banshin could go off, do battle and show it who was Boss. Hopefully, it would be a clean taming and they wouldn't have to kill the beast or even worse, witness Banshin's death.

'Why can't we capture a baby, Sir?' asked Candera. 'Wouldn't that be safer and more humane?'

'Who knows how long it takes for it to grow and besides, what's the fun in that? Probably have to kill its mother anyway to get to the little buggers.'

'How are we going to track them, Sir?' asked Banshin, the hairs on his neck beginning to stand up, now that his moment was near.

'Shit, Banshin, shit. Those things shit a lot, great big mounds of the stuff. Then, it's a case of follow your nose. Nothing smells like a pack of wild Anracs. I have to wash my beauty every day or she wouldn't be allowed inside the city.' Turinus stroked his Anrac with as much affection as he could muster.

And so the search for the smell started.

'Shouldn't we be able to smell it by now, Sir?' Banshin wanted to know.

'Well, the thing is these Woods are bloody massive. Keep on going, we'll smell it soon enough. Nothing like the heady aroma of Anrac shit.'

They kept on walking and came to a clearing in the Woods.

'I smell something, Sir,' said Banshin.

'That's just Necarius farting, Sir,' said Magins.

'Shut up Magins, no fart can smell like Anrac shit.'

They all started to sniff but no one could discern the direction of the smell.

157

'We need a bloody bloodhound,' said Turinus. 'Right, we were walking in this direction when we first smelled it, so we just keep going straight.'

'Maybe my daemon can help, Sir,' offered Necarius.

'Yeah, all we need is another bloody mouth like Magins. Well, we'll need the thing for the fight and it should all be over within the three hours. Fair enough, evoke, Necarius.'

Necarius started to evoke, summoning through the blue magic of the jains. Soon enough they heard the familiar 'Hiya, how you doing? Need some help, your Majesties, I'm here to help. Yo, Magins, how you doing?'

'Fine, Enraefem, we're smelling shit, it's awesome, you any idea where it's coming from?'

'Let's go beyond the clearing.'

'You reckon Anracs are there?' asked Morovius.

'Not a clue, just seems like a good idea.'

'Fair enough,' said Magins and spurred his horse on, encouraging her across the clearing.

The rest followed, Turinus muttering under his breath about bloody neccies and their evil daemons and stupid boys who didn't know when to shut up, what had he done to deserve this and so on.

As they trudged along and the smell became stronger, it appeared that the daemon might have stumbled across the right direction, after all.

'Right guys, keep quiet, we don't need to warn these things. Magins and Enraefem, I'm speaking especially to you. First, we need to track down the pack and then find one that's moved away a little.'

They kept going and eventually Banshin noticed that the smell was altering.

'That's the smell of Anrac, all right,' pronounced Turinus. 'Our fun is about to begin.'

Suddenly, as the group went over a rise in the land they could see them in the distance, a huge herd of the lumbering, magnificent beasts meandering through the Woods, the occasional one stopping to graze upon some grass or a low lying branch. As the herd moved their bulk on tree trunk legs, the ground shook and occasionally a flock of birds would take flight from a nearby tree. The party dismounted from their steeds.

'Right,' Turinus said quietly, 'now we just follow them and wait for a straggler.'

'What about that one, Sir?' Candera asked, pointing.

'Wait, it's too close to the pack at the moment.'

So, they waited. The Anrac seemed preoccupied with the earth, digging away. Occasionally, it appeared to find something of interest and its head would come up, its jaws moving, presumably feeding on a piece of root or a nut. Banshin decided he liked him and hoped desperately that he would not rejoin the herd.

Banshin's luck was in. The rest moved on and the Anrac continued to be preoccupied. At last Turinus decided that the time was right and that Banshin could fight the Anrac without alerting the herd. Banshin prepared himself and adjusted his armour nervously. He remembered his lesson, a quick charge, a shield bash, cutting blows with his broadsword but making sure none were fatal so that Candera could eventually heal the wounded beast.

'Go,' ordered Turinus.

Banshin started to jog, concentrating on building up his magic power, Enraefem hitching a free ride on his shoulder. Magins prepared to provide him with a permeable bubble, while Candera was ready to heal his friend should an injury occur. Necarius concentrated on his mind link with Enraefem who appeared to be preoccupied with hamstringing.

Eventually, Banshin had built up enough magic power to begin his warrior's charge. Magins threw his protective permeable bubble around him, Enraefem jumped off and began to circle the beast so that he could attack from the rear.

The Anrac looked up at the last moment only to be greeted by a massive blow across the face from Banshin's shield bash. The beast staggered as Enraefem started sinking his fangs into his hind legs, the beast reared in pain, exposing his tender underbelly. Banshin jumped up, ten feet into the air and slit the beast from beneath, not enough to kill but enough to blood and weaken the creature over time. Blood spilled to the ground, the fight was going well.

But, the Anrac showed its unbelievable speed by swinging his head around and catching Banshin in the arm with one of its long twirled horns. Banshin was impaled as the beast started to toss him in the air. Enraefem jumped on his back and started biting furiously, trying to distract the animal. Candera shot out a bolt of healing but he missed his target because Banshin was being tossed so furiously. Morovius started to prepare a spell to kill the Anrac and save his friend.

Suddenly, Banshin was flung from the horn by the speed of the Anrac's thrashing. Blood had started pouring from the Anrac's back, Enraefem had found an artery. Candera blasted Banshin with healing magic and his arm started to reform. It was, however, too little, too late. The Anrac charged and tried to stamp the life out of Banshin. Luckily, Banshin stopped the Anrac's stamp with his shield but it was only a matter of time before his strength gave out and he would be crushed.

'Now, Morovius,' ordered Turinus.

Morovius was prepared and immediately shot off a large fire arrow. It went straight through its target at speed and exploded against a nearby tree. The Anrac fell over dead, Enraefem still chewing on its back.

Banshin got up, wearily, tears in his eyes. His Anrac was dead and he had failed. What was the point of a warrior without his Anrac? By the time he had stood upright and dusted himself off, the others had approached.

'I'm sorry, Sir,' said Banshin.

'Not to worry, these things happen, very few warriors defeat their first Anrac. Let's look on the bright side, we have plenty of meat for the campfire tonight. Right, let's get our mounts, track down the herd again and look for another straggler.'

The youths chopped off huge chunks of meat for later, mounted up and started tracking down the beasts again. They were disappointed to see that the Anracs were all together and this time there were no stragglers. So, they followed the herd for an hour. It was not difficult because as Turinus put it, 'Those buggers smell so bad, you haven't got to worry about being upwind or downwind or any of that crap.'

At last, Banshin noticed a cow who had separated off to munch on a tree that had taken her interest.

'All right, Banshin, this will be harder, her head isn't buried in the ground. Just charge up, jump in the air and shield bash her.'

'OK, Sir.'

'Right you are beastie, prepare for some biting,' said Enraefem.

'Enraefem, stop worrying about hamstringing, bite her gonads, get those ovaries, the pain should distract her.'

'Ah, but hamstrings are my thing, my speciality, my reputation.'

'This is not about you, it's about Banshin. Go for the gonads.'

Banshin set off, Enraefem on his shoulder, building up magical energy. Eventually, he had enough energy and was close enough to start his warrior charge. Enraefem jumped off to start his circling manoeuvre. A permeable protective bubble surrounded Banshin.

As Turinus had predicted, the Anrac noticed Banshin but not soon enough to take evasive action. Banshin leapt into the air and smashed the beast as hard as he could on the chin, a stunning blow. Simultaneously, Enraefem bit the Anrac from behind.

'The things I do to get away from the boredom of the Netherworld,' he thought.

It worked. The Anrac reared up in pain. Banshin wielded his broadsword into the Anracs rear left thigh, cutting an artery, blood flowing in huge gushes from the gaping wound. Enraefem proceeded with great enthusiasm to tear at the creature.

The Anrac was in desperate trouble and knew it. She jumped back and attempted to impale Banshin, the daemon causing all kinds of mischief from behind could be dealt with later. But, the creature was still stunned and Banshin easily avoided her horns and managed to get in a blow cutting at the Anrac's neck.

The animal started to stumble.

'Shield bash her, Banshin. Show her who's Boss,' Turinus shouted.

Banshin hit the Anrac as hard as he could on the nose and backed off. The bewildered animal had no answer to the attacks and slumped.

Turinus came charging up on his own Anrac. 'Banshin, stare into her eyes, show her you are her master and for fuck's sake, Enraefem, leave the thing's ovaries alone.'

'Now he tells me, like the taste, might go for gonads not hamstrings in the future.'

'Necarius, get your disgusting daemon off her.'

Necarius used his mental link to Enraefem to coax the daemon back to him. He stroked him affectionately as Enraefem sat on his shoulder, as if the daemon could be hurt by Turinus's words.

'See how I jumped, in the gonads, munching away, I was awesome, in fact I was legendary.'

'Sure, Enraefem, it was quite amazing. Seems you have a new tactic there,' agreed Magins.

'Bloody male gonads are normally well protected by codpieces in battle though. This requires more thought, might just stick to the ol' hamstrings.'

Banshin, oblivious to the chatter behind him, stared into the Anrac's eyes.

'Heal her,' he told Candera.

Candera set about the healing, shooting large blue bolts at the Anrac, but it was difficult. The creature had lost a lot of blood and her hind quarters were a mess.

'Just carrying out orders,' Enraefem said defensively.

The Anrac opened her eyes and looked at Banshin hopefully. She was desperate, a pack animal, now she was severely wounded and all alone. All that was left of her world was this strange human. She tried to stand up but fell over.

'Please try, Candera,' Banshin pleaded.

Candera said nothing, but concentrated deeply. He imagined the form of a healthy Anrac, intact, powerful, majestic and tried to imbue the injured beast with this image, constantly filling her with healing magic at short range.

The beast gave a huge sigh, her sides moving visibly and lay down.

'Is she dying?' asked Banshin.

'Maybe she's having a rest,' offered Enraefem.

'Actually, the daemon might be right,' said Turinus. 'She's either dying or just resting. Candera, stop, you can do no more. You can't replace loss of blood with healing magic. Banshin, keep looking into her eyes.'

Banshin kept looking into her eyes trying to delve into her mind. Eventually, the beast stirred and began to stand up.

'Get on her back. You've earned the right.'

Banshin did as he was commanded and stroked the shaggy creature. The Anrac looked back at him and Banshin could feel, really feel the creature. Her power, her beauty, her love of grass and trees, roaming with her herd, the Queen of the Woods. The mind meld had started. Banshin could feel her past, roaming through the Woods, growing up in its serene, idyllic beauty. How the Anrac had awoken each day to the beckoning sun and slept as darkness approached. Her feelings of belonging in her Woods and now, her dedication to her new Master.

Turinus turned his Anrac around and Banshin followed.

'Come on Banshin, let's find a place to set up camp for the night. These lesser mortals can ride donkeys.'

CHAPTER 9

They settled down ten feet from the clearing they had previously passed and set up camp as it was too late to proceed home. The boys collected dried wood while Turinus waited for them, preparing a bed for the fire. When they had enough kindling, Turinus sparked the flint and began the fire.

They skewered three lumps of Anrac meat with a sharp wettened stick and proceeded to roast it, taking turns to turn the skewer. This was a rare treat and one the boys would be unlikely to repeat. Anracs, because of their value in war, were totally protected, not even the King was allowed to hunt them. The only time anyone could eat Anrac was in a failed taming. Even then, you had to bring some of the meat back to the Royal family as tribute.

The meat was eventually roasted, the skin bubbling and dripping with fat from the lit fire. The taste was sublime, juicy, yet subtle, and not like chicken at all as Magins was quick to point out. A little like beef Morovius supposed, but it had a stronger flavour. Magins was of the opinion that on the way back they should kill a peasant's horse and eat it. Test out the theory that Anracs had come magically from horses. See if it tasted the same. They laughed, even Turinus and Necarius.

'But well done, Banshin, my friend,' said Morovius. 'You never gave up even after your first failure. You kept on going and just look at the beast you now have at your command.'

'Yeah,' Banshin agreed. 'Tasting this meat and looking at how beautiful she is, I'm glad I failed initially.'

168

'Don't half stink, though,' said Magins.

'The stench of success,' Turinus told them. 'Banshin will wash her before we enter the city. We'll reach the River Rimplin on the way to Bogloris. Only a fast flowing river can wash a recently tamed Anrac. After that, Banshin, you'll need to wash her every day, it's essential. Can't have a whole herd of stinking Anracs running around Bogloris, the King'll banish us to some godforsaken peasant village. Those peasants already stink enough and won't notice a couple of Anracs.'

They laughed and Banshin promised that he would take good care of his new steed. They all looked at her grazing next to Turinus's Anrac as if they were the best of friends. It was difficult to believe that mere hours previously, she had been running wild with her herd. She only showed minor wounds from her battle, mainly on her hindquarters courtesy of Enraefem. Candera had done excellent work in healing her. They all felt that she had now found her destiny. She had become a war beast.

'Sir,' asked Morovius, 'why can't I wear armour?'

'Anyone know?' asked Turinus. 'Come on, some of you at least attempt to read, unlike your friend Morovius.'

'It's because of the jains,' said Candera, 'but I'm not sure why, Sir.'

'Necarius. You are allowed to speak.'

169

'As far as I am aware, the jains allow physical but not ethereal magic, Sir.'

'Yeah, we're not sure exactly how it works, but that is what happens in practice. Warriors amplify their already existing physical strength and speed. Somehow, even wearing armour we can access the jains for that. Actually, Morovius, you probably could as well with practice but not to the same extent as a naturally endowed warrior. But ethereal magic, fire bolts and arrows, the Neccie blue bolt, protective magic, healing and summoning just don't work. No one has yet been able to harness the power of the jains for ethereal magic wearing armour.'

'Sir, may I ask another question, please,' asked Necarius.

'Sure, I'm in a good mood, bloody rare occurrence so take advantage.'

'Do you hate my daemon, Sir?'

'Not really.'

'What is it then, Sir?'

'Well, you do know your daemon can't die, at least on this plane of existence, don't you?'

'I have read a bit about that, Sir.'

'But, Sir, I have been told that if I blast a daemon hard enough, it'll die or something,' said Morovius.

' 'Something' is the crucial word. You see, if a daemon is blasted or wounded enough, the summoner's hold weakens or the daemon chooses not to be summoned. Either way, back to the Netherworld it goes, to lick its wounds, repair its pride and be ready to come back again. If its neccie dies, it can even be summoned by a new neccie.'

'I wondered why Enraefem seemed so experienced, Sir,' said Magins.

'Oh, yes, I'm pretty sure the way Enraefem talks that he's strode our world before. I suppose people are wary of neccies because they are in contact with the Netherworld, the unknown and warriors like me find the beasties they evoke a pain in the arse.'

'Sure are, or the gonads, Sir,' said Magins.

'I'm talking metaphorically. They are in some ways the perfect fighter. No fear, because they cannot die but they are not foolhardy. If they are injured enough, they are banished back to the Netherworld and if their neccie dies, well they could be there for a bloody long time. So your average daemon has just the right amount of fearlessness and caution. Damn formidable.'

'I'm lucky, Sir,' said Necarius.

'I'm also lucky, Sir. Just look at my Anrac.'

'We're all lucky. Sure, only Morovius knows for sure, but most of us would probably have been damn peasants if we had not been endowed with magical abilities. Imagine that, living with those flea bitten ignorant hags.'

They sat there contemplating what might have been if they had not been so blessed. The dire toil and degradation of the peasantry. Even Novus on his worse day was preferable to that. They had an education, they were respected and they had no fear of hunger. It wasn't even as if the peasants avoided the war, they provided the bulk of the troops as bowmen, pikemen and simple warriors. Imagine that, back breaking, stultifying work only to be punctuated by being called up for battle. Even then in battle they were not respected, forming the lowest paid and least regarded of the troops.

War and privation – a peasant's lot.

'Right, it's time we slept. Let's arrange the rota for the lookout. Nothing will happen, but it's army protocol and besides, no harm in being on the safe side,' ordered Turinus.

The rota was arranged and the group made preparations for bed. Soon they were all asleep apart from Morovius who had volunteered for first look out. Best to get it over and done with, he reasoned. The night seemed peaceful enough so Morovius settled down and thought of what had been discussed. It must be awesome to be a mage in chain mail armour but it was his fate to be a clothie.

Morovius continued his watch and as Turinus had predicted nothing happened. He heard owls hooting and some other scrapings presumably of small creatures. Maybe if he'd read any books he might have an idea what the noises signified but who cared, what had woodland night sounds to do with the important things in life like fighting battles? He watched tree branches rustling in the wind, their movement outlined against a full moon. He began to wish something might happen to relieve the boredom, when he estimated that the moon had moved enough to awaken Candera.

'Hi there,' he said, gently shaking Candera's shoulder. 'Wakey, wakey, your turn to get bored.'

Morovius prepared to sleep as Candera began his watch. Candera observed similar nocturnal sights and sounds as Morovius. His greatest wish, however, was that Banshin would give his Anrac a damn good wash as soon as possible.

Then there was a rustle which didn't quite fit in with the rest of the sounds. It was different and seemed to emanate from a position lower down than the treetops. Candera lay on his front and strained his eyes. There were shadows, moving shadows, men? But, only one party was allowed into the woods to tame an Anrac at a time. Poachers? It would take one hell of a brave peasant to risk the inevitable torture if discovered hunting Anracs.

He was about to awaken Turinus when he heard voices, strange voices in an accent he had never encountered before. This was not good at all. He wondered over to Turinus.

'Sir,' he gently tapped Turinus on the shoulder. Turinus opened his eyes.

'We have company, Sir.'

Turinus put his forefinger to his lips to signify silence. He listened carefully. Eldarans, he could recognise the accent, he had heard it often enough on the battle field. What were they doing here? What was the point? They needed to neutralise the enemy and take a captive to find the answer.

Turinus quietly awoke the others and similarly motioned them to silence. The only lad he spoke to was Necarius with the command to keep that damn imp quiet. Luckily, Enraefem had enough experience to immediately assess that this situation did not call for his usual delightful repartee.

They huddled together and Turinus spoke.

'Right, lads, this is it, your first contact. We have the element of surprise, so we should be all right. How many fire arrows can you control Morovius?'

'Three, Sir.'

'No 'Sirs' now. Keep our words to a minimum. Now, Morovius, blast them off. Whilst you do Banshin and I will charge them. Enraefem, you're on my shoulder, permeable shield Magins and Candera get ready to heal.

'Now, we must take one of them alive. This is imperative. We have to find out what the hell they're doing here. It makes no sense. Candera, if it looks like they're all going down, get ready to heal one of them. We must take one alive.

'All right you lot, know your roles?'

They nodded assent.

'Good luck, men.'

It was the first time he had called them men.

Banshin and Turinus quietly got on their Anracs, each gripping handfuls of fur, preparing their mind melds. They started to trot towards the enemy, invoking the magic of the jains to prepare for their charge. Meanwhile, Morovius began building up the blue magic between his hands preparing for his first fire arrow attack.

The arrows gradually took form and Morovius shot them off towards three previously selected targets being careful to avoid the now charging Turinus and Banshin. Magins covered the warriors with a greenish permeable bubble and Necarius cast a blue bolt. Enraefem was uncharacteristically quiet, concentrating on the job at hand, hamstringing and if possible, gonading.

Something was wrong. One of Morovius's arrows burnt out in mid flight and the other two weren't as strong as they should have been, glowing orange instead of the usual bright red. It was still impressive for a mage of his age but nothing like Morovius had produced in training in Bogloris. What was wrong?

Nevertheless, two of the arrows hit their mark, one for each magic wielder. The enemy spun around, there must have been eight of them, two dropping from Morovius's fire arrows. One was dead, a black hole smouldering in his chest, the other severely wounded, missing an arm. The enemy healer went straight into action to heal his wounded comrade.

Another cloth wearer moved into action, he had to be the defensive mage, damn, he was unscathed. Enraefem leaped and bounded at maximum speed, easily able to outstrip an Anrac over a short distance, trying to get behind the upcoming defensive wall. The wall shot up, Necarius concentrated on his mind meld, Enraefem had made it, he was behind enemy lines.

Turinus and Banshin hit the magic wall with a shield bash together. They could see Enraefem bounding towards the enemy, cause mayhem you little prick thought Turinus, go for those gonads. He looked over his shoulder, good, Morovius and Necarius were preparing to attack the enemy magic shield. Hopefully, Enraefem could cause some chaos and with the pressure they were putting the shield under, they might achieve a breakthrough.

The two warriors shield bashed and hit the defensive wall with their broadswords, noticing with satisfaction the fireballs and blue bolts smashing against it above them. What's going on? Morovius's fire bolts although acceptable, had been far more powerful in practice. Had he lost his nerve?

Enraefem reached the enemy, easily dodging a fire bolt and swings from the two advancing warriors, he ignored them, clothies, he wanted the clothies. The healer was closest, he'd have to do, have that, try to walk without hamstrings, you bastard! Enraefem sank in his fangs, the healer screamed in pain and prepared to heal himself. Enraefem bounded off, he had to be fast or those bastards would have him. Where's that damn defensive mage?

There he is, at the back, Enraefem went for him, no time for niceties, he's getting it in the face. The daemon tore at the mage's face, biting off his nose, claws scratching at his cheeks. A scream, shouts of 'hold the defence', the defensive mage's concentration wavered for half a second, Enraefem jumping off to avoid attacks and cause more mayhem.

There was a momentary hole in the defensive wall and Banshin seized his opportunity. Luckily, Magins had little to do since the beginning of the attack and was concentrating carefully. He kept on maintaining Banshin's permeable shield and then the defensive wall closed. Magins could no longer provide a shield. Banshin was through but alone, he needed to act quickly.

Every instinct in Banshin's body screamed to attack the warriors as he shouted his battle cry, broadsword flying, shield up defensively. No point, the healer would just heal them. Getting the healer would be most satisfying but ultimately useless, he was totally outnumbered. He had to get the defensive mage, destroy that shield, enable his friends to join in the battle. Where was that damn mage?

He looked around as he chased through on his Anrac. Confusion reigned, men running everywhere, the black blur of Enraefem, bouncing around, all thought of hamstrings and gonads gone, just biting where he could, distract the healer, cause chaos. Banshin looked away from the daemon and concentrated, where the hell is that mage?

177

He heard his name above the shouting and chaos.

'Over here, Banshin, over here.'

It was Enraefem, there the bastard was, the defensive mage, Enraefem jumping around him, biting at random. Enraefem was off to cause more mayhem. Banshin could see out of the corner of his eye, the enemy's necromancer ready to finish his evocation. Forget him, get the defensive mage, he's the key.

A burning pain in his shoulder, a fire bolt had glanced him, pain, never mind, Candera would deal with that if only he could destroy the enemy shield. Banshin let out a huge incomprehensible battle cry tinged with his pain and urged his Anrac on in a straight line, no time for evasive manoeuvres to put off his attackers, just get that damn defensive mage.

On he went, straight for his foe, he approached, his Anrac towering above the figure of the diminutive mage, he could see fear in the mage's eyes. Banshin leapt from his Anrac, sailing through the air, shield facing the fire mage, a fire bolt bouncing off. Onwards he went towards his intended victim.

With a massive yell, he lowered his shield and swung his broadsword with enormous force, its sharp blade swinging straight at the mage, slicing through him, the mage falling to the earth in halves, blood pumping arbitrarily from sliced arteries.

'Heal that, bitches,' he yelled.

Banshin could hear Enraefem.

'Hiya, Banzoon, I've always wanted to get you.' He glanced briefly, the enemy daemon was evoked, a huge beast, horned, knobules all over his body, some oozing puss, he was a dark purple colour, two fangs jutting downwards from his upper jaw. Banshin hoped Banzoon had gonads, Enraefem would need something to work with. Banshin leapt back onto his Anrac to meet the charging enemy warriors who were on foot. He could feel cool healing magic envelop his shoulder, well done Candera.

Turinus came charging through as a blue bolt and two fire arrows shot past him, unerringly heading for their targets. Let the clothies sort each other out, he needed to defend his outnumbered pupil. He headed straight for the warriors, only killing blows would work, their healer was fully intact. Even Enraefem couldn't cause any more mayhem, he would undoubtedly be occupied with the enemy daemon for some time.

Banshin charged and did his jump again, swirling his broadsword against a shield which his opponent had managed to raise just in time. Turinus, didn't dismount but just hung down from his Anrac and held his broadsword out with a stiff arm. The broadsword went straight through the neck of the nearest warrior, his head spinning off crazily through the woods.

Turinus looked around. A clothie, presumably the fire mage had dropped, the tell tale smoking hole through his chest, another was being healed, presumably a victim of Necarius's blue bolt. Get him! Turinus set off towards the clothie that was being healed.

Banshin faced up to his opponent, warrior on warrior. The warrior was older and presumably more experienced. Banshin tried a shield bash, which his opponent easily sidestepped. The enemy warrior waved his broadsword in an arc as he pirouetted away from Banshin, slicing him down the back, luckily not a killing blow, he could feel Candera immediately respond with healing magic.

Enraefem jumped around furiously, biting where he could, desperately trying to avoid Banzoon's swiftly moving clawed hands. Eyes, I've got to get his eyes, blind the bastard, if he grabs me, I'm finished.

Banshin went to attack his foe with an uppercut, his broadsword moving swiftly upwards. His more experienced opponent jumped to one side and moved to shield bash Banshin, catching him a glancing blow. Banshin went spinning, down on one knee, raising his shield to block his opponent's inevitable attack. The attack never came, his opponent falling to the ground, Morovius's signature fire arrow leaving its smouldering black hole through his chest.

Turinus continued to charge the fire mage, dodging his attempts at fire arrows. One did manage to catch his arm but Candera immediately responded with a heal. Screaming loudly, Turinus jumped down to confront the mage. It was no contest. There was no way a cloth wearer could deal with an armour clad warrior at close quarters. Turinus despatched the mage with one mighty blow of his broadsword.

Enraefem was attempting to solve his dilemma, eventually Banzoon would catch him and that would be the end of this particular battle for him. Gonads, daemons had none, but it gave Enraefem an idea. He jumped down to the ground between Banzoon's feet and jumped upwards biting furiously at Banzoon's hind quarters. It worked, Enraefem was in, within his daemon foe, biting at his insides.

'Get me now, you bastard,' Enraefem thought.

Banzoon grabbed furiously at himself. Their healer started to try to heal the daemon but was stopped by Turinus's broadsword at his throat and promises of dire consequences if he proceeded.

Enraefem proceed to chomp away at Banzoon's insides, wreaking all sorts of havoc. Banzoon could think of no solution and felt his link to this world waver. His master was dead, his return to the Netherworld would be a long one. Banzoon could feel himself giving up, the Woods becoming a distant haze, the Netherworld beckoning. He suddenly disappeared and Enraefem plopped to the ground, wiping his lips, savouring the taste of daemon.

Turinus had his broadsword against the healer's throat, he had captured one of the enemy alive, answers would be forthcoming. The healer looked at Turinus and smiled. There was a cracking noise as the healer bit hard on a tooth and the smell of bitter almonds filled the air. The healer collapsed.

'Heal him, Candera,' Turinus yelled but it was too late, The healer was dead, taking the secret of why the Eldarans had ventured into the Anrac Woods with him. Turinus slammed his broadsword against the ground in frustration. Damn!

Candera, Necarius and Morovius ran up to join their comrades only to hear the sound of Enraefem chatting.

'...did you see me? I was awesome, behind enemy lines, I got their defensive mage, gave Banshin a chance to be a hero, gonads and hamstrings everywhere, their healer didn't know what to do. See me take on Banzoon, big bastard that Banzoon, hard as nails, I got him, chewed him up, did you see me in action, played your part, but where would you have been without me?'

'Dispel him Necarius, please,' Turinus told his pupil, a note of desperation in his voice. 'For God's sake, his neccie was dead, it was just a matter of time before his daemon was dispelled.'

'Ta ra, you'll miss me when I'm gone, I'm awesome...' Enraefem's voice trailed away as Necarius banished him to the Netherworld.

'Pain in the arse,' said Turinus.

'He was essential to our victory, though,' said Banshin.

'Yeah, don't tell him I said so,' said Turinus.

'I'll tell him, don't you worry,' said Necarius.

'Oh and by the way, boys, the battle is over. You will address me as 'Sir'.'

'Yes, Sir,' they murmured.

'Morovius, what happened, I have seen you far more powerful in training.'

'I don't know, Sir. I just don't feel as powerful in the Woods.'

'It can't be the Woods, there are plenty of jains here and the rest of us are just as powerful. Is it battle? Please tell me, you can be honest, battle is hard, it's not easy to kill.'

'I don't think so, Sir. I could feel that I had less power when I entered the Woods before any battle took place.'

'Well, you need to try and sort it out. The more immediate concern, however, is what the hell were the Eldarans doing here?'

'Perhaps they wanted Anracs,' said Morovius. 'Their warriors were on foot, Sir.'

'Makes no sense,' replied Turinus. 'They have plenty. If anything the Eldarans have more than us. I'm sure they protect their woods as well as we do. No, it was something else.'

'Maybe they wanted to kill our Anracs, deprive us of our battle steeds, Sir,' guessed Banshin.

'Perhaps. Hell of a risky thing to do. Anyway, I'll have to report this back to the authorities in Bogloris.

'This means war.'

CHAPTER 10

Turinus was up before the Council. He had already sent a messenger to inform the King that he had news of great delicacy and importance. The King convened a meeting of his closest advisors. In attendance were the King himself, his Queen, Elbeth, his chief advisor, the Chief Exchequer, Amran and Archmage Marinus.

Turinus stood before them and outlined what had happened in Anrac Woods.

'It must be a matter of great importance and there must be information that the Eldarans are desperate to keep secret. Why would they equip their own men with poisonous teeth? I must admit I have no idea why they would send a party into our woods. They have plenty of Anracs of their own and we saw no sign that they were slaughtering our Anracs in order to weaken us. It just makes no sense.'

'I don't care about the sense,' said King Almein, 'we must mobilise a retaliatory attack. This outrage cannot go unanswered.'

'I'm pretty sure that when their party fails to return, the Eldarans will realise they have been compromised and will expect retaliation,' said Chief Exchequer, Amran.

'Well, they're getting retaliation whether they expect it or not,' answered the King.

'I just wish we knew what secret the enemy were hiding,' said Archmage Marinus. 'It could well be crucial. As Turinus has pointed out, it must be of some importance for them to equip their own party with suicidal teeth.'

'I just can't think what it might be,' said Turinus. 'I have thought of nothing else since the incident. It's almost as if the truth is staring us in the face and we just can't see it.'

'What I do know is I am sick and tired of this unending war,' said Amran. 'I have been thinking that we need some new tactic, something we haven't tried before, something to give us a decisive advantage.'

'Have you had any ideas?' asked the King.

'Well,' Amran replied, 'as you know I study warfare and tactics carefully, hoping to find something new.'

'Not an easy task,' said Marinus. 'Everything has been tried over the centuries. It would require something most unusual to give us a decisive advantage.'

'I can assure you it is unusual,' replied Amran. 'I have been reading about sieges and how tunnels have been dug to undermine the foundations of castles and fortifications.'

'That was a long time ago and there are no castles in no man's land, but please continue,' said Marinus.

'Yeah, I know,' said Amran, 'but it got me thinking. A tunnel dug under enemy lines.'

'How would that help?' asked King Almein. 'A certain shock value if troops emerged, but they would be isolated and soon wiped out. Would it be worth all the effort of digging a tunnel for that?'

'You see, I was thinking the same, Your Majesty,' replied Amran, 'and then I had a moment of folly or perhaps inspiration. I thought about gunpowder.'

'Oh, the stuff the dwarves use for pretty fireworks,' said Marinus. 'Our best experts are still trying to work out how we can use the stuff to propel projectiles, but the bloody tubes keep blowing up.'

'Exactly,' said Amran. 'Maybe we are thinking along the wrong lines. Why would we need tubes? Just put a load of gunpowder at the end of the tunnel underneath our enemy, send a fireball down the tunnel and blow them up.'

King Almein looked astonished. 'Bloody hell, that would give them a fright.'

'and cause some major casualties, Your Majesty,' said Turinus, 'but I agree the shock factor would be tremendous. A major attack on clothies behind their defensive wall could really cause all kinds of mayhem.'

'Dwarves,' said Marinus.

'What about them?' asked King Almein.

'Well, Your Majesty, the little guys are always digging after gold and so forth and they're the ones with the gunpowder.'

'That's all well and good,' said Almein, 'but dwarves are strictly neutral. How are we going to enlist their help?'

'Gold, Your Majesty,' answered Amran. 'Little buggers love the stuff. About five hundred gold should do the trick. That and guarantees that we'll keep them well hidden so that the Eldarans never find out they were involved. They won't be able to resist. Five hundred gold to dig a tunnel. By the time the battle starts they'll be well away. That'll guarantee their continued neutrality'

'Five hundred gold,' said King Almein. 'Those little guys don't come cheap.'

'It'll be worth it, Your Majesty,' said Turinus. 'The confusion could cause a major breach in Eldaran defences and enable a major, decisive push.'

'Well, we have to talk to the dwarves first. Little guys aren't too fond of strangers and they really want nothing to do with our war,' said Almein.

'We need a negotiator of skill and intelligence,' said Marinus.

'Someone who isn't threatening,' said Turinus. 'We turn up at the Windborne Mountains to see the dwarves with an army and they will think of war.'

'Who can we use?' asked King Almein.

'May I make a suggestion?' asked Queen Elbeth.

'Sure,' answered the King. 'We're at a loss.'

'What about the Assessor?'

They all looked at one another. The Assessor certainly had intelligence, was widely travelled and should be non-threatening. It looked as if the Queen was right. Certainly, no one could think of a better candidate.

'He'll need a party,' said Turinus. 'I recommend the boys I took into the Woods. They are young enough to seem non-threatening to the dwarves but they have been blooded and I can vouch for their effectiveness.'

'I agree,' said Marinus, 'that Morovius is certainly very powerful and his friends are more than competent.'

Turinus said nothing about Morovius's apparent reduction of power in the woods. No point mentioning something he did not understand and besides, even with his relative loss of power, Morovius still remained formidable.

'That would seem to be it. When is the Assessor next due back in Bogloris?' asked Almein.

'In three days, Your Majesty' said Amran.

'Tell him what is needed. We'll need those dwarves to start working as soon as possible. It'll take us and the Eldarans about six months to prepare our armies. The tunnel and gunpowder will need to be ready by then.'

They all agreed that this was the most viable plan.

'Oh, and Amran,' said the King. 'Well done. We desperately need thinking outside the box like you've displayed. I really thought there was nothing new in battle tactics. I am pleasantly surprised that you came up with something.'

'Thank you, Your Majesty. I must admit to being rather pleased with myself when I first thought of it.'

They all agreed to tell no one else about the plan. Secrecy was all important as shock value was essential for success. There was an air of excitement in the room. For decades everyone had been trying to think of ways forward without success. Using gunpowder to propel projectiles, how to stop defensive barriers from having a greenish hue, how to overcome the three hour exhaustion suffered by magic users and now this. The Chief Exchequer had come up with a plan that was totally original. This could be good. An explosion behind enemy lines, a break in the defensive wall, a decisive push into the heart of enemy territory, it could be a splendid victory.

Meanwhile, Morovius, Banshin, Candera, Magins and Necarius sat in a circle in Morovius's bedroom oblivious to the fact that they had been discussed for the upcoming mission. They were just excited that they had come through their first contact successfully. Banshin had his Anrac, now thankfully a damn sight cleaner after her bath in the River Rimplin and they had destroyed the enemy. All thoughts that Necarius could have evoked a more imposing daemon were forgotten. Enraefem, although at times a right egotistical pain in the arse, had proven his worth.

Candera suggested that given how they had come through their first battle unscathed, they should all cement their friendship with a ritual. Comrades in arms, friends forever. Necarius wanted Enraefem present and Magins, of course, was all in favour of seeing his talkative friend again. Morovius was worried whether Enraefem would disrupt the solemnity of the occasion but as Necarius pointed out, rituals could be both solemn and fun. It was agreed that Necarius could evoke Enraefem, after all, he had been an essential part of their victory even if he did continue to make sure that everyone knew exactly how awesome he was.

'Hiya, how's you all doing? Any daemons for me to eat today? Yo, Magins, did you miss me?'

'Of course, great to see you. I just have one thing to tell you.'

'What's that?'

'You're awesome.'

'Great, I know it, every daemon knows it, glad to see you puny humans are catching on. I was good wasn't I, see how I chomped through Banzoon, big bastard that Banzoon, no chance against me, though, quite the talk of the Netherworld I am.'

The friends looked at Enraefem and wondered about the Netherworld. Must be some daemons damn pleased he had been summoned away. They wondered how much Enraefem had teased Banzoon and what the other daemons thought. They would never know. Not even Necarius could enter the Netherworld again.

'Right, let's do this ritual,' said Candera, eager to proceed and not wanting to spend an entire night listening to a daemon boasting, however awesome he might be.

The friends proceeded to draw out a pentagram in chalk, Enraefem offering hints about angles and demonology which were of no help whatsoever. They put the appropriate symbols on each point of the pentagram. A bowl of earth in the North, incense signifying air in the East, a candle for fire in the South and a bowl of water in the West. Spirit they left empty for later in the ritual.

They made a circle around the pentagram by holding hands and began to evoke the spirits of each element, asking them to bless their ceremony. Enraefem looked on from Necarius's shoulder, quiet for the time being, seemingly his work was done in his excellent advice for drawing the pentagram.

They asked the spirits to look kindly and bless their union of friendship. Then at the climax of the ritual, they each had to prick a finger and place a drop of blood signifying spirit, their spirit, the mingling of their blood, the communion of their comradeship.

Each youth dropped a little blood on the point of the pentagram, saying, 'With this my blood, I dedicate myself to the greater unity of my group. Friends and comrades in arms forever.'

When the five had done this, they noticed that their blood had started to bubble, the spirits were answering. Enraefem spoke up, 'Needs a bit of daemon juice, got no blood, so I'm going to spit on it.'

Before they could consider whether this was a good idea, Enraefem had jumped down and spat on the blood before bouncing back onto Necarius's shoulder.

'That should do the trick, bit of daemon spittle. Spirits like that sort of thing.'

It started to smoke in the middle of the pentagram and the blood and spittle boiled and disappeared. The smoke was thin and wispy, rising up into the air in spirals. They were mesmerised looking upwards, straining to see if the spirits had blessed their ritual, trying to see patterns in the smoke. Eventually, they looked down.

There, in the middle of the pentagram, was a small image of a beautiful maiden. They could see through her, as if she had not fully materialised.

'Hiya,' said Enraefem while the youths stared open eyed at the apparition.

The lady did not respond. She turned around looking at each in turn, saying nothing. They waited, even Enraefem was quiet. Eventually, she turned to Morovius and stared at him.

'Morovius,' she said, 'Morovius, amongst all here you have been endowed with the feminine.'

The apparition disappeared. They all looked at Enraefem for some idea as to what had just happened.

'Don't look at me, not a clue, bloody strange lot those spirits, always talking in riddles. We daemons are far more straightforward, more trustworthy.'

'But what did she mean?' asked Morovius.

'She meant amongst all present you have been endowed with the feminine,' said Enraefem.

'Yes, but what the hell is that supposed to mean?'

'No idea, as I said, they're a strange lot those spirits. I've never had a clue what they're on about.'

'So you have seen them before?' asked Necarius.

'Ah, past lives, past necromancers. They're of no consequence now, all lost in the past. I'm a live it up in the present kind of guy.'

The friends were at a loss. The feminine, how the hell did that apply to a man? It made no sense. They decided that Necarius should go and do some reading. He knew the most about this evocation stuff and besides he was great at reading. As Morovius had said if it was up to him, it would take years as he wasn't too keen on the old reading even if it was of direct importance to him. In the meantime, they swore each other to secrecy. If Novus or Turinus found out, there could be trouble. Novus, in particular, had no time for anything to do with women, regardless of how manly Morovius might appear.

They spent a week pondering, whilst Necarius studied every night in the library. Morovius looked at himself carefully, nothing feminine that he could see. He even asked his mother if perhaps she had wanted a little girl instead of a boy.

'Whatever makes you ask that?' Belinda replied. 'All I have ever wanted is you. You are my pride and joy, a son any mother would be proud of.'

Eventually, Necarius came back to talk to them. He had been able to find little of importance.

'Well, there are some who talk of a feminine and masculine principle,' he said, 'but it's all a bit vague. Things about active and passive which don't make a lot of sense. There's stuff on Banshees, but they are all women, dangerous and unpredictable. I'm not sure, but for all their dangers, they are very powerful. Maybe it's a metaphor for you being such a powerful fire mage. It's just a guess and it doesn't make much sense because for all your power, you have the blue magic of a typical fire mage while the Banshee's female magic is black by all accounts.'

'Maybe it has something to do with you being able to understand your mother when you were a baby,' suggested Candera.

'That could be it,' said Necarius. 'You had a major connection to your mother and I suppose, still have one. Maybe it's that. Maybe, it's just that you have some of the power of a Banshee. I really don't know, nah, that makes no sense, your magic is blue, how can you have the feminine without black magic? I just don't get it.'

'I suppose the fact I have always known my mother could lie at the heart of it,' said Morovius.

'Look, we need to keep this quiet,' said Candera. 'Any notion that you are a bit like a woman would be an utter disaster.'

'Enraefem told me that spirits tend to help,' said Necarius.

'What, by totally confusing me?' asked Morovius.

'Well, the feminine in your life is your mother,' suggested Candera. 'I suppose you just keep intact your special bond and we all keep an eye out for anything unusual.'

They all agreed this was all that could be done. It was especially important that they told no one else about it. No good could come of the authorities thinking that Morovius was a bit of a woman or whatever it was that the spirit had been talking about.

The friends were still busy contemplating the apparition's strange message when they were summoned before Marinus. Did he know? What could it mean? Marinus sat them down in his study and swore them to secrecy, not even Novus was to be told what they were about to hear. More secrets?

Marinus outlined the tunnelling plan to the group and how they needed to contact the dwarves.

'But why us, Sir?' asked Morovius.

'It is essential that the dwarves do not feel threatened. A group of experienced warriors would send all the wrong signals. Bad tempered, those dwarves, they might just attack. Their attitude to anger management is attack first to settle the nerves. As far as they're concerned if you listen to the other's point of view then it just causes confusion. Not known for their great philosophers are the dwarves but bloody good at digging. We need fresh faced youths like you lot who won't seem a threat. On the other hand, Turinus reckons you can handle yourselves, so you're ideal for the job.'

'But, Sir, how are we going to negotiate with the dwarves? We don't know anything about them or how to approach them,' Morovius said.

Marinus smiled. 'But, I know a man who can. Come in,' he shouted. The Assessor walked into the room with Marcus.

'Any of you know this man?'

No one did.

'Oh, but he knows you. This is the Assessor, he chose you to come here. Morovius, it was his idea for your mother to come here with you. Cost me a bloody fortune that did. Anyway, this man has been instrumental in all your lives.'

They looked at him, there he was, the man without whom they would all be peasants. Morovius mouthed a thank you and the Assessor sat down.

'I'm not one for formalities, neither am I one to mess around,' said the Assessor, 'so let us be clear. I know you magic users look down on us ordinary folk but in this case you haven't a clue.

'You know little of what lies outside the city walls, how people think, their fears and aspirations. That is my job and is essential to the success of this undertaking. I expect to be obeyed at all times. If there is any fighting, then sure, that's your job but I know far more about tactics than you lot. You'll need to do the fighting but even then I expect to be listened to without question. You are young and know nothing. All the negotiations and the tactics are up to me. Do you understand?'

'Yes, Sir,' they said.

'We need to be clear, the King has entrusted me with this important mission. You are merely there to enable me to reach the dwarves and negotiate with them. I don't need your opinions or advice, you need mine. Is that clear?'

'Yes, Sir,' they all said in unison.

'Good, we understand one another. We leave in the morning. Banshin, you can use your Anrac, the rest of you will be with me in the coach. My guard, Marcus, will drive us.'

'Are you happy with your escort?' asked Marinus.

'Do I have a choice?' asked the Assessor.

'No'

They all left Marinus's office to prepare for their journey tomorrow.

CHAPTER 11

The following morning, they all awoke early for their journey to the dwarves after a peaceful night's sleep. The youths had already ascertained that although the Assessor might not have the violent abilities of a Turinus to back up his orders, he was not one to be messed with. Besides, as the Assessor had argued, what did they know about the world outside Bogloris? Virtually nothing of any significance. The Assessor, on the other hand, was widely travelled because of his job.

As for the dwarves, they knew nothing whatsoever. They were aware that the dwarves lived far away in the Windborne Mountains and were stubbornly independent. As such, the dwarves had hitherto played no part in the war and hence no part in their education. Come to think of it, what did the Assessor know? The youths hoped he knew a lot more than they did which actually wouldn't be too difficult.

They all met up in the courtyard and as previously agreed, Banshin was proudly astride his Anrac, while Marcus sat on the seat of the coach ready to give the signal to move. The Royal insignia was prominently displayed on the coach's doors.

'Are you lot happy with what I told you yesterday?'

'Yes, Sir,' they replied.

'It is essential you accept my authority. If you don't say now and I'll find another escort.'

'Sir, we are happy with your command.' answered Morovius. 'As you have told us, we lack experience of the outside world.'

'Thank you. We all have to face up to reality at times and some of you magic users are a bit too overly impressed with your own abilities.'

'Sir,' asked Magins, 'we were wondering. We know you understand a great deal, but what do you know about the dwarves?'

'Not a lot I'm afraid, but who does? I'm going to have to do a great deal of thinking on my feet. Maybe, if we approach them peacefully they will respect that and if they say 'No' then so be it. Apparently, though, the little guys like gold and I've got enough to hopefully entice them.'

'So, we have to protect the gold on the way there as well?' asked Morovius.

'Oh yes, the journey's not plain sailing. Up to Anrac Woods is easy enough, no peasant would dare attack a Royal coach, but further North is bandit country. It's pretty cold and poor land for crops, makes people pretty desperate. They see a coach, even if it is accompanied by a warrior on an Anrac, they could get interested.'

'Maybe we should all be outside the coach, Sir,' suggested Candera. 'If they see a whole group of magic users, they could be deterred.'

'Maybe, but I think not. We'll lose the element of surprise that way. Why let any potential enemy know exactly what they're up against?'

They nodded their agreement. The Assessor certainly seemed to know his stuff.

'We have experienced a contact,' said Morovius 'but we were under Turinus's command, Sir.'

The Assessor smiled. 'Don't worry, I know a thing or two about battle tactics. Will you follow my command?'

'Yes, Sir,' they answered.

'All right, first off, Banshin rides his Anrac in front. Any attack will try to neutralise him. Magins be prepared to shield him on my command. That'll absorb their opening attack and expose their positions. After that, listen to me. Is that acceptable?'

It certainly was. The youths were impressed with the Assessor's reasoning.

'Oh and Necarius, does your little guy enjoy hamstringing? Those little daemons usually do.'

'Well, Sir, hamstrings and lately he's developed a taste for gonads.'

'Well, he could be in for a treat. Most bandits can't afford codpieces.'

They all laughed and took their positions in the coach, with Banshin in the lead on his Anrac. Marcus slapped the horses with the reins, signalling to them it was time to go. They made their way through the streets of Bogloris and out through the front gates.

The journey to the Anrac Woods in the North East went boringly as the Assessor had predicted. The area was thoroughly settled by a peasantry used to subservience towards the nobility of Marcovia. The Marcovian crest on the coach was enough to ensure a peaceful passage, even without the presence of a powerful warrior on an Anrac. They approached the Anrac Woods, travelling the jutted road which went around the Wood, following the outline of the trees.

Morovius prodded Candera and whispered in his ear. 'I can feel a loss of power.'

Candera looked at Morovius and studied the surrounding countryside and the Woods.

'Maybe it's the Woods, perhaps something to do with the Anracs. They are, after all, magical beasts,' Candera whispered.

'Not sure,' replied Morovius, 'maybe I only reach full power in Bogloris.'

Candera thought about this. Homesickness was a powerful force, maybe that's how it manifested itself in Morovius.

'Well, at least no man's land is relatively close to Bogloris. That's when your magic will be really needed.'

Morovius nodded. Maybe it was just the case that the further he went from the city, the less powerful he would become. Frustrating to say the least, but an ordinary fire mage was still formidable, the main magic attack force of any army. Maybe, he just had to accept that if they were to have an encounter now he would only be able to conjure up two fire arrows. Still, two enemies killed in one attack, that was still enough to give any marauding bandits plenty of food for thought.

They continued as the road straightened, by skirting the Woods, heading north towards the Windborne Mountains. They could see the dense, lush Woods on the right, the scene of their recent victory and the contrasting farmland on their left. Small parcels of land, most abundant with crops responding well to the fertile soil and pleasant climate, interspersed with patches of fallow soil, left undisturbed to recover so that it could bear fruit the following year. They could see peasants scattered about, tending crops, weeding, even one in the midst of harvesting, collecting the wheat he had so patiently cultivated since Spring.

Occasionally, they could see small villages with children playing with makeshift peasant toys. Balls made of cloth were being thrown between friends and small wooden homemade coaches pulled along by little boys and girls. A childhood they would have had, if it not been for the intervention of the man sitting alongside them, the Assessor.

Whatever happened in their lives, whatever fate befell them, it was all down to this man who had assessed them worthy to be magic users. A man whose intervention none of them could possibly hope to remember and whom they would never have seen again if it had not been for this present mission. How strange life can be! Everything spinning on the decision of one man over whom you have no influence, no say. Morovius found himself wondering whether Flavin, if he had been chosen for this mission, would be looking upon these peasant children with envy, at least they knew their mothers. Maybe, he would look at the adults working tirelessly in the fields and thank the Assessor for giving him the opportunity to grow up in Bogloris and be a fire mage?

The Assessor decided they had travelled enough and he decided to stop at an Inn which was apparently comfortable and had the redeeming feature of selling a local ale and not being confined to mead.

They sat around the table drinking a mug of ale, quiet, none could discuss what was on his mind with the Assessor. What would be the point? Not even Magins could see one. The Assessor had selected them and that was that. The only justification he needed was the fact that we live in a time of war and magic users are essential to our war effort. They had all developed into magic users thereby justifying by their own success the Assessor's initial decision. It is what it is.

Magins, being Magins, could take the silence no longer. He wished there was an excuse to evoke Enraefem, who would soon liven things up, but there was none, it wasn't as if any of the Inn's patrons needed their gonads readjusting. But there was no way silence could win the day when Magins was around.

'Sir, can you tell us anything more about the dwarves?'

'What do you want to know?'

'Anything, Sir.' This was true. For Magins, anything was preferable to silence. 'Any information could be useful in our upcoming mission.'

'Well, I don't know a great deal. I mean, they're easy to recognise, short stocky types, you can't mistake a dwarf. The main thing is they are fiercely independent. They really want nothing to do with human affairs and our war and who can blame them? They made it clear long ago, that any aggression of any sort from Eldara or Marcovia will be met by a massive assault from all the dwarven clans.

'I believe them. Apparently, they enjoy a drink and a good punch up between themselves, but anyone messes with them and all inter-clan rivalry will be forgotten and you'd face a major attack.

'Of course, such an attack would spell disaster for either side. Let's say the dwarves attacked us. We might be able to defeat them but the Eldarans would take full advantage. They would attack us and we would be potentially annihilated having to fight on two fronts. Even a small Eldaran force which could be mobilised at short notice would be too much. So, together with the Eldarans, we just leave them alone.'

'Until now, Sir,' said Candera.

'Until now. The success of our mission depends on three things, their love of gold and who doesn't love gold, me convincing them they can dig the tunnel and the Eldarans never finding out. They walk away five hundred gold richer with their independence intact.'

'Why don't we dig the tunnel, Sir?' asked Banshin.

'Yeah, I wish we could, but just digging a hole in the ground isn't as easy as it sounds. There's all sorts of things to consider and we only have about six months to complete it. Both Kingdoms are mobilising as we speak. Not only that, but those little guys have loads of gunpowder and that is essential.'

'The thing could collapse, couldn't it, Sir?' Morovius commented as he considered his own tunnelling experience with Flavin.

'There's all sorts of things that could go wrong. To be honest, I know less about tunnelling than I do about dwarves. I'm not even sure how good they are at digging. All we know is that they apparently do a lot of it in the mountains, looking for gold or something.'

'Well, Sir, if those guys can dig through a mountain, a tunnel under no man's land should be child's play,' said Magins.

'Let's hope so. What for them is a simple tunnel and they walk away with five hundred gold. They will be well away before the battle even begins. Anyway, all I know is I'll have to think on my feet during negotiations, hopefully get inspired or something.'

They returned to their drinks, Magins grateful that silence had been broken, albeit temporarily. Marcus looked at the Assessor. 'If anyone can pull this off, it'll be the Boss,' he thought.

The next morning they resumed their journey. The scenery subtly and gradually changed as did the weather. As they proceeded Northwards and beyond the Anrac Woods it became colder, the wind harsher and the agricultural land more scattered. Instead of occasional fallow land breaking up the rows of crops, there were large sections of rocky areas which only the toughest heathers could call home. They rarely encountered a village, the population density being insufficient to support a central hub of shops and an Inn. The occasional street they did encounter was largely deserted, and the road they travelled became wilder, tough grasses attempting to recolonise their old spaces.

The Assessor stopped the coach and walked up to Banshin.

'Hopefully, the warning I'm about to give you is totally unnecessary but I've always found a little paranoia to be useful. If we are confronted, you must hold your nerve and remember, Magins is there to shield you.'

'Yes, Sir.'

'You do trust Magins, don't you?'

'With my life, Sir. A warrior needs a defensive mage and I've the best supporting me.'

'Well done.' The Assessor returned to the coach and hoped that Banshin's faith in his friend would not be tested.

They did encounter the odd person alongside the roadside, but instead of the salutes and stares of amazement to see an Anrac, the figures slinked off. Hopefully, it meant nothing more than folk in these parts didn't like strangers.

The land became more mountainous as they continued their approach to the Windborne Mountains. They eventually came to an area, the Assessor told them was the Windborne Pass. The road, such as it was, went through the pass, surrounded on both sides by mountainous terrain, about a hundred feet high.

'This is it, lads. We get through here and we should be on course to see the dwarves without incident.'

True enough, perhaps, but this also looked like the perfect place for an ambush. Everyone was on alert and the Assessor told Marcus not to be an heroic fool but to disappear through the trapdoor beneath his seat at the slightest sign of trouble. As the Assessor said, 'We have magic users here for a reason.'

They could see three horsemen approaching at the end of the pass. Travellers or was this trouble? The area was ideal territory for an ambush, but no point in ambushing a coach by initially announcing your presence. The men continued their approach, Banshin sat bolt upright on his Anrac, the youths inside the coach began to build up their blue magic in case it was needed. The Assessor watched matters carefully through a slit in the coach.

'Good day,' one of the men shouted to Banshin. Banshin nodded to him noting that the men stayed out of reach. Banshin began to build up his magic in case he needed to wield his broadsword.

'Hold firm, Banshin,' the Assessor whispered. 'Marcus, get ready to drop through the trapdoor.' Marcus undid the latches which held his seat in place.

'We have a proposition,' said one of the men.

Banshin said nothing.

'You see, we know you are a brave and potent warrior and I'm sure you are a person of fine moral principles. Sure, one on one, you could kick our butts, but you have to realise this. There are many of us, most are hidden, you haven't a chance. Now, dismount from your Anrac, allow us access to your coach, we promise merely to relieve the occupants of some of their possessions. You can then be merrily on your way, hey, only the rich are in coaches, all their possessions at home will be safe and most importantly, you'll all have your lives. What do you say?'

Banshin said nothing. Those inside the coach imbued themselves with the power of the jains, Enraefem was summoned and was quiet, realising the urgency of the situation.

'They have bowmen in the mountains.' said the Assessor. 'Wait for the arrows, then shield Banshin and his Anrac. The arrows will reveal their positions, blast them. Little guy, you're up those mountains, it's gonad time for you.'

They waited for the enemy's initial attack.

'Right, you mute bastard, I'm going to count to three. You'd better give me an answer that makes me happy.'

Banshin grabbed his broadsword and his shield and said nothing, sitting bolt upright.

'One,' shouted the bandit, holding up one finger. 'two,' he paused looking at the silent Banshin, 'three.'

A flurry of arrows came shooting down towards Banshin from both sides of the pass. Marcus activated the trapdoor, the seat swung around and he was gone. Magins jerked his hand, throwing an impermeable shield around Banshin and his Anrac. Necarius and Morovius jumped out of the left side of the coach, Enraefem shot out of the right hand side, bounding up the mountain. It was gonad time. The arrows bounced harmlessly off the shield Magins had created.

'Make the shield permeable,' Banshin shouted and it immediately took on a greenish hue. Banshin charged the three bandits with Candera ready to heal if any arrows made their way through.

Necarius was blasting the mountain up above with blue bolts and Morovius with his stronger fire bolts, both trying to remember where they had seen the arrows emerge. Enraefem continued to jump upwards, easily avoiding an arrow shot in his direction.

Three arrows penetrated Banshin's permeable shield and although the shield slowed them it was not enough to prevent them penetrating Banshin in the arm, chest and thigh. Candera, immediately cast a healing spell, Banshin's wounds closing up, forcing the arrows out of him to land harmlessly on the ground.

Banshin laughed. One on one, are you joking, you three have no chance. Morovius and Necarius continued to blast away at the mountain to their left, shattering boulders, causing mayhem, Morovius straining to make out any distant figures. He could see a man taking aim with a bow and arrow.

The bowman didn't have a chance to test the permeable shield which now surrounded Banshin, Necarius and Morovius. A fire arrow struck with unerring accuracy and obliterated his head. Morovius smiled, I might not be as powerful as I am in Bogloris but you'd still better not mess with me.

Banshin charged, taking glee in the terrified faces which greeted him. Two of the bandits managed to hold up their shields just in the nick of time. They needn't have bothered. Banshin wielded his broadsword with such force that it smashed through one shield, sliced through a bandit and continued its journey to embed itself in the next bandit.

'Two down with one blow,' thought Banshin. 'You won't insult me with this one on one nonsense again.'

He turned to chase down the third bandit who was frantically urging his horse into a gallop. Idiot, a horse outrunning an Anrac, who had ever heard of such a thing? It was Banshin's pleasure to kill him as a fleeing coward, slicing off his head. 'Enraefem's gone to the right,' he thought, 'I'll go to the left.' Banshin turned his Anrac to ascend the mountain.

Necarius looked into his mind meld with Enraefem. He started to blast with his blue bolts to the right, to support his daemon. 'I'll back up Enraefem, you support Banshin,' he told Morovius.

'Morovius clear a way for Banshin's Anrac. Just enable him to get up there,' shouted the Assessor. 'Magins give Banshin a normal shield, only make it permeable when Banshin is in melee range.'

Necarius started to cast his blue bolts to his right, supporting Enraefem. He explored his mind meld. Enraefem had made it and seemed to be pre-occupied with one thing and one thing only, gonads.

Enraefem jumped up and sank in his teeth, tasting gonads. The bandit archer screamed so loudly, they could all hear it. Good boy, Necarius thought as he smiled to himself. He was even happier to see a bandit archer jump up to avoid Enraefem, exposing his head to Necarius who blasted him with a blue bolt. It wasn't enough for an outright kill, after all, Necarius was not a fire mage, but the archer would never recover without the help of a skilled healer.

Enraefem continued to leap around, biting whoever and wherever he could, preferring the gonads, but not particularly fussy. The archers were panicking, shooting at Enraefem as best they could, one even managing to shoot one of his comrades in the chest. They just couldn't believe it, why would so many magic users be this far North?

213

Meanwhile, Banshin was moving up the mountainside, arrows deflecting harmlessly off Magins's impermeable shield, his Anrac showing surprising agility in an animal so large. He encountered a large rocky outcrop which his Anrac had no chance of climbing. Banshin was wondering about a way around it when a fire bolt shot past his left-hand side obliterating the outcrop. The way ahead was clear. He climbed to the top and with a flick of his hand, Magins made his shield permeable.

Banshin screamed and launched himself into the archers. They didn't have a chance. A magic warrior with a permeable shield and a healer on call. What did an archer have in melee? A small dagger. The odds were horrendously against the bowmen and they started to flee.

This was an equally futile option. What chance did they have to outrun an Anrac? Perhaps they thought if they all went in different directions, one of them might at least escape. Banshin had other ideas. One by one, he charged them down and dispatched them. He played a game with himself, attempting to achieve a clean decapitation with each blow, sometimes succeeding, on others it was more messy, but it was a kill nevertheless.

Enraefem's opponents didn't choose to flee, but kept on trying to shoot him as he dodged around taking bites where he could, a trail of bodies lying on the ground, groaning in agony, blood pouring from their groins. Necarius kept blasting away, eventually enlisting the support of Morovius, just keep them distracted and let Enraefem work his magic.

Perhaps the horror of Enraefem's attacks concentrated an archer's mind, perhaps it was blind luck, but he managed to shoot the daemon straight through the body. The daemon disappeared and the arrow dropped to the ground. There were only three archers left unwounded and they ran, leaving their screaming comrades bleeding profusely, the results of Enraefem's gonad fetish.

'Enraefem's gone,' said Necarius.

'I don't think there's anyone left to fight,' said Morovius.

'Well, there might be,' said Magins, 'but Banshin's dealing with that.'

They all laughed, thinking how ridiculous it was. A bunch of archers faced with Banshin, it hardly seemed fair.

The Assessor emerged from the coach. Turinus had said this lot could handle themselves.

'You can come out now, Marcus,' he shouted. 'Did any get away?'

'Yes, Sir,' replied Necarius. 'They got my daemon before he could dispatch them all.'

'Guess they'll let everyone know it's best to leave us alone. What the hell is all that screaming?'

'Gonads, Sir. Enraefem got most of them in the gonads.'

'Well, let's get out of here as soon as possible. That noise is getting on my nerves.'

They looked up. Banshin was descending his side of the mountain. He had dispatched all the archers.

They took their positions as before and Marcus was told to make good speed as the Assessor felt that the screaming and sobbing was getting him down and it was quite possible it might put him off his dinner.

'Sir,' Necarius asked. 'How long will it be before I can summon Enraefem again?'

'Was he badly injured?'

'An arrow straight through him, Sir.'

'Ah, a death blow. It takes most daemons a week to recover.'

They continued onwards, sure in the knowledge that the escapees would spread the word and the bandits had learnt a good lesson.

It was time to meet the dwarves.

CHAPTER 12

The group, now in high spirits, continued onwards at a good pace until they could no longer hear the screams of the dying men. Necarius hoped Enraefem would be all right, but the Assessor assured him being a daemon, he was as tough as nails, and would be back as good as new. Magins certainly hoped so, the end of the battle wasn't the same without the 'I am awesome and I'll tell you why speech,' from Enraefem.

Instead, they had to settle for assurances from the Assessor that they were fine warriors who knew the balance of following orders and showing initiative. They now had two contacts under their belts and had successfully negotiated both. The youths were still too young to fight in no man's land as they had not reached their full magical potential, but the Assessor was confident that they would nevertheless, acquit themselves with honour and bravery.

'Mind, you, no heroics with the dwarves. We cannot win. Even if we won a battle, we would lose. The Kingdom cannot afford a war with the dwarves under any circumstances.'

The time for fighting was over. It was down to the Assessor now to successfully complete the mission. The youths had done all they could. They'd gained safe passage to the Windborne Mountains.

After a somewhat uncomfortable camp by the roadside and uneventful boring watches, they continued their journey until the Mountains rose up before them. The Windborne Mountains were huge, rocks jutting out of the ground, allowing nothing but sparse ledges where only the toughest grasses and heather could survive. But life has a way of hanging onto the harshest of environments. The odd goat could be seen, high up, somehow existing on the meagre offerings of the mountain.

'This is it, lads. Time to be non-threatening.'

The youths were not quite sure how they could go about this, their entire training being dedicated to making them the most dangerous warriors possible. It was definitely time to listen carefully to the Assessor, they were in completely unknown territory.

They followed his instructions and all left the coach, while Banshin dismounted. The party walked along holding up white flags which Magins in particular found distasteful.

'Are we surrendering, Sir?' he asked.

'We're doing whatever we have to in order to gain an audience with the dwarves.'

They continued their walk and eventually saw flashes of sunlight from the mountains.

'That's probably them observing us through eyeglasses,' said the Assessor. 'Just keep walking and lads…'

They looked at him.

'Let me do the talking.'

As not even Magins had the slightest idea what he'd say to a dwarf, this was an instruction easily followed. Somehow, 'We come in peace, take us to your leader' didn't sound like it would be enough.

They kept up their steady walk until they heard the sound of hooves.

'That'll be the dwarves,' said the Assessor.

'What's that sound?' asked Morovius.

'Rams. The dwarves ride mountain rams.'

They stopped walking and waited. They'd been spotted and the dwarves were approaching. Well, it was up to the Assessor now. His instructions were clear. If the dwarves attack, just shield and heal. No offensive moves of any sort were allowed. We can't afford to offend these little guys.

They could see about twenty dwarves in the distance mounted on white furred and horned rams coming up towards them. The dwarves mounting them were in full mail armour and bore axes.

The dwarves approached.

'What do you knaves want with us?'

'I would like to have the opportunity to talk to your leader. We require the services of the dwarves.'

'And why should we serve humans, we want no part in your dealings.'

'Because we can pay. I have a hundred gold in the coach and can pay a further four hundred gold.'

'What can we do that would justify such an amount?'

'Dig us a tunnel.'

'Dig your own tunnel.'

'We lack the mining skills of the dwarves.'

'There has to be more to this than a simple tunnel.'

'There is. Please allow us safe passage into your Kingdom and I shall explain everything in detail. If our offer is unacceptable, we will just leave and you will have lost nothing. If our offer is acceptable, you get five hundred gold for a tunnel.'

'There has to be a catch.'

'It is a bit more complicated but to explain things fully I need to sit down and carefully go through everything.'

'If you are trying to trick us...'

'We cannot. You know full well we are at war with the Eldarans. We cannot possibly afford to offend the dwarves with trickery or deceit. Please, all I am asking is the chance to make my offer. You can always say 'No'.'

'and if we say 'Yes'.'

'Then you are five hundred gold richer.'

The dwarf stared at the Assessor. He had the huge bushy beard typical of his race, and broad shoulders. At his side was a large axe which the Assessor was sure he could wield with great expertise. The dwarf smiled.

'Human, you intrigue me. We will listen if for no other reason than I am most curious why you'll pay five hundred gold for a simple tunnel.'

'I'm sorry, but I never said it will be simple.'

'Ah, a complication.'

The dwarf nodded and the rams moved to one side.

'Oh, and humans,' the dwarf said as they walked past, 'stop waving those silly flags and get in your carriage. I know your kind are stupid enough to wage a war with no chance of victory but not even you lot are crazy enough to mount an attack with such a meagre force.'

The youths and the Assessor stepped back into the coach and Banshin mounted his Anrac. Ah well, they were in. The Assessor had gained an audience. Now the hard part was about to begin.

They were allowed passage into the Dwarven Kingdom in Windborne Mountains on passing through a small opening in the mountainside which barely allowed the coach entry. The party were thankful they could enter proudly as warriors, particularly Banshin on his Anrac, rather than as those who had surrendered with white flags. There was silence in the coach, no one could do anything now apart from the Assessor who was thinking furiously. However, it didn't help. He knew enough about negations to realise that however prepared you were what usually mattered was how well you replied spontaneously to questions or a problem you hadn't anticipated. Whatever that box thing was, the sooner he thought outside it, the better.

They passed through a huge stone cavern. They wondered how much of it was natural and how much had been designed by the dwarves. If they had dug most of it, then no wonder they had come to them for their tunnel. Anyone who could dig this deeply into a mountain certainly knew how to mine. A tunnel would be child's play to such folk.

They looked at the myriad colours which painted the walls. There were minerals and crystals of various colours and hues and shadows and light caused by the multitude of burning torches which adorned the walls. The mountain outside, while impressive in its magnitude, seemed sparse and

222

devoid of life. Inside, it had a raw and natural beauty. Everywhere they looked they could see the dwarves, short maybe, but proud of stature, stocky and solidly built.

They were told to stop and obeyed. One of the dwarves accompanying them went into a side room and the delegation waited patiently for him to return. Hopefully, the mention of five hundred gold for a tunnel would arouse enough curiosity to grant an audience with the presumably important dwarf who sat inside.

It wasn't long before they were asked to enter and the Assessor asked permission for his entourage to accompany him. 'Don't worry, they won't talk,' he assured the dwarf.

'If they know what's healthy for them, all they will do is breath and that quietly,' the dwarf replied.

They entered the room and the Assessor took his seat at the table, the rest of his companions remained standing alongside the walls. Across from the Assessor sat a majestic dwarf, long of beard, flecked with grey to denote his seniority. Behind him stood ten dwarves, each with a hand on his battle axe.

The Assessor took a deep breath and began. 'Thank you for allowing us safe passage.'

'You're not welcome, I would rather you had not come, but the small size and youth of your party show you have no violent intentions. You have assured my men that if I refuse your offer, you will just leave us in peace.'

'Absolutely.'

'Well, carry on. Let me warn you. My mind is already made up to say 'No'. I want nothing more from humans than to be left alone. Your mad war is proof enough of your stupidity. I doubt you have anything worthwhile to offer us.'

The Assessor thought of the one hundred gold pieces he had on him and the promise of four hundred more to come. He obviously had something to offer, otherwise he would never have been granted an audience.

'Well, as you have undoubtedly been told, we need a tunnel'

'Yes, five hundred gold for a tunnel. Simple enough. Now tell me the complications and don't hold anything back.'

'We are mobilising for war against the Eldarans.'

'No doubt they are also mobilising.'

'Certainly. Now we wish to dig a tunnel under no man's land up to their position. This tunnel will be about two miles long. The important thing is and this is crucial, very few of our side and no Eldarans know about this tunnel. If you agree, every effort will be made that dwarven involvement will remain unknown to the Eldarans. It will maintain your independence.'

'So you want a tunnel for a surprise attack?'

'Well, yes, but not of our warriors. We want you to pack the end of the tunnel with gunpowder. Now, once you have done this, your men can depart. No dwarf will be around when the battle commences. We'll use a fire mage to ignite the gunpowder.'

'and for this you will pay five hundred gold?'

'Yes.'

'What if we fail to dig the tunnel on time?'

'Well, it's only two miles and you have six months.'

'Oh, you simpletons, you think mining is that simple. What is the state of the ground under no man's land, how much support will the tunnel need, what measures are in place to remove all the excavated soil, what angles are required to allow a fire ball access, what unseen obstacles are there?'

'I don't know. That is why we need dwarven expertise.'

'All right. I ask again. What if we fail to dig your tunnel in time? We have no idea what obstacles we may need to overcome under no man's land.'

The Assessor thought. Here it was, the unexpected question and, of course, the dwarf was right. There was no guarantee of success. He had no idea what a tunnel really involved and couldn't even make an educated guess as to their chances of success.

'Three hundred gold.'

'If we fail?'

'Yes, three hundred gold for failure, five hundred gold for success. One hundred to be paid now up front.'

'That seems fair. However, you are asking us to put at risk our neutrality for a mere five hundred gold?'

'Every effort will be made to ensure that the Eldarans remain totally ignorant of dwarven involvement.'

'I'm sure that's true and if you could guarantee that, I would be inclined to accept your offer but you cannot possibly guarantee it.'

'Your men will be underground, digging. How can the Eldarans ever know it was you?'

'Can you guarantee it? Have you a crystal ball that can predict the future? Let's say one of my men takes a piss in the moonlight and is spotted by one of their sentry towers. Your war starts, big explosion in a tunnel, they saw a dwarf, put two and two together. What's a dwarf doing around here, oh yeah, there was a tunnel and a bloody big explosion. They'll soon suspect us.'

It was true. One sighting of a dwarf and the whole thing could be exposed. Hell, the Eldarans might even suspect through logic alone. Dwarves are excellent miners and have gunpowder; the Assessor knew he could not guarantee Eldaran ignorance.

'OK. Well, firstly every effort will be made to ensure dwarven anonymity. The tunnel will start behind one of our towers which is easily big enough to shield you from prying Eldaran eyes. Just tell your men to be careful when they have a piss.'

The dwarf started to look annoyed.

'Seriously, your men will have to be careful. So, firstly, chances are you will not be discovered. The point is, all the work is underground, by definition out of sight. I promise you, even Marcovian knowledge of dwarven involvement is absolutely minimal.'

'Fine, fine, but what if the Eldarans do discover what we've done?'

'Right, let us presume they do. What can they do?'

'Attack us in revenge.'

'Really? You think so? The Eldarans attack the dwarves and we will take full advantage and launch an offensive, even if we only have our standing army present. The Eldarans know this, as do we. If the Eldarans attack you, they will inevitably face an attack from us. There is no way they can survive an attack on two fronts. I know this, because neither can Marcovia. The dynamic ensuring dwarven neutrality and independence from human meddling remains intact.'

'Maybe, maybe, but why incur their wrath?'

'Will you? Actually, if I were Eldaran, my attitude would be, bloody good idea that tunnel, dwarves are the ideal race to build it, I'll go and offer them five hundred gold to build us one.'

'and so we get involved in your war?'

'Maybe, but at no risk to yourself and making five hundred gold a time. But this is just the worst case scenario. Facts are, your dwarves will be working underground, out of sight. Very few people indeed know about this plan even on our side. The most likely outcome is, your guys go in, dig a tunnel. Plant it with gunpowder underneath the Eldaran lines and go back to the mountains before the battle even commences. We blow it up and everyone presumes we did it ourselves.'

'So we win regardless of whether our involvement is discovered or not?'

'Exactly. The dynamic guaranteeing dwarven independence and freedom from human meddling remains intact, regardless of what happens.'

'You may leave. Wait in the main hall for our decision.'

They walked out, the Assessor earning approving glances form the youths and Marcus.

'Damn clever fellow, my Boss,' thought Marcus with great pride. 'Who could have thought of that? If things go totally wrong, you still win. Who can reject an offer like that?'

The Assessor sat down in the coach. Well, he'd done everything he could, managing to think on his feet. Anyway, he shouldn't feel too proud, of course the dwarves would want to know what would happen if things went wrong. He should have anticipated their question but was happy that even if he had he couldn't have answered any better. Damn it, if I was a dwarf, I'd accept the offer, how could they refuse?

They couldn't. It wasn't long before a dwarf emerged from the chamber with the good news that they would spare ten of their best miners. The terms were acceptable, and just by the way, where was the one hundred gold pieces they had been offered up front?

The Assessor handed over the gold and as promised ten dwarves approached, leading their rams behind them. The rams each had bags balanced over their shoulders. Gunpowder they were told. More would soon be put into the carriage. The Assessor had succeeded. He just hoped the dwarves now managed to dig the tunnel in time otherwise he would have to explain to the King why they had to pay a further two hundred gold for failure.

'Now you can go and I hope never to see you again,' the dwarf who had led the negotiations told them. The Assessor wondered who he was, probably some sort of King, who knows how these dwarven clans worked?

'Thank you. We will be quite safe. We encountered some bandits on the way here. I'm sure they now know not to mess with us.'

The dwarf laughed. 'You will be accompanied by ten dwarves in their prime on rams. Bandits learnt long ago that their best course of action was to leave dwarves alone.'

The Assessor smiled. He had done it. His shoulders relaxed. Just a simple journey to Bogloris and he and Marcus could go back to searching the Kingdom for magical babies and infants.

He walked up to Marcus. 'We did it.'

'You did it, Sir.'

'Yeah, it was touch and go for a bit.'

'Well done, Sir. Many would have failed.'

'Thank you. Anyway, let's hope we have a boring journey to Bogloris. I have had quite enough excitement these past few days.'

The Assessor's hopes were well placed. The few bandits who survived had told their stories to anyone who would listen and all those who valued their lives and gonads quickly realised that challenging a coach with the royal insignia was not a particularly good idea. They had long ago realised that the best thing you can do with a dwarf is to leave him alone.

They set off on their uneventful journey back to Bogloris. As they did, the Assessor had to tell Banshin something that had been on his mind.

'Banshin, you know that Anrac of yours?'

'Yes, Sir.'

'As soon as we encounter any water, be sure to give it a damn good wash.'

'Certainly, Sir.'

It is often thus. Once the important things in life have been achieved, the more mundane regain their former importance.

CHAPTER 13

The party set off on their journey. Banshin in front on his Anrac, the ten dwarves following in two single files of five, the rest of the party in the coach. They only saw a few people in the Bandit Lands who were always in the distance and ran away. They approached the edge of Anrac Woods knowing they were about to enter more populated territory.

The Assessor approached Gimlin who had been nominated as head of the dwarves. As he had been told, Gimlin was in charge of human affairs in this operation and all negotiations were his concern – leave the other dwarves alone.

'Gimlin,' the Assessor said, 'we are now going to encounter more people and the road is much safer. You need to be hidden.'

'That makes sense. This is after all, a secret mission.'

'Right. So you dwarves get in the coach and we will ride the rams into Bogloris.'

'Bit of a squeeze, isn't it?' asked Gimlin.

'Don't worry, you're small enough.'

Gimlin grimaced but decided it wasn't time for a diplomatic incident just yet.

The dwarves crammed into the coach with expletives and cries of 'get yer elbow out of my face' and so on. Eventually, things calmed down and the magic users mounted four rams, the rest being tethered to the coach's horses. The Assessor who was damned if he was getting on one of those rams, sat next to Marcus up front.

They proceeded towards Bogloris, this time getting more stares. Few had seen rams before, especially not mounted by magic users. Imagine their surprise if they knew there were a bunch of dwarves crammed into the coach!

They went into the coach house in Bogloris and cleared the place of all staff. Only then were the dwarves allowed to emerge, saying things like, 'Bloody uncomfortable, that coach,' 'Who the hell thought it was a good idea to ride in a box when perfectly good rams are available,' and such similar grumblings. The magic users were told to go and tell no one of their little adventure. The Assessor and Markus waited with the dwarves until nightfall.

Nine of the King's most trusted guards arrived to join Marcus with their horses. The dwarves, hidden inside a woolen bag, were mounted on the backs of the horses, and off they rode to no man's land, the rams tethered to the horses.

The party arrived at the lookout tower and disembarked behind the tower so that prying Eldaran eyes could not see what was happening. Ready for them in the tower were picks, shovels and torches to provide light in their tunnel. They peered around the corner into no man's land. The jains glistened heavily in the moonlight. The rams were led to the bottom of the tower.

'Right you are,' said a guard, called Frank. 'Marcus and me have been elected to guard the tower. Any problems, just tell us and we'll see to it.'

'Ale,' said Gimlin.

'What?'

'Ale, we need ale, lots of it. Thirsty work is digging.'

The other guards set off back to Bogloris for ale. The dwarves immediately began to dig, pickaxes and shovels on the go. Markus and Frank were suitably impressed and went inside the tower.

The first crisis was reached after the first shift.

'Is that it?' shouted Gimlin.

'What?' asked Marcus.

'That barrel of ale?'

'Sure. What's wrong with it? You haven't even tried it yet?'

'One barrel! There are ten of us you know.'

'Do you want more?'

'A lot more and why have we only got one tankard each?'

'For drinking?' guessed Marcus.

'I know that, but what about singing? We need a tankard for singing,' shouted Gimlin.

'All right, all right,' said Marcus. 'Frank, go and get ten more tankards and more ale.'

Frank was off and the pattern was set. The dwarves would dig a night shift of nine hours with their rams helping to remove the dug earth to the surface. The trusted guards would get rid of the debris and the shift would end. Then, the dwarves would quaff ale, a great deal of it, and sing. That was when the extra tankard came in useful. Dwarven songs are much better when accompanied by a great deal of tankard banging against a table and who wants to risk spilling precious ale with a full tankard?

And so it continued. The dwarves dug a diagonal down twenty feet before they started to go horizontally towards Eldara. The guards kept bringing wood to shore up the tunnel and provide flooring as the rams in particular would have badly cut up the earth. In turn, the guards' horses pulled away barrel loads of jain sparkled earth. Digging, drinking, singing, tankard bashing and the odd punch up were the order of the day. Eventually, Marcus was summoned before the Court to report on progress.

Marcus had not been too happy to be separated from the Assessor in the first place and now this. Up in front of the Court where no doubt he had to answer loads of questions and what did he know? The dwarves were digging away but Marcus really didn't have a clue what was going on underground – how could he?

He walked into the Court and was glad to see the Assessor sitting there. Unfortunately, not only was the Chief Exchequer, Amran also there but so were King Almein and Queen Elbeth.

'Guard,' said the King, 'what's going on with those damn dwarves?'

'They are digging, Your Majesty,' said Marcus.

'Well, I should bloody well hope so. I'm paying enough,' said the King, 'but how are they doing?'

'They seem fine, Your Majesty.'

'Tell me guard, do you and your friend have a drink problem?'

'No, Your Majesty.'

'Well, how come I am getting reports of untold barrels of ale being delivered to your sentry post?'

'It's for the dwarves, Your Majesty.'

'Bloody dwarves? They're only small, how can they drink so much?'

'I am not sure, Your Majesty.'

'What do they do up there all day?'

'Well, they sing songs Your Majesty, drink ale and sometimes they fight.'

'Fight? I can't have this. I've paid a lot of gold for that damn tunnel. I want no slacking. Amran, go and find out what the hell's going on.'

'Your Majesty, the guards report that they are removing plenty of earth. I'm sure the dwarves are working hard.'

'Amran, are you questioning me? Go and see those bloody dwarves and find out about all this drinking and fighting.'

Amran looked weary as Almein stared at him. 'Certainly, Your Majesty.'

A rather crestfallen Chief Exchequer left the Court with Marcus to find out about dwarven culture. He was not looking forward to it.

As they approached the sentry tower, Amran turned to Marcus.

'Markus, you may speak freely. Do you have any advice to offer me on talking to the dwarves.'

'I'm afraid not, Sir.'

'What? You've been with them a month.'

'I've found that they are best left alone, Sir.'

'Damn! I wish that was advice I could follow.'

They approached the tower.

'Ask that Gimlin fellow to come down, will you?'

Gimlin emerged, bleary eyed.

'What the hell do you want?' he shouted.

Amran sighed. This was not the start he was hoping for.

'Just a friendly visit, that is all.'

'Well, we're dwarves and you are human. We are not your damn friends, so bugger off.'

'Come now. We are paying you, after all. I just want to know if we can help.'

'Well, make sure that we have good quality wood for shoring up the tunnel and for flooring. Some of the stuff we've had is shocking.'

'Well, I can certainly help there. Anything else?'

'More ale.'

'Ah, now. Are you quite sure you and your men should be drinking quite so much?'

Gimlin stared at him through bloodshot green eyes. His beard shaked. Amran though he was going to explode.

'What the hell do you know about digging?'

'Very little,' conceded Amran.

'Right. Bloody hard work is digging and we need our sleep.'

'Certainly,' answered Amran unsure about this particular piece of dwarven logic.

'Now, ale helps us sleep. Prepares us for the work ahead. Understand?'

'Makes sense,' conceded Amran, uneasily.

'Get more ale in.'

'Certainly.'

Gimlin started to walk away but Amran had to ask one last question.

'Say, my good fellow.'

Gimlin turned wondering what this stupid human could possibly want now.

'Are you chaps getting along all right?'

'What the hell are you on about?'

'You're not fighting, are you?'

Gimlin took in a deep breath and seriously considered hitting Amran. He thought of gold and decided diplomacy was the better option.

'Listen to me, you bloody human. You lot have been fighting some stupid war for no one knows how long for no good reason. Do you think us dwarves are stupid enough to do anything that wasteful and ridiculous?'

240

'Certainly not.' Amran was beginning to see that he had underestimated dwarven logic.

'Right, so bugger off out of dwarven affairs. You have no advice of any value to offer us. Understand?'

'Certainly.'

'We are working our arses off to dig your stupid tunnel. If we encounter a problem we'll tell you.'

'Certainly.'

'Oh, and Chief whatever you are.'

'Yes?'

'Make sure the ale keeps coming.'

'Certainly.' Amran walked off wondering how the Assessor had managed to bargain with the dwarves in the first place. He mounted his horse and determined that he would tell the King the dwarves were splendid fellows doing a great job.

The dwarves continued digging the tunnel and the Chief Exchequer was true to his word. He ensured the wood for shoring up the tunnel was of the finest quality and that the ale kept coming.

The dwarves were also true to their word and kept to themselves unless they encountered a problem. As happens with anything as complex as a two mile underground tunnel, they encountered a problem.

Gimlin approached Marcus. 'We have a problem.'

'Is the ale alright?' asked Marcus.

'With the tunnel. In fact we have two major problems. Probably best that you take me to see that Chief bloke and his group.'

'What? You want to see His Majesty?'

'Yeah, he'll do. Whoever's in charge. These two problems will take some solving and some decision making. Whoever is paying will have to decide what to do.'

'Can I tell them what's up?'

'Yeah, shale and air.'

'I don't understand.'

'Shale, that's loads of compacted small stone and we are having difficulty breathing down there.'

Marcus set off for the Court and arranged for Gimlin to have an emergency meeting with Amran, King Almein and Queen Elbeth. Unfortunately, the Assessor was not available. Gimlin was smuggled into the Palace at night-time.

'Before we start, may I just ask that we all remain calm and discuss this rationally,' said Amran.

'For once I agree with the wee man,' said Gimlin, without a trace of irony in his voice.

'All right,' said the King. 'Please tell us the problems and remember, we are not miners.'

'Alright. Air and shale. I'll explain it,' said Gimlin. 'We've hit shale.'

'What's that?' asked Amran.

'It's compacted small stone. Now, it might not sound like much, but it's a big problem. We're twenty feet down and Anracs and who knows what have been tramping over that ground in the centuries before. The small stones are compacted together and we can't get through.'

'No way of digging through, is there?' asked Amran.

'It would take forever with a pick and shovel. We could try blasting with gunpowder but that would alert the Eldarans. See, if it were solid rock we could crack the rock and remove large parts at a time. This stuffs a nightmare. All you can do is chip away a bit at a time and that would take too long.'

243

'Well, you're the miner. What do you recommend?' asked Amran.

'We dig down until we come to the end of it. Just know, while we dig down we are not making any progress towards the Eldarans. We'll have to go vertically downwards. Now your fire ball isn't going to go at right angles, so once we've dug beneath the shale we'll have to dig a diagonal shaft back to the main tunnel.Then, we'll block off the route to the right angle at the shale with sandbags so that your fire ball will go down the diagonal and along the route to the gunpowder in the chamber at the end.'

'Damn, that's going to use up time,' said the King.

'Yes, unfortunately, but there is a positive. Once, we are underneath the shale, we won't have to shore up the roof as much because the shale is so compact and we should make good progress.'

'Well, there appears to be no alternative,' said the King.

'Well, we could go left or right, but who knows how wide this shale layer is.'

'All right,' sighed Amran. 'Now, you mentioned air. What about it?'

'We've got very little. It's getting hard to breath down there.'

'What?' said the King. 'It's a tunnel, air can go down a tunnel, surely?'

'Your Majesty, you've got ten dwarves working, even if I say so myself, very hard. Three on the face, four shoring up and three moving all that earth with rams. We breathe hard'

'More like breathe ale,' thought Amran, but realised saying anything would be a huge mistake.

'Now, the air is being used up more quickly than it can be replenished. It's getting impossible down there.'

'I don't mean to be rude, but why didn't you mention this problem before?' asked Amran.

'It just happened.'

'What? Didn't you already know about this with your experience of mining? What do dwarves normally do?'

'We don't normally dig such narrow tunnels which are this long. We just haven't encountered this problem before.'

'Air, you say?' asked Queen Elbeth.

'Yes, air is the problem,' answered Gimlin.

'Bellows,' said the Queen.

'Bellows?' asked King Almein.

'Bellows,' answered the Queen. 'A blacksmith's bellows push air. Push air down the tunnel through a tube if necessary, and the dwarves will be fine.'

'They will need to be big bellows, operated by a mighty powerful man,' said Gimlin.

'No problem,' said the King. 'We have these huge powerful oafs called warriors. One's magic power lasts for three hours. There is already that young one you've met, we'll just have to recruit another two.'

There were general nods of agreement and smiles all around. Then Gimlin grimaced.

'Sorry, our problem with bellows. How can we see?'

'What?' asked the King. 'Will it be too windy to see?'

'Yes, our torches will be blown out. We won't be able to see a thing. Dwarves will get hurt, what with picks being thrown all over the place.'

'Damn,' said the King.

They all sat there contemplating this latest development. It appeared that every solution merely involved inviting new problems. Amran sat there, light without a flame, where had he seen that before? He had it.

'Daemons,' he shouted, standing up.

'What?' they asked.

'Daemons, those big ones. Bedines have shiny, red glowing eyes.'

'So?' asked the King.

'Well, he stares down the tunnel, flashing his eyes, giving the dwarves light.'

'What about when the tunnel goes down a diagonal?'

'We use mirrors.'

They all started thinking about the daemon. Would the light be strong enough? Would the daemon agree?

Suddenly the King laughed. 'Imagine a large Bedine, with his butt in the air staring down a hole for three hours.'

They laughed at the thought but had unanswered questions. Questions only a daemon could answer. Rather than call in a new necromancer who had such a daemon, too many people already knew about the tunnel, they decided to call upon Necarius. Maybe his daemon could advise them and besides, Necarius already knew about the tunnel.

Markus set off for Necarius and called the rather nervous young man into the Court. Necarius's nerves were not calmed by the long corridors and the paintings of past monarchy. He was overawed by the throne room itself, decorated with huge tapestries, tables and high chairs of finest oak and golden statues.

All sensed the youth's nervousness. 'Don't worry young man. We just need to talk to your daemon.'

'He's a little rude, Your Majesty.'

Amran looked at Gimlin, this was all he needed.

'Does he talk?' asked the King.

'Incessantly, Your Majesty.'

'Good, evoke him.'

Necarius did as bidden, moving his hands with the blue glow, the plop of evocation and the

inevitable, 'Hiya, hey this place looks the same, some things never change, bit like the Netherworld,

you're new though,' Enraefem said, pointing at the King.

'I've been King for fifteen years.'

'A mere hair's breadth in the sliver of time. Why do you need me, any gonads need adjusting?'

'No,' said Amran uneasily repositioning himself. 'We need information.'

'Go on, I'm all ears.' Enraefem shook his head and his normally small ears became as large as his

head.

They outlined the plan for Enraefem and asked about the Bedines with glowing eyes. To everyone's

amazement, Enraefem said nothing out loud, he just whispered in Necarius's ear.

'Your Majesty, he wants to be banished, something about rules.'

'What rules?' asked Almein.

'Your Majesty, he is not clear about that, he just says he will not say any more.'

Enraefem looked at them, wide eyed and with an obstinately closed mouth. They had no option but

to banish him and wait uneasily for the ten minutes the daemon had said he needed to check on the rules. They looked at each other wearily, wondering what those rules could possibly be and what the little imp had in mind.

Thankfully, the ten minutes expired and Enraefem was evoked again. He appeared to be back to his normal chatty self.

'Checked with the Boss, Coronzon, don't want to get on the wrong side of him, rules are rules.'

'Fine,' Amran said, 'what can you tell us?'

'Well, your plan won't work. The Bedines do have glowing eyes, that's true, but it would never light a tunnel. Not strong enough, you see. However, seeing as you are on the right track I can show you something. Just remember an Eldaran imp will show his necromancer the same thing - rules are rules, balance and all that.'

'What, a bloody imp is going to tell the Eldarans about our tunnel?' shouted Almein.

'Not the tunnel. That is a human plan, not our fault. An imp will show them what I am about to show you, no more and no less.'

'Well, what is it?' asked Amran.

'Only show, no tellings, rules are rules. Coronzon said so.'

They all looked at the now silent imp dumbfounded. At last Almein spoke. 'Go ahead, as long as one of you bastards doesn't tell them about the tunnel, I don't care.'

Enraefem said nothing. He just shook his head, his ears now back to their tiny selves and opened his mouth. A strong burst of light shone forth from his throat between his razor sharp teeth brilliantly lighting a tapestry above the King.

They gasped.

'Brilliant!' shouted Gimlin. 'Can you talk when you shine your light?'

Enraefem closed his mouth and started to speak. 'No, it doesn't work that way.'

'Even better,' said Gimlin.

Plans were set in motion. Two new warriors and two necromancers were made privy to the plan. The bellows were made and operated by warriors in three hour shifts and the imps sat on dwarven shoulders lighting the way. The dwarves who had been assigned to carry out the earth in sacks on the rams had to work in the dark as they traversed the tunnel but at least those working at the face for the shift could see clearly.

The dwarves continued to dig down, hoping to arrive quickly at the bottom of the shale.

CHAPTER 14

While the dwarves were desperately digging downwards with thankfully silent imps on their shoulders, both Kingdoms began the arduous task of mobilising their armies. Both knew they could call upon approximately four hundred magic users and pay for three hundred mercenary crossbowmen. There were a handful of upper nobility who could afford the full chain mail armour and the stocky warhorses needed to carry such a load. The three richest landowners even had a retinue of full time knights and bowmen they could automatically call upon. Even so, this only amounted to approximately a further two hundred men.

Fielding the rest of the army to bring it up to the usual five thousand strong required delicate negotiation. Originally, perhaps, it had been easy. King Almein, in theory at least, owned the entire Kingdom of Marcovia. Actually He only ran the relatively small demesne around Bogloris. The rest of the land was held by various landowners in return for providing armed men in time of need. The larger the land, the greater the obligation to provide troops. In particular, the King needed knights, pikemen, bowmen and swordsmen.

However, over the centuries, matters had evolved. Indeed, they had evolved a great deal. Certain landowners hit hard times, a poor crop, for example and were bought out. Sometimes a lesser knight could keep his land but only under the condition that his new liege Lord was his neighbouring knight who would then negotiate with the King on his behalf. Contracts were made between different Lords and knights, whereby one had to provide a certain percentage of another's troops for favours, like protection from another avaricious Lord.

Lords were not even above killing each other. Lessons were learnt. For example, don't play chess with Lord Rufus. Rufus played chess with the conventional large pieces. This normally tranquil chap became somewhat animated when playing chess. Once when playing a neighbouring Lord, his neighbour was in the unfortunate position of actually winning. Highly discontented, Rufus repeatedly brained his opponent with a large chess piece, with the good fortune that he thereby won the match by default and indeed took over his neighbour's land and military obligations.

Another common story was circulated to show that women should listen to their husbands. Lord Manning did not need the excuse of chess in order to become excited and he was very excited indeed about his neighbour, Cedric's land, so he invited him over for dinner. Suddenly, acquiring an interest in hygiene for which he was not renowned, he demanded Cedric have a bath. While Cedric was naked, Manning donned full armour, burst upon him and bludgeoned him to death with his shield. Manning's wife, the good Lady Rosemary, pointed out this was not a gentlemanly way to treat a neighbour, so she got a good thrashing, which everyone agreed she deserved.

The lesson learned was not to go to Manning's for dinner, or indeed any meal, and certainly have a bath before you went on urgent business. Manning remained undeterred by his lack of friends. As he put it, 'I've got loads of land and they're all wankers, anyway.' He suspected they might be jealous of his recent good fortune. He also has, needless to say, an obedient wife.

Another factor that complicated matters was motivation. There were rumours that long ago, people were patriotic and some were even mercenary types looking forward to a bit of pillaging. This was the stuff of legend. The war had been going on for so long to say enthusiasm had waned would be putting rather a pleasant gloss on things. Any thoughts that had ever existed of the pleasures of raping and pillaging had long evaporated. The great set pieces on no man's land inevitably ended in stalemate in a land that however, exhilarating it might be for magic users, was essentially a desert. As a peasant who as a result was executed had said, 'So there's loads of jains. So what? You can't eat jains.' No one argued this openly any more, but the sentiment was there.

Furthermore, even though the battles were usually fruitless, casualties could still be high. Now it's not just your strapping six foot four young peasant who does not want to die but, perhaps more importantly, neither does his Lord want to lose him. In a world where food shortages were common in a harsh winter, a strapping peasant was better employed on the land, or at least that was the thinking of many Lords.

To say cynicism was widespread is a bit like saying that the sea contains a little salt. In fact, the only way the King could actually raise his army was with the threat of magic users. Four hundred magic users turning up at your doorstep was not to be welcomed even if you got them naked in bath and they have a proclivity for playing chess.

So, everyone negotiated. Even the top nobility would try to provide only their personal retinue and nothing else. The smallest landowner was not immune from trying his luck as well.

The knight Bentham was an apparently simple case. He clearly owned a little land directly from the King, so no complications there. His due was his own services as a knight and one healthy peasant pikeman. Even the experienced Sheriff thought this would be an easy task. Not so.

'What the bloody hell is this? That peasant can barely hold the pike he's so bloody small.'

'Well, you see,' said Bentham, 'he is highly skilled. In fact, I trained him myself.'

'I don't care how bloody skilled he is. Look at him! He can barely walk with the pike never mind run into battle. This is ridiculous.'

The peasant looked at the Sheriff, hopeful that he might get out of this battle, but determined to look the part remembering Bentham's words, 'You'll hold that pike and hold it well or I'll poke out your eyeballs with a sharp stick.' To be fair he was holding the pike with all his might, but said might is somewhat limited in a man four foot ten.

'Guards,' screamed the Sheriff. 'Search the huts, hovels, Bentham's home, everywhere. Find me a bloody big peasant.'

They eventually emerged with a fine looking lad, broad shouldered, well over six foot.

'Right,' shouted the Sheriff. 'What about him?'

'Unskilled,' said Bentham. 'Very stupid, can't even wield a hoe never mind a pike.'

'Look, you little runt, give that pike to the big fellow.'

The small peasant gratefully rid himself of his burden.

'Right, he can hold a bloody pike, that'll do. He's going to gloriously serve His Majesty on His Campaign.' The Sheriff crossed off Bentham's name from his list. 'Any objections Bentham?'

'None,' Bentham said dejectedly.

'Right,' said the Sheriff, 'see you in three months in Bogloris. Oh, and Bentham.'

'Yes.'

'You'd better make sure you feed that big lad and train him or you'll be having an intimate meeting with a daemon. I've heard one has developed a taste for gonads. All right?'

'Yes, all right.'

The Sheriff rode off with his guards.

While all this chaotic recruitment was going on above ground, the dwarves continued to dig down, feeling the shale hoping to find soft ground. As the new shaft was vertical, the dwarves were having to carry the newly dug soil up the shoring to the horizontal section, where the waiting rams could be loaded. Banshin and two other warriors were assigned to the bellows. Tubes were attached to ensure that fresh air reached the dwarves. Holes were made in the tube on route, so that dwarves and rams bringing soil back to the surface could also breath. The imps sat on dwarven shoulders lighting the way at the front of the tunnel.

It was all rather disheartening. Working hard while making no real progress towards the goal of reaching the Eldaran line. They kept going downwards. Another ten feet and the shale was still there.

Gimlin did his best to keep up spirits.

'Keep going lads. This shale can't go on forever. Remember, it's an extra two hundred gold if we succeed.'

Down they went. A set routine was followed. Picks chopping through the ground. Shoring up the sides with the good quality wood that Amran ensured they received. Dwarves climbing up the shoring with the newly dug soil, loading the rams and traversing the horizontal section to the awaiting guards at the surface. The guards were dumping the newly dug soil across the ground two miles outside Bogloris. It was a well oiled machine that was still making no real progress towards the Eldaran front. Failure was looking imminent.

They dug down another ten feet, checking the front, hoping for soft soil. They were down a total of forty feet.

'Look,' shouted a young dwarf called Amlin. 'Gimlin, Gimlin, come here, look, look.'

Gimlin, who was shoring up, came crawling across, labouring over the dwarves who were digging.

'Gimlin, it's soft, it's soft.'

'Hold your rams,' said Gimlin feeling the surface. 'It might only be a soft pocket. Damn, it certainly feels soft. Look, keep digging, let's make sure.'

They kept on digging down with renewed vigour, checking that all the soil that was exposed in front of them was soft. They were there! A whole layer of soft earth. They had done it.

Gimlin filled a bag with the newly dug earth and started to ascend using the shoring as a ladder.

'I'm going to tell the guards myself.'

He climbed the vertical shaft and proceeded along the horizontal corridor with the laden ram, eventually reaching the surface.

'Tell your King we've done it. We're forty feet down and we have hit soft soil. We'll dig about ten foot horizontally to make sure and then dig back a diagonal to the main tunnel to ensure a path for your fire ball. We've done it. Tell your King. It's game on.'

They dug ten feet horizontally. Sure enough, they were below the shale and as Gimlin predicted, they proceeded quickly as the roof of the tunnel now needed only a little shoring, the shale being so hard. It was game on indeed!

They dug a diagonal from the bottom of the shale to intersect with the original horizontal tunnel. To make sure that the fire ball went down the diagonal and not straight into the shale wall, they packed

258

the intersection with sandbags. Progress was initially very good. Not only did the shale roof not need much shoring but the redundant horizontal tunnel between the diagonal intersection and the shale wall could be packed with the newly dug soil, so the soil did not need to reach the surface. Eventually, the redundant section was filled with soil and they needed to take the newly dug soil to the surface again. They kept going determined to succeed, for reasons of pride and gold.

So harmony was restored. The old routine without anxiety continued. Dwarves using picks to remove the jain laden earth, shoring the tunnel and earth removal with the help of the rams. Shift over, back to the watchtower and mass drinking of ale and the odd punch up with plenty of singing and tankard bashing. All the dwarves would look back on these times with fond memories. Miners united, working hard, playing even harder.

They continued onwards and a new fear developed. How long would the shale roof last? There was no way they could dig up through it and build a chamber for the gunpowder. It had to stop sometime. They had dug one and two thirds of a mile towards Eldara and were beginning to fret. Again the search for soft earth was a preoccupation. They kept digging, checking the ceiling for soft earth.

They need not have worried. They soon encountered soft earth above them, well before the Eldaran line. They could begin digging a gentle diagonal incline up to the intended chamber. It was smooth enough for the rams to easily negotiate. Shoring up was more complex as they were surrounded on all sides by soft earth, but the main thing was it was dry. It rarely rained in no man's land, its flat surface allowing clouds easy passage.

If the Sheriffs above had known about the dwarves they would have been envious. Their problems were far more complex. Trying to deal with Lords and knights who although owners of the land, were never there was hard. Such Lords lived off money rents, not a portion of the produce and usually resided in the city of Bogloris. They had little idea of the details of their land, but instead entrusted its administration to clerks and lawyers. One was even mad enough to entrust the land to his wife while he sampled the pleasures of the city!

It was necessary for the Sheriffs to find out who knew what and as these peasants paid rent they regarded themselves as independent. But small holdings held by one peasant were not eligible for the draft as he was needed to tend his land. Yet, one Lord owned a great deal of this land and was eligible. Sheriffs had to conduct deals whereby the peasant could be a soldier and neighbours were sworn to tend his land for the short period of time he was away, but negotiations were delicate.

Expenses also had to be considered. The further from no man's land a man was, the more expensive it was for him to travel. Ale was the usual sticking point and the Sheriffs had to insist that two pints a day was enough for any man, although any dwarf would have laughed at such rations. Accommodation at inns along the way also had to be negotiated.

Then there was the pay. Six silver for a knight per day, two silver for a pikeman and swordsman, one silver for the rabble. However, as the battle rarely lasted longer than a day, this was poor reward for risking your life. Sheriffs readily resorted to the threat of magic users and eventually everyone heard of the imp who took such a strong interest in gonads.

The King also tried every propaganda trick he could think of and enlisted the aid of the Church. He approached the Arch Cleric and told him of the encounter in the Anrac Woods, a clear motivation for war. The Arch Cleric told his Bishops who told all the clerics and matters were set in motion.

Soon pulpits resounded with sermons of how the Eldarans were raiding Marcovia and trying to kill all the Anracs. Not only this, but it was only a matter of time before they would resort to rape and pillage. Everyone was at risk. But, there was hope. Figures varied, but as many as fifty Eldarans had trespassed into the Anrac Woods and a mere six magic users, five barely youths, had killed them. The gonad chomping imp was particularly applauded. So there was a great threat but also great hope, this could be our chance to finally reunite the Kingdoms under its rightful heir. It was finally a chance to right the wrongs of a long forgotten past when Eldarans had chased Marcovians out of their land before the Marcovian defence in no man's land.

Overall, it worked as well as could be hoped and men allowed themselves to be volunteered. They started practising with great vigour, whether it be the knight on horseback, the mercenary crossbowmen, the archer or swordsman. Their lives depended on their prowess. Even what was termed the rabble practised with pitchforks or whatever implement was at hand. The Sheriffs promised them they would be given simple swords and shields when they arrived in Bogloris.

The accountants started to earn their pay in earnest and collated all the information relayed to them by the Sheriffs. The expenses, the wages, the cost of arming the rabble and of course, the five hundred gold and untold ale for the dwarves. The total was a staggering thirty five thousand gold. The treasury just could not afford it as Chief Exchequer Amran was quick to point out.

261

The King and Amran had to go to the port at Inlein. It was a long journey South East but they had no option. The merchants would not lend the money unless they saw the King in person. Negotiations were difficult and it was always the same question from each merchant, 'How do I know you'll pay me back with interest?'

The King and Amran resolved upon the normal measures – increased taxation. They also pointed out that they couldn't double cross the merchants, they were hugely dependent upon trade. A merchant boycott of Marcovia would ruin the Kingdom, they had no option but to pay.

So, the Sheriffs were sent to work again, this time to collect the hearth tax, a tax on each adult who was not totally destitute. Rumblings grew.

'But, I'll be bloody destitute myself and then who will pay your damn tax.'

'So, I risk my life to fight for the King and he taxes me more than my wage. I am paying for the privilege of risking my life.'

'If the rich didn't waste money, we could afford to wage war without this tax on the already downtrodden peasant.'

The clerics went into overdrive at the behest of the Bishops. Always the same, we can win this time, the Eldarans will plunder us all if we do not raise an army, our magic users are the best ever, we are loyal to King and country. The taxes were quietly eked out of a desperate population, with the promise of riches for all in the event of victory.

King Almein just wished He could tell the people about the tunnel to give them hope, but He could not. Its very success depended utterly on the Eldarans knowing nothing. It was hard. He had the answer to give people heart, but could not say a word about it. He was sure that the tunnel was going well. All the reports were positive.

The dwarves continued to dig up through their gentle diagonal incline. The picks kept flying into the soft earth, timber shored up the newly dug section and rams took all the dug earth to the surface. The ale kept flowing. Gimlin kept encouraging his men and confidence was high.

At last they came to within ten feet of the surface directly beneath where the Eldarans would stand in war. It was time for the chamber. They still had a month left so success was virtually guaranteed. They continued digging.

It was better now that they had more space. No climbing over each other, trying to avoid rams. The imps sat on wooden shoring on the walls, lighting up the whole of the growing cavern. A nice open space, reminiscent of the caverns back home but on a smaller scale. They kept going, eventually digging a cavern five foot high, ten foot deep and twenty foot long. They made sure to shore up the roof with great care. The last thing they needed was a collapse and the Eldarans being alerted. Talk about grabbing defeat from the jaws of victory.

It was time for the gunpowder brought from the Windbourne Mountains and the Kingdom's own reserves. The rams were laden with two bags each and gently led by the dwarves to the chamber. A two mile trek over the floorboards which by now, everyone knew by heart. The gunpowder was stacked into the chamber. The dwarves started to feel a little disheartened. Their great adventure was coming to an end and they would never see the final result – the explosion.

It took one week of hard labour to fill the chamber. One final task. The tunnel entrance to the chamber had to be blocked off with sandbags. As Gimlin explained, the explosion will seek out the easiest escape route. An open tunnel would greatly reduce the explosive force upwards, which was the whole point of the enterprise.

The tunnel was blocked with sandbags and a small tube inserted. This would ensure that at least some of the fireball would make it to the gunpowder. Gimlin and his men had completed their task. Four hundred gold still to be paid. They had succeeded. If you need a task done, ask a dwarf!

They were bundled at night into a coach and their rams were tethered to the horses. It was time to go home. As before, there were various curses and moans as they were crammed into the coach.

'You would think that they could have provided us with two coaches,' moaned Amlin.

'Forget it,' said Gimlin. 'We have the gold and they have their tunnel.'

They were set free after Anrac Woods and mounted their rams. As they rode off Amlin looked puzzled.

'What's wrong?' asked Gimlin, riding alongside.

'Well, I'm thinking of my Aunt Izzie,' said Amlin.

'Do you miss her?'

'Not at all,' replied Amlin. 'Terrible temper.'

'Terrible,' agreed Gimlin.

'Well, the thing is she had a mole.'

'What, on her arse?'

'No, in her garden.'

'Oh, that sort of mole.'

'Yeah, terribly destructive. Her turnips had no chance. The mole even teased her. She'd see a molehill trembling and she would run and kick the hill, only for another molehill to appear next morning.'

'What did she do?'

'Well, you know her temper. She stuffed a hole with gunpowder. Not as much as we have, but enough.'

'What happened?'

'Bloody big hole and when a bird flew to the bottom it died. Reckon there was loads of poisonous gas down there.'

'Did she kill the mole?'

'Think so, never saw it again, but she was never able to grow any turnips either.'

'And your point is?' asked Gimlin.

'Well, they're going to blow that gunpowder.'

'Sure are.'

'Bloody great big hole filled with poisonous gas.'

'Yep.'

'Well, this is the thing. How are they going to charge through a bloody great big poison filled hole?'

Gimlin thought for a moment.

'Not our problem,' he decided.

The dwarves continued on their merry way.

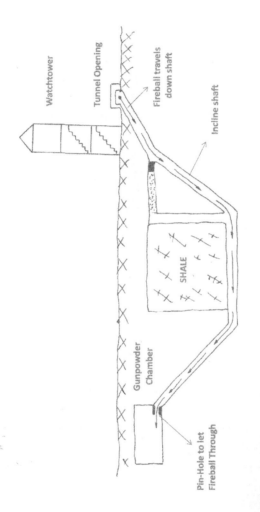

THE EXPLODING TUNNEL

Watchtower

Tunnel Opening

Fireball travels down shaft

Incline shaft

SHALE

Gunpowder Chamber

Pin-Hole to let Fireball Through

CHAPTER 15

Morovius and his friends stood on a mound watching the men who would form the newly assembled army. The friends were still too young to enter into the war. The reasoning being, they still had to perfect their fighting skills, so why risk wasting a magic user who had not fulfilled his full potential?

Many of the untrained peasants entering Bogloris, referred to as the rabble, walked around in amazement. All they had known hitherto was a village which at most could boast four buildings of any substance. Here, the streets were aligned with buildings of all sorts. Huge models of shoes, leather saddles, dresses, horseshoes and needles were outside the shops advertising the wares within. Shopkeepers who were not busy, stood alongside their signs shouting about the quality of their wares.

And the smell! Many of the peasants who had been accused of being unclean for most of their lives were amazed. While the King's mansion and imposing buildings like the mage tower had primitive sewerage systems, taking advantage of the River Rimplin that ran through Bogloris, the ordinary townsfolk had no such luxury. Sewerage was thrown out of windows which would hopefully enter the gutters. Ordinance after ordinance had been proclaimed about proper waste removal but to little effect.

The men kept marching through Bogloris which could only accommodate the Lords and their retinues and the magic users who had permanent residence in the city. The rest of the army had to reside in tents outside the city. Sheriffs went around making sure that the enlisted men had actually turned up.

'Well done, Bentham. Glad you left that runt at home and brought the big fellow.'

Bentham nodded, what else could he do?

Furious efforts were made to assess the viability of the army and to determine payments. Exact figures were derived. There were four hundred and five magic users, three hundred mercenary crossbowmen, seven Lords with retinues between them of two hundred and twenty one knights. There were a further two hundred and two independent knights. The trained peasants consisted of five hundred and twenty two pikemen, six hundred and thirty eight bowmen and one thousand, three hundred and fifteen swordsmen. To bulk up the army, three thousand, one hundred and two rabble had been recruited. They had come armed with whatever they could find, knives and pitchforks being the most common implements.

The King's workmen had managed to make two thousand swords, which although not the fine workmanship of a knight's longsword were better than nothing. These were distributed amongst the rabble lucky enough to receive them, who then gave their unwanted home-made weapons to their unlucky comrades. Overall, things did not look too bad. The figure of five thousand needed to launch a successful battle had been exceeded.

The Watchtower guards kept a constant lookout. Far in the distance, past no man's land, they could just see movement outside the Eldaran capital city of Bleddin. No doubt the enemy were making similar manoeuvres, let's just hope that their army consists largely of rabble.

While preparations were being made, a battle council was held in the throne room. As well as the usual attendees, Almein, Elbeth, Amran and Marinus, the seven Lords who would lead sections of the army were in attendance. Berin had also been asked to attend.

'Well, I suppose it'll be the usual,' said Lord Manning. 'Magic users kicking shit out of each other for three hours and us lot waiting for a chance to enter the fray.'

'That might be sooner than you think,' answered King Almein.

'What do you mean, Your Majesty?' asked Lord Rufus. 'That's the way it always works. It's getting a little boring, sitting there for three hours while the magic users have all the fun.'

'Well, we have a trick up our sleeve,' said Amran.

'What trick can there possibly be?' asked Lord Manning. 'The terrain is flat, we have tried everything before. There are no surprises left.'

'Gunpowder,' said Amran.

'What, you've perfected the tube to shoot projectiles?' asked Manning in amazement.

271

'Not quite. We've dug a tunnel with a shedload of gunpowder at the end with which we are going to blow the Eldarans sky high.'

There was a pause with a couple of gasps.

'Keep it quiet until the moment is right. We are just telling you as you are Lords and leaders. When the explosion occurs we should make a huge gap in the enemy's defences. We can hopefully rush through, get up close up to the magic users and win a decisive victory,' said Amran.

'Lord Manning, we want you to take up position in front of the third Watchtower,' said King Almein. 'The explosion will occur in the Eldaran ranks opposite you. We want you to lead the charge.'

Manning's chest puffed up. 'It will be a great honour, Your Majesty.'

'How will the gunpowder be ignited?' asked Rufus.

'That's where Berin comes in,' said Archmage Marinus. 'Berin, you are to be taken to the opening of the tunnel behind the third watchtower. On the King's signal you will send a fireball down the tunnel. Manning, your section of the conventional army will be in front of the tunnel. When you see the gunpowder blow, wait for Berin. Berin will lead our section of magic users opposite their destroyed front. You'll have shielders with you.'

'Manning, your fine fiery temper is well known to all. You will charge through with Berin and cause mayhem amongst the enemy,' said King Almein.

Manning's chest virtually burst with pride. 'This could be the decisive victory we always wanted, Your Majesty.' He paused. 'I hope I shall be allocated some land as a reward.'

'Well as King, I shall control the reunited Kingdom, but as your liege Lord, I shall allocate you the finest land in Eldara.'

Manning's eyes glazed over. This would be more fun than braining that bastard, Cedric, in the bath and more lucrative. There was hope in the room. No one had come up with a new battle tactic apart from endless attrition since no one knew when. Now this, there was a chance after all.

Those assembled rode out to join the bulk of the army outside the city gates. Almein stood on top of a mound to address his troops.

'Men, for you are men, the finest in the Kingdom. This is a great day. For too long has this war worn on. You have heard of our victorious skirmish in the Anrac Woods and how we defeated the cowardly enemy that day. That was a portent for things to come.

'Do not waver, do not falter, do not worry, our time has come. A great event is about to occur. Please don't ask me what because I cannot tell you at this point, but all will become clear. Your leaders have developed a perfect plan and when it is put into action you and the Eldarans will be astounded. You with delight and them with horror.

'For too long have we toiled under Eldaran threats and barbarity. For too long, have the best of us sacrificed ourselves against the infidel. For too long have our women and children been fearful of the rape and pillage that the Eldarans have intended for our land. For too long has our land been divided.

'Today, begins the start of the healing process, whereby we shall reunite the lands so that Marcovia will be great again. Eldara will be consigned to the dustbin of history. Their vicious attacks and occupation of our lands a forgotten memory.

'Our day of deliverance is at hand.'

Troops cheered at the speech although they were somewhat mystified as to what this new plan could be. Nevertheless, they banged swords on shields, raised their voices, shook fists in the air and swore undying loyalty to their fatherland.

They arranged into formations, the seven Lords each leading a section of the army. Almein rode out in front with Amran and Marinus. When they reached the edge of no man's land, Almein, Amran and Marinus stopped and were joined by twenty messengers who would relay their orders to the Lords. The rest of the army kept marching. Berin took up his place behind the third watchtower next to the tunnel opening.

The Eldarans were in sight. Both armies kept on advancing towards one another. The shouting started, expletives burning into the air. Swords rattled against shields, magic warriors chanted atop

274

their Anracs, crossbowmen and archers waved their weapons in the air. Magic users began to feel the effect of the plentiful jains in no man's land, some even starting to take on a bluish sheen. Still, they marched.

When they were close enough, the magic users started to invoke their blue magic and the necromancers to evoke their daemons. As well as the imps and the Bedines, those great purple puss oozing daemons like Banzoon, there were the Flanteins and the Cathrens. Flanteins were huge green legless daemons who rippled along the ground. Although large they were not renowned for their attack power. Rather, they were damage absorbers, capable of taking great punishment before being dispelled back to the Netherworld. Cathrens were the beauties of the Netherworld. Long limbed with dark flowing hair and lithe bodies, these female daemons shot arrows tinged with black magic at great speed. Up close, they wielded the anthren, their barbed whips. They could almost have passed for human females of unsurpassed beauty if it were not for their forked daemon tails.

Turinus screamed 'CHARGE!' atop his Anrac and the melee fighters, magic warriors and daemon, tore into battle to face the upcoming Eldarans. Defensive mages put up impermeable shields around them. Archers and crossbowmen started shooting and all of a sudden the air was black with arrows and bolts, a strange darkness descending upon the battlefield. Then came the real firepower. The blue bolts from the necromancers and the awe-inspiring fire bolts. Cathrens shot off their magic arrows mingling them in with the lesser arrows of mortal men. The mercenaries after letting off their bolts, quickly set about wrenching their crossbows for the next attack.

The defensive mages set to work. Greenish permeable shields shot up, allowing their comrades' attacks through, but blocking much of the force of the incoming attacks. Fireballs shuddered against the shields of air, exploding into flares of red, green and gold. Bolts and arrows, magic and ordinary, shuddered against magic walls of air before splintering and falling harmlessly to the ground.

The magic warriors started their impossibly fast charge, eating up ground as they approached each other, outstripping their daemon allies, smashing into each other with their shield bashes, their permeable shields offering some protection, still blood poured from broken noses and cheeks, their designated healers, offering up the soothing blue magic of their trade. Now, the battle was on. The opening salvo had stated death's intent, now it was time for death to really show his face.

Turinus had an imp on his shoulder who bounded off through the enemy's permeable shield in an attempt to cause havoc with the enemy and preoccupy their healers. Turinus's Anrac smashed into an enemy Anrac, locking horns as best they could through the permeable shield. Turinus shuddered on his Anrac, the shock of the clashing beasts penetrating his shield.

Turinus, glowing blue with the plentiful jains, screamed and swung his broadsword at his enemy, managing to break through his opponent's permeable shield and hit his upper arm. The blow although slowed by the magic shield, was enough to cut through his enemy's chain mail and slice into his upper arm. All concentration, he pushed up his shield just in time to block his opponent's attack to his face.

'Round one to me,' Turinus thought as blue magic enveloped his opponent, stemming the flow of blood and healing his wound. 'Never mind, he's lost some blood and his mail is damaged.'

276

Fireball bolts and arrows, magical and mundane rained above Turinus, attacking both defensive walls. Fireballs and blue magic orbs lighting up the sky, while the projectiles tried to penetrate the magic shields. Small amounts of fire, blue magic and magic arrows managed to get through the permeable shields, burning and embedding in the foe. Healers immediately cast their magic to aid their comrades. The defensive mages were a study in concentration, maintaining the large defensive walls of air and most able to provide a further two mobile permeable bubbles, usually one for a magic warrior and one for a daemon.

A Bedine fought alongside Turinus, alternatively attempting to bite his opponent's Anrac and rake the damage absorbing Flantein. The opposing Flantein was doing his best to block Turinus, taking blows intended for the warrior, frustrating Turinus.

Still Turinus managed to get in another blow, surely this was a warrior of extraordinary skill, slicing through his enemy's leg armour, cutting through his thigh. Again, came the blue healing magic, but his enemy had lost more blood and armour integrity. This was going well.

All across the front, melee were engaged in similar battles, none able to inflict a killing blow protected as they were by permeable shields slowing down their enemy's attacks. Any damage caused was not fatal and quickly healed. The defensive mages kept to their task with dogged determination and offensive ranged attacks continued to batter at walled defences of air. The time was right.

Berin stood next to the tunnel entrance, watching the battle, too far away to do anything. It was his purpose in life to do the boring, while others were in the thick of it. He had trained Morovius when

277

he was a baby and missed the opportunity to see him really develop – just sums it up, who knows if this whole tunnel, gunpowder thing would work anyway? He kept his eye on the King. The time was right.

King Almein observed the battle. It was like a game of chess where all your positions are in a perfect defence and there is a devastating attack awaiting which your opponent hardly suspects. He had all the aces up his sleeve. He looked at Amran and then at Marinus. The time was right.

He raised his right hand and waved a red handkerchief signalling that the time was right.

Berin conjured up blue magic between his hands invoking as much power from the plentiful jains as he could bare. Knowing his luck, nothing would happen.

With a jerk, he propelled the fireball down the tunnel.

The fireball shot down the initial diagonal part of the tunnel, the wooden shoring smouldering in its wake. Onwards it went, obediently following the path so carefully prepared for it by the dwarves. Down it went beneath the shale shelf, powering through. It was coming to the fulfilment of its journey, the upper diagonal towards the sandbags. It hit the sandbags with a bang that alerted the Eldarans, largely dissipating against the sandbags, burning cloth, but the tube had been carefully placed. Enough of the fireball made it through to the gunpowder.

BANG!

A huge mighty explosion rocked a section of the Eldaran front, momentarily halting the battle. Almein jumped off his horse in delight. The explosion ripped at the eardrums of all on the battlefield, blasting a mountain of earth into the air, limbs flying separated from their bodies, a head ripped off its shoulders propelled upward while its body disintegrated. A thick fog of jain encrusted soil reaching up to the Heavens.

What new sorcery was this? How could the Marcovians have produced such magic? The earth, the jains themselves have become a part of Marcovian magic. Silence descended upon the once screaming, blade shattering chaos of battle. Marcovians started to cheer, Eldarans looked around in panic.

Then, as suddenly as it had erupted, the noise abated, the jain laden soil started to settle after twenty seconds, men started shouting once more, Berin mounted his horse to join the battle, Manning started to bark orders at his knights to prepare a charge and most importantly, a section of the Eldaran shield collapsed.

Turinus was one of the first to react. This was the moment he had been waiting for and he realised immediately that his opponent's permeable shield was down. He wielded a wide arc with his broadsword and sliced off his opponent's head. What was it Banshin had yelled, ah yes, heal that bitches. He needn't have concerned himself. His decapitated foe's head was beyond healing and besides his foe's healer was long dead in the explosion that had annihilated him and his comrades in the death shattering blast.

He looked around for another man to kill. There was none. There was a warrior comrade alongside him but he too had taken advantage of his unshielded opponent. The two of them set to work on the Flantein with the help of their Bedine, carving huge swathes through the daemon. Even a Flantein can only take so much damage. It was only a matter of time before it was banished. What then? Turinus knew that he and his comrade needed reinforcements if they were to advance on the broken Eldaran line.

Berin joined Manning and the order was yelled out to 'Charge!' The cry was taken up by the fifty five knights in Manning's company and they began their charge in Turinus's direction. In their confusion, the Marcovian fire mages and necromancers saw the break in the Eldaran defences and immediately began to shoot their balls of destructive magic in that direction. They need not have bothered. All the Eldarans in the break in their defence shield had long been killed by the initial explosion. Those that were wounded were actually behind the still intact sections of the defensive wall and were being rapidly healed.

The Eldarans desperately tried to mend the breach in their defensive wall but could not as too many defensive mages had been killed in the explosion. Those that remained were needed to keep intact the still remaining defensive walls. The Eldarans were vulnerable. Some of the more aware fire mages and necromancers suspected what would happen and prepared for the inevitable Marcovian attack.

Manning led his troops onwards charging towards the breach and reached Turinus and his warrior comrade. This was the glory of battle, the blood stirring, the stuff of war, what a real man was made for. This great Lord could already smell the grass of the new lands he would win in Eldara. A

Lord? He would be like a god amongst mortals, his renown celebrated in ballads for all eternity – the victor in the Battle of the Exploding Tunnel!

The Marcovian division under Manning sped on towards the Eldaran breach, their defensive mages making sure that they were all protected behind a non-permeable shield. A famous victory was in sight.

The Eldarans started to organise in panic.

'Make the existing shields non-permeable,' was the order in Eldaran ranks.

'Prepare for the attack.'

'Fire mages, necromancers, Cathrens, archers, concentrate on defending the breach.'

'Aim at the breach when the enemy comes through.'

It was mayhem.

Manning's division kept up their charge, secure behind their magic shield. The Marcovian ranged attacks kept banging against the non-permeable Eldaran shields, merely attempting to exhaust the Eldaran defensive mages, as there was no way their attacks could penetrate. The Eldarans stopped attacking as they could not get through their own shield. Even melee attackers stopped due to the Eldaran non-permeable shield. All eyes were on Manning and his advancing division doggedly going forward, relentless, death in their eyes, the battle hinging on their every move. Manning had never felt more alive.

They reached their objective and encountered a huge lip of earth before the crater, blasted out by the gunpowder. All that jain laden earth had to go somewhere and it had come to rest on the edge of the crater forming a high lip of earth which would not be easy to traverse.

Simultaneously, Manning's division was now in range of the enemy's missiles as the enemy could see them from behind their non-permeable shield. Manning's defensive mages started to take the strain and made it clear that they could not continue indefinitely.

Manning had to decide. It was time for him to show true leadership and he was damned if he was going to fail this test.

'We go onward,' he shouted.

'No,' screamed Turinus, 'we'll be sitting ducks in that pit.'

'Nonsense coward, our defensive mages will protect us. We can ascend and attack, those bloody clothie magic users will be of no use with my steel through their hearts.'

'Damn you, Manning, those aren't some naked simpletons you can bludgeon to death in your bath. We have to retreat.'

'Coward! Berin, you defensive mage, you healer and my knights. Come with me.'

Manning, Berin, the two mages and the knights ascended the lip of the crater. They descended down into its depths, balls of magic, arrows and bolts being harmlessly deflected by their non-permeable shield. A pikeman on Turinus's orders peered over the lip at Manning's battle charge.

He saw them charge down the incline to the depths of the pit and watched to see if they would be able to climb out and attack the Eldarans fulfilling Manning's dreams of a date with destiny.

It did not happen.

Manning, Berin and their companions slowly fell over and lay on the ground. They even looked peaceful as their defensive shield slowly collapsed. They were obliterated by the mass of Eldaran fireballs which greeted their corpses.

The pikeman rushed back to Turinus who ordered an immediate retreat.

The battle continued around them as the Eldaran commanders once again ordered their shields to be permeable.

CHAPTER 16

Turinus led the retreat of the remaining division which now only consisted of the peasant section and one defensive mage. Their shield was of course, non-permeable as they were all exposed melee fighters at great risk. There was the odd fireball to contend with, but the Eldarans, seeing their shield, largely ignored them. Turinus led them all the way back to the Marcovian line to ensure their safety.

He returned to the fray, noticing a Marcovian Bedine fighting an Eldaran imp and a magic warrior. He built up his magic and charged onwards, the imp not noticing his approach until it was too late, his broadsword slicing the imp in half returning him to the Netherworld as he shield slammed the opposing warrior in the face.

The warrior lurched, almost falling off his Anrac, his permeable shield offering some protection and waited for the soothing healing to arrive. The enemy warrior's defensive mage sensed the danger realising that Turinus was no ordinary magic warrior and made the Eldaran warrior's shield non-permeable as soon as he saw his warrior enveloped in a healing blue glow. Turinus and the Bedine attacked the shield attempting to exhaust the defensive mage. The Eldaran defensive mage was presumably attempting to maintain a defensive wall around the Eldaran main line as well.

Arrows, bolts and balls of magical destruction continued to dominate the skyline, slamming into the opponent's shields, some finding a way through, occupying the healers. The knights were largely engaged in attempting to despatch the imps who had made it into their ranks, hamstrings and faces being attacked, healers compensating.

284

One such knight was Dinran, Cedric's son, a newly anointed knight. Dinran was the only Marcovian who had taken some pleasure in Manning's failure and could now see the way forward to becoming the new Lord of the combined lands previously ruled by Manning and his late father. He was careful not to become injured, instead preoccupied with the task that lay ahead to prove himself when the knights went into action. Manning's old domain would be bound to resist a new upstart knight becoming their Lord. Be careful now, then prove yourself in the real battle, that is what he needed to do. Dinran had to impress his new subjects, hopefully he would not follow Manning into the halls of folly.

King Almein was back on his horse, his head in his hands. He looked reproachably at Amran, the father of the scheme which had failed to achieve fruition. Amran was pale, shocked that what had seemed to be such a foolproof plan had backfired so spectacularly. At least they had killed a number of the Eldaran mages.

Almein put his hand on Amran's arm.

'Don't worry. We all agreed to the tunnel. At least we were able to try something new. It'll show our troops that we have some innovation and can attempt the unexpected.'

'Thank you, Your Majesty. I am sorry it didn't work out as well as expected. Please forgive me.'

'Nothing to forgive, nothing to forgive. Oh, and Amran.'

'Yes, Your Majesty?'

'Look on the bright side. We've got rid of Manning who was causing all kinds of crap in the Kingdom. I mean, if every Lord was like Manning, our nobility would be frightened of baths and they would all stink like peasants.'

Amran and Marinus laughed.

'Still, Your Majesty,' said Marinus, 'there could well be a struggle for his land now.'

'Ah well,' said Almein, 'what will be, will be.'

They turned their attention back to the battlefield.

Something was happening in the Eldaran front. The permeable shield looked intact, but they could see that more of the Marcovian fireballs and blue bolts were penetrating. The Cathren arrows seemed to penetrate at will and were barely slowed by the permeable magic wall. Eldaran healers were furiously turning their attention to the wounded.

'Look at that, Your Majesty,' said Marinus, 'a cross bolt got through.'

Sure, the bolt was sufficiently slowed by the shield to cause no damage but who had ever heard of a cross bolt penetrating a magic shield, permeable or not? In contrast the Marcovian permeable shield was allowing only the same amount of hostile firepower through as it had at the beginning of the battle.

'Could the tunnel explosion have caused this?' asked Amran hopefully.

'I don't know,' said Almein, 'maybe they were a little poisoned or something?'

'That can't be it, Your Majesty. Their wall is failing across the entire front. If it was the explosion, the effects would be stronger around the crater,' said Marinus.

'That's true,' conceded Amran somewhat deflated.

They continued to examine the battlefield.

'Even their attacks have weakened,' said Marinus.

As a mage himself, he could see clearly that the Eldaran fire balls and blue bolts lacked their former potency. How could this be? The battle had been going on for two and a half hours, the three hour window was still open. Why would the Eldarans be tiring?

They noticed messengers furiously running from the Eldaran King, issuing orders. The Eldaran magic warriors started to retreat towards their lines, leaving the daemons to preoccupy the Marcovian warriors to enable their escape. When the magic warriors had made it back to the Eldaran lines, their shield went non-permeable.

Of course, this would protect troops, but it also made any Eldaran attack impossible. Was this some clever trick? It was virtually an admission of defeat, a statement that Eldara could not cope with the Marcovian ranged assault.

'What do you think?' asked Almein. 'Is this a cunning ploy?'

'If it is, I cannot see what they hope to achieve. Even if their magic users do nothing, they will still be unable to cast after the three hours, they have already expended too much energy,' said Marinus.

'I would hate to be wrong twice in one day, but I agree,' said Amran. 'I can think of no cunning plan. We must attack with all our might, try to break down their shield.'

'The Eldarans are making no sense. They trespass on the Anrac Woods provoking this battle and now this,' said Almein.

Almein thought about this new development. He could see no point in holding back.

'Order an all out attack,' he told his messengers who sped on horses to the Marcovian line to relay the order.

The messengers ran down shouting for an all out attack.

'We've got half an hour, give it everything you've got.'

'They're on the ropes, they are fully defensive, all out attack.'

And throughout the ranks Lords, knights and anyone else who felt brave enough to join in shouted, 'Attack, Attack, Attack.'

The sky darkened once more with arrows, magical and mundane, and bolts. Mages discharged their fire bolts and blue bolts, lighting up what was otherwise a darkened sky. Tiring crossbowmen again redoubled their efforts to winch in their weapons, preparing the next salvo.

It was true, something was going on. Even though the Eldaran shield was non-permeable and should have stopped any attack, still some of the Marcovian ranged attacks managed to get through. Even some mundane bolts and arrows were piercing the wall, albeit being much slowed. Enough of a particularly strong fireball got through to incinerate an Eldaran fire mage. Everyone could see healers working furiously, while it was obvious who were the defensive mages. They were showing strain and breaking sweat.

Turinus led the melee charge. Turinus, his fellow magic warriors atop their Anracs, the Bedines and the Flanteins rushed the Eldaran shield wall. Just to be on the safe side, they had impermeable shields on their march up to the front which was made permeable as the magic warriors launched their magic charge, slamming the Eldaran defensive wall with their Anracs and shields. The Eldaran shield appeared to lurch uneasily. The warriors started to hack at the defensive wall in the hope that they could destroy it before the three hour deadline and start to inflict real damage.

Fireballs flew in furiously above them, looping over their heads and then going on a downward trajectory towards their targets. The impermeable shield was still largely holding but the defensive mages were showing real strain. The problem was that Turinus could feel his own body starting to tire, the dead exhaustion of magic usage setting in. It was a race against time. No need for niceties or any fancy complex tactics. Just expend as much destructive power as possible.

Turinus glanced behind him. He could see a Cathren, shooting off her black magic arrows at great speed. All seemed well but it was not. The Cathren was translucent as was the Bedine, raking with his claws alongside him. They did not have much time. Time might well wait for no man, it would appear that it didn't wait for daemons either.

One last effort, they could sense it, all they had to do was break down the defensive wall and that would be it. One blast of ranged and melee attacks and it would all be over, victory would be theirs. Turinus could see the Eldaran knights preparing themselves for their charge. They sensed that the end of the magic battle was in sight.

And indeed it was. The Eldaran defensive wall began to collapse but the daemons were also dispelling back to the Netherworld. Turinus could feel the exhaustion settling in, he could barely hold his broadsword, so he placed it in the sheath on his Anracs side. His whole body felt heavy, barely able to move. His muscles did not ache so much as shut down.

He knew magic users across the battlefield would be feeling the same way. Bodies like lead, moving slowly away from the battlefield, leaving it now to the knights and the footsoldiers of the army. Turinus activated his mind meld with his Anrac and ordered it to retreat before his shield collapsed. One thought entered his head as he joined the other magic users who were leaving the battlefield, 'Imagine if we had a mage of Morovius's power with us today, what could we have done? We were so close.'

Turinus's Anrac raced back to the Marcovian line just in time to see the Lords and knights assemble. Six Lords were now left leading their individual divisions. Alongside them were their knights, those who had sworn fealty to them.

Lord Rufus stood proudly, his squire alongside flying his pennant, which showed a knight chess piece. He thought it was a reasonable gesture. As Manning had died, Cedric's son, Dinran, in an act of historic irony, had taken lead of what remained of the dead man's division. A good show today and he could lay claim to his father's old manor and Manning's land as he had led left no heirs. Dinran was the only male contender.

Behind Dinran was the knight Bentham who had no illustrious thoughts of glory. As he had told his pikeman, the big fellow, the object of this battle is to stay alive. Who knows how many were looking forward to the battle to prove their worthiness in society and how many concentrating mainly on self-preservation?

Whatever their motives they had to begin their charge as soon as possible. It had long been established that it was a waste of time trying to launch a mounted attack against enemy knights who were on foot surrounded by pikemen. The pikemen killed the horses of the charging knights and allowed the defending knight to easily kill the unseated rider who was still struggling to his feet.

This had led to a code of honour, the battle must commence with knights charging at each other, lances under their armpits, attempting to use their horse's full momentum to attack fellow knights.

Speed was also essential to avoid missile attack. Crossbow bolts in particular could breach chain mail armour, so each side wanted to engage the enemy as quickly as possible. When both sides met, ranged attack was nullified against melee fighters, because who could shoot a target in the confused mass of armoured men and horses? The ranged attack then had to be satisfied with shooting at each other.

So, the knights charged each other, attempting to use their shields to deflect or block incoming arrows and bolts. The sturdy warhorses built up momentum and started into their gallop. Cedric's son, Dinran, having the most to prove, led the charge. Seven Marcovian knights and six Eldaran knights were dismounted, victims of missile attacks. A further twenty on both sides were unseated, as missiles took out their horses. They ran onwards, having to be content with fighting on foot against the up rushing melee fighters. One of the unseated was Bentham. Although he regretted losing his horse, he could see the positives in joining battle late with his trusted pikeman. He might make it out alive, after all.

'Let's protect each other as best we can, Ledine,' he told his pikeman. 'Try and get in a blow of sorts or distract them and I'll finish them off.'

The cavalries charged into one another, lances held horizontally attempting to dislodge their opponents while at the same time the knights had to weave away from attack. This was the time for all those years of training as a pageboy and then a squire to be tested.

Dinran led the charge and at the last moment he ducked, while holding his lance true. It worked, Dinran managed to dislodge his foe, while remaining seated. He rode his horse up to the enemy, threw his lance away and jumped off holding his well crafted longsword and shield. His opponent was desperately attempting to regain his feet, struggling with the weight of his armour. The Eldaran knight had one hand on a knee and was about to arise when Dinran ran his longsword through his visor. Blood poured out freely as the knight fell to the ground in a death convulsion. Dinran had the first kill. Not only his personal first but also the first of the charge. Cedric's son felt like nothing could stop him. He looked around at the tunics the knights wore over their armour, looking for the Eldaran green circle and trying to avoid the Marcovian blue cross.

Lord Rufus came to the culmination of his charge, he and his opponent both missing one another, but Rufus spotted the green circle of Eldara on an unseated knight ten yards away. He sped to the Eldaran, holding his lance at a diagonal angle above his head to enable a downward blow. Damn! Rufus missed again. Time to dismount.

Bentham and Ledine reluctantly came up to the fray, well it had to happen sometime, Ledine holding his pike straight out to defend himself and his master. They kept marching into the dust bowl of war. More by luck than judgement, Ledine hit someone.

'Is it one of ours, Sire?' he asked.

Bentham had no option but to investigate, trusting to his vision, armour, longsword and shield. He could make out a knight stumbling, but the knight's back was to him so he could not see what faction he belonged to. Bentham moved in and span the knight around with his shield to disorientate him. If the knight was friend, he could always apologise, but it was foe, the green circle of Eldara clearly visible.

Bentham was able to strike the first blow against the disorientated knight, catching him high up on the right arm. The Eldaran knight's armour protected him but Bentham hoped the blow had stunned his sword arm. His foe went to bash him with his shield, clearly his right arm was at least temporarily out of action. Bentham ducked and struck out with all his force at the knight's left leg, catching him high in the thigh. His opponent stumbled, but before Bentham could take advantage, Ledine thrust his pike square at the knight's chest, drawing blood. The knight collapsed.

'Right, Ledine, that's the spirit. Let's try to stay alive.'

'Sire, killing Eldarans appears to be the only way to stay alive.'

'Hey, not just Eldarans. In all this mayhem, a Marcovian could well end up attacking us.'

'Right you are, Sire. Anything attacks us, we kill 'em.'

The rabble descended upon the mass of fighters. Relatively unskilled they were seen as just cannon fodder, although some had fought in battles before. Besides, the rabble had their own honour to protect. It was their chance to kill noble oppressors, albeit from the other side, but what the hell, to kill a noble had to be good.

With great yells, inferior swords and pitchforks, the rabble descended, adding to the chaos. Jain filled dust from this dry stretch of land started to fill the air, shouts and incoherent orders split the air while the groans and cries of the wounded and dying provided the backdrop. Most of the knights had dismounted by this point and panicking horses, baying at the sky, attempting to flee just added to the confusion. The jain saturated earth started to be christened with the blood of men.

Dinran kept on fighting with zeal. He could barely contain himself and had to concentrate with all his power just to attack those wearing the green circle. Dinran felt like he could beat all on this battlefield. Surely, this would be noticed, he had definitely earned his spurs and as the only male heir he could inherit his father's and Manning's territory.

Dinran shouted orders to what used to be Manning's battalion, some of them even coherent.

'Stand firm.'

'Aim carefully.'

'Keep each others' backs.'

Dinran noticed three rabble from Eldara, this would be fun and set off to show them hell. He easily deflected a pitchfork with his shield and decapitated its wielder, blood satisfyingly spurting over the jain laden earth. A sword caught Dinran high on the shoulder, but it was a peasant's and of poor quality, his armour easily protecting him. A thrust into the heart and another kill. The third peasant ran away – coward, these peasants are scum who need to be shown who their betters are. No skill, no intelligence, they are barely better than pigs only fit for slaughter.

Lord Rufus trod carefully, attempting to shout orders to his division. Things were not going well for him. Rufus had seen three of his knights fall, he hoped they were only injured and could be healed tomorrow. He ordered his division to group up, safety in numbers, they needed to defend.

Rufus arranged four pikemen around him for protection, promising them that he would in turn launch forth when needed to deliver the killing blow. The tactic worked well. A young over-eager knight, seeing a Lord with his plumed helm, rushed forward to gain a memorable kill. Two pikemen jabbed at him, knocking the wind out of him. It was easy for Rufus to dispatch him with a cutting neck blow.

'Well done, men. Let's keep this up and we could well see tomorrow.'

Through the mayhem a bugle blasted a retreat for the Eldarans. Dinran started to run after them but was pulled back by Rufus.

'Wait. It could be a ruse. This is an old tactic. Orderly retreat, look at them, they are not panicking. We chase them, lose our structure, they turn on us and it's a sure defeat. Wait lad, wait.'

Sure enough the Eldarans were retreating in an orderly fashion and after fifty yards, they lined up again. Now ranged attacks could come back into play in the centre of the battlefield. Bolts and arrows from both sides started to rain down on the now separated melee forces. The knights with their armour and shields were able to withstand this attack, but the peasantry, especially the rabble were suffering, falling under this death from above. Something had to be done.

Rufus was considering an orderly attack on the Eldaran line when the enemy trumpet sounded a quick series of notes. They were asking for an end to the battle.

King Almein had to think quickly. 'What do you think, Amran?'

'Well, Your Majesty, our superiority lies with our magic users. The conventional armies are about equal. Accept and we can prepare for the next battle when our magic users should be victorious. The Eldarans clearly have a problem maintaining magic for the full three hours.'

'I agree,' said Archmage Marinus. 'Remember, Your Majesty, Morovius will be ready for the next battle and he is turning into a superb fire mage.'

'Yes, that makes sense,' agreed Almein. 'Sound our agreement,' he told his trumpeter, 'we can regroup and win the next battle. If this Morovius is as powerful as you say, we should win that easily.'

The Marcovian trumpet answered its Eldaran counterpart with an agreement for a ceasefire.

Both armies shoulders' dropped and many men fell to one knee. The shouting and orders of battle stopped and all that could be heard were the screams and moans of the dying and wounded.

Chivalric protocol asserted itself and men returned to their original lines, those who could, attempting to bring a wounded comrade with them.

It was a point of honour now that had simply been respected since time immemorial. Each side scoured the battlefield for their wounded and brought them back as gently as they could to their own side. Of course, the nobility were carried first.

It would be a full twenty three hours before the healers who had fought in the battle could heal again. Students who had not fought would be brought out immediately to see what they could do. Most of the wounded would have to be cared for as best they could until the combatant healers were ready. Hopefully, the majority could last that long.

The dead were stripped of their armour and weapons. Dead knights and Lords were brought back for a decent and heroic funeral. Peasant corpses were left.

A murder of crows had started to circle overhead. When all was calm they descended to feast on peasant meat.

CHAPTER 17

Candera and five other student healers were adjudged to be sufficiently skilled to try to heal the wounded. Candera was by far the most advanced. He noticed the strength of the jains as he approached no man's land, power surging through his body.

Naturally, the Lords and knights were the first to be healed as they were the most important. Candera leaned over a rather imposing knight who had extremely serious injuries and had almost lost an arm. He expended all his skill but doubted if even an experienced healer could have helped as the knight had lost too much blood. He worked on the knight for half an hour, sending in wave after wave of blue healing and managed to mend the knight's arm. However, the blood loss was too great and the knight eventually died.

Candera moved on to the next knight who had been selected for him and again tried to heal. And so it went on. Eventually, the healers had done all they could for the nobility and proceeded onto the skilled peasants for the last forty minutes. They were left unfinished. The rabble were not touched at all.

The healers departed and the medics did their best to comfort the wounded and keep them alive until tomorrow when the battle weary healers would be ready.

Candera left the scene disheartened that he could not have done more, but it is difficult so late after the battle when the wounded have lost so much blood. Hopefully, some of the peasants he could see who only suffered from broken bones would fare better.

The next day the Council was convened to discuss the battle. In attendance were King Almein, his Queen, Amran and Marinus and the six remaining Lords. Guards adorned the room adding to the gravity of the occasion.

'Firstly, let us discuss the tunnel,' said the King. 'It was in my opinion a worthwhile effort, but unfortunately did not work as well as we planned, as often happens with new ventures. Manning's bravery will always be remembered.'

'That's right, Your Majesty,' agreed Marinus. 'Manning showed great bravery and it was not his fault that the crater was filled with poisonous gas. How was he to know? All reports are that the gas could not be seen.' Marinus deliberately omitted the fact that Turinus had seen the descent into the crater as folly. After all, even without the poisonous gas, how were they going to be able to maintain their magical shield long enough to ascend against close up firepower?

However, it mattered not. The nobility needed their plaudits and even the odd memorial to keep up their spirits. Who cared, especially since Manning was now dead. It did not matter now what anyone said about the oaf.

'Perhaps we should have a memorial,' suggested a Lord.

'Well,' hesitated Amran, 'it was ultimately a failure. Maybe we should remember that. After all, I admit it was my plan and it failed. I would not like a memorial to myself which celebrated a failure. I doubt Manning would have wanted one either.'

There were murmurs of ascent, everyone remembering Manning and grateful that a man who had proven so inhospitable would not be getting a memorial.

'Now, onto the most important event of the battle. What happened to the Eldaran shield and magic attacks? Perhaps, you can help us Marinus?' asked the King.

Marinus spoke. 'Well, clearly, their shield started to fail before the three hour mark and their attacks withered. All right, I am just stating the obvious and I have wracked my brain all night trying to determine why, but I cannot.'

'The important thing,' said Amran, 'is that somehow they are weakening. We must launch another attack as soon as possible, ideally with that new powerful mage, Morovius.'

'I agree,' said Almein, 'but things have to settle in the Kingdom first. That is always the way it is. The nobility and indeed the peasants have to make new arrangements to account for the casualties.'

It was true. New power struggles inevitably broke out internally after a battle. Who would replace a Lord or consolidate his lands, which squires were good enough to become knights, who was entitled to the land vacated by dead peasants and what fealty would they owe their new Lord? These things always took time. Besides, everyone wanted Morovius at full strength. They sat pondering the new power dynamics in the land. One was particularly pressing. What would happen to Manning's estates? Certainly Dinran had distinguished himself on the battlefield but he was young and not Manning's heir.

'Well, Your Majesty,' said Amran, 'Lady Rosemary and Dinran have requested an audience to discuss their particular situation.'

'Yes, I thought something might happen there,' said Almein. 'Show them in.'

Dinran and Lady Rosemary entered the chamber. Dinran walked in shoulders back and chest puffed out fully aware of his great achievements the previous day. Lady Rosemary was tall and stern, her face newly made up, her gown flowing.

Both started speaking simultaneously and were thus incomprehensible.

'That's enough,' ordered Almein. 'One at a time. Lady Rosemary, you may go first.'

'Thank you, Your Majesty.' Dinran looked at her with disgust. 'My position is simple. My husband died as a brave and valiant soldier in defence of our glorious Kingdom. Yes, he is without an heir, but I am fully capable of administering his estate.

'Dinran is too young and filled with hatred for my dead husband. He will treat our people poorly in revenge to the detriment of our lands and the Kingdom. Production is bound to fall due to his youth and anger. This is no way to proceed.

'I, on the other hand, am fully cognisant of all the intricacies of the land. Although I am of the fairer sex, I have excellent well-established advisors and will be able to fulfil our lands' full potential.

302

'Finally, Dinran has no claim on the land. He is not my late husband's heir and did not inherit his father's former lands on his death. He has no legitimate claim.'

The Court was silent for a moment. Lady Rosemary might be a woman but the argument she put forward was sound. They all looked at Dinran for his repost.

'Your Majesty, my Lords,' said Dinran. 'Far be it for me to malign a Lord who fought so valiantly for our kingdom, but we all know the circumstances of Lord Manning's acquisition of my father's lands. It is well known that Lady Rosemary, herself, did not approve of his methods.

'I shall say no more about this topic for it is not my intention to talk badly of the dead, especially one who showed such chivalric bravery on the battlefield. I personally honour his memory, despite his questionable actions towards my father.

'We also have to consider a woman ruling the largest estate in the Kingdom. Even Lady Rosemary concedes her own inferiority as she, herself, has to argue that she will need good council to run the estate well. Lady Rosemary condemns my youth, but I have shown my maturity on the battlefield, she has done no such thing.

'As my father's heir, I shall inherit his former lands. As Manning has no heir and the lands are at present consolidated, I shall have rulership over the united lands. Your Majesty can rest assured, I shall serve you well and furnish your army with men who will fight honourably, following my example.'

303

The Court was silent. This too made a great deal of sense. They could see no option but to ask Dinran and Lady Rosemary to move outside while they considered the matter.

The discussion went on for thirty minutes, but proved inconclusive. No one could argue clearly or make up their mind in favour of either candidate. There were positives and pitfalls with both. Both arguments made equal sense.

'I suppose we can't ask them to get married,' said Almein.

Everyone laughed.

'Unfortunately, Your Majesty,' said Amran, 'that appears to be the only solution we can think of that makes any sense and it is quite impossible. I can't imagine Dinran marrying his father's murderer's widow.'

'They'll just have to sort it out themselves,' decided Almein. 'If we leave them with half the land each, there will just be perpetual conflict to the detriment of the Kingdom.'

Lady Rosemary and Dinran were recalled to the chamber and informed of the stalemate. They were told that they had to resolve matters themselves but in an orderly fashion. They had one month in order to marshal their forces. Battle must take place away from agricultural areas so as to minimise damage to crops. Battle could only take place over one day and not be ongoing as a long drawn out conflict would be destructive to the Kingdom's prospects. Any infractions of the rules would incur the wrath of fire mages against the offending party.

Lady Rosemary and Dinran had no option but to agree and walk off to make preparations for battle. Dinran's power base was the land his father had controlled, while Lady Rosemary went to her late husband's original lands.

The two had a month to prepare and both repeated the arguments they had put to Council with the additional accusation that the other was bound to favour the land they originally owned. Thus, Lady Rosemary was able to overcome prejudice against her sex by arguing that Dinran would tax more heavily Manning's original land. Dinran was bound to favour those that he knew for social advancement as knights and advisors. It would be a disaster for all concerned if he were to win the battle.

Dinran argued exactly the same with the added moral justification of Manning's original cowardly attack on his father and the horror all would experience in being ruled by a woman. Both knew the best way to invoke support from a populace was to appeal to their self-interest.

Their pasts and gender did however, lead to different advice. Lady Rosemary sensed correctly that there were doubts about a woman running so large a territory. She was determined to prove herself.

'I shall don armour,' she told her assembled nobility. 'I will show you that I am no weakling. I shall lead you into battle and show bravery beyond even that of my late, dear husband. You shall know that you are led by one worthy of this great land.'

In contrast, Dinran's advisors were keen to cool the impassioned youth.

'Sire, you have already proven yourself in battle. The upcoming fight depends utterly on your survival. Stay back, if you should die, all will be lost for how can we pronounce you Lord if you are dead? This is not dishonourable, for you have already shown yourself worthy in the Battle of the Exploding Tunnel. Remember, the King himself does not enter into battle, but rather observes, using his messengers to make his decisions known. You must do the same. Stay back and direct the action. It is imperative that you stay alive.'

Dinran was slow to be convinced, relishing the thought of yet again indulging in clashing steel and seeing his foe vanquished. Above all, he imagined the glory in killing Lady Rosemary, thus avenging his father's death.

'But, Sire, our Kingdom will soon attack the Eldarans again. Everyone knows this. You will have your chance to prove yourself again, this time as the fully fledged Lord of the largest estate in Marcovia. Resist the temptation to indulge yourself now. You need an old head on young shoulders.'

This convinced Dinran, the appeal to be mature, to act contrary to his youth. Thus, the two opponents experienced contrary pressures. Lady Rosemary to be active in battle due to her sex, whilst Dinran was pressurised to be passive in an attempt to compensate for his youth.

They both mobilised their armies, the knights and peasants of their lands. They had the usual archers and pikemen and a vast array of rabble, some of whom were still armed from their time in the Battle of the Exploding Tunnel. Dinran was sure it would be a glorious conflict. No magic users to confuse matters, no cowardly defensive magic walls, just good honest battle.

They lined up opposing each other as planned on land which had been allowed to lie fallow. Regardless of the King's orders, it was in neither of their interests to destroy crops in the land both sought to win. Lady Rosemary was filled with trepidation. This was it. A chance to actually rule as a woman without that ghastly man she had married. She was not foolhardy. She arrayed her knights around her. They would also advance more slowly, surrounded by pikemen for defence. She realised, as much as Dinran, that her survival was crucial for victory.

Troops on both sides started to march towards one another, shouting expletives, swords banging on shields, mighty warhorses trotting forward, clad in protective padding. They were in range. A pause. A silence descended across the battle field. The armies could clearly see the patterns of the opposing army's tunics. Dinran had chosen a bathtub as his army's pattern as a reminder to all of Manning's dishonesty and cowardice. Lady Rosemary's troops had the outlines of a fire, a symbol of courage and their destructive potential.

One of Lady Rosemary's archers shot a single arrow. It started its flight towards Dinran's army.

It was the signal to commence hostilities.

The sky immediately darkened with arrows, the cavalry began their charge and the infantry started to run.

The cavalry sped out in front to encounter the enemy and obscure themselves from enemy projectiles. Lady Rosemary proceeded more slowly into battle surrounded by her knights and limited by the speed at which the pikemen could run.

The cavalry attempted to topple each other with their lances. Most were unsuccessful, but four from each side were knocked off their horses. The knights were now at close quarters and lances were discarded and they equipped themselves with the shields and longswords attached to the sides of their horses. The sky remained darkened as the archers shot at each other. The infantry were running to join the fray, Lady Rosemary and her knights alongside them. She was sure to win the day, she had a slight numerical superiority.

Knights slashed at one another, kill or be killed, there was no other way. Some chose a more defensive stance with shields raised, others decided that the best defence was to kill and maim and slashed away with their longswords.

The pikemen were advancing, The knights had little time left on horseback, the pikes would soon be able to impale the horses making them useless.

'Dismount,' went up the shout and it mattered little which side was issuing the order as all had to obey. Horses' flanks were slapped to encourage them to leave the battle field.

Lady Rosemary and her knights now had an unexpected advantage as they were still mounted being slower to join the fray. They realised this and started to gallop leaving their protective pikemen behind determined to press home their advantage. The six of them charged up and managed to lance four of their opponents. Lady Rosemary was amongst the successes and was beginning to prove that fairer sex be damned, she could inflict death as well as any man. Lady Rosemary and her knights dismounted, shield and longsword in hand.

The pikemen, swordsmen and rabble arrived, bringing with them their class hatred, determined to kill a noble, often forgetting in their zeal the opposing infantry. To kill a knight, that would be glorious, something to celebrate for all eternity.

Lady Rosemary's pikemen joined her, keeping formation, determined to protect their Lady from the unlikely young upstart. The battle was going well. She had numbers and the tactical advantage on her side. Lady Rosemary noticed with satisfaction the arrows overhead. The archers would take care of each other, this fight would be decided by melee and she was winning.

Dinran could see defeat at hand. The youngster had proved himself worthy in battle, he was a dervish, and he had listened to foolhardy advice. Lady Rosemary was proving herself worthy and Dinran was looking like a coward. No wonder his side was losing. Dinran needed to think, ignore the counsel of supposedly wiser, older men and act. It was time for the impetuosity of youth to show its hand.

Dinran rode up to his archers, his shield over his head to protect himself from the incoming arrows.

'Men,' he shouted, 'We need drastic action. Follow me, who cares about their archers. We need to kill Lady Rosemary. Follow me. Use your daggers. When you get to the fight, take swords, take pikes from the fallen, arm yourselves. We need to kill Manning's widow. Remember, she will never forget or forgive that you fought against her and will be your oppressor.'

It made sense, it was their only hope. Dinran charged atop his battle steed into battle, his lance pointing forwards. Behind him, his archers threw down their bows and ran forwards, daggers drawn, eyes searching the battlefield for better weapons.

Dinran chased straight at Lady Rosemary's group, lance ready, and managed to strike one of her knights in the throat killing him outright. He dismounted, longsword and shield at the ready. He risked a backward glance, the archers had followed his orders and were descending towards the melee.

Dinran hacked his way through, shouting encouragement to his troops who took heart at their master's presence.

'Reinforcements arrive, reinforcements arrive. Kill Lady Rosemary, that's all that counts. Men, for you are all men, her death is all that counts.'

Dinran's archers joined the fray, easily finding better weapons amongst the fallen. One even found an exquisitely handcrafted longsword from a fallen knight, friend or foe, it mattered not. A peasant with a longsword, a glorious day.

Under Dinran's leadership, his troops bore down on Lady Rosemary's group, Dinran at the heart, protected on all sides by his own knights. They were so determined that they even ignored attacks from the side, some falling in the process. It was of no consequence, they had to take out Lady Rosemary.

Dinran's pikemen engaged Lady Rosemary's pikes, each nullifying the other. Dinran and six of his knights managed to get to Lady Rosemary's group and started to engage them. The group walked steadily as the blood underfoot was making progress difficult. Still they went onwards. Dinran was indeed the dervish of battle, youthful, dashing, blood coursing through his body. Dinran received a blow to his helm, still he went onwards, slashing furiously in his dazed state, his knights alongside him.

The battle raged on furiously.

Dinran was close enough now and hacked a way through one of Lady Rosemary's knights, opening a path to her. This was Dinran's chance, he would kill her, the land would be his, glory would descend upon him again.

It was not to be. A lowly peasant archer, who had sheathed his dagger instead of abandoning it when he picked up a sword, saw his chance. He loved his dagger and played a game with his brother where they had thrown daggers into targets on trees. The peasant usually won. He could see Lady Rosemary clearly. The peasant lifted his dagger to his eye to steady his aim and threw.

The dagger sailed through the air, somersaulting its way towards its adversary. All those years of playful competition with his brother payed off. The dagger went through Lady Rosemary's visor, through her eye and into her brain.

Lady Rosemary toppled.

Dinran screamed out, 'No' the prized kill denied him.

As Lady Rosemary toppled, the fighting began to abate.

'The Lady is dead, the Lady is dead,' went up the cry from both sides.

The whole point of the battle had been won or lost. Men looked around at the fallen, some wondering if it had been worth it, how many could the healers from Bogloris save, some even beginning to think it might have been better if Dinran and Lady Rosemary had just fought it out between themselves in a joust.

One peasant archer whooped with delight.

The battle ground to a halt, the men appearing to move in slow motion. It was over.

Over the following weeks, Dinran sent messengers to all parts of his new estate proclaiming that all would be treated equally, regardless of whether they lived in Manning's old lands or not. All of

Lady Rosemary's knights and advisors were congratulated on how well they had served their former mistress and were pardoned as long as they now swore fealty to Dinran.

Calm settled over Dinran's new estate and thoughts turned to the inevitable upcoming battle with Eldara.

CHAPTER 18

The War Council was held in the Palace's inner chambers as the prospect of war with the Eldarans approached. Foremost on everyone's minds were the questions of why was Eldaran magic so weak in the last battle, how were preparations going for the upcoming battle and how powerful were the new magic users, particularly Morovius?

In an attempt to find answers, a large number were assembled. There was no need for secrecy now. No one, least of all Amran, had any new tactics to discuss. In attendance were the usual, King Almein, Queen Elbeth, Amran and Marinus. Joining them were the Assessor, Turinus, Novus and the seven Lords of the Kingdom. As befitted the occasion, guards adorned the walls, resplendent in their tunics, plumes swaying from their helms. Marcus stood proudly, pleased that at least on this occasion, the Assessor would have no need of his advice.

The King started proceedings. 'Right, We have summoned you here today to hear ideas about the magic display of the Eldarans in the last battle and to hear any ideas anyone of you might have about their problem with magic towards the end of the three hour period and our appropriate response.'

There was silence. No one had a clue why the Eldarans had failed to match them and their magic had grown weaker towards the end of the battle. The King tapped his hand on the table, showing his frustration.

'Well, Your Majesty,' said the Assessor. 'It stands to reason that something is happening in Eldara. No man's land is the same for both sides. The Eldarans have shown over the centuries, they are as naturally adept at magic as us. They also had about the same number of magic users as us. Yet, somehow, their magic waned towards the end of the battle.

'So, that eliminates anything in no man's land, their innate ability or numerical superiority. It couldn't have been the exploding tunnel. The decline in their abilities occurred far later and across the entire front, not just at the site of the explosion. The crucial thing is what we could see in the battlefield was not the cause as far as we are aware. It must, therefore, be something in Eldara that they are keeping secret.

'I am sorry to state the obvious, Your Majesty.'

'Not at all, not at all,' said the King. 'It might be obvious once someone has stated it, but no one has said it that clearly before. We have to determine now, what is happening in Eldara?'

'Your Majesty,' said Amran. 'As we have no contact with Eldara, we can only track major events like a mass mobilisation of troops. People talk of spies but sadly they are a myth. No one will risk going over no man's land.'

'Will the merchants tell us?' asked Dinran.

'Not a chance,' said King Almein. 'The only thing they will discuss is the price of goods and loans. They are making a fortune out of the war because we refuse to trade directly with the Eldarans and will not allow trade across our borders making us dependent on the merchant ships. You can rest assured, if the merchants know, they will not tell us.'

'I wonder if it had anything to do with the incursion into Anrac Woods?' asked Turinus.

'Could be, could be,' said the Assessor. 'If they knew they would be at a disadvantage, then they would try to kill our Anracs to weaken us.'

'Not sure about that,' answered Turinus. 'We saw no evidence of hunting and there are so many Anracs it would take an army to depopulate them, not a small party.'

'I thought there were seventy of them,' said Lord Rufus.

'Don't believe everything you hear,' answered Turinus.

Everyone looked around waiting to see if anyone else had any ideas. No one did.

'As a magic user myself,' said Novus, 'I have to say I can think of nothing that would cause difficulties for the Eldarans. The thing is, we have never experienced anything like it ourselves. This makes it difficult, if not impossible for us to guess what is going on.'

'I agree,' said Marinus, 'we have no frame of reference.'

316

'Ah well,' said King Almein. 'I suppose we had better leave it at that. Now, how are preparations for the upcoming battle proceeding?'

'Very well,' said the Arch Cleric. 'My bishops report that sermons are going well. We are using the usual arguments plus we have the added bonus of showing everyone that our leaders are trustworthy. Just look at the originality of the exploding tunnel.'

Everyone looked at Amran, who decided to go red in the face and look at his shoes.

'But more importantly,' continued the Arch Cleric, 'people can sense victory. We are not the only ones who saw Eldaran magic wane at the end of the magic battle. The masses noticed it as well. It has given people heart. Some are even talking about how they will take over the best parts of Eldaran land.'

'Nothing breed success like success,' said Lord Rufus, who knew this from his own experience in winning at chess.

'Excellent,' said King Almein. 'Recruitment should be easy this time around. Hopefully, the Eldarans will encounter difficulties due to demoralisation.'

'Or, Your Majesty,' said the Assessor, 'they might recruit heavily because of a desperate population. They hardly relish the thought of us invading.'

They paused, looking at the tapestries hanging from the walls. All around them were depictions of war. Magic users casting spells, fireballs breaking down air barriers to immolate their opponents. Hopefully, it was a portent of things to come.

'Any ideas about tactics?' asked King Almein.

No one said a thing. Slowly, eyes moved to Amran.

'Don't look at me,' he said. 'Let's be honest. The tunnel was not a great success. I am out of ideas.'

'Come now,' said Almein. 'We are all friends here and we all agreed with the tunnel. As the Arch Cleric has said, it did show our people that we are actively pursuing new strategies and giving them hope. Now, Amran and the rest of you, any ideas?'

Silence. No one could think of anything.

Turinus just ventured a thought. 'Your Majesty, it seems to me that we have to mount an all out magic attack as the conventional forces are about equal.'

The Lords stared at Turinus.

'I mean no disrespect. I know you all fought valiantly. It is just that magic is the Eldaran weakness at the moment.'

They had no alternative but to murmur agreement.

'Talking about magic,' asked Almein, 'how are the current crop coming on? Is this Morovius as powerful as we have all expected?'

'I was certainly impressed by him, Your Majesty,' said Novus. 'He was far more advanced that the others.'

'He is certainly very powerful in training,' said Turinus, 'the most powerful fire mage I have ever seen, but...'

Open eyes turned to Turinus.

'but, well, I noticed a decline in his power when he moved away from Bogloris. In practice he shows his true power, but in the Anrac Woods, he lacked the same strength.'

'I agree,' said the Assessor. 'I noticed that as well on our journey to the dwarves. By the time we hit the Windborne Pass, he was just like a normal mage.'

'Is he scared of battle?' asked Almein.

'I don't think so, Your Majesty,' said Turinus. 'He was active in the fight and showed no sign of cowardice.'

'Maybe, he gets homesick,' said the Assessor. 'After all, no one is exactly certain how magic actually works.'

'Well, at least no man's land is relatively close to Bogloris,' said Almein.

'The plentiful jains should compensate as well,' said Novus.

'Let's just hope he can fulfil his potential,' said Almein. 'Anyway, we have such superiority in magic we should do well, but if he can really perform we'll be in with a great chance. What about the other youngsters, Turinus?'

'Your Majesty, they are a highly accomplished group. There is still a lot of animosity between Flavin, Orken and Morovius and his friends but that should dissolve in battle. Banshin, in particular, is a fine warrior and that bloody imp Necarius summons is quite deadly.'

Almein laughed. 'He did me good. The only thing around here that shows me no respect. Taught me I am only here for a short time, while these hallowed walls have been here for aeons and long may they last.'

'Long may they last,' went up the murmured agreement.

There was not much more to discuss but as is the way with meetings, they talked for another half an hour to ensure that nothing had been left out of the discussion. All that happened is that they largely repeated what had already been described. Everyone just hoped that Morovius would deliver, if he did they could achieve victory. Turinus was advised to give all the new magic users a good inspirational send off in their last day at school.

Turinus found the advice useless, if he had not already inspired the class in the preceding years, what difference would one day make? But they had all agreed on its importance and who was he to argue? The day of battle was drawing near, men had started to arrive in Bogloris with their weapons and his pupils had become excited. All those years of training and now their time had come. It appeared as if Turinus was going to find it easy to inspire his pupils.

'Right class, settle down, I know this is our last glorious day together but that is no excuse for slackness.'

The class settled, looking up at Turinus, waiting expectantly for what he had to say. You never know, a last pointer in the right direction from the experienced warrior could mean the difference between life and death.

'As you know,' Turinus started, 'our leaders devised a brand new tactic for the last battle, the exploding tunnel. This proves that our leaders do not rest, our King is always alert to new possibilities. The resultant explosion shocked all who saw it and no one who witnessed the incredible event, at least those who survived, will ever forget what happened.

'For years, people have tried in vain to come up with an original tactic. All, except Chief Exchequer Amran, have failed. He alone came up with that ingenious plan.'

A hand went up.

'Yes, Flavin?'

'Sir, will there be more exploding tunnels in this battle.'

'I'm afraid not. There were unforeseen circumstances, which no one, not even our leaders could have predicted. These make future tunnels impractical. Besides, we have no need for new tactics this time. Can anyone tell me why?'

Hands shot up. Everyone, at last knew the answer to a question.

'Go on Orken. Tell us about it.'

'There is significant evidence, Sir, that the magic of the Eldarans, especially the length of time the Eldarans can last in battle, is in decline.'

'Correct. I was there and it was quite remarkable. The Eldaran shield weakened and much of our magic was able to penetrate even when the shield was impermeable. A great responsibility thus lies with the neccies and especially the fire mages. Your bolts have a real chance of causing the enemy irreparable damage. Further, you neccies who can evoke Cathrens are in for a treat. Many magic arrows were able to penetrate their shield.'

Banshin put up his hand.

'Yes?'

'So, it's just an all out attack then, Sir. No special tactics?'

'I'm afraid so. There will be no pleasant surprises, like the ground exploding. I am sure the Eldarans know as well as us the battle plan. The enemy must be aware of their weakness and that we will attack with everything we've got and they will be desperately defending. Of course, the Eldarans will attack as well. After all, they have their own neccies and fire mages, but hopefully, our shields will hold true. Theirs on the other hand, well, here's hoping.'

Candera put up his hand.

'Yes?'

'Sir, I saw many horrific injuries when I healed after the last battle. Do things become very confusing, I mean, who do I heal when so many are injured?'

'Interesting. Sure, some of you have experienced minor contacts, but let us be clear, these were minor. You could hear instructions clearly and see the entire conflict.

'War is different. It is quite frankly, chaos. Some orders get through, others do not. Too much is happening for anyone to get a clear picture. I am sure that even the planners observing, just like Our Majesty, find it difficult to be sure what is happening all around them. It is just too complex.

'What happens is your vision narrows, it has to. No one can comprehend the entire battle so your focus shifts to specific fights. The warrior you are engaging, the group you are in, the shield wall you are trying to penetrate, the shield wall and bubbles you are maintaining. All focus on the specific, you have no choice. You will do much, seemingly instinctively, without thought. That is why your training has been so extensive.

'That is the nature of war.'

The pupils allowed his words to sink in. Trepidation was added to their initial excitement. Had their training been thorough enough? Had all they learnt been enough? Maybe, thought some, I should have read some books. Perhaps, thought others, I should have read more. In particular, Morovius and his friends began to realise that the encounters they had been involved in so far were only a minor appetiser compared to the main course of war.

They walked out of the school for the last time, kicking pebbles on the ground as they went. There was general hollering and whooping, they had done it, they had graduated and were now fully fledged magic users. Some stole wistful glances back at a past that was never to be repeated.

Candera, Morovius, Banshin, Necarius and Magins began the walk back to the huts they would be sleeping in for the last time tonight. As newly qualified soldiers, they would from tomorrow be expected to sleep in the Barracks in Bogloris. Luckily, the five friends had arranged it so that they would be billeted together. With the end of their schooldays, their minds turned to the future and to war.

'So tell us, Candera.' said Magins, 'what was no man's land like. Is it true what they say about how powerful you feel there?'

'Oh, yes,' Candera replied. 'The ground glistens with jains. You can feel it in your bones, the power surging through you as you approach the area. I saw other healers positively glowing with a blue aura.'

'Fantastic,' said Banshin. 'Magic dealers must do great deeds there, worthy of any chivalric poem.'

'Well, I suppose so, if by great deeds you mean great destruction,' said Candera. 'Frankly, it was quite shocking. I am sure it's all good fun when the battle is raging, but to see all those dead men, crows picking at their corpses, mangled bodies, the groans of the injured, it really was a sight. I did all I could, you know, but I couldn't save that knight. I was too late, he'd lost too much blood. Seemed a handsome sort of chap, as well.'

They pondered this piece of information.

'They don't tell you about that in the poems,' said Banshin.

'Well, we have killed before,' said Morovius. 'This will just be on a larger scale.'

'I wonder how much death Enraefem has seen,' said Necarius.

'Well, it doesn't seem to bother him much,' said Magins, 'he's pretty cheerful. Nothing gets him down. Didn't you tell us he wasn't even respectful towards the King?'

'Yeah, that was an embarrassment,' agreed Necarius.

'But he's a bloody daemon,' said Candera. 'You can't expect him to have feelings.'

'Nor us,' said Morovius. 'Whether we like it or not we are soldiers. We have no choice in the matter, we never have. Our feelings don't count, just our efficiency.'

They carried on walking towards the huts, no one able to answer Morovius. They naturally went to Morovius's hut. The others had Aunties who kept changing but Belinda was the one constant in their lives apart from their friendship. She was going to become an Auntie herself and was moving to a smaller hut to care for a young boy. She was busy in the garden, tidying things for the new occupant.

'I've made cookies. Help yourselves,' she shouted. 'Can one of you bring me a glass of water?'

Candera volunteered and went to her. She looked upon him kindly, he was after all the one who had initially stood up for her son.

'Are you all right, you seem a little pensive.'

'Well, Belinda, it's war. It's going to happen. There will be death.'

Belinda paused in her weeding and stood up.

'Yes, there will be death, but you are a healer. You save people.'

'I never saved that knight. I merely prolonged his agony.'

'But your intent was good. Look, in life we tend to blame ourselves. It helps us think that we are in control. If it's our fault then we could have done something about it and had a better outcome. You have been taught to strive, that you are the best amongst people, a magic user, someone special. But there are limits to what even someone special can achieve.'

'I suppose so.'

'Don't blame yourself, Candera. This war is not your fault, it's none of our faults, it was established before we were even born. All you can do is your bit, that is all. Do your best to heal, to save life.'

Candera smiled. He felt better. 'Thank you,' he said, simply. They walked together to join the others. The chatting continued, what would the billets be like, how would they organise things, who would be in charge of what and most importantly, what would war be like?

The newly qualified soldiers were not the only ones obsessed with war. It was unavoidable in Bogloris. There were soldiers everywhere, men called up from all over the Kingdom, fulfilling their duties to their ultimate Liege Lord, the King. There was trepidation, of course, but there was also hope.

Hope that at last victory might be in sight. In the past, people had heard so many stories and sermons from the pulpits about how this was the final battle, this could do it, the enemy is weakening, we have a great original plan, but now it was different. All who had survived the Battle of the Exploding Tunnel had witnessed how Eldaran magic had failed. There was real hope at last.

If the Marcovian magic users could obliterate the enemy's mages, then it would be magic users and Marcovia's conventional army against Eldara. They could not lose. And for once there would be rich pickings. All that land in Eldara would be theirs. Peasants dreamed of better land to till, prosperous peasants thought of how they could afford armour and a warhorse and perhaps become knights, knights dreamed of land acquisition and who knows, maybe a Lordship.

Even the relatively contented and unambitious, like the knight Bentham started to dream.

'You see Ledine, if I could get some major land in Eldara, well, you could run my lands in Marcovia, even become a knight.'

'Really, Sire?'

'Sure, but you know what?'

'What?'

'In order for that to happen there is one major prerequisite.'

'What is that?' asked Ledine, not even sure what this 'prerequisite' animal was.

'We have to live. Let others be heroes, we must live. I'll charge behind the other knights out of the way of the real action. When I dismount, you come and join me. Together, all our practising will pay off and hopefully, we'll survive again.'

'I hope so. I like your plan, anyway, Sire.'

'It's the best plan of survival I can think of. Come, let's have an ale.'

They went into the busy Inn, whilst all around men talked of acts of bravery they would commit, how they would show those Eldarans, once and for all, this was their chance, one day peace would descend on this fair land again.

You never know, one day, peace might reign once again in this pleasant land.

CHAPTER 19

The morning of the Battle had arrived. The five friends climbed out of the bunk beds and started to adorn their war clothes. Banshin, alone, was able to wear chain mail armour. His friends helped him to dress, putting on his helm and lacing up his armour. The mail went down to his knees like a skirt. He put on his leggings.

'Leave the codpiece to me, Magins. I'll do that myself.'

'You sure,' replied Magins, 'looks like you need some help. Sure I couldn't rearrange things down there for you, make you feel a little more comfortable?'

'Ha, bloody ha.'

'Come now Magins. It's his first real battle. We don't want to excite him any more than necessary,' said Morovius.

They all laughed. This was what true comradeship was like. The bawdy humour, donning battle garb, real men with a real purpose. And of course, the Marcovians could win a great victory. It was a glorious day. Finally, Magins helped Banshin put on his tunic, the cross of Marcovia showing his allegiance.

The ethereal magic users put on their robes, which were also decorated with the blue cross. They offered little if any protection, if their garments had done so they would be unable to channel the

330

jains. Instead they were dependent on their destructive power and the air mages for defence. At least, they had codpieces to protect them against any Eldaran imps that had developed Enraefem's particular fetish.

They made their way out of their billet. Banshin mounted his Anrac, its size and smell prohibiting her from entry into the billet. She was lucky because as it was the day of the battle, she had been allowed this far into the city. The scene was busy with similarly attired magic users milling around, swapping stories, wishing each other well and, in particular, encouraging the new recruits.

'You lot are really lucky. Imagine being on the verge of victory in your first battle. All we have ever known is stalemate.'

'Good luck, young 'uns, enjoy yourselves.'

'Fine Anrac you have there, boy. May she serve you well.'

They started to make their way down the main gates where the horses awaited. Not warhorses for battle, but the more timid, ordinary sort that were merely for transport. Various magic users formed into pods, a fire mage, a defensive mage, a magic warrior and a healer. Ideally, they also included a necromancer. As the friends had formed such a pod long ago, they were not involved in the last minute negotiations.

They started their ride out of Bogloris into no man's land. It was not long before Morovius noticed a change.

'Lads, I can feel a loss of power,' he said.

'Damn, that's all we need,' said Magins. 'What is this thing to do with Bogloris and you losing power?'

'I wonder if that spirit going on about the feminine is the answer,' said Banshin.

'What, you mean I'm a wet girl's blouse?' asked Morovius.

'Not at all. I really don't get what's going on,' said Banshin defensively.

'Try not to worry,' said Candera. 'As we approach no man's land, the jains will kick in.'

'I certainly hope so,' said Morovius.

They could see the flicker of the jains as they approached the flat expanse of no man's land. Beyond the watchtowers the land took on a bluish tinge, inviting them onwards, promising them unimaginable power. It was as if Morovius took heart from the sight.

'I feel better now,' he proclaimed.

The friends smiled and Candera leaned over and gave him an encouraging pat on the back.

'You five, over there on the left flank,' came the order.

The four on horses dismounted and started to walk while Banshin continued to ride his Anrac. They could see the huge crater from the Battle of the Exploding Tunnel. All around it brought gasps from the new warriors. They had heard it was large, but it was huge, that must have been one hell of an explosion. Some wished they had seen it happen.

The five comrades took up their positions. Across no man's land, they could see the Eldarans clearly with their green circles denoting their allegiance. They certainly didn't seem weak, their mages tall and upright, their warriors huge and daunting on their Anracs. Were the stories of their weakness a myth to bolster spirits? It couldn't be. Too many people had witnessed their plight.

The two armies lined up facing each other, the archers and crossbowmen on their flanks. Behind them the knights and infantry were milling around, their time to fight was a long way off. Behind all the troops were King Almein, Marinus and Amran mounted on horses, ready to instruct the waiting messengers. Morovius noticed a knight and his servant were particularly keen to be at the rear.

'Common Ledine, back here will do nicely,' said the knight Bentham.

Morovius looked to his right. He groaned inwardly. 'Look over there.'

The friends looked and saw Flavin and Orken.

333

'Oh, no,' said Banshin.

'Don't worry,' said Candera, 'we are all comrades in arms today.'

Turinus rode up on his Anrac.

'Banshin and Orken, with me on the charge.'

A deathly silence descended over the battlefield, broken only by murmurs as necromancers started evoking. The plopping sound of daemons coming into existence was the sign for battle.

'Off we go,' piped Turinus's familiar high pitched voice, as Enraefem jumped onto Banshin's shoulder.

'Come you oaf, charge!' said Enraefem.

Banshin started to charge. Alongside him were Orken and Turinus, Enraefem screaming expletives. Morovius started conjuring a huge blue ball between his hands, feeling the power of the jains, a radiant blue glow surrounding him. He turned the blue into red, yellow and orange wisps darting form the ball's surface, smoke smouldering. He gave a jerk and shot off the fireball. As it sped off, Magins put up the permeable shield protecting his part of the line and shields around Enraefem and Banshin.

The fireball went screaming overhead, followed by Necarius's lesser blue bolt.

'Damn, that's big,' shouted Turinus.

'That will be Morovius at work,' confirmed Banshin.

Morovius's fireball smashed into the Eldarans permeable defence, splintering into a myriad kaleidoscope of colours but not dissipating entirely. A small part of the fireball shot straight through the permeable wall at its target, a mage, setting him alight. His healer set to work immediately.

A cheer went up from the Marcovians. The Eldarans were in shock. What new sorcery was this? Nervously, they checked the ground. Who could cast such a spell? Morovius smiled and prepared another.

King Almein couldn't help clapping. Even amid the myriad fireballs, blue bolts and projectiles, Morovius's fireball stood out prominently.

'I told you he was good, Your Majesty,' said Marinus.

'You should have seen the mess he made of my ceiling when he was a baby,' said King Almein.

'I did, Sire. It was most impressive,' Marinus confirmed.

'Oh, of course, you were there.'

'I paid for the repairs, Your Majesty.'

'This is awesome. Victory will be ours, I can feel it.'

'I certainly hope so, Your Majesty,' said Amran.

The magic warriors hurled themselves at each other with a loud crash, Anracs smashing into one another, locking horns. Enraefem jumped off Banshin, determined to go for gonads. Banshin went to shield bash his opponent who was young like himself, but his foe had the same idea and they smashed their shields together, the shock waves travelling up Banshin's arm. Suddenly, his foe's Anrac reared up and let out a roar of pain, it must be gonad time, as Banshin slashed across its stomach. Keep the healer preoccupied with the Anrac.

Necarius operated his mind meld with Enraefem. 'Get the warrior, quickly, while his healer is dealing with the Anrac.' Enraefem complied, jumping up, going for the calf muscle above the stirrups. Just cause pain, distract him, Banshin can sort him out.

Morovius cast a sidelong glance as he let off another fireball. There was a Cathren, magisterial in her beauty, letting off her magic arrows with great speed. Her lithe body, slim and slender, with firm breasts, mesmerising. The Cathren continued, unabashed, firing her deadly arrows. Morovius started to conjure another fireball, happy to see that a portion of his last one had made it through the barrier, this time immolating a healer, his intended target.

Magins kept up his concentration. His shield was largely effective, only allowing through the strongest of magic arrows and a little fire. An arrow penetrated his thigh, but Candera was quick to heal him, the arrow being pushed out by the regenerating flesh. Magins tried to not let it distract him, keeping up his shield on Banshin and Enraefem, feeling the strain of the assault on his main shield.

Flavin kept on throwing his fireballs and noticed with disappointment that not much of his fire was able to penetrate the permeable shield. Those that did were moving so slowly that they were easily avoided.

'Damn.'

'Keep trying,' said his shield mage nearby. 'Just keep going. These Eldarans will tire and then you will have your day.'

Orken had the misfortune of being matched up against an experienced warrior, an Eldaran Turinus. He was concentrating on parrying his foe's thrusts with his shield, looking for an opening to counter-attack. All those years of training had to pay off. He suddenly could see his opponent's rib cage after a strong thrust had put his foe slightly off balance. He thrust his broadsword swiftly, digging it in about six inches. His opponent slumped and operated his mind meld with his Anrac to steer away, giving his healer time to cast his magic. Orken chased after him, hearing a 'Well done lad' as he did so, from Turinus.

Fireballs, arrows, bolts and blue bolts of magic kept passing overhead. Messengers ran from the King shouting instructions that few could hear and fewer cared about. Just concentrate on the task at hand. Keep the fireballs going, wear them down, concentrate on the defences, keep your eyes peeled for any injuries that need healing. Flavin noticed with pride that enough of his fireball had penetrated with sufficient speed to hit his target, another fire mage.

'Yes,' he said to himself.

Orken's foe had been healed and wheeled to face the upcoming warrior, but Orken had the advantage as he was on the charge. They shield bashed each other and his foe was sent reeling over the back of his Anrac. Orken slashed down with his broadsword for what must surely be the killing blow, but his opponent's experience kicked in and he quickly righted himself, his Anrac being sliced, needing healing. Orken and the experienced warrior squared up once again.

Banshin could see an opening he had manufactured. He feinted to go for his young foe's legs and when the shield was lowered, quickly switched position for an upward thrust to the neck. As his sword moved upwards, a Flantein leaped up under the mind meld instruction of his aware necromancer and took the blow, absorbing it easily before slinking down. Enraefem started chewing at the warrior's back, anything to get him off guard, c'mon Banshin, get him!

Morovius set off another fireball, arcing over the pitched melee battle into the defensive shield, he had to get that healer, he was really getting on his nerves. He really should have gone for the defensive mage, but he just could not stand how the healer was nullifying his attacks. The fireball arced in a beauty all its own, smoke trailing, wisps of fire emitting from its red hot core. The

338

fireball hit the shield with a crash and sparks, still enough got through, straight at the healer. Got him! Two healers from adjoining pods immediately set to work to aid their comrade. He'll live, but damn, that's gotta hurt.

Candera kept straining his eyes. It was just mayhem out there. Keep an eye on Banshin, make sure he is all right, you can't let your friend down now. Keep an eye on the projectiles coming through, make sure your comrades alongside you are in good shape. He started to fret, he hadn't had to heal in a while, was he doing nothing while the battle raged all around him? His time would come.

Banshin saw another opening, only to his opponent's arm but it was still an opening. He could see out of the corner of his eye that the Flantein was out of position and swung. It was a mistake, an Eldaran ploy that a more experienced warrior like Turinus would never have accepted.

As Banshin's broadsword came in, the warrior shifted his position and hit Banshin who was leaning forward with a mighty shield bash across the side of his body. Banshin was caught with an almighty blow and as large as he was, could not keep his seat on his Anrac. He toppled off, his Anrac wheeling around expecting Banshin to jump back on, but Banshin was reeling, stunned by the blow.

Enraefem furiously went for the warrior's visor to block his vision, but the warrior could see past him. He was after the dismounted Banshin, a sure blow and trampling from the Anrac would finish Banshin off. Candera threw healing magic, as much as he could, and although it immediately cured his bruising, the magic could not help his dazed state. Banshin started to panic, adrenaline pumping, trying to clear the fog from his brain.

339

Banshin held up his shield hopefully, trying through his confusion to get into position. Suddenly, he felt a sharp pain in him armpit, but the warrior hadn't hit him, what was going on? He felt himself fly through the air towards his Anrac. It was Turinus. He had seen his young protégé's plight and rode from his own private battle, lowered over and threw Banshin upwards before turning to face his own foe.

Banshin used his mind meld to direct his willing Anrac and was back on top, his enemy yelled with frustration and charged but Banshin was now relatively clear headed and he returned the charge. They clashed shields, equals again, the fight still on. Enraefem returned to the warrior's back, Banshin trying to get past the Flantein, who was determined to greet everyone of Banshin's thrusts with its broad expanse.

Orken was struggling. Why couldn't he have faced a newbie like Banshin? It was taking all his training, guile and cunning to deal with this warrior. At times, it seemed as if his foe possessed second sight, the ability to anticipate Orken's every move. He supposed it came with experience and he could see how Orken was going to thrust, parry or shield bash by his preparatory moves. Orken tried to resort to short jerks and quick shield thrusts to disguise his intent. It almost worked, a quick shield bash glanced his opponent's face.

Meanwhile, the battle raged. Apart from Morovius's fireballs, few ranged attacks were able to penetrate the permeable shields with any real effectiveness. This did not dishearten the Marcovians. They kept going remembering that in the last battle the Eldarans had displayed their weakness after two and a half hours. There was no need for complex strategies like exploding tunnels, this was a war of attrition. Hit the enemy with everything you've got in the sure knowledge that your defences are stronger than theirs.

Messengers kept relaying the same messages from the King's party.

'Keep it up.'

'Maximum attack.'

'Don't slack.'

'Don't worry. They will tire.'

'Good work Morovius, keep it up.'

Morovius kept on sending his huge fireballs. Each exploding like some crazed firework against the Eldaran shield. Yet, consistently, parts were penetrating, emblazoning his enemy, causing work for the healers. He told himself that although he had not yet managed a kill, not to worry. It was all about the last half hour when the battle would really take place. Every heal was taking something out of the opposition, making tiredness a real possibility.

Still, he wanted a kill, what the hell, let's try some fire arrows, a bit of accuracy, that's what's needed. He sent off five to gasps of amazement, most mages could only manage two or three. They flew true, over the heads of the melee scrummage and down towards the Eldarans.

Four were a waste, the reason why fire arrows were rarely used at this point in the battle. Lacking the power of a fireball, four of them broke up in an anti-climatic puff of smoke when they hit the permeable wall. One, however, managed to find a weak spot or perhaps it was imbued with unusual strength, because it managed to penetrate the shield and barely slowed in its trajectory.

It went straight for its target, guided by Morovius's mind. The necromancer began to move, but it was too late, the arrow went straight through his heart, blood spluttering, dead beyond healing. Satisfyingly, a Cathren started to disappear out of this existence, back to the Netherworld.

Morovius wished that one of his arrows meant for a healer or defence mage had made it instead, but what did it matter, he had a kill.

'Got one,' he shouted.

Necarius nodded his appreciation, concentrated on his mind meld with Enraefem and continued casting his blue bolts of magic.

Morovius was tempted to cast five more fire arrows. Three sets of five went off, surmounting the melee fighters, honing in on their targets but to no effect. All the arrows spluttered out of existence upon hitting the defensive wall, lacking the substance of a Cathrens' solid arrow, they failed to penetrate. Was it just luck that had allowed one through? Who knows? Morovius went back to his fireballs.

Everyone else at range was doing the same, the war of attrition. Cross bolts being winched in to send bolts at tremendous speed, but the crossbowmen could only manage two bolts a minute. The archers were faster although with less velocity and penetrating power. The mages kept up their fire bolts and blue bolts. All the time they were being urged on by the King's messengers. Wait until the half hour mark, wait until the half hour mark, the Eldarans will tire, they are bound to, it happened last time, it will happen this time as well. Some started to doubt, but all kept up their ranged attacks. Meanwhile, the Marcovian permeable defensive wall held up well. The attacks it allowed through were not enough to cause any damage the healers couldn't easily deal with.

Candera kept examining the battlefield. Orken was moving out of his own healer's line of sight nearer to Banshin. It was now Candera's role to heal them both. He strained forward noticing the little shape of Enraefem trying to keep Banshin's enemy off guard. Orken still appeared to be on the defensive looking for a suitable opening.

Banshin jabbed at his opponent from behind his shield, exposing his arm. His opponent was quicker, his broadsword coming down towards Banshin's arm. Banshin anticipated the move and drew his arm away but not quickly enough to avoid a cut. It was not major and Candera could soon heal that.

Candera started to invoke his healing magic when he noticed that the experienced Eldaran warrior was bearing down on Orken. With a mighty shield bash he exposed Orken's side, slashing at his ribs, a significant injury. Candera was going to heal Orken first, then turn to the relatively uninjured Banshin. But, Banshin was his friend, he was part of his pod, what if his injury was disorientating him, how could he heal Banshin second? Banshin was his main responsibility.

343

Candera made a split decision.

He healed Banshin.

Immediately, Candera started to invoke again, this time to heal Orken who was beginning to slump. He could hear Flavin shouting Orken's name, Candera had to get this right, he should have healed Orken first, it was a mistake, unforgivable. Candera shot off his healing bolt towards Orken to right the situation.

It was too late. The experienced warrior took advantage of the slumped Orken. He hammered through Orken's permeable shield with all his might, connecting with the back of Orken's head, breaking skull bone and slicing through the protective cowl. Orken fell off his Anrac, lifeless, Candera's healing magic arriving too late, you cannot heal the dead.

'No,' screamed Flavin. 'Candera, why didn't you heal him first, you bastard!'

Candera said nothing and just kept concentrating, beads of sweat breaking on his brow.

'Don't worry about him,' said Magins, 'he was not part of our pod. You did your best to save Banshin and Orken.'

Candera just stared grimly ahead.

The sight of the falling Orken gave Banshin new vigour, he had to dispatch his warrior quickly. The experienced Eldaran warrior who had killed Orken would be looking for a new youngster to kill. Banshin decided to throw caution to the wind and jumped off his Anrac, onto the enemy, shield bashing him. He used his mind meld with his Anrac to order the animal to stand still.

Banshin's shield bash and unusual tactic disorientated the young Eldaran warrior and he lurched back. Banshin had his chance, he thrust with all his magic enhanced strength through the permeable shield and into the man's stomach. The permeable shield slowed the thrust but not enough to stop the broadsword from penetrating the youth. Could that be healed? Well, what about this? He twisted his sword in the warrior's gut and jabbed upwards through his heart. That should do it. He jumped back onto his Anrac to greet the upcoming experienced warrior.

He realised now why Orken was so defensive, this warrior was good. Banshin kept his shield up to block and used his broadsword to anticipate incoming blows. He saw an opening. Was it a ruse? He feinted as if to go for the opening, but pulled back just in time to see his foe ready to strike a huge blow as Banshin leaned forward.

Luckily, Banshin had pulled back from his thrust and could see that his opponent's chest was bared. As he came down, Banshin thrust his broadsword up. The warrior's downward momentum plus Banshin's thrust, sent Banshin's broadsword through the permeable shield and into the warrior's chest killing him.

Fantastic! Another kill and this time against a warrior Orken couldn't handle. What a start to his career as a warrior in battle! Banshin looked around, filled with confidence, looking out for his next victim.

Back in the Marcovian lines, they began to notice a difference. More of their attacks were getting through, it wasn't just Morovius who could cause damage now. Even Necarius's blue bolts were penetrating and Candera noticed a mundane arrow penetrate the Eldaran permeable shield. The Eldaran melee began to withdraw.

'Banshin, to their wall. It's starting,' shouted Turinus.

Again, as in the last battle, the Eldarans were beginning to tire. The Marcovian shield was still permeable to allow their attacks to penetrate and now was the time to take advantage.

'Attack!' went up the cry in Marcovian ranks, with their melee fighters chasing the fleeing Eldarans. Their way was impeded by Eldaran daemons, willing to sacrifice themselves to ensure a successful retreat. Banshin's Anrac crashed into a huge Flantein, Enraefem on his shoulder urging him on.

Morovius was now using his deathly arrows as he could now target five enemies at once with deadly force. He jerked his arrows away, over the melee fighters, swooping down towards their targets. Yes! Each one shot true, barely slowed by the failing permeable shield, each one a head shot, instant death to the Eldaran magic users.

Cheering went up amongst the Marcovians. This was the moment they were waiting for, the famed half hour of carnage they would inflict upon the hated enemy. The reunification of the lands was at hand, they would all be heroes.

The Eldaran melee forces made it back to their lines and the shield became non-permeable. The Eldarans could not attack, but hopefully, they could weather the storm for the next twenty-five minutes. Their big problem was that tall, well built mage. He had penetrated their walls well before the problems started. Where had the Marcovians found a mage of such power?

The Marcovian bombardment continued and their own shield went down, there was no need for it as the Eldarans could not attack through their non-permeable shield. Magins' battle was effectively over unless the Marcovian melee fighters broke through to confront the Eldarans and needed permeable shields. He slumped to the ground.

'That's it Morovius. Keep going. Their whole shield will fail soon,' Magins said encouragingly.

Initially, the Eldaran shield held well as it was non-permeable, but the Marcovians could see that the shield mages were showing strain, sweating heavily. Morovius could see that all their troops were shouting, no doubt encouraging their defence mages.

Morovius started to send in his largest fireballs, time was of the essence, they had twenty minutes until both sides collapsed exhausted. He noticed with dissatisfaction that none of his fireballs were penetrating substantially. The Eldarans have to break some time soon.

Banshin and Turinus stood side by side, shield bashing and hitting the magic shield with their broadswords. They could feel the shield shuddering under their blows, giving them encouragement and would soon achieve a warrior's dreams, to be up close to a clothie. Let's see how well a fire mage does with a broadsword up his gullet.

All along the Eldaran front, warriors attacked with shield slams and slashing broadswords. Bedines hacked away with both tooth and claw, growling their rage. Flanteins hurled their huge bulk, smashing into the defensive wall. Imps, like Enraefem, clawed and bit with great speed.

The offence continued. Time elapsed. Desperation grew on both sides, can our shield hold, their shield has to go down, will we be denied glory, if the Eldaran shield lasts then the whole battle will have been a waste, will this be another forlorn hope signifying little like the exploding tunnel? King Almein jumped from his horse screaming orders no one could hear.

Then it happened. There were barely minutes to go. The shield of magic air started to shimmer, vibrating in the air. Could this be it? Defence mages strained, attack could be possible, this could be what the whole battle was about.

Banshin and Turinus tore through to attack the Eldaran magic users. The Marcovian defence mages put up permeable shields to protect them. Eldaran daemons, whose outlines were becoming faint, rushed at them, determined to protect their masters. Eldaran warriors, whose magic was now almost exhausted, stood their ground. Behind them stood the clothed magic users, daggers drawn, determined to do their best in unfamiliar melee combat.

348

Morovius sent off another five fire arrows now no longer impeded by a magic shield of any sort. Flavin was able to shoot in two. Necarius had to content himself with his blue bolts while using his mind meld with Enraefem to survey the Eldaran front line. Enraefem showed his worth, avoiding the upcoming daemons and warriors and went for a fire mage's neck, ripping at his jugular, rejoicing in his blood. He had never killed a fire mage before. Right, who's next?

All along the Marcovian front, death rained down upon the Eldarans. Cathrens shot their arrows with a new found determination, accurately piercing the melee ranks, avoiding their own warriors and impaling Eldaran magic users.

'Quickly Banshin,' Turinus ordered, 'we don't have much time.'

This time, the warrior who faced Banshin was no match for him. Banshin had a permeable shield and a healer at his disposal, his opponent had no such luxuries. Banshin dismounted and hurled a shield bash. The warrior stood no chance and went reeling to the ground. Banshin realised that the warrior's own magic was practically exhausted. Banshin was still fully charged and brought his broadsword down into the man's chest. Another kill.

Eldaran knights started to charge the Marcovian melee fighters in an attempt to defend what remained of their magic users. There could only be a couple of minutes to go and then surely the Marcovians would tire as well. Just keep them off for two minutes. The Eldaran magic users prepared to flee.

The Marcovians started to kill the knights, hacking at their horses, impaling them as they fell, fire arrows blasting through their midriffs, leaving perfectly circular smouldering holes in their chests. Even Necarius's blue bolts were killing. It was glorious.

A Marcovian trumpet sounded. It was time for their magic users to retreat. The three hours were about to expire.

Morovius slumped. His muscles ached, he could barely sit down in an undignified manner. His eyes hurt. He put his head between his legs and gulped in gasps of air. He had been warned about this but never realised it would be like this. He looked around and saw his comrades in similarly inert states. All the daemons were gone, their necromancers no longer able to sustain them in this plane of existence.

As Banshin withdrew, he looked around. It was carnage, yes, some of the Eldarans had escaped but look at all those bodies. The flower of the Eldaran magic fighting force was ruined. Corpses littered the blood soaked ground like rose petals strewn in a romantic encounter.

He looked at Turinus who smiled at him.

'This is it. We might not have achieved outright victory in this battle, but the next will be ours. They have been decimated.'

Banshin nodded. So, this is what victory felt like. He slumped over his Anrac, grateful that he was going back to the Marcovian lines, back to his friends.

350

Orders were being shouted.

'Magic users, I know you're tired, get back. Your battle is over. The knights take over now.'

Morovius started to walk back through the knights, stumbling as he went. He noticed the bright jains whose power he had always taken for granted, but now they had forsaken him. He had never felt such exhaustion.

He passed a lonely bush, a rare specimen who had managed to eke out an existence on the edge of no man's land. He admired its waxy, sharp needles, warning any herbivore that they would regret taking a bite. It is incredible how plants can cling to life.

Behind the bush, Morovius saw a young peasant, one of the rabble. His poor quality sword was lying on the ground and the peasant was tearing at the earth with his bloodied hands.

'The tunnel must be here, it must be here.'

Morovius became red in the face. His anger forced its way through his exhaustion enabling him to make one last effort in the battle. He grabbed the peasant by the throat.

'Look you miserable cowardly piece of shit, we have done our bit, now get out there and fight.'

The peasant gibbered something incomprehensible.

'Look, you have two choices. Get out there, fight and be a hero or I shall personally rip out your throat and you can bleed to death a coward.'

Morovius grabbed the peasant by the throat, put his poor quality sword in his hand and gave the him a push towards the front line. The peasant stumbled onwards.

King Almein surveyed the battlefield with satisfaction. So, it came down to this. Victory was not the result of some great new tactic or solving the three hour problem but due to some inexplicable weakness in the enemy. He prepared to launch the conventional attack.

'If I might be so bold, Your Majesty,' said Amran.

'Yes, what do you have in mind?'

'We are bound to win the next battle, Your Majesty. I estimate that they have lost two thirds of their magic users.'

'That makes sense and they are bound to have their half hour problem again. In the next battle we shall definitely be totally victorious.'

'So why waste our knights and Lords now, Your Majesty?'

'What do you mean?'

'What will a conventional attack achieve now when we are guaranteed a magical victory in the next encounter, Your Majesty? Next time around our magic users will wipe out their entire army.'

'I agree with Amran, Your Majesty,' said Marinus. 'Let's keep our casualties to a minimum for the siege of Bleddin and the subjugation of Eldara.'

Almein pondered his options. The advice made sense. Almein told the trumpeter to signal the Eldarans for an end to hostilities. The series of notes announced themselves over the battlefield.

The Eldarans did not respond.

'They know their magic users have taken a thrashing,' said Marinus. 'They must be hoping for a conventional victory to compensate.'

'Let's go defensive,' said Almein. 'If they want to charge a phalanx of pikemen, that's their loss. They have already lost many knights, let them lose them all.'

The messengers were sent out. Dismount, dismount, the classic defence manoeuvre.

The knight Bentham turned to Levine.

'Ah, well, at least I don't have to go charging off.'

'Yes, Sire, don't worry. I'll protect you.'

'Thank you, Ledine.'

Bentham decided to take up a position on the extreme left flank. You never know, he might be out of harm's way.

All along the Marcovian front, the knights dismounted and their pikemen stood alongside them, pikes firmly pointing outwards. It was the classic defensive formation, let the enemy charge, the pikemen will kill the horses and then our knights will dispatch the dismounted riders. If the Eldarans want another massacre, so be it. Their blood will be on their hands.

Almein ordered the archers and crossbowmen to the flanks. Their orders were clear, just shoot at the incoming knights as they charge, killing as many as possible. If you can't get a clear shot on a knight, kill their war horses.

The Eldarans lined up, knights in one line to the fore and the rest of their melee behind. Like the Marcovians, they had their archers and crossbowmen on either flank. They pondered the situation, was this going to be another massacre? The Marcovians seemed determined to be defensive and were refusing the conventional chivalric charge.

Everyone waited.

The reply came from an Eldaran trumpet. A request for an end to hostilities.

King Almein did not hesitate in signalling his trumpeter to agree.

The Battle of the Failing Shields was over.

Morovius looked behind him. On the extreme left flank of the Marcovian melee line a knight and a rather tall, well built pikeman could be seen dancing together, obviously well pleased with this unexpected turn of events.

Candera walked off with his friends. He looked straight ahead, oblivious of his surroundings.

CHAPTER 20

That night the five friends went into the deep sleep which only exhaustion can bring. The sound of snoring could be heard clearly from their billet, the contented sounds of men who had completed their first mission. Only Candera awoke briefly from time to time. He could see an image of Orken's wounds. He reassured himself that he had done his best, Orken was not in his pod and went back to sleep.

The next day the friends talked about their experiences.

'Enraefem was a big help,' said Banshin, 'the way he jumps around causing havoc, it's really something.'

'What about my shielding?' asked Magins. 'I'd like to see you feel the full weight of those blows. You wouldn't stand a chance.'

'All right, all right,' Banshin conceded. 'Those shields come in pretty useful.'

'What about Candera's healing?' asked Morovius. 'We all rely on that.'

'Of course, of course,' said Banshin. 'Every warrior needs a good healer.'

They looked at Candera, who smiled.

'Thanks,' he said.

'Well,' said Morovius, 'I think we make a great team. We haven't lost anyone yet and have plenty of kills under our belts. I don't think anyone can doubt our performance.'

'I'm not too sure,' said Candera. 'Flavin seemed pretty upset I didn't heal Orken.'

'Ah, screw Orken,' said Morovius. 'He wasn't in our pod and besides, look at how they beat me up when I was a kid.'

'That's right,' agreed Magins, 'and if it hadn't been for you Candera, they might have killed Morovius when he was a youngster.'

'Yeah,' agreed Banshin, 'you certainly led the way there and risked expulsion by healing Morovius.'

Candera smiled and looked away. Maybe expulsion would not have been a bad idea. He noticed a bluebird outside pecking eagerly at the ground with great determination. Eventually, it started to pull and managed to drag a large earthworm out of the ground. The way of the world.

'Candera, Candera,' said Magins. 'Are you all right?'

'Yeah, fine,' said Candera, dreamily, 'just watching a bluebird get his breakfast.'

'Ah, they are beauts, aren't they?' said Magins. 'I'd like to be one, flying around, not a care in the world, building nests, crapping on people from on high.'

'Yeah,' said Banshin, 'and chirping away non-stop, getting on everyone's tits.'

They all laughed and continued with the banter.

'Hey, Necarius,' said Magins, 'get Enraefem in here. He's part of the crew.'

'Well, there's no real need,' said Necarius.

'Why do we have to need him?' asked Magins. 'Just get him here for a chat. I wanna see his charming face again.'

'Yeah, go on Necarius.' said Morovius. 'He's the only thing that can shut Magins up.'

Necarius agreed and evoked Enraefem.

'Hiya,' came the familiar voice, 'what's afoot, what you need a doing?'

'Nothing much,' said Magins, 'just wanted your company.'

'Ah, bless,' said Enraefem, 'they're missing their dear ol' imp. Warms the cockles of me heart, that does.'

'Don't get too big headed,' said Banshin. 'We were just getting tired of listening to Magins.'

'What do you mean?' said Magins. 'I'm the heart and soul of the crew. You know you'd miss me if I was gone. You'd have to deal with awkward silences if it were not for me.'

'No problem, I can always evoke Enraefem,' said Necarius.

'Of course, always at your service,' said Enraefem. 'Always happy to see you guys.' Enraefem looked around. 'My, this is a cosy set up you guys have got here.'

They all looked around. All they could see was a simple, if strongly built hut with bunk beds. What was Enraefem on about? The little log fire to stop them freezing in winter? The only touch of home was a medium sized painting of Belinda that Morovius had commissioned. They all looked at Enraefem.

'What the hell you on about 'Raef?' asked Magins. 'I've seen a whore's armpit more cosy than this.'

'Well, I'm sure you guys snuggle up together, just lovely,' said Enraefem. 'Bring each other the warm comfort of home.'

They all looked curiously at Enraefem.

'Whose stupid idea was it to summon that bloody imp?' asked Magins.

'Yours,' they all answered.

'Me and my big mouth,' said Magins. 'One day it'll get me into trouble.'

They were somewhat perplexed as to why it hadn't happened yet. And so the banter continued.

Enraefem's three hours were almost up when he turned to Necarius and asked to go for a short walk with him. 'I want time with my buddy,' he said.

Necarius and Enraefem walked out of the billet into the sparse military camp.

'What is it?' asked Necarius.

'I don't need time with you, it's just something I need to tell you.'

'Sure, what is it?'

'Candera. Watch him. He could be in trouble.'

'What? He seems calm enough to me.'

'Yeah, too bloody calm. I have seen it before, it's not a good sign.'

Necarius knew Enraefem well enough to realise that the imp wouldn't have taken this step unless it was important.

'OK. I'll keep an eye on him and mention it to Morovius.'

'Candera might need to talk.'

'Fine, I'll tell Morovius.'

Later that day, Necarius took Morovius to one side and told him what Enraefem had said. Morovius nodded and took the next opportunity to have a quiet word with Candera.

'Mate,' he told him, 'I know we're rough and ready, but remember, we're always here for you.'

Candera smiled.

'Seriously, we all have each others' backs. You're my friend. You possibly saved my life when I was young, I'll never forget that. Hell, my mother still mentions it from time to time. If ever you need anything, just ask.'

'Thanks,' said Candera. 'Your mother is a good woman.'

'Yeah,' agreed Morovius, saying nothing further, mindful that Candera had never known his own mother.

That night, they were all sleeping soundly when Candera suddenly jolted upright, wide awake. Tears tore down his face, his heart beat quickly, his palms were sweaty. He clenched up.

'Orken,' he said.

All he could see in his mind's eye was Orken's gaping wound, a rib clearly exposed, nothing else.

The others awoke.

'What is it, Candera?' asked Morovius.

'Orken, I should have healed Orken. I can see his exposed rib. I'm a healer, I should have, I should have.'

'Bloody hell, Candera,' said Magins. 'He wasn't in your pod. He had his own healer. You did your best.'

'No. I should have healed him. Orken, Orken, Orken.'

'But I was injured,' said Banshin. 'I needed healing.'

'Not as much as Orken. I should have healed him first, you had time. Orken, Orken, Orken.'
Candera buried his head in his hands.

'Crap,' said Morovius. 'What are we going to do?'

'He's stuck,' said Necarius. 'I've read about this. Combatants get stuck. He needs to talk to someone who can help.'

'Who the hell is that?' asked Morovius. 'If we tell the authorities, they might think badly of him.'

They pondered this for a while. Who could they go to, who would not judge Candera, who understood him, who could help?

Necarius suddenly turned to Morovius.

'Belinda, your Mum.'

'Of course,' said Morovius. 'Candera, can I take you to my mother?'

'Yes,' said Candera, smiling, weakly.

They all looked at one another. If anyone could help it was Belinda. She knew Candera well, liked him and had never forgotten that he saved Morovius. She knew about army life and might be able to help. If she couldn't, Candera was in serious trouble.

Morovius led Candera out of the Barracks into the main street, his arm around Candera's shoulders.

'Don't worry Candera, not far to go and we'll be at my mother's. If anyone can help you, it's her.'

'I should have healed him, I should have healed him.'

They kept on walking, past the empty shops, skirting a Tavern that was still open to early morning drinkers and into the grounds where the infants slept. Morovius went to the third hut on the left and tapped his mother's window.

Belinda appeared in her nightdress at the window.

'Morovius, what is it? What's wrong?'

'It's Candera. He's stuck, he's stuck. You must help.'

Belinda looked at the hunched form of Candera.

'Of course, come in. Go round the front.'

Belinda let the two into her simple hut. She sat them both down.

'What is it Candera?'

'I should have healed him, I should have healed him.'

'Who Candera, who?'

'Orken, Orken, now he's dead.'

'That's all he'll say,' said Morovius, 'he's stuck, I tell you, he's stuck.'

'All right, all right. Morovius, leave us alone. He can stay here tonight.'

'Can you help him, Mum? Can you help him?'

Belinda smiled, a tear in her eye. 'I'll certainly try.' Morovius left the two together. Belinda left Candera on the seat staring into space and made a cup of tea.

'First things first, Candera. Have a cup of tea.'

'Thank you.'

She waited patiently for him to drink half a cup of his tea.

'Right, now tell me what is going on?'

'I'm stuck, I'm stuck. All I can see is Orken's wound, his rib showing, I should have helped him, I should have healed him.'

'All right. You're stuck. I'll help you. You have to trust yourself, you're a good person. You have to believe in yourself.'

'I'm useless, I failed, I should have healed him, I should have saved him.'

'All right, let's try. Tell me what you see.'

'All I can see is Orken's rib. Nothing else. It haunts me. I should have healed him. If I had everything would be all right. I should have healed him. I should have.'

'Tell me about Orken. What did he look like?'

'A large warrior, an impressive young man. He had his chain mail armour and his tunic.'

'What was on his tunic?'

'The blue cross.'

'What does the cross mean?'

'It meant that he was a proud warrior of Marcovia. A wounded warrior, a warrior I should have healed.'

'Right and was he standing up?'

'No, he was on his Anrac, he was a little slumped, but he was on his Anrac, a proud warrior.'

'Tell me about his Anrac. I haven't seen many Anracs.'

Candera proceeded to describe the Anrac, a huge beast of an animal, even bigger than Banshin's, twisted horns, surprising in its agility, an animal now bereft of its master, a master Candera should have healed.

'Right, thanks for that. Now tell me what was around Orken.'

Candera described the experienced warrior Orken was fighting, the glow on his face at the blow he had delivered, proudly astride his own Anrac, a magnificent animal, the warrior who would kill Orken, Orken whose greenish permeable shield would not be sufficient to prevent the killing blow, a blow which would never have been made if Candera had acted earlier to heal Orken.

'Right. Now please help me again. I have never seen a battle. Sure, I have seen plenty of soldiers, magical and mundane, but never a battle. Please tell me about it.'

Candera described the flashing of weapons, the greenish permeable shields, the fire bolts, the blue bolts, the sky black with arrows and crossbow bolts, the shouts, the screams of the wounded, the cries of triumph, the silence of the dead, Orken was dead, never to make a sound again, dead because Candera had never helped him.

'Wow, that sounds quite chaotic.'

'It was, thousands of men shouting, crying out, I have never been so confused.'

'Tell me. How long did you have to make your decision to save Orken?'

'It was still my fault.'

'I'm not saying it wasn't. I would just like to know how long you had to make your decision. A minute, a second, what?'

'Well Banshin was also wounded, not a bad wound, he would have been all right for a while.'

'All right, so how long did you have to make your decision?'

'I don't know. Time seemed to stand still.'

'How long Candera?'

'A second, I suppose.'

'So please correct me if I'm wrong but it seems to me that everything was chaotic, your friend was injured...'

'Not badly.'

'Not badly, let's call it a minor injury and you had to make a split second decision when you were a little confused.'

'Well, it's still my fault.'

'I never said it wasn't. But, still, you had to make a split second decision in chaotic circumstances when your friend was injured, albeit, not seriously.'

'I suppose so.'

'You suppose so or is that what happened?'

Candera sighed. 'That is what happened.'

'Yes, that's what happened. Dear boy, you seem quite tired. Use my bed, I'll sleep on the couch.'

'I can't do that.'

'You have to. If the infant awakes and leaves his room, you'll give him quite a shock if he sees you on the couch. Now go and sleep in my bed.'

Candera did as ordered and slept soundly. Belinda noticed his snores with satisfaction.

'A troubled lad, a troubled lad,' she said to herself.

In the morning, Belinda awoke Candera and asked him if he would like to come back that afternoon. He readily agreed and so their second meeting was set up. Belinda started their meeting.

'Yesterday, we discussed how you made a split second decision in the midst of a chaotic situation. Have you thought about that at all?'

'Well, it has been on my mind constantly. The problem if you are a healer is that you spend a long time doing nothing, while all around you people are busy. Then all of a sudden there is plenty to be done.'

'Sounds difficult.'

'I found it hard. It would be easier if you were always busy. I have also been wondering if I hated Orken and that was the reason that lay behind my decision to heal Banshin first although his wound was relatively minor.'

'Did you purposely not heal Orken so he would die? Was it a preformed plan?'

'No, I was just wondering if that lay behind my decision to heal Banshin first.'

'But you weren't conscious of it at the time?'

'Not at all.'

'All right. You were enemies as children.'

Candera went through how they had been enemies, particularly when Orken and Flavin had bullied Morovius. It just seemed so unfair, it wasn't Morovius's fault that he knew his mother.

'And how do you feel about the fact that you don't know your own mother?'

'I have never really thought about it. It is just the way things are.'

The next day they explored the issue of his mother more closely. Candera just didn't know. Maybe, she was not a nice person, who wanted to be a peasant anyway, it was better the way things had worked out. He just wasn't sure.

Their daily sessions continued for one month, Candera exploring how things had worked out, the chaos of war and how little control he had over his life. Fate had decreed that Candera was a healer and the Kingdom of Marcovia had decided what he should do with his healing abilities. Belinda wanted to know if Candera felt any anger about the whole situation. Initially, Candera denied any such emotion, but eventually he felt the stirrings within his heart.

'It's just so unfair. I mean, we are humans, who can think, capable of making decisions and yet we are denied any choices in our lives. My heritage, my background, all my relatives have been denied me. Who am I? I am only what the King wants.

'This whole war just doesn't make any sense to me. We want a united Kingdom, so do the Eldarans. Why don't we just join up, reunite and carry on. It makes no sense. All around us is a war whose beginning none of us can remember, a war whose perpetrators are long dead. What can we possibly owe them?

'I have a great gift. These hands can heal. I could do so much good, but instead I am reduced to being a war machine.'

'What are you going to do?' asked Belinda.

'I have only one option. To keep on going and look after my friends. They are the only things that count now. My friends are my family.'

'And the war?'

'I'll keep healing. The war could be over soon anyway. There is something seriously wrong with the Eldarans. Besides, we have the most powerful fire mage in existence – Morovius.'

Belinda smiled. It seemed that their meetings had come to a natural conclusion. Belinda told

Candera that he would probably be troubled by his thoughts for some time, but just to work through

things. Finally, she told him that if he ever wanted to talk to her, she would be glad to listen.

CHAPTER 21

Recruitment for the next battle began almost immediately. Under King Almein's orders, the Sheriffs were told to muster all the men in four months. However, agriculture was beginning to suffer as so much time had been taken up with the war and time consuming travel to and from no man's land. The Sheriff approached the knight Bentham with not particularly high hopes. He wondered what sort of excuse the knight would have this time. The Sheriff had determined that as far as chivalry went, Bentham was not exactly a shining exemplar.

The Sheriff sighed inwardly on his approach. Bentham was working in the fields with his peasants, not exactly the best example of knighthood, but production had dropped in his lands recently. The Sheriff approached Bentham.

'You know what's required, Bentham,' said the Sheriff.

'But as you can see, I'm busy. The crops really need tending.'

'What are you doing? Isn't that peasant work?'

'All hands are needed. Our crop yield this year will be low. We face possible starvation this winter.'

'I see. So your excuse this time is that you are desperately needed for production?'

'I wouldn't be doing peasant work otherwise.'

'Well, I suppose there is Article 143.'

'What's that?'

'An exemption from military service may be granted if the man is urgently needed in the production of essential goods.'

'These are pretty essential. It is food after all.'

'All right. You are granted an exemption, but Bentham.'

'Yes.'

'You will forfeit your rights to the spoils of war as a non-combatant.'

'I accept that.'

'Well, there we are then.'

'Oh, Sheriff. Couldn't I have used Article 143 before? I've never heard of it.'

'There is a good reason few such as yourself have ever heard of it. Good day, Bentham.'

'Good day.'

The Sheriff rode off with his retinue, while Bentham smiled broadly. At least one thing was sure. He was going to outlive this particular battle. Ledine wanted to know if a dance were in order, he felt like dancing. Bentham agreed but felt it appropriate to wait until the Sheriff couldn't see them. 'Then we can do all the dancing we like,' he said.

Bentham was the exception. The other Lords and knights and even many serfs were eager to enlist. Victory seemed assured. The Eldaran magic users had been virtually wiped out and those that remained were strangely affected by the half hour phenomenon. The spoils of war would surely go to the Marcovians and those that partook of what must surely be the final battle.

Back in His palace, King Almein called an emergency meeting of His most trusted advisors, Amran and Marinus. The only guards in attendance were Markus and Frank who had proven their discretion and trustworthiness in the tower supervising the tunnelling dwarves.

'This is a matter of great delicacy,' said the King. 'It requires careful consideration. The thing is Archmage Marinus, Amran has raised a matter of great concern. A concern that could totally nullify all the good that will come from our upcoming victory against the Eldarans.'

'What is it, Your Majesty?' asked Marinus.

'Well,' said Amran, 'it concerns five of your best pupils. They could be a problem.'

'My pupils?'

'Yes,' continued Amran, 'Morovius and his friends, but in particular Morovius.'

'What could be wrong with our most powerful mage?'

'His power, his great power,' said Almein.

'You are worried about how powerful he is?' asked Marinus.

'Exactly,' said Amran. 'He is extraordinary.'

'Isn't that a good thing?' asked Marinus. 'Isn't that why we allowed his mother to stay here? Isn't this what we have always wanted ever since he was a baby?'

'It's a case of being careful what you wish for,' said Almein. 'Please continue Chief Exchequer. Make the Archmage aware of our concerns.'

Amran proceeded. 'We are basically in a position where we are guaranteed victory over the Eldarans. There is no way they can survive the next battle. Even without their half hour problem, which as far we are aware, still exists, their magic users have been decimated and they even lost many knights.'

'A good thing, surely?' asked Marinus.

'An excellent thing,' said Amran, 'but we must consider the aftermath of victory, the peace dividend. Now the war with Eldara has ensured balance. The magic users have something to do, a war to wage, in the process of which they thin their own numbers. Basically, they keep each other under control.'

'And that ends with the peace?' suggested Marinus.

'Exactly,' said Almein. 'Continue Amran.'

'That dynamic ceases to exist with the end of the war. The magic users lose their reason for existence. Sure the healers can go around healing people, feeling good about themselves but what about the warriors, what about the mages, what about the most powerful fire mage, Morovius.'

'You are worried that he will make a bid for power,' said Marinus.

'Exactly,' said Almein. 'You are beginning to see our problem. The magic users will lose their purpose in life. They will see their great power, a power which will be lying idle. Idle hands, especially powerful idle hands, are dangerous.'

'Your Majesty is right,' said Amran. 'After victory we will have an idle, incredibly powerful fire mage on our hands who will not have an enemy. It is inevitable that his mind will turn to how he can build up his own power base. We see it after every battle, look at Lady Rosemary and Dinran.

They had to fight to see who could control Manning's land, neither leaving any room for compromise or any way to divide the spoils of war.'

'You think that Morovius will challenge the throne,' said Marinus.

'It is inevitable. He will challenge the throne, challenge everything, even challenge you the Archmage. Could you deal with Morovius at the head of an army of magic users?'

'No, I could not,' conceded Marinus.

'Neither could we,' said Amran. 'We have to deal with him, we have no option. We have to take him out, now, before he can cause any trouble.'

'I see, but isn't he needed in the upcoming battle?'

'Not really,' said Almein. 'Victory is assured without him. The Eldarans are so weak, we don't need Morovius. Besides if we wait for the final victory, it could well be too late. You can bet if we are considering our options after the victory, so is Morovius.'

'I see your predicament,' said Marinus.

'Not just ours, but yours as well,' said Almein. 'Surely you wish to remain Archmage?'

Marinus nodded. There was a pause. 'So, where do I come into this plan?'

'Marinus, you know the magic users better than anyone,' said Amran. 'Do you know the best way of dispatching Morovius and hopefully his friends as well?'

'I suppose it has to be done at night, Morovius and his friends will be asleep then. Then, there is a fire mage called Flavin. There is no love lost between Flavin and Morovius.'

'Can you organise this?' asked Almein.

'Um, well, let me see. Flavin is upset that Candera, Morovius's friend, did not heal Orken, who was a close personal friend of Flavin's. That might present me with an opening I can play with. Let me see, I need to stoke the whole Orken episode. I can say that we suspect Morovius and his friends of treachery. That could be the only excuse Flavin and some others need.'

'Excellent,' said Almein. 'Please proceed. After all you are not even really lying. Morovius will soon become treacherous. We are just anticipating things a little.'

'The only thing is,' said Marinus, 'what about the future? You are still going to have idle magic users.'

'That problem my friend,' said Almein, 'is for future leaders to solve. Maybe they can start another war, get those damn dwarves that have my gold or something. Our concern is the present. If we eliminate Morovius and his friends we will have stabilised the situation. In the present, magic ranks have been sufficiently thinned to ensure order and stability. The future will be the future.'

'I see,' said Marinus.

'So, you'll deal with this matter?' asked Almein.

'Consider it done,' said Marinus.

The meeting disbanded and the men went their separate ways. Markus, who had a troubled look on his face, went straight to the Assessor.

'Assessor, Assessor, you always told me to be honest with you, to tell you what is going on.'

'That's correct. What is it? Another harebrained scheme like the tunnel? What do they want me to do now?'

'Nothing to do with you, Sir. They plan to kill Morovius and his friends.'

'What? Why would they want to kill their most powerful fire mage?'

'Because he is the most powerful. They fear him, Sir.'

Markus recounted the discussion he had just heard to the Assessor. The Assessor just sat there and said nothing, not even interrupting Markus for clarification. All the while he thought of the little baby and his fondness for grass, the innocent gullible peasant mother, the Court's excitement at

381

such a powerful baby. He thought of their encounter with the dwarves, their battle at the Windborne Pass, how his young charges had displayed such faith in him, their bravery.

'Markus, you have done well to tell me of this. Don't repeat what you have said to anyone else.'

'What shall you do, Sir?'

'I shall right a great wrong before it is committed.'

The Assessor went to Morovius's billet and asked for a quiet word with Morovius alone.

'You know Morovius, there are times when we feel safe, but the thing is we are never safe in a time of war. There is always danger.'

'What do you mean?'

'There is always danger. Mark my words carefully.'

'I will. Thank you.'

The Assessor walked off. Morovius went back into the billet and told the others of his brief conversation with the Assessor. To say the least, they were puzzled.

'I know one thing,' said Banshin, 'the Assessor doesn't pay us social visits. Something's afoot. Something important.'

'Yeah,' agreed Magins. 'The only thing that can explain it is that we are in great danger. We have to be careful, wary of everyone.'

'Tell no one of this,' said Morovius. 'The Assessor was circumspect, no doubt to protect himself and his source. We can't let our guard down.'

'Not even at night,' said Candera, who was grateful that his sessions with Belinda had come to a recent conclusion. This new matter required all his attention.

'One of us will always have to be awake at night,' said Morovius. 'The rest of us will have to be prepared to go into action quickly.'

'We don't leave our billet alone,' said Magins. 'Candera, have you finished with Morovius's mother?'

'Yes, I can see her whenever I want, but for now we have finished.'

'Good. So there is no need for anyone of us to go out alone,' said Magins.

'I wonder what it could be?' asked Necarius.

'Might be an Eldaran spy,' suggested Banshin. 'They might want to take out the most potent Marcovian fire mage.'

'That makes sense,' said Magins.

'I wonder how the Assessor got to know about an Eldaran spy?' asked Necarius.

'No idea,' said Morovius. 'All I know is that he gets around, talks to all sorts, hears all kinds of things. Maybe he went to Port Inlein on his travels and a drunk merchant told him.'

'Makes sense,' agreed Banshin.

They decided to be wary of an Eldaran spy, never to go out alone but always as a group and to appoint a rotating watch while the others slept. Only Banshin could see a problem with the plan.

'There'll be no escaping Magins then.'

They all laughed while Magins promised he would be his chatty best in order to keep them all amused while they waited for the spy.

Meanwhile, Marinus took steps to approach Flavin. He sent him a message asking to see him in his quarters in the mage tower. Flavin was under strict instructions to come in the middle of the night and to ensure that no one knew of his whereabouts.

Flavin knocked nervously on the Archmage's door.

'Come in,' came the instruction.

Flavin carefully opened the door and stepped slowly into the Archmage's chamber wondering what he had done now.

'Sit down, Flavin. I have a matter of great urgency and delicacy to discuss with you.'

Flavin sat down. Surely, this was a matter for that great, heroic pod of Morovius that everyone was going on about. Flavin maintained his silence.

'It would appear that we have a traitor in our midst.'

Flavin's eyes widened. Who would do such a thing? Why would they do it with Marcovian victory in sight?

'Who could that be, Sir?'

'This is going to be a bit of a shock. I shall just tell you straight and truthfully. It is Morovius and his pod.'

Flavin was startled. He had never liked Morovius, but a traitor! This really was news!

'I am surprised, Sir.'

'We are all deeply shocked. After everything we have done for that boy. We even allowed his mother to come to Bogloris with him. We thought he would be our most loyal follower.'

Marinus allowed his words, especially the reference to mothers, to sink in.

'What evidence do you have, Sir?'

'Now, Flavin, a good soldier does not question his superiors. We have the evidence.'

'Certainly, Sir. I did notice that Candera wouldn't heal Orken.'

'There you are. The first act of treachery. Can you imagine Morovius and his pod going rogue in the final battle.'

'It would be carnage. It could scupper our certain victory.'

'Indeed it could.'

They sat there, motionless, contemplating how a rogue Morovius could cause mayhem and death within their ranks. He would be behind their shield, he would be devastating.

'What would you like me to do, Sir?'

'Well, Morovius is very powerful. You have to take him out at night, take them all out. Can you do it?'

'Sir, I can certainly rely on my pod to deal with a traitor and there is another pod we are very friendly with. That makes nine in total. If we attack when they are asleep, we can do it. Remove the threat from our lands.'

'Excellent! How many fire mages will you have?'

'Including myself, two Sir.'

'That's fine. Two huge fireballs to start with, then put up a permeable shield and finish them off if they are not already dealt with. Nothing clever, just dispatch the traitorous bastards.'

'Yes, Sir.'

Marinus nodded at Flavin who stood up and made his departure. He'd always known it. No good could come of a Mummy's boy. To think, they had almost been friends! A traitor. It all made sense. That was why Candera had not healed Orken. That's the thing with traitors. As hard as they might try, a traitor's allegiance always comes through. No one can keep up a pretence forever.

Flavin went back to his pod with the distressing news. They all discussed how much damage Morovius could cause. He would be behind their shield, they would be unprepared, he could really

387

cause mayhem. It all made sense, it was the only chance the Eldarans had, they must have contacted him somehow and offered him great riches. You just couldn't trust that pod. They were always together, not fraternising properly. Hell, recently, they didn't even go out on their own, but were always together, glancing furtively, distrustful of others.

Once you realised that Morovius and his pod were traitors, it all added up. There was no other explanation. Not only that, but they had hard evidence. Candera had not healed Orken. It was as Flavin argued, a traitor always betrays himself, he cannot help it.

They approached the pod they were friendly with and discussed their revelations. The other pod could see it as well, it all fitted together. Besides, they had the Archmage's word for it. They needed to act and to act quickly, the whole future of Marcovia depended upon it. The Eldarans and their spies had to be stopped. Who knows how many secrets Morovius had already told them? Time was of the essence. The two pods would strike tonight. Their leader, the Archmage, had entrusted them with a sacred task, they would not let him down. The youngsters would prove themselves worthy of Marcovia's great cause.

As far as Magins was concerned, being on guard had to be the worst duty of war. There was no one to talk to, hell, he couldn't even talk to himself as it would have awoken the others. Worse still, it was night time. Not a soul stirred. The most exciting thing that happened was an owl hooting and something like a mouse scuttling by. Knowing his luck, the owl would kill the mouse, decide to be quiet and then there would be no noise at all. They should have been billeted near the Tavern. At least he could have seen a drunken brawl or two, but oh no, they were soldiers, an elite apparently, tucked away in some corner of Bogloris. Not only that, they were well disciplined, no late night

388

revelries, just go to sleep, ready for the day ahead. After the war, he determined to join a more interesting army, one with prostitutes and midnight shenanigans. Any army had to be better than this.

He heard a sound, a twig snapping, that was no mouse. A 'Sh' sound. Someone wanted to be quiet, that must be our cue, the spies are coming. He nudged Morovius next to him, who awoke the others. They took their positions and started to invoke their blue magic, ready for action. Magins was especially alert. Everything depended upon him erecting a shield at the last possible moment so as not to alert the spies.

It was quiet but someone was outside the billet. They could hear breathing. Was it just a foolish prank or the danger that the Assessor had warned them about? Morovius could not just blast a fire bolt at some innocent prankster gluing their lock. Come on Magins, make sure that shield's up if we need it.

There was the sound, the whoosh of magic, it could even be a fireball, Magins jerked his hands and up went an impermeable shield. Let's see what this is about. Two fireballs tore through the door and the front of their hut, smashing into the shield, dissipating harmlessly, exploding in a cascade of myriad colours.

'Permeable,' ordered Morovius and the shield took on the familiar greenish hue with a flick of Magins's hands.

Morovius had been conjuring the blue magic between his hands to ensure a fireball of great size and let it off as a plop announced Enraefem's appearance. Banshin jumped up, ready for action.

The huge fireball sped off illuminating the small group outside. Screams filled the air as the fireball tore through clothing igniting the men, searing through chain mail armour, cooking the men within. Magins threw a permeable shield around Banshin and Enraefem.

'Get one of the spies alive. Marinus will want to interrogate him,' said Morovius.

Banshin ran and Enraefem leapt through the permeable shield which allowed anything to exit but blocked most incoming damage. If these attackers had employed a permeable shield, it had not done much good against Morovius's huge fireball at such close quarters.

One of the warriors managed to stagger towards Banshin. Banshin carved his broadsword through his head, the attacker's helm offering scant protection. Time to be careful, that one won't be offering any evidence. Banshin looked around. There were figures in agony, writhing on the ground, smoke billowing off them. Candera would have to be quick if even one of them was going to be saved. It could be like the skirmish in Anrac Woods all over again.

Banshin looked around anxiously. He noticed one was writhing with great vigour – a possible sign he might live? Who knows? Banshin grabbed him and pulled him towards Candera.

'Bloody hell, Banshin. Kill the rest. Their screams will wake up the entire barracks,' said Morovius. 'Candera, save this one. Necarius, check his teeth. We don't need any suicidal heroes.'

Banshin went into the fray, slicing at throats, dispatching the dying into deathly silence. He started dragging the bodies into the hut. He could see other soldiers coming towards them from the other huts. Best to hide the bodies until we know what's going on.

The bodies were inside and Candera was desperately hurling healing magic at the spy, while Necarius held his mouth open with a piece of wood. Banshin and Morovius went outside.

'Don't worry,' said Morovius to the advancing soldiers, 'my experiment just went a little wrong.'

'Why don't you do your bloody experiments in the daytime. We thought war had broken out or something.'

'Sorry. You're quite right. It won't happen again. Very sorry.'

'Morovius, you're a damn idiot.'

'Yes, sorry. It was rather stupid of me.'

'Stupid, more like imbecilic. We are trying to sleep.'

Morovius and Banshin went back into the hut. Magins was busy hiding the bodies in the bunk beds, while Candera was desperately throwing as much healing magic as he could at the burnt man. Enraefem was looking intently at the victim.

'Far be it for me to correct your esteemed Sirs, but isn't that one of your own guys? Is he a spy? Look at the others. Pretty familiar, aren't they?'

Magins, Morovius and Banshin started examining the faces of the corpses while Necarius and Candera looked at the badly burnt survivor. There was silence.

'These are our men,' said Magins.

'That's Flavin,' said Morovius. 'I should know, I've punched that face often enough.'

'They can't all be spies, surely,' said Banshin. 'I mean, I was never Flavin's biggest fan, but a spy? Besides, how did he manage to convince the others? There's got to be two pods here.'

'Is it revenge because I didn't heal Orken?' asked Candera, still desperately trying to heal the sole survivor.

'What, two whole pods in a petty revenge attack?' asked Morovius. 'It makes no sense. Necarius, leave him alone, he's not Eldaran. I doubt his teeth are a problem.'

'Can you speak?' Morovius asked the man whom he recognised as a defence mage from another pod.

'Yes, but I'll tell you nothing, you filthy spy.'

'Me, a spy!' said Morovius. 'You're the spy, trying to take me out for the Eldarans.'

The defence mage flared with anger. 'I am no spy. We were acting under Marinus's orders.' He clamped his mouth shut, realising he had said too much.

'Marinus,' gasped Necarius. 'This is serious.'

'No shit,' said Magins. 'People trying to kill you when you are asleep is normally considered a serious matter.'

'Serious and a total mystery,' said Morovius. 'Why would Marinus think that we are spies? If he did, why didn't he send in the whole camp to attack us?'

They looked at one another. 'Maybe,' said Necarius, 'only this lot were stupid enough to believe him. Imagine trying to convince everyone that we are spies.'

'Well, why didn't you heal Orken?' asked the defence mage.

'I made a terrible mistake in the heat of battle,' said Candera. 'I thought I had time to heal Banshin and Orken.'

'But, Banshin wasn't badly wounded, Orken was. You should have healed Orken first.'

'Yes, that is true. I made a terrible mistake in the chaos that is war. I only had time for a split second decision.'

The defence mage's eyes widened, he started muttering to himself, 'It can't be, it can't be.' He looked around urgently, seeing the dead bodies, trying to make sense out of what had just happened.

'You've been played for a fool,' said Morovius. 'Your friends are dead. Tell us what you know.'

The defence mage hesitated.

'You do realise that we will torture you, then heal you and then torture you again until we obtain the information we require. Why protect your source? He's played you.'

The defence mage's shoulders slumped, he appeared to relax.

'Flavin, it started with Flavin. He told us that Morovius was an Eldaran spy. Marinus himself had confirmed it. Candera showed his true colours when he didn't heal Orken. That's all I know.'

'This makes no sense,' said Magins. 'Why would Marinus do such a thing? Was Flavin lying in order to organise an attack to get revenge for Orken's death?'

'This attack could have been orchestrated from on high. We've obviously done something we aren't aware of,' said Morovius.

'Could we explain things to the Archmage?' asked Candera.

'How? We don't know his motives or whether Flavin just made the whole thing up to enlist their support. I mean the Archmage can't really believe we are spies. Nothing makes any sense. We have to find out what is really going on.'

'The Assessor,' said Magins. 'He knows, he warned us, we need to get to the Assessor.'

They agreed, it appeared to be the only way of finding out the truth. The Assessor had warned them, he must know what was going on. He moved in all types of circles, the answer lay with him. They decided to go straight to him.

'What about your mother?' asked Candera.

'What about her? She can't be involved in a plot to kill me.'

'If all of us are in danger, she could be as well. They might even try to get to us through her,' said Candera.

'Oh shit,' said Morovius. 'Mum. If anything happens to her...'

'Don't worry, we'll go to her first and then go to the Assessor,' said Magins. 'Then we can make some sort of plan.'

They securely bound and gagged the defence mage and set off to the infant quarters.

CHAPTER 22

They rushed off to Belinda's hut as fast as they could and Morovius knocked on her window in a flustered state. Belinda answered in her nightdress.

'Mum, let us in. We have a big problem'

'Is it Candera?'

'No, it's far worse, just let us in.'

They went around the front and Belinda opened the door to the hut. They quickly recounted recent events.

'I just can't see Flavin organising this entirely on his own and lying about Marinus. This must be an order from on high.'

'But why?' asked Magins. 'What have we done to deserve this? How can they possibly expect us of spying?'

'It would appear that the Assessor has the answer,' said Belinda.

They had only one option and that was to see the Assessor. Luckily he was present in his usual quarters in Bogloris which lay a mile away. Belinda quickly dressed and they made their way to his house.

The once familiar streets of Bogloris that had been home for so long seemed oddly unfamiliar. Every person they passed could be a potential enemy, every dark alleyway could be filled with danger. It was essential that no one knew who they were, that no reports made their way back to those in authority.

They started to speculate. Presumably, Flavin was under instructions to report back the success of his mission. How long would that take? How much time did they have? Enraefem was still out. His presence might alert people that something was wrong. Necromancers did not normally evoke their daemons for social occasions. Necarius hid him beneath his cloak. Luckily, the only people they encountered were late night revellers stumbling uncertainly home.

They made the mile to the Assessor's house in good time. Morovius banged on the door. He wanted to be discrete, but the Assessor was bound to be asleep. A rather tired Marcus answered.

'We need to see the Assessor urgently,' said Morovius. 'An attempt has been made on our lives.'

'He's asleep.'

'Well, wake him up.'

'No can do. We have a busy day tomorrow.'

'Look, I know he helped us, but you are going to have a busy five minutes if you don't do as I say. Think you can handle five magic users?'

Marcus looked around. He had no option.

'Come in. I'll see what I can do.'

They went into the Assessor's drawing room and waited anxiously. The speculation continued. What had they done wrong? Surely Candera not healing Orken could not be interpreted as a sign that they were all spies? Even if they were spies, what information of any value could they possibly have for the Eldarans? Surely they had proven their discretion by being quiet about the dwarven tunnel?

'There is no point playing this guessing game,' said Belinda. 'Only the Assessor has the answer.'

'He'd better be bloody forthcoming with the answers,' said Morovius.

'Just remember,' said Belinda. 'You owe him your lives. If he hadn't warned Morovius, you'd all be dead.'

'I remember now,' said Enraefem.

They all looked at him expectantly. Had he heard anything, perhaps Enraefem had perceived something from the Netherworld or another daemon had told him something?

'This house used to belong to the Chief Medic. Long ago. Right butcher he was. Believed in leaches. Used to bleed people dry while they waited for a healer. Strange bloke.'

They all looked at one another, mystified.

''Raef, do us all a favour,' said Morovius.

'Sure.'

'Shut the fuck up.'

'No probs. Doing the shutting up now. If you aren't interested in history, it's your loss.'

Magins laughed while the others looked exasperated.

The Assessor appeared with Marcus, bleary eyed in his white nightgown. He lit the candles in the darkened room.

'I feared this might happen,' he said. 'Try to do people a favour and it rebounds in your face. I do hope you haven't implicated me.'

They looked around avoiding eye contact, the defence mage, he was still alive and they had mentioned the Assessor in front of him. They looked at each other quietly.

The Assessor apprised the situation quickly. 'Of course you did. You left a survivor didn't you? Let me see, who would be so indiscrete?'

They looked at Magins who went red faced.

'Of course it was Magins,' said the Assessor. 'Who else could it be? Tell me what happened.'

They recounted carefully the recent events, how Flavin and two pods had attacked them, the defence mage and his accusation that they were spies. Their total mystification about the whole series of events. How could this have happened just because of the Orken incident, it was a split second decision in the heat of battle, Orken wasn't even in their pod?

The Assessor listened carefully.

'Clever, clever,' he said. 'Look guys, the whole spy thing is a red herring. Who cares what the Eldarans know about us, there are no secrets to tell them. Our plan is simple. We just blast them because we have more magic users and presumably they still have their half hour problem. The only mystery is that half hour phenomenon. We might need an Eldaran spy, the Eldarans don't need us to tell them anything. Besides, this whole spy thing is, as far as I am aware, a myth. Apparently, there are all these spies running around. Ever met one of ours?'

'No,' said Morovius.

'Exactly,' agreed the Assessor. 'No one ever has.'

'So, what the hell is going on?' asked Necarius.

'Power, it's all about power. Morovius is too powerful.'

'What?' asked Belinda. 'They are worried that their army is too powerful in a time of war?'

'Oh, in war his power is fine, everything they could have hoped for. It's the peace dividend that they are worried about.'

'Peace dividend?' asked Morovius.

'Yes, what you'll do when the war is over. They think you'll challenge them and make a bid for power as head of the magic users. They think victory is assured, which it must be and they are worried what such a powerful fire mage will do upon victory.'

They all looked at one another, mystified. None of them had even considered what would happen after the war.

'I'm not even interested in politics,' said Morovius.

'Hell,' said Magins, 'he doesn't know anything about such stuff. He's hardly read a book.'

'Well, in life,' explained the Assessor, 'we tend to think that others will do as we would. King Almein, Amran and Marinus are power hungry and ruthless. They had to be to get to where they are now. If those three had your abilities they would make a bid for power, so they think you'll do the same.'

'So,' said Morovius, 'I'm condemned because of their power hungry natures.'

'That just about sums it up,' agreed the Assessor.

'The thing is, what do we do now?' asked Belinda. 'We are not safe in the entire Kingdom of Marcovia.'

'Unfortunately,' said the Assessor, 'that now includes me and Marcus. It was Marcus who tipped me off.'

They all murmured thanks to Marcus, who nodded.

Silence descended as they considered their options. Their minds were blank. The entire Kingdom was unsafe. Sure, they had a powerful pod, but could never take on the Kingdom's entire army. Gradually, heads turned to the Assessor who sighed.

'Why is it whenever there's a problem it's let's go to the Assessor, let's ask the Assessor. Got a problem with dwarves, want a tunnel, let's go to the Assessor. It's always the same.'

'
'Cos you're the best,' said Enraefem. 'Anyway, you're a damn sight better than that blood sucking Chief Medic.'

The Assessor ignored this obscure reference to the Chief Medic and continued.

'We have three options. Two not really viable and one which is most distasteful. Before I proceed I must demand that you include Marcus and me in the escape, seeing as how Magins has so kindly implicated us.'

They readily agreed. The Assessor was a fine asset in any party.

'The entire Kingdom is unsafe, we have to leave. Three places we can go. First, the dwarves in Windborne Mountains. A difficult, long journey which will give the King plenty of chance to attack us. We are bound to be seen, especially in the relatively well populated area before the Anrac Woods.

'Then, will the dwarves accept us? Problematic to say the least. Candera, as a healer, has a great deal to offer, but the rest of us? Also it flies in the face of dwarven neutrality and we have no gold to tempt them as we did with the tunnel.'

They looked at one another, option one was to say the least, problematic.

404

'The second option. We go to Port Inlein and try to join a merchant ship. Now, the merchants don't overly care about upsetting the King, but they would rather not. We have a similar problem to the dwarves, we have to make a long dangerous trip and what do we have to offer? Magic doesn't work at sea and even Candera would, in their eyes, be useless.'

This option seemed similarly problematic, even more so.

'What's the third option?' asked Belinda.

'You're not going to like it, not one little bit, but the journey is short and they really need us. They are desperate for magic users, they are losing a war, on horseback we could be there quickly. They are our only hope and we might be theirs.'

Eyes widened, the group looked at one another, attempting to gauge what the others were thinking. Could they do such a thing? It went against everything they had been taught, everything they had lived for, it was an act of the greatest treachery.

'Join the Eldarans?' asked Morovius.

'Have you got a better plan?' asked Belinda.

'We can't,' said Banshin. 'It goes against all honour. The Eldarans are barbaric.'

'Barbaric enough to kill their most powerful fire mage?' asked the Assessor.

'We are certain to lose,' said Necarius. 'The Eldarans are finished.'

'Anyone got a better plan?' asked Belinda again.

They sat quietly for a few minutes.

'I hate to point this out,' said the Assessor, 'but we don't have the luxury of time. Decide quickly.'

No one could think of anything better. Slowly, reluctantly, they nodded their heads in agreement.

'That's settled,' said the Assessor. 'Markus, get the white handkerchiefs, we'll need them. Banshin, go and get your Anrac. The rest of us can mount our horses. We'll meet outside the gates of Bogloris in fifteen minutes.'

They all agreed and set off. Belinda did not have a horse, so she sat behind Morovius. Luckily for Banshin his Anrac was near the city gates, because of the famous Anrac smell. Only one person saw him mounted and he was so drunk he would not remember anything in the morning. The rest rode their horses out of the city without incident. No one knew how much time they had, how long Marinus would wait until he realised something had gone wrong.

They assembled outside the gates and made their way towards no man's land, hoping that they would not encounter anyone. However, if they were to encounter anyone, it was a big problem.

Banshin atop his Anrac was a definite giveaway. If anyone reported a party of eight with a magic warrior heading to no man's land, the Marcovian authorities would know exactly what was happening.

They decided not to ride the main road used by troops marching to battle, but rather the lesser used side tracks. It would take longer but the chances of anyone seeing them were reduced. They had proceeded two miles without incident when Morovius turned to Candera.

'It's strange. We have left Bogloris and I feel no loss of power.'

'Good. We'll need you in top form if they send an army after us.'

'If they send an army after us, not even me in top form will be of any help. We just have to get past the guards into no man's land. Magins's shield should be so strong that we will be able to make our escape then, even if chased.'

They kept on, seeing no one, everything was going well, too well, what was happening in Bogloris? By now, they must have discovered that Flavin's attack had failed. Would the Marcovians realise that they were about to become traitors? Eventually, the silence was inevitably broken by Enraefem.

'I want to go on Banshin's shoulders.'

'Why?' asked Necarius, somewhat offended.

'I can see the furthest, what with being a daemon and all, atop the highest point I shall be able to see even further.'

Necarius reluctantly agreed and Enraefem jumped onto Banshin's shoulder.

'He just wants to be on a bloody Anrac,' said Necarius. 'Probably as blind as a bat.'

Needless to say, when they did encounter a problem, it was not Enraefem who spotted it, as he was at the time intent on examining his finger nails.

'Crap, someone's coming,' said Banshin.

'Let's just keep going,' said the Assessor. 'He's not coming from Bogloris, he probably knows nothing about us.'

A peasant and a donkey came into view.

As they approached, Morovius said, 'Let's kill him. Dead men tell no tales.'

'You're not killing an innocent peasant just for being in the wrong place at the wrong time,' said Belinda. 'We'll just have to think of something.'

They all looked at the Assessor who sighed inwardly as his brain steadily worked to solve this latest problem.

The peasant looked terrified as he had never been this close to magic users and certainly not an Anrac.

'John, John, John'll help me.'

'Who the hell is John?' asked Morovius.

'Be wary of John. If you hurt me, John will get you. John'll never let anyone hurt me.'

'Oh crap,' said the Assessor. 'John must've gone into hiding as we approached. Enraefem, off you go. Find this bloody John.'

'Shall I get his gonads?'

'No,' shouted Belinda. 'Just tell us when you've found him.'

Enraefem bounded off into the distance. Trees grew thickly on either side of the road, Enraefem easily bouncing between them, jumping from branch to branch. Necarius employed his mind meld.

'Enraefem can find nothing.'

'So much for his bloody eyesight,' said Morovius. 'Right peasant, tell us where this John is or I'll hit you.'

Belinda snarled at Morovius.

'Look, it's his own bloody fault if he wants to conceal John.'

'John, John, help me John!'

'Let's hit him,' said Morovius, 'that'll bring John out of hiding.'

'No one's hitting anyone,' said Belinda. 'Look, he's terrified. Do you really think threatening him is helping the situation?'

'If he doesn't come clean about this almighty John fellow who can take on five magic users, I'm going to do a lot more than hit him.'

'Relax Morovius.' Belinda moved towards the peasant and put a reassuring hand on his shoulder. 'Look, no one's going to hurt you. We just need to know where John is. Tell him to come out of hiding.'

The peasant stared into Belinda's eyes and looked a little confused. His eyes moved towards the donkey. They all followed the peasant's gaze and stared at the donkey, who seemingly oblivious of the commotion around him, was quietly eating some roadside grass.

'Call back Enraefem,' the Assessor told Necarius.

'This doesn't solve the problem of what we're going to do with this peasant,' said Magins.

'I'll shut him up,' said the Assessor.

'If he's dead, he'll shut up for sure,' said Morovius.

'Morovius' Belinda said sternly. 'I've had enough. Get lost. You have nothing constructive to offer.'

Morovius walked off in a huff muttering something about bloody civilians not understanding the way of the world even if it was your own mother. Belinda ignored him.

'Assessor,' she said, 'I'm sure you've thought of something.'

'Yeah, Marcus, come here.' He started whispering in Marcus's ear. 'I want you to stand next to the hind leg of the donkey. Every time I move my foot, pinch the donkey.'

This made no sense to Marcus, but by now he knew he was best off placing his full trust in the Assessor. Marcus took up his position ready to pinch the donkey.

The Assessor walked up to the peasant.

'Do you know what we are?' he asked him.

'Powerful warriors,' said the peasant.

'Exactly and we have magical abilities. Do you know what magical abilities we have?'

'You can make fire.'

'Yes and many other things. Did you know that I can speak donkey?'

'What?' the peasant's eyes opened in amazement.

'John, I can talk to him and he can understand me.'

'Never!'

'Oh, yes.' The Assessor leaned over and spoke into John's ear. 'John, you understand me, don't you?' He moved his foot, Marcus pinched, John the donkey stopped grazing, his head shot up, 'Eeyore.'

The peasant stared intently at the scene before him, utterly speechless.

'Right, now I'm going to have a chat with John.' The peasant nodded. 'John, you know we are here on a secret mission, don't you?'

Another pinch. 'Eeyore,' John cried in agreement.

'John, you know it's a really good idea for you and your master to tell no one of us, don't you?'

'Eeyore.'

'Even if the King himself were to ask, it's better that you both say you know nothing.'

'Eeyore,' went John in agreement.

'Good. So you've got it. Both you and your master will never ever tell anyone about us.'

'Eeyore.'

'Now, what will happen if you or your master say anything about us?'

The Assessor's foot moved three times, 'Eeyore, Eeyore, Eeyore!'

'That's right. We will come to your village and kill you and your master.'

The Assessor looked at the peasant. 'Do you understand?' he asked.

'Oh, yes. John was quite clear,' said the peasant.

'Good, if you and John want to live, you'll keep your mouth shut. Besides, no one expects a peasant and his donkey to know anything.'

'Me and John will never say anything.'

'Good,' said the Assessor. 'Come, we'll be on our way.' The party set off towards no man's land leaving a rather startled peasant and John the donkey behind.

They proceeded towards no man's land, this time without incident. Whatever was going on in Bogloris, it did not seem if anyone had worked out their plan. Perhaps, after accusing them falsely of being spies, they could not conceptualise that they would actually become traitors. A case of not being able to believe your own lies.

They approached no man's land. They went up to the nearest Marcovian tower and hailed the guard. Hopefully, the plan to kill them had not reached the towers yet. A rather surprised man came down to see them.

'Can I help you, Sirs?' he asked.

'We are just going on a reconnoitre. See the lay of the land, that sort of thing,' said the Assessor.

'Well, I am sure that will be OK.'

'Thank you.'

They carried on into no man's land. Now there was no going back, they were deserters. The guard would report what had happened and the whole game would be up. Never mind, soon it will be too late for the Marcovians to do anything. The Marcovians will just have to carry on preparations for the upcoming battle.

Morovius stumbled. 'I've never felt power like this, not even when I was in no man's land before.'

They all looked at him and indeed, Morovius was covered in a blue aura, his body readily absorbing the power of the jains.

'Come on,' ordered the Assessor. 'We have no time for speculation.'

They proceeded onwards. On the Assessor's instructions, they dismounted and walked, waving white handkerchiefs on sticks. They approached an Eldaran tower.

'What are we going to say?' asked Magins. 'We come in peace, take us to your leader?''

'Something like that,' said the Assessor.

There was a plop as Enraefem disappeared back to the Netherworld, his three hours had elapsed.

They continued their slow walk to the Eldaran tower.

CHAPTER 23

Morag and Boran were sitting bored in their Eldaran watchtower. Got a boring job that no one else will do, got a vacancy no one will fill, want someone to stand around doing nothing, get a guard. He'll do it. Morag and Boran had been on guard duty at this particular watchtower for four years. Four years of boredom, nothing ever happened. It was always the same. There was no subtle event to indicate an enemy manoeuvre. Both sides had to engage in such laborious and visible operations to raise their armies so each knew exactly what the other was up to. The one time the Marcovians had tried something new with their exploding tunnel, the guards hadn't noticed a thing.

'That's the thing, Morag,' said Boran. 'Nothing ever happens but at least we get paid.'

'Boran,' said Morag looking out of the tower.

'The thing is,' continued Boran, 'at least we get on well. That really is a good thing, imagine if we hated each other. It would be a nightmare.'

'Boran.'

'We are also going to receive a decent pension. You need to look on the bright side, things could be a lot worse.'

'Boran!' shouted Morag.

'Yeah, what is it?'

'Something's happening. Look out of the window.'

Boran looked out of the window. Approaching them was a small group, one on an Anrac. They were waving white bits of cloth in the air.

'Bloody hell,' said Boran. 'There's that powerful Marcovian fire mage everyone is talking about after the last battle.'

'You and your big mouth, complaining nothing happens. What do we do now?'

'Um, you rush off and report this to the authorities in Bleddin. I don't know, I suppose I'll just try and delay them.'

'The authorities will be asleep.'

'Well, bloody wake 'em up. This is important, really important.'

'Will you be all right, Boran?'

'Let's just hope those white flags are sincere. Now go, now.'

Morag ran down the stairs of the tower and mounted one of the horses. He sped off to Bleddin hoping that nothing untoward would happen to his friend. The fire mage, he was so powerful, there was nothing Boran could do. What was the fire mage doing? Was this another Marcovian trick like the exploding tunnel? Morag carried on riding.

Boran watched the group as they came towards him, white handkerchiefs wafting in the breeze while they waved their free arms. Well, they certainly weren't trying a sneaky approach. Boran had to think quickly. While it would be eventual suicide for such a small group to attack, in the short term there was little he could do. If they wanted to kill him, he was dead. He decided to wait.

One of them was shouting, the older man, what was it? Boran leaned out of the tower and strained to hear what was being said. It couldn't be, no one would ever shout that. No, there it was again, it could only be one thing.

'We come in peace. Take us to your leader.'

Clearly, these Marcovians didn't have much imagination, but with that fire mage, did they need any? Boran decided to respond.

'Sit there at the bottom of the watchtower,' he shouted. 'My friend has gone to get our leader.'

To Boran's relief, they obediently walked up to the base of the watchtower and sat down. Maybe, with victory imminent, the Marcovians had come to parley, to offer terms of surrender. It was all

Boran could think of. Well, if that were the case, there was nothing he could do, he had no authority to parley.

'Hurry up,' the grey haired man shouted. 'The Marcovians will soon be alerted that we have switched sides.'

'They'll be here soon,' shouted Boran.

So, they want to switch sides. Why? Why would anyone want to join the losing side? Did that powerful mage want a challenge? If so, he had come to the right place.

They sat waiting for an hour, Boran studiously watching them, noting that from time to time one would say something to another, but at no point did any of them attempt to invoke any magic. Eventually, Boran could see an Eldaran party coming to investigate. Boran ordered the group to remain where they were and rode off to meet the party.

At its head was Archmage Cender and Boran's friend, Morag. He rode up to the Archmage.

'Sir, they are waiting at the foot of the watchtower.'

'Have they tried anything?'

'No, Sir. No hint of any kind to invoke magic.'

'What do they want?'

'Sir, they say they want to switch sides.'

'Join us, what the hell for?'

'I don't know, Sir. They didn't say.'

'Anything else?'

'I am afraid not, Sir. They are just waiting for you but they do seem anxious. They say the Marcovians will soon realise that they have deserted.'

Cender rode up to the watchtower with thirty Eldaran magic users in attendance. It was true. There sat that powerful fire mage who had caused so much damage in the Battle of the Failing Shields. None of this made any sense.

'I am Archmage Cender,' he said. 'The guard tells me you wish to switch sides. Why?'

'We'll tell you everything, but we must move into Eldara immediately,' said the Assessor. 'The Marcovians must know by now we have deserted and could send in magic users to catch us. We need to get away from here, unless you want a skirmish.'

'That makes sense,' admitted Cender. 'You have put me in a difficult position. Mount up and we'll take you to Bleddin. Note, you will be surrounded and if you try anything we will kill you. I am sure one or two of these guys are itching to launch an attack on that fire mage.'

'We accept your conditions,' said the Assessor.

'Well done, you two,' Cender told Morag and Boran as the party set off to Bleddin. It was odd, but on leaving their homes, they had to keep to obscure roads and watch every shadow with fear. Now, riding deeper into enemy territory, they were completely visible and able to take the main thoroughfare.

They rode away from no man's land, along the main road used by troops to march into battle. Vegetation and trees lined each side of the highway.

There were questions. Why had these Marcovians turned traitor, will the Eldarans accept us, will we find out the riddle behind the half hour problem? So many questions on all their minds, all best left until they could sit down and talk properly.

The group reached Bleddin, a huge walled city which had diverted a river to make a permanent deep moat. Guards walked around the top ramparts and crossbowmen could be seen in some of the apertures. This was a city on alert, a walled fortification prepared for a siege.

Within, preparations were even more obvious. There were huge mounds of hay to feed livestock and men were working in the early morning hours to fill the silos. Like Bogloris, shops had huge models outside and shopkeepers shouting their wares, but the shouts were different. They shouted about preparing yourself, making sure you had enough when things became scarce. Early morning shoppers walked along the streets, hoping to beat their neighbours to a bargain.

'We have no time to lose,' said Cender. 'I am sure King Alphonse will be eager to hear your story and if you want my advice, you'd better make it a good one. I wouldn't want to be in your shoes if he is left in any doubt as to why you deserted.'

The Marcovian traitors and their Eldaran escort arrived at the main palace, an imposing if somewhat bewildering building. Its basic square shape had been added to over the years, as fashions changed, so did the additions. Circular towers were erected at odd intervals and gargoyles in various hideous forms lined the top of ivy covered walls. The palace had been added to and built upon until there was no room left for its expansion.

The entire party went into the palace and dismounted in the courtyard. They made their way inside along curving corridors, unlike the straight corridors that were the feature of the Palace in Bogloris. However, the palace here shared with Bogloris one important principle. The dead from ages past looked down on you as you made your way to the King. Grand ladies with little fluffy dogs, young Princes, some with lurches, others with hunting birds of prey and fierce Kings, steadfast in their pride.

Eventually, the entire entourage arrived in the throne room. At the back of the room, King Alphonse sat on his throne with his Queen, Sandrine. To his right, was Chief Exchequer, Rincin. Cender went to take his seat on the left as Archmage. The Eldaran magic users moved towards the guards

423

alongside the walls, ready to protect Their Majesties should the Marcovians attempt to invoke any magic. The Marcovians remained in the centre.

'This is it,' thought Magins. 'Our lives depend upon the Assessor's explanation.'

'Why are you here?' asked King Alphonse with great clarity. His voice was deep and denoted one in authority, only undermined somewhat by his brow furrowed by long nights of anxious thought.

'I'll tell you as honestly as I can, Your Majesty' said the Assessor. 'It started when my guard, Marcus over here, came to me with distressing news.' The Assessor then proceeded to recount recent events from his own perspective to ensure as much honesty as possible. He left speculation to a minimum and stuck closely to his own experiences. He covered the Marcovian rulers' plan to kill Morovius and his pod and the subsequent attack and flight.

There was silence when the Assessor had finished. Alphonse, Rincin and Cender looked at one another. The story hung together and was consistent, but then they had had plenty of time to rehearse it. How could they tell it wasn't just a ruse to get that fire mage and his buddies behind their shield to attack their already depleted stock of magic users?

'How do you know that we won't think the same as the Marcovians?' asked King Alphonse.

'We don't, Your Majesty,' said Morovius, 'but there are two factors to consider. We had little choice but to try to join your forces and secondly, you need us more than the Marcovians. They are looking at certain victory, you, I am afraid, are not.'

'Ah, choice,' said Chief Exchequer, Rincin. 'It would appear that no one here has much of that luxury.'

'What do you mean?' asked Alphonse.

'Your Majesty, if I may speak freely,' said Rincin. 'After all, our frailties were out there for all to witness in our last battle. We have lost two thirds of our magic users. We have failing walls before the three hour window is up. The Marcovians know this well. In our state how can we refuse help from the most powerful fire mage in the lands? If this is a trap, then so be it, we have no option but to take the bait.'

'This could be our undoing,' said the King.

'Your Majesty, we are already undone. This might be our only hope.'

Alphonse's shoulders slumped and he let out a sigh. 'I see your point.'

'But, Your Majesty, as long as the monster exists, we have no chance, regardless of this mage's ability. We have to be able to maintain our shields' said Cender.

'What monster, Sir?' asked Magins. 'Is he the reason your shields are failing?'

'All in good time, all in good time,' said Rincin. 'First, let's see how this Morovius does in the dampening pit. We need to assess what you're really made of.'

'What's a dampening pit, Sir?' asked Morovius. 'Is this a test?'

'Of sorts,' replied Cender, 'but don't worry. You can't be hurt. We just want you to throw a fireball at a scarecrow, see how powerful you really are.'

'Let's go,' said Alphonse.

The entirety of those assembled made their way out of the throne room. The Marcovians were surrounded by the Eldaran magic users, just in case this was another Marcovian trick. They made their way through the palace into the back gardens. In the centre was a bricked rectangular structure with a wooden door allowing entry.

'That,' said Cender, 'is the dampening pit. Morovius, you are to enter through that door. Your task is simple, stand there and fireball a scarecrow on the opposite wall.'

'You think I can't cast a fireball, Sir? Surely, you saw the last battle?'

'Just do it and all will be explained.'

Morovius entered through the gate and closed it behind him. The assembled took up positions on the ramps and the walls in order to observe him. Morovius looked around and gasped. He felt a huge decline in his power. Morovius looked down and recognised what was so unfamiliar. Where were the glistening jains? He bent over and grabbed a handful of earth, examining it. Jains were there but not their normal brilliant selves; they were dull and seemingly lifeless.

Jains are jains Turinus had taught them. Well, apparently not. Morovius cast his mind back over their trip to Bleddin. Had the jains been weaker there? He couldn't remember, so much had been on his mind and it had been dark. His mind clicked, so this was a dampening pit, a pit where jains were weak. This was his test.

Morovius started to conjure up blue magic between his hands. He strained to absorb what he could from the depleted jains. He kept trying on the principle that although depleted, the jains still had power. He would just need to take longer than normal to harness their energy. He kept going, the blue ball becoming larger. It was nowhere near as large as he was used to casting but it should be enough to blast a straw man.

He concentrated on turning the blue ball into fire, this was up to him, his speciality, he had harnessed as much of the jains' power as he needed. Satisfying curls of smoke arose from the fireball. That should do it. He jerked.

The fireball shot off, smashing into the straw man, incinerating it as it continued on its path. It hit the brick wall with a crash and bathed the brickwork in a dazzling fire. The bricks slowly began to crumble under the intense heat and eventually a hole was left in the wall. Morovius inhaled a deep breath after his exertion.

'Excellent,' shouted Cender. 'Just what we need. You can come out now, young mage.'

Rincin leapt over to King Alphonse and whispered in his ear. 'We have to trust them, Your Majesty. The Assessor's story rings true and besides we desperately need them. With them we have a slight chance, without them, defeat is certain.'

'I agree,' replied Alphonse. 'It just doesn't make sense for the Marcovians to have planned sending them over as a cunning ploy. I don't see what they could hope to achieve. Surely, as the Assessor has stated, all the Marcovian efforts are expended in raising a large army for the final confrontation.'

'So, Your Majesty believes their story?' asked Rincin.

'Why not? If we were in the Marcovian position, we might well have done the same. Dismiss our magic users, we need to tell Morovius and his friends about the monster.'

The Eldaran magic users were dismissed and Morovius rejoined his friends.

'How have you managed to make a dampening pit, Your Majesty? How long have you been able to do this to the jains?' Morovius asked.

'Ah, all will be explained to you,' said Alphonse. 'As it is a matter of magic, I'll hand you over to Archmage Cender. Archmage, if you please, explain our little predicament to our guests.'

'Everything, Your Majesty?'

'Everything. Our little band of heroes are going to kill our problematic monster. Morovius has proven to be effective where the jains are weak.'

They looked at one another, puzzled. This reference to a monster again. What was this blight upon Eldara and why were they trying to kill it? What was going on with the jains? They looked at Archmage Cender for an explanation.

'To start at the beginning,' Cender said, 'as you undoubtedly know, this war started when the Marcovians invaded and pushed back the Eldarans. Eventually, we were pressed back to no man's land where our magic users put up a heroic defence and the present border between Eldara and Marcovia was established. No doubt, your knowledge that the Eldarans are victims aided you in your decision to join us. It must be difficult fighting for a side that you know are in the wrong.'

The friends looked at one another mystified but realised that it was best to say nothing.

'A stalemate then continued for as long as anyone can remember until the emergence of the monster. Almost five years ago, we noticed that in the North West part of our Kingdom, around the Baranu Cave, the jains were becoming duller and lacked their normal potency. A group went into the cave to investigate but never emerged. Realising that something was wrong, we launched an attack of fifteen magic users but they were defeated and six were killed.

429

'The monster is an amorphous blob, glowing blue as it absorbs the power of the jains. It grows larger and more powerful as it absorbs more and more power from an ever greater area. We have been unable to launch an all out offensive against it as this would leave Bleddin vulnerable to a Marcovian attack.

'So matters have continued, the monster keeps absorbing the power of the jains and it has recently been making an impact on our edge of no man's land. Our half hour problem revolves around these factors. Firstly, it has been a major impediment to our training and secondly as it now affects us in our area of no man's land, our magic users are finding it impossible to be effective for the full three hours.

'Presently, we have lost two thirds of our magic users in the Battle of the Failing Shields. Our half hour problem and the difficulties we experience in training remain. You have to kill the monster if we are to stand any chance in the upcoming battle. Morovius has proven that he has power even in jain depleted territory.'

Morovius and his friends looked uneasy.

'What makes you think we can succeed, Sir?' asked Morovius.

'We don't know if you can, but you were able to cast magic in the dampening pit which is filled with earth taken from near the Baranu Cave. Your pod has a better chance than anyone. Well, at least you are the only ones who have any chance. Besides, idle speculation is not necessary. Your pod must kill the monster. It's the only chance we have against the Marcovians.'

430

Silence descended as they all considered the onerous task that lay ahead.

Magins raised an arm. 'What else can you tell us about this monster, Sir?'

'Only that he is a great blue blob. He emits blue bolts, much like a necromancer's, but far more powerful. He moves slowly but appears to have an enormous capacity to absorb damage, like some sort of super charged Flantein.'

'No weak spot, Sir?' asked Necarius.

'None that we know of. Just a huge blob of hatred and destruction. He must be destroyed.'

They contemplated this new challenge. If what they were being told were true then they had to deal with this monster. It was the only way forward.

'Sir,' asked Banshin, 'one thing I don't understand. If you are so weakened, why did you provoke a battle by trespassing on Anrac Woods?'

'We had little choice. Our own Anracs have been affected by the monster and the loss of power of the jains. They have become far weaker. Our warriors now need your Anracs. In fact that was the tenth expedition we had smuggled into Marcovia.'

So that was why they had been in Anrac Woods. So much for the guards and the watchtowers. Unless you walked up to them shouting and waving white flags, they were basically useless. They just seemed to be there to make people feel more secure, like the stories about mythical spies. Just one matter remained to be resolved.

'How are we going to find the cave, Sir?' asked Magins. 'We are not familiar with Eldara.'

'I shall appoint you a Sheriff,' said King Alphonse. 'He shall have my royal seal allowing you and him access to the entire Kingdom. He will accompany you to Baranu Cave.'

They nodded in agreement. That seemed to answer all their questions, that is everything apart from the rather important detail of how to kill the monster, but the Eldarans seemed to have little to offer in that department.

Arrangements were made for them to stay in the main Tavern in Bleddin. They could rest there for the night. In the morning, the Sheriff would accompany them on their mission. Only the magic users were needed for the mission. Belinda, the Assessor and Markus could stay in the Tavern until suitable roles were found for them.

They walked off accompanied by a guard who was to pay for their stay in the Tavern. They maintained silence in front of the guard until they had reached their destination. Once alone they started to speculate.

How were they going to achieve victory where all others had failed? How could the Eldarans possibly believe they were the victims in this conflict? Weren't the Marcovians the victims as they had always been taught? Had they been fed a falsehood their entire lives? Only yesterday morning, life had seemed so simple, now there were just a mass of questions to be answered. In particular, how could you fight a monster with greater damage absorption than a Flantein who also shot off powerful blue bolts?

They were just going to have to hope that Morovius could burn the bastard.

CHAPTER 24

That night they all rested well, apart from Morovius, who slept in fits and starts. The others just seemed to take it in their stride that they had turned traitor, but not Morovius. Everything he had been taught, everything he believed in was challenged. From those early days with Berin which formed his earliest memories, through to his first day at school with Novus, then his training under Turinus – all of this had been for one sole purpose, to fight for Marcovia. He had not just betrayed Marcovia, he had betrayed his entire life.

And what was this about the Eldarans being the victim in the war, wasn't Marcovia the victim? It made no sense. How could both sides claim that the other was the aggressor? What was the truth, who had been the foreign invading army? Nothing rang true anymore.

His thoughts turned to Novus, Turinus and Marinus, his mentors, his leaders. What would they think of him? Surely, they would realise that he had no choice. The authorities were trying to kill him for no good reason. What option did he and his friends have? They had to join the Eldarans. He was sure no one in Marcovia would understand. They would just be branded as traitors. Probably make up some lie that they had done it for the money. If the authorities had claimed he and his friends were spies, then they were capable of saying anything.

That was another thing. How could Marinus have said that they were spies and how could anyone have believed him? As the Assessor had pointed out, there was no useful information anyone could give the Eldarans. Everyone knew that Marcovia was preparing for an all out attack in the next battle, a battle Marcovia were sure to win.

434

What were Morovius and his friends going to do now? They were joining the losing side. The Eldaran magic forces had been decimated. Even with Morovius and his pod, they were still vastly outnumbered. Let's say his pod did kill this monster and the half hour problem was solved, what did it matter? How could the Eldarans take on a vastly superior army? Even if Morovius was at full strength and the riddle of why he seemed to lose power on occasions had been solved, it would still be impossible to win the battle.

His seemingly random loss of power still troubled him greatly. Why was he losing power on occasions and not on others? It couldn't be as simple as leaving Bogloris because he had performed well in the damaging pit. Was it because he was only fighting a scarecrow? Was he a coward? Did the thought of fighting a real enemy intimidate him? He didn't feel like a coward, sure he felt fear, didn't everyone? Even so, wouldn't fear actually drive him on and make him more powerful, more eager to draw upon the power of the jains? How were they going to face the monster if he lost his normal power?

Once, everything had been so straightforward and then the Marcovian authorities had decided he was a threat. That made no sense, he was no politician, damn he'd hardly read a book and knew nothing about politics. Court intrigue bored him. He was ultimately a simple soldier. Simple, that was it, he liked it simple, everything had become far too complex.

And, what was this monster? Why didn't they have one in Marcovia? Why was it trying to destroy the Eldarans? It couldn't be trying to help the Marcovians, damn, the Marcovians didn't even know it existed. What was it hoping to achieve? Was it just simply bent on destruction, a being of pure evil?

Simple, try to keep things simple. OK, we are Eldarans now, we have to kill their monster. Then, we have to join their army for the upcoming battle. Hopefully, with the monster's death, the half hour problem will be over. Perhaps not, the Eldarans had also blamed their poor quality training over the previous few years for that problem. Forget that, we'll kill the monster and that will hopefully sort out the half hour problem. Then with me in the Eldaran army, I'll hopefully be at full strength and we'll beat the Marcovian army or at least fight them to a stalemate and balance will be restored.

That's it, problem sorted. Well, as sorted as it'll ever be, Morovius supposed. He fell asleep hoping he would not experience a loss of power when he encountered the monster. The depleted jains were enough of a problem.

The next morning, the friends, Belinda and Marcus sat down for breakfast. It was decent peasant fare of brown bread, salmon and assorted vegetables. Conversation was meagre and the others were showing no sign that they had been assailed by doubts similar to Morovius. Anyway, there wasn't a great deal to discuss. They just had to wait for the Sheriff and hear what he had to say.

Eventually, a tall, well built man arrived and announced his presence by standing in the middle of the dining area and looking around at everyone. That must be him.

'Are you the Sheriff?' asked Magins.

'Yeah. Sheriff Quince at your service. You the heroes who are going to kill that monster?'

'Not too sure we are heroes,' said Magins, 'but we have been asked to kill a monster in Baranu Cave. We were told a Sheriff would show us the way and grant us safe passage.'

'Aye, that'll be me. Well, I hope you're lying and that you are all a bunch of heroes. You'll need to be to kill that blight upon our land. Eat up, I'll meet you outside; Ma'am,' he doffed his hat to Belinda.

He walked off and Belinda noted her surprise at being called Ma'am. What would he do if he realised she was just a peasant Auntie? They all laughed.

Eventually, they finished their meal and made preparations to leave. There were goodbyes all around and the Assessor, Markus and Belinda wished the magic users good luck and told them to be careful. Belinda gave Morovius and Candera a hug and they were ready to go.

'I just hope I don't lose power, Mum.'

'Well, you are bound to lose some. They told us the jains are sorely depleted near the monster.'

'I don't mean that. I mean the loss of power I have felt before when I left Bogloris.'

'Right, but you didn't experience it this time.'

'No.'

'There we are. Hopefully, you'll be fine.'

Morovius, Banshin, Necarius, Magins and Candera made their way out of the Tavern to join Sheriff Quince who was waiting patiently outside. Together with Quince, they went around the back of the Tavern and all except Banshin mounted their horses. Banshin would have to walk to the city gates where the Anracs were housed, as the Eldarans shared similar views to the Marcovians about Anrac smell.

The city was bustling, trade was brisk as people bought as many essentials as they could afford to prepare for what must be the inevitable siege. The Sheriff led them through the winding streets which had seemingly been put together in as chaotic a manner as possible. Eventually, they reached the city gates and Banshin was able to mount his Anrac. It was time to leave Bleddin and make their way to the monster.

The young men and Quince started their journey through the countryside, ignoring the children who were running up to see an Anrac. Banshin's Anrac just plodded on, oblivious that she was the centre of so much attention. The surrounding fields were lush and filled with healthy crops.

'It would appear,' Sheriff Quince told them, 'that with the declining power of the jains, the crops are doing better. As you know, nothing can grow in no man's land where the jains are so plentiful.'

The magic users pondered this ironic state of affairs. The source of all their power was actually bad for the peasants and their crops. It all meant that if it came to it, Bleddin would be well supplied and could withstand a lengthy siege.

They carried on for the rest of the day, the friends looking nervously at Morovius. Was he going to lose power? This whole expedition depended upon Morovius being at full strength, if he started losing power, what were they going to do?

That night they went into a small Inn and settled down in the dining area while Quince went off to order food. It appeared that this Inn specialised in a variety of broths, so broth it would be. While Quince was ordering the food they turned to a worried looking Morovius.

'Well,' Magins asked, 'how do you feel?'

'I feel all right, I'm not sick or anything,' said Morovius. 'However, I can definitely feel a loss of power.'

'Oh crap!' said Magins. 'Maybe it's just the diminishing power of the jains as we get closer to the monster.'

'Have any of you felt a considerable loss of power compared to when we were in Bleddin?' asked Morovius.

'No,' they all murmured.

'Well, there we are,' concluded Morovius.

'What are we going to do?' asked Necarius.

'We carry on,' said Banshin. 'That's all we can do. We can't go back to the Eldarans and say we didn't even try.'

'It could be suicide,' said Magins. 'The monster has beaten all previous attempts to neutralise it.'

'It has never faced our pod,' said Banshin.

The group looked at Banshin and hoped that his faith was not misplaced. Silently, they waited for Quince to return. There really was nothing else they could do. They spent a quiet night, contemplating what lay ahead.

The following morning, at breakfast, the party were disturbed by a peasant woman rushing in.

'Sirs, Sirs,' she said agitatedly, 'please, please can you help me? Please help me, only you can help me.'

'What is it?' asked Quince.

'My husband. He's fallen off a cliff three miles from here. He's quite broken up. Only a healer can help him now. I've been told you are powerful magic users with an Anrac. One of you must be a healer. Please help, I'm so sorry to inconvenience you, so sorry, I know you have better things to do, please help!'

'I'm not sure we have the time,' said Quince.

'What?' said Magins. 'That monster's been there for five years or something. A three mile detour is not going to make any difference.'

'I'll help,' said Candera. 'I'm the healer.'

They procured some rope and the peasant mounted up behind Candera, thanking them all the time, sure they had better things to do, how grateful she was and so on.

They let her talk, convinced that if she shut up, she would pass out with worry. Better that she keep on talking, besides, they needed her for directions. They went down a narrow pathway between crops of wheat, until they came to the cliff.

Candera leaned over the edge and could see on a ledge fifteen feet down, the form of a man. His leg was at an odd angle, clearly broken and there was a loss of blood from a nasty gash to his head.

'I can heal him,' said Candera, 'but I cannot compensate for the loss of blood.'

'That's great,' said the peasant woman. 'Please heal him, once you have, we'll take care of him.'

'Give him plenty to drink,' said Candera as he started to invoke his healing magic.

The woman stood mesmerised by the blue ball slowly forming between Candera's hands. Perspiration broke out on Candera's brow, the effort of invoking where the jains had been depleted. He kept on concentrating, the ball gradually increasing in size. He jerked.

The blue ball of healing shot downwards at the injured man, enveloping him in soothing magic. His leg straightened, resuming its normal position, bones setting into place. The gash on his head closed over. He groaned.

'Throw down one end of the rope.' Magins told Banshin. 'Good man, tie the rope around your midriff. My friend will haul you out.' Magins turned to the peasant woman, 'He does know how to tie a rope, doesn't he?'

'Of course,' she replied.

'Good.'

The man proceeded to tie the rope around his midriff, securing himself with a stable knot. He held onto the rope with his hands to secure himself. Banshin started to pull slowly and the man began to rise. He used his feet to stop himself from banging into the cliff face. Up he came until his pale face was visible. Necarius and Magins helped him over and he lay on the ground panting.

'Thank you, good Sirs, thank you, good Sirs,' exclaimed the peasant woman. 'We have little but please accept this.'

They all laughed and told her to keep her money. The man murmured some thanks but was still clearly not well as he had lost a lot of blood. Candera told the woman he would take the man on his horse back to the hut which lay one mile away. Candera set off while the peasant woman followed on foot, expressing her gratitude all the time.

They waited for Candera to return.

'Ah, well,' he said, 'even if we don't beat this monster, we'll have done some good.'

'It won't be of much use if you don't kill the monster,' said Quince. 'If that monster lives, then we are certain to lose the war and all this land will lie in waste after the Marcovians pillage.'

Magins was going to say something but Morovius put his hand on Magins's arm and shook his head, denoting that at this point in time, silence was the better option. The entourage with Quince leading the way, carried on their journey, through the crops of barley, wheat and rye. It was the same pattern for four days. Night at a local Inn where broth always appeared to be the speciality. Sleep and then breakfast and on the party would go, stopping only for a packed lunch they had procured at the Inn.

Whenever the magic users had the chance and Quince was out of earshot, the others would ask Morovius how he felt. It was always the same, he was experiencing a steady loss of power. It seemed to all of them that he was turning into just an ordinary fire mage. How were they going to cope with the monster?

As the group continued in a North Westerly direction, it became colder and the crops became more sparse. Eventually, they came to an Inn which Quince told them was their last stop before the monster.

Quince went to his room, whilst the rest went into the bar area and ordered an ale each, hoping it would not be their last. The friends all had one thought on their minds. How were they going to deal with this monster with Morovius reduced to the level of an ordinary fire mage? Everyone would have severely reduced powers as the jains around here were harshly depleted. Necarius wasn't even sure he could sustain a proper link with Enraefem. It just wasn't looking good. The friends were diverted from their musings by the sound of a peasant talking loudly.

'… so these magic users, what good are they? Eldara will soon lose this war, meanwhile, those magic users haven't done a day's work in their lives. I tell you, they never earned their powers, it was just a case of being born lucky. Without their powers, they are nothing. I could snap one in half with my little finger.'

'Be careful, Sandin,' said a peasant woman, looking anxiously over at the friends.

'I'll not be careful, why should I be, those magic users are useless. I'll be silent for no man.'

444

Morovius leaned over to talk quietly to his friends. 'It's that peasant's unlucky day.'

'Why?' asked Candera.

'My mother's not here.'

Morovius walked over to the peasant and smiled at him.

'What do you want?' the peasant wanted to know.

Morovius said nothing but just smiled. He quickly reached out and grasped the peasant by the back of the neck, smashing his face into the table. He pulled his head up by the hair with his left hand and hit his jaw as hard as he could with his right. A satisfying crack of breaking bone filled the room.

'See,' said Morovius to the crowd, 'no magic. Now my friend, you have two options, either of which is equally satisfying to me. You can keep your pride and walk around the rest of your life with a broken face. Your face will tell people all they need to know about magic users. Either that, or you can crawl over there, beg for forgiveness and maybe, just maybe, my friend will heal you.'

Morovius dropped the man who fell to the ground and walked back to his friends.

'Arsehole,' he announced as he rejoined them.

The man came crawling up on all fours, muttering as best he could through his broken jaw how sorry he was, that he would henceforth respect all magic users and he now realised they were doing their best for Eldara. Would they please consider healing him?

Candera could take no more. 'Shut up,' he told the man as he began to laboriously invoke healing magic trying to absorb what power he could from the depleted jains. He managed to build up a blue ball of moderate size and cast it at the man's head. The jaw bone slotted back into place and the gash on the man's forehead healed over.

'Let's go,' Candera said, 'time for bed. Big day tomorrow.'

The friends stood up and went upstairs to their rooms. There was total silence in the bar.

The next morning they set off to meet the monster. Quince tried to offer some advice but he had little to add to what they had already been told. Just that the monster was a massive blue blob, shot out blue bolts of great power and seemed to have an enormous capacity to absorb damage.

'That sure sounds easy enough,' said Magins sarcastically.

'Just make sure your shields are of good quality,' said Banshin.

'I'll try my best.'

'Yeah, I know. Sorry, I'm a bit nervous.'

'Aren't we all,' said Morovius.

'You guys don't sound too confident,' said Quince.

'Oh,' said Morovius, 'is that so? We are going to fight an invulnerable monster where the jains are severely depleted. How could that possibly undermine our confidence?'

No one said a word.

They continued onwards to meet the monster.

CHAPTER 25

The blobule was dying.

She knew it. It was obvious. Deep within the mounds of flesh which encased her, she could feel

organs beginning to fail. Maybe, she had grown too big, her organs unable to fuel her ever

expanding mass.

She knew so much. The jains had told her everything. Every time she absorbed some of their power,

they would tell her of this land, the land they called Eldara. Its monumental struggle against the

Marcovians, how she was depleting their jains, how their crops were now more plentiful, how they

were preparing for the siege of Bleddin.

More than this, she knew details of their lives. How families worked the land, the Lords and Ladies

and how they frivolously wasted their lives on the backs of others' labour. The petty arguments, the

affairs, the jealousies and the hopes. She knew all of this, the jains told her and yet she could tell no

one.

But, for all she knew about others, she knew little about herself. What was she, where had she come

from, what was her purpose, was she pure evil sent here to destroy the Kingdom? She didn't know.

As far back as she remembered she had been in this cave. She had absorbed the power of the jains,

it was the only sustenance she needed. The jains, with their sweet magic, invigorating her, giving

her power.

She had speculated as to what she was. She had an affinity to the jains, that much was obvious. Was she a magic maggot, who had grown fat on their power? The Anracs were magic horses, was she a magic maggot that could never crystallise? Maybe she was a virus, a bacterium, living off and absorbing, parasitic upon the land. She liked to think that perhaps she came from another planet, an interstellar traveller who had alighted on this land. She liked this thought because it meant that out there, somewhere, were others like her.

Only to meet another like her, to have a mate, that is what she really wanted. She had all this knowledge and no one to share it with. Where were the others? She did not know. Maybe she was unique, condemned to eternal loneliness. Maybe she was dying of a broken heart, she had sensed people saying that was possible.

She was dying and now this group of adventurers, these Marcovians were coming to kill her.

She waited.

Morovius's pod and Quince reached a ridge, behind which lay the Baranu Cave. Quince turned to them.

'Guys, this is it. Just over the ridge you will find the cave and your monster. If you guys have a clever plan, you'd better come up with it now.'

'Any last minute advice?' asked Magins. 'Anything you've forgotten to tell us. We don't want to hear after the fight that you'd forgotten to tell us about an important weakness.'

449

'Sorry, I've told you everything I know. At least the monster isn't subtle, just blue magic bolts and a huge capacity to absorb damage.'

'You keep saying that,' said Morovius, 'but just how much damage can this thing absorb?'

'Well, one party had three fire mages blasting it and they never succeeded in hurting it. Plus, the jains are more depleted now.'

'Bloody hell!' said Morovius.

'All right,' said Banshin. 'Quince, leave us alone while we plan our strategy.'

Quince rode off.

'What strategy have you got in mind, Banshin?' asked Candera.

'None. I just didn't want Quince to see how weak we are.'

'Well, without Morovius at full strength, we really have a problem,' said Magins.

'You think?' said Necarius.

'Guys, I'm really sorry,' said Morovius.

'It's not your fault,' said Candera. 'What are we going to do?'

'I don't even know if I can evoke Enraefem properly,' said Necarius.

'Look,' said Banshin. 'We have no option. Magins, keep up permeable shields, making them non-permeable when you see big blue bolts. Enraefem and I will just have to attack the creature. Necarius and Morovius cast whatever you can and Candera, get ready to heal a lot.'

'A cunning plan,' said Magins.

'Got anything better,' came the curt reply. 'I'm all ears.'

'Afraid not,' Magins conceded. 'Necarius, evoke Enraefem now. It's time for battle.'

'All right, I shall do my best. Say, do you think we will be affected by the half hour problem?'

'I sincerely doubt that will matter,' said Morovius. 'The chances of this battle taking longer than two and a half hours are exceedingly slim.'

Necarius started to evoke Enraefem. It took longer than usual and the daemon, when he did appear, was almost see-through.

'What's going on?' asked the daemon.

'We have a problem.' said Morovius. 'A big problem, we just hope that Necarius can keep you in this plane of existence.' Morovius outlined the situation to Enraefem and their plan to battle the monster.

'Sounds easy enough,' said Enraefem.

They all looked at the daemon. 'Hey, I didn't say it would be easy to win, just that it would be easy to follow the plan.'

'Look 'Raef.' said Banshin. 'Apparently, this monster doesn't have an obvious weakness and can absorb a huge amount of damage. You gnawing at it isn't going to achieve much. The only chance you have is if you see an opening, jump in there and chew away at its insides like you did to that Bedine in the Anrac Woods.'

'Sure, here we go again. Got a disgusting job, give it to the daemon.'

'Have you got a better idea?' asked Banshin.

'Nope.'

'Then it's monster eating for you.'

'This is it guys,' said Morovius, 'unless someone has had a sudden burst of inspiration.'

He took their silence as confirmation that no one had anything further to offer and started to walk over the ridge.

The blobule knew that they were coming, the jains had told her. She wondered if they knew that she was dying and was why the Eldarans had sent this party, but no, these boys did not, they hadn't a clue. None of them even knew why the fire mage had lost potency and she was not going to tell them. This would be her last adventure. Yet, so much seemed to depend upon it. Those Eldarans sure had a lot of faith in that fire mage. She had already damaged the Eldarans enough, was it fair to kill off the only hope they had left?

She crawled out of the cave, concertinaing her huge bulk out of the entrance. Whatever happened, she would face her last battle honourably, face her potential vanquishers and would not sulk guiltily in her cave.

The friends emerged over the hill and saw the monster for the first time.

'Bloody hell!' said Magins.

No description could possibly have prepared them for what lay ahead. The monster must have been at least thirty foot long and ten feet wide. It glowed with the blue intensity of the jains it had absorbed. Its skin was a wrinkled, convoluted mass. Facing them were a whole series of eyes atop what they supposed passed for a head. They could see no other openings, no nostrils or mouth.

'Well, 'Raef,' said Banshin. 'Reckon you're going for the eyes.'

Enraefem didn't move. He thought he had seen everything, having been summoned to this land since the days of the earliest necromancers, but certainly nothing like this. Even in the Netherworld, he had never seen anything that looked vaguely like this creature. How the hell had such a monstrosity come into being?

Magins, Morovius and Necarius started to invoke their magic, laboriously, almost in slow motion, attempting to extract what power they could from the depleted jains. Banshin started to invoke and just hoped he would be able to muster the strength to wield a shield and a broadsword. Enraefem sat perched on Banshin's shoulder. He could feel the pull of the Netherworld and strained to maintain his place in this plane of existence.

'Let's go,' said Enraefem and Banshin started his charge. Up went the permeable shields around the casters, Enraefem, Banshin and his Anrac. It shimmered in its greenish glow and Magins just hoped it would not allow too much of the monster's bolts to penetrate.

Luckily, Banshin's Anrac was unaffected by the poor quality of the jains in the area and started her gallop. Banshin made one final attempt to invoke the power of the jains and was able to pick up his shield and broadsword. It was shield bashing time. Necarius and Enraefem concentrated, Enraefem's body becoming clearer and losing its translucence.

The blobule watched with interest the up rushing warrior. How could such a small group hope to defeat her? The youths and their daemon certainly seemed a game bunch, no doubting their spirit, although their sanity was certainly questionable. Ah, the warrior was shouting, they tend to do that, makes them feel imposing. Let's see what this group of magic users are made of.

The blobule twitched.

A blue bolt shot off from beneath her eyes and sped past Banshin. Simultaneously, Necarius and Morovius let off their bolts of blue and fire. Enraefem leapt up into the air, determined to find out if those eyes were vulnerable.

The fire and blue bolts hit the monster's skin, there was the smell of burning flesh, was the monster vulnerable? Immediately, blue flesh closed over the burnt patch, healing the wound.

The monster's blue bolt hit Magins's shield, mostly dissipating, but some made its way through, straight for Morovius. He screamed in pain as the blue fire engulfed him. Luckily, Candera had prepared a healing spell and immediately cast it at Morovius.

Banshin shield slammed the monster while Enraefem bit at one of its eyes. The shield slam merely resulted in a rippling effect on the monster's copious flesh. Enraefem bit an eye, tearing at it but a sharp flick of the monster's body and Enraefem went flying. He somersaulted through the air, landing neatly on his feet. He looked up, the eye he had mauled was already beginning to heal.

Banshin kept slashing at the monster, his broadsword easily cutting through the blubber that encased the creature. However, once his broadsword was removed, the flesh closed over, the blubber reknitting to heal the monster.

'Bollocks to this,' shouted Morovius.

'Keep going,' said Magins. 'Nothing is invulnerable.'

'The person who made up that saying obviously never met this bastard.'

Morovius and Necarius prepared to cast again. It really was looking quite hopeless. They cast their bolts just as the monster sent a magic bolt their way. Magins expertly allowed their bolts through and then made the shields non-permeable. Banshin halted as he could not attack and watched the blue bolt dissipate harmlessly against Magins's shield. At least that's something, he thought as Morovius's and Necarius's bolts hit the creature.

Magins had protected them against the monster, but their own bolts were hardly effective, the creature absorbing most of the bolts, showing a little damage and then healing. Enraefem jumped up at the eye again, clawing and biting but it all seemed rather cosmetic. There was nothing behind the eye for him to penetrate and as he moved onto the next eye, he could see the injured eye beginning to heal.

The blobule looked at her attackers. This group certainly showed spirit. The last lot had run away as soon as they had seen her. She could feel their dismay that the fire mage was not at full strength, but what did it matter? Even at full power, that fire mage would be totally unable to penetrate her blubber to attack her vital organs. But, she was dying, what really was the point in all of this?

'Go for the eyes, Morovius,' screamed Necarius. 'It's our only chance, use fire arrows.'

Morovius started to conjure as many fire arrows as he could, but could only manage two and one of those was not at full strength.

'What the hell?' he thought as he cast them flying towards the monster's eyes. A direct hit, would that give Enraefem an opening? Was there a brain behind those eyes?

Enraefem realised what was afoot and jumped at one of the blazing eyes, chewing as fast as he could. It was to no avail. The monster gave another shake and Enraefem went flying off again, the eye healing behind him.

'Just keep going, that's all we can do,' commanded Morovius.

Banshin kept slashing, the mages kept casting bolts, Enraefem attacked the eyes, they kept at it against these insurmountable odds. But, something was up. Why wasn't the monster attacking? Was it toying with them?

The blobule was thinking. She realised her deepest desire. A desire to meet at least one of her kind, to have a mate, to live a life in peace. Instead, she realised she would be forever alone, always at war. By her very nature, she had ruined the Kingdom of these men, condemned them to defeat in their upcoming battle. That was why they kept on attacking her. They could think of no other way to protect their Kingdom.

The blobule considered these men who now attacked her. They were young, healthy, they had a life to live. The Eldarans didn't have much chance against the Marcovians, but she supposed they did have a chance. She had no chance, she was dying. These youngsters could go on, meet others of their kind, have a mate. They had a life to live.

She carefully considered her next move and made her decision. She lifted the front half of her body, exposing her underside to the aspiring warriors. It was her decision and it felt right.

Banshin stared at the underside of the monster. A bright pink patch of vulnerable looking flesh was clearly visible. It stood out markedly from the mounds of blue glowing blubber that surrounded it.

''Raef, come here quickly,' Banshin shouted.

He pushed his broadsword with all his might into the pink flesh. The broadsword sliced through with ease and the monster shuddered. He withdrew the sword and this time the flesh did not heal and reform around the wound, but left a gaping hole oozing puss.

''Raef, get in there, do it.'

Enraefem leapt in and began to chew and claw his way into the monster. This time, there was no healing. He kept on going and could hear a rhythmic beating sound – a heart? Who knows what was buried inside this monster? Enraefem kept chewing his way towards the beating sound. He suddenly broke through into a chamber. Above him was a large beating organ, it must be the heart. This was it. He leapt up the chamber and started to bite and claw at the organ, tearing away chunks and

458

throwing them away. Blood cascaded all around him, the heart tremored, it was becoming irregular and then it stopped. Enraefem could feel himself falling as the monster slumped forward to its death.

Magins slowly let down his shields, Morovius slumped to the ground, while Necarius rushed up to the monster to see if Enraefem was all right. Banshin dropped his broadsword to the ground, exhausted by trying to wield the huge blade single-handedly relying only on depleted jains for assistance.

'Look,' said Banshin. He pointed to the ground. The jains nearest the monster were beginning to glow, to regain their power. Slowly, gradually, the circle of glowing jains spread from the monster. In death, the monster was giving back to the land all it had stolen in life.

Morovius, Magins and Candera came walking up.

'What the hell happened?' asked Morovius. 'It didn't seem to want to fight us.'

'Who cares,' said Magins. 'We've won, we're heroes, just look at the jains, they're regaining their potency.'

They looked at the jains regaining their normal, sparkling lustre.

'I can feel the return of power,' said Necarius. 'Enraefem, you in there?'

A muffled sound could be heard from inside the carcass.

'Maybe I should dispel him. It can't be much fun inside there.'

'Nah, he's a daemon,' said Magins. 'Daemons love being inside monsters. It's what they're built for.'

Morovius laughed. 'Magins, I swear there's a sadist somewhere inside you.'

They waited for Enraefem who eventually appeared through the blubber with his familiar 'Hiya.'

The friends soon wished that Necarius had dispelled him as they were regaled with tales of how Enraefem had single handedly killed the monster, he was awesome, the bravest daemon ever and they had to listen to a detailed description of the monster's heart and how Enraefem had dismembered it.

'Anyway,' said Magins, 'at least we have our old power back.' They all looked at Morovius.

'I am more powerful,' Morovius said, 'but not at full power. I feel like I did in Anrac Woods and when we went to meet the dwarves in the Windborne Mountains. Sure, I'm a fire mage, but full power, no, not at all.'

They looked at each other mystified. Eventually, Candera broke the silence.

'Look, there's a pattern, we're just not seeing it. Right, there is the obvious pattern of depleted jains near the monster, plentiful jains in no man's land and so on that affect us all, but clearly there is some underlying pattern affecting Morovius as well. We just have to work out what it is.'

'Well, every time I left Bogloris, I lost power,' said Morovius.

'Even when you went to no man's land to fight in the Battle of the Failing Shields?' asked Necarius.

'Initially, I lost power and then I regained it when I hit no man's land,' replied Morovius.

'Right,' said Candera, 'so the two patterns were at work. The obvious pattern of plentiful jains in no man's land made you more powerful, that applies to us all. However, in your case the underlying pattern was also at work and your power reduced.'

'So he could be even more powerful in no man's land,' said Banshin.

'It would appear so,' said Candera.

'Hang on,' said Necarius. 'It can't be a simple thing like Bogloris. What about the dampening pit? Other fire mages struggle to ignite a scarecrow, Morovius took out the damn wall.'

'Yeah,' said Candera. 'What happened the last time we left Bogloris, when we were fleeing?'

'I felt no loss of power. I thought it was just because my adrenaline was pumping.'

461

'That can't be it. Your adrenalin must have been pumping on your way to your first battle,' said Necarius.

'We have a clue,' said Banshin. 'That spirit said Morovius had the feminine within.'

'So something feminine is about, within him or something' said Candera, 'and Morovius is potent. Without it he loses power. He needs something feminine to be potent? Something that was there when we fled and at the dampening pit?'

They all looked at one another in amazement. Morovius eventually broke the silence.

'Mum?'

They all nodded, Enraefem did a cartwheel. 'Think about it,' said Candera. 'You told us when you were a baby you could understand your mother, you were incredibly powerful and she was there. Remember the spirit, you have the feminine within you, that's your link to your mother, when she's nearby you are fully potent.

'Remember how we were the conduit for Necarius so that he could find his daemon, your mother is your conduit. When she is nearby, you can harness your full power.'

'What about the Battle of the Failing Shields. I was hardly weak then.'

'But you did experience some loss of power on leaving Bogloris. Then you felt more power when you got to no man's land because of the plentiful jains. Besides, no man's land is not that far from Bogloris. Your mother probably had some influence as the conduit although not as much as if she had been standing nearby.'

'Makes sense,' said Banshin.

'It makes total sense,' said Necarius.

'But that means I'll be even more powerful in no man's land in the next battle if Mum is near me.'

'Yep,' said Magins. 'An even more powerful Morovius. This could be the big break we have needed.'

'Maybe,' said Morovius, 'but it's still going to be difficult. I'm not omnipotent and we're going to be vastly outnumbered.'

'At least now we have some hope,' said Banshin.

CHAPTER 26

They rode back to Quince, watching the jains light up all around them as if announcing their victory to the world. Quince greeted them with a broad smile.

'So you did it! Never thought you would. You killed the monster. You really are heroes. I heard stories about Morovius at the Battle of the Failing Shields but I never realised he was that potent. Well done, I say, well done!'

'Hold your horses,' said Enraefem before any of them could say a word. 'It was a team effort. I personally did the killing. Ripped apart the monster's heart, I did.'

'Marvellous, absolutely marvellous.'

'Well,' said Banshin, 'at least Enraefem isn't saying he killed the monster single-handedly.'

'Yeah,' agreed Magins, 'be grateful for small mercies.'

'Grateful!' said Quince. 'Our gratitude will show no bounds.'

'Look Quince,' said Magins. 'You have to organise an audience with Archmage Cender. We've worked out a way Morovius can become even more powerful.'

'More powerful! That's amazing. I'm certain the Archmage will want to hear about that.'

The victors and Quince sat astride their steeds and watched as the jains lit up, moving away from them across the barren northern landscape. The authorities in Bleddin would know of the young magic users' victory before they arrived, the reinvigorated jains announcing to the entire population of Eldara how victorious they had been. The Marcovian traitors were heroes.

The party started their journey back to Bleddin. At every Inn, they heard talk of how the jains had returned to normal. Ordinary people didn't know the reason and the victorious group didn't offer any explanation. Obviously, the monster and his effect upon the land had been kept a secret because no one in authority wanted the Marcovians to know of their problem.

Morovius, his friends and Quince made their way back to Bleddin without incident, but on arriving there, things were different. Ten trumpeters announced their arrival and magic users lined their way to the Palace. People were cheering and some even tried to touch one of the heroes who had killed the monster. Chief Exchequer Rincin was personally waiting for them outside the Palace, along with Belinda.

Belinda ran up and hugged Morovius.

'I'm so please you are all right, all of you. I was so worried.'

'You needn't have been Mum, it was all in a day's work.'

'So,' she said, looking around, 'you all escaped unscathed?'

'Yes,' they assured her.

'We did it, Belinda,' said Magins. 'We did it. We're all heroes now.'

'You've always been heroes in my eyes,' said Belinda.

'So, I can take it that you killed the monster,' Rincin said.

'Yes, we've handled your problem, Sir,' said Morovius.

'That's just fantastic, quite fantastic. We knew you were powerful, but really you have succeeded where all others have failed. His Majesty will see you immediately.'

'We really need to see Archmage Cender, Sir.'

'He'll be there, come with me.'

The returning victors went through the circular corridors and negotiated the maze that was Bleddin Palace. This time the figures depicted in the paintings seemed more benign, gazing down upon them in admiration. Banshin puffed up his chest with pride.

'We're bloody heroes,' he said.

'Yeah,' agreed Magins, 'and even better, Enraefem isn't out to take all the credit.'

'How do we tell them that the monster didn't put up much of a fight?' asked Morovius.

'We don't,' said Magins. 'After all, heroes don't brag.'

They all laughed.

The young men entered the Courtroom. Everyone rose to greet them, even King Alphonse and Queen Sandrine. A trumpeter heralded their entry with heroic sounding blasts. All around the walls the Eldaran nobility broke into applause.

'Greetings, my fine warriors,' said King Alphonse. 'We can see by the enlivened jains that you have achieved a famous victory. Why, even the dampening pit has fully functioning jains. Our gratitude knows no bounds. Our magic users will be able to practice properly at last. You have given all my people hope.'

'Thank you, Your Majesty,' they said together.

'But isn't one of your party missing? What is a necromancer without his minion?'

'He's not here, Your Majesty.' said Necarius. 'He's a little rude.'

'He's not talkative, is he?' asked Cender.

467

'Very,' said Magins. 'I personally like him, Sir.'

'Do you know him, Your Majesty?' asked Necarius.

'I think we might have met,' smiled the King. 'Get him out.'

Necarius started to evoke Enraefem who plopped into this plane's existence.

'Hiya. Yo King! Long time no see, how's it hanging?'

'It's hanging fine Enraefem. I suppose you killed the monster single-handedly.'

'I did have a little help from Banshin but you're right, it was largely my doing. I was in there King, right up that monster, big bastard he was an all, I was there inside him, ripped up his heart, I did the killings.'

'Well done and I suppose your friends did a little to help?'

'Oh, King, they did their bit. They're a fine supporting act.'

The King and the entire Court laughed. Necarius looked shocked, his daemon certainly had been around.

'Yo, King, one thing,' said Enraefem pointing at Queen Sandrine. 'She's new.'

'Yes, she is. Queen Alexandra unfortunately died in a hunting accident.'

'Ah, I'm sorry, I liked her, very active she was.'

'Yes,' Alphonse looked down at the floor, contemplative. 'But let us rejoice, this is a great day, we at last have a chance against the Marcovians.'

'I hate to be a doomsayer,' said Rincin, 'but we are still vastly outnumbered.'

'Yes,' agreed Cender. 'We will be lucky to achieve a stalemate in the upcoming battle.'

'We do have some advice,' said Morovius. 'We have worked out how I can become even more powerful, Your Majesty.'

There were gasps around the Court.

'We need to discuss matters with Archmage Cender, Your Majesty,' continued Morovius.

'Well, I am here,' said the Archmage.

'We would prefer to talk alone with you, Sir. We need to discuss magic.'

King Alphonse nodded his approval.

'There is a side room over here we can use,' said Cender.

They walked off to the side room whilst there was a general mummer of speculation in the Court. Was there a problem? Hadn't the heroes vanquished the monster? Was there some matter everyone had overlooked?

'What is it?' asked Cender, as he sat himself behind the desk.

Morovius standing upright addressed the Archmage. 'Sir, I have over the years experienced a waxing and waning of my powers, independently of the strength and quantity of jains present. It was all rather confusing but we think we have finally solved the problem.

'We have determined that my mother is my conduit. When she is near me, I am at full power, when she is far away I am reduced to the power of a normal fire mage.'

'Did this happen when you met the monster?'

'It did, Sir.'

'Then. how did you manage to kill it?'

Morovius outlined the battle, including how the monster had reared up and exposed its weakness.

'We must keep this quiet. You are heroes, you have given us hope, we can't let it be known that you won due to some random fluke. OK, let me think, you were very powerful in the Battle of the Failing Shields and your mother was not nearby, how did that happen?'

'Sir, Bogloris is not that far from no man's land, but we believe that if my mother is near me in the next battle, I shall be even more powerful.'

'Excellent,' Cender clapped his hands excitedly. 'This is great news. Tell me, does your mother have any magical abilities?'

'None, Sir.'

'Then she can't be a conduit. A conduit channels his magical power into another.'

'Magins and Candera did that to me, Sir,' said Necarius. 'To help me evoke Enraefem for the first time.'

'A glorious event,' said Enraefem.

'Exactly,' said Cender. 'Conduits channel their magic into another magic user. Your mother is an extremely rare phenomenon I have never encountered before and only read about. She is a catalyst.'

'A catalyst, Sir?' said Morovius.

'A catalyst,' whispered Necarius, 'I remember reading about them.'

'Ah, a necromancer, always the best students.' said Cender. 'What do you remember?'

'Not much, Sir. They are enablers.'

'Why didn't you say anything?' Morovius wanted to know.

'I didn't realise it applied to you until now,' said Necarius.

'Indeed,' said Cender. 'Catalysts are difficult to spot due to their rarity and their nature. You see, a catalyst is not magical, they have no magical abilities of their own. They enable a particular magic user while remaining totally unchanged themselves. Nothing happens to them, they are only noticeable by their absence. Your mother is a catalyst.'

'Can you arrange for her to be near me at the next battle, Sir?' asked Morovius.

'We are so desperate that any advantage we can gain will be welcomed by the King. Your mother can be with the King, Rincin and myself and watch us coordinate the battle.'

They all agreed that that would be the best strategy, Belinda would be close enough to act as a catalyst and still be out of danger.

'Right, I'll have you lot shown to your quarters. Oh, just a small point Enraefem, you have been unusually quiet, anything to say?'

'Rule are rules.'

'Of course they are, of course they are.'

As they left for their barracks the friends quizzed Enraefem as to whether he knew Belinda was a catalyst all along. The now taciturn imp would say very little, only that rules were rules. They were shown to their billet.

'Damn,' said Morovius, 'I've forgotten Mum's painting.'

'After what we've achieved,' said Magins, 'I'm sure the Eldarans will be happy to commission another.'

Meanwhile, Cender asked to speak to King Alphonse and Rincin in the side room and told them about Belinda.

'That's just marvellous,' said Alphonse. 'Can this day get any better? He was powerful enough to kill the monster without his catalyst and in an area of depleted jains. Imagine how powerful he'll be in the next battle in no man's land.'

Cender kept quiet about the strange nature of the battle against the monster, while Rincin pointed out that they were still at a huge numerical disadvantage. Not only had they lost two thirds of their magic users, they had also lost a substantial number of Lords and knights in the charge to defend the surviving mages. All they could hope for was to achieve a stalemate.

'Sure,' said Alphonse, 'but we have promoted people to replenish the lost Lords and knights.'

'Yes, Your Majesty,' said Rincin, 'but the new knights in particular lack experience.'

'We need to maintain morale,' said Cender. 'Let's get Chief Cleric Andrin in here. He'll know what to say, it's his job.'

'I thought his job was talking to God,' said King Alphonse.

Rincin laughed. 'Maybe it is, maybe it isn't, Your Majesty. Let's just hope that God inspires him with some exalting propaganda.'

They went back into the Courtroom and all were dismissed except for Andrin.

'Andrin, old boy,' said Alphonse, 'we need you and your clerics to prove their worth. We are going into battle with reduced numbers and inexperienced knights. We need to keep up morale. What can you and your clerics do?'

'Your Majesty, surely news of this great fire mage and the death of the monster will be all the propaganda we need.'

'Maybe, maybe, but any fool can see that our magic ranks have been seriously depleted. We need people to be invigorated, to sacrifice all, not just rely on one mage. They need to have a purpose.'

'Ah, Your Majesty, religion is all about purpose and destiny. Who we are, where we're going, our role in life.'

'Yeah, yeah,' said Rincin, 'what's that in common language?'

'Let me think,' said Andrin.

Andrin paused and looked into the distance. 'He's talking to God now,' whispered Rincin to Cender who just sniggered.

'Let's see,' said Andrin. 'The fire mage and his party have joined us out of moral necessity. They realised that our Kingdom is the victim in this war and being heroic warriors, they couldn't fight for the wrong side. That gives us the moral advantage.

'Then God Himself has enabled them to kill the monster. Now it's dead we can tell everyone about him. Doesn't matter if the Marcovians find out about him now. That's it, God Himself showed his approval of the heroes' act in joining us by enabling them to kill the monster.

'But, as you say, we cannot just be passive and rely on the fire mage. He leads us by example. We must follow his lead, train hard, be willing to sacrifice everything for what is right and proper.

'That's it. We have God and right on our side. God will not let us down in battle with the Marcovians, just as he did not let down the fire mage in his battle with the monster.'

Alphonse, Cender and Rincin looked at the Chief Cleric. This religion certainly was a fine motivating force. Even Rincin felt like praying.

'Get on with it,' said Alphonse. 'Tell your Bishops how we are right and with God. Get all your clerics pronouncing it throughout the land. With God on our side, we cannot lose.'

Andrin smiled. He had proved his worth once again. He set off to meet with his Bishops.

And so it was that the pulpits of Eldara sang the same song, how hope had returned to the land, the mystery of the diminishing jains was made public along with great stories of how the powerful fire mage and his friends had killed the monster. We faced our darkest hour in the Battle of the Failing Shields, now Eldara has turned the corner, we have passed our test, just as we did in that long forgotten day when the Eldaran magic users had heroically defended us against the aggressive Marcovian army in no man's land.

Eldara had defended herself against the Marcovians then and would do so again. Everyone had to follow the bravery of the heroes, be willing to face insurmountable odds, laugh in the face of defeat because everyone knew we would be eventually victorious, just like the fire mage and his party.

476

They were victorious because they had right and God on their side and we will follow in their footsteps.

But this was no excuse for slacking, there could be no room for overconfidence. The fire mage himself, did not just accept his God given gifts, but practised hard and read widely. Indeed, there was not a magic book in the Kingdom he had not read and studied carefully. His example was there for all to follow.

Peasants must work hard and produce the food needed for a healthy army; swordsmen and archers must practice every day. Knights, especially those newly promoted, must practice with great vigour, perfect their charges with their lances, Lords must learn with great diligence the art of leadership and command. All magic users must learn their art, perfect their skills, for on them was a most onerous task, to fight for three hours whilst outnumbered.

But most importantly, no one must ever lose heart. All must know, we have the most powerful fire mage on our side, the vanquisher of monsters. Most importantly, we have God and right on our side. We cannot, we must not fail. We will preserve our Kingdom, we will ensure that the evil Marcovians will never despoil our land, enslaving our children, raping and pillaging, destroying all we have worked so hard to build.

The clerics' words had a good effect. Their sermons explained why the jains had stopped glowing and how they had resumed their normal lustre. Survivors of the Battle of the Failing Shields verified that there had indeed been a mighty fire mage amongst the Marcovians. Citizens of Bleddin confirmed he and his party had joined the Eldaran forces. Surely, God had tested them, Eldara had endured and now with the passing of His test, victory was assured. No one would lay siege to Bleddin, the land would be secured, no one from Marcovia would ever be able to despoil their lands. Hope was in the air.

Troops began to converge on Bleddin. Forges blazed night and day as blacksmiths relentlessly, machinelike produced swords and shields for the rabble. Knights rode up on their warhorses, resplendent in their chain mail, their tunics proudly displaying the green circle of Eldara. Even the rabble who were unable to procure swords, proudly sharpened their knives and pitchforks, everyone determined to serve their Kingdom.

Guards in the watchtowers used eyeglasses and could see that the Marcovians were also amassing their troops in the distance. Pennants waved in the air and a huge encampment had been set up. It appeared to be that the Marcovians were building as large an army as possible, anticipating their final victory. Word was sent back to Bleddin.

A War Council was held. Present were Alphonse, Rincin, Queen Sandrine, Cender and the ten Lords who would individually lead the ten divisions of the army.

'All right,' said Alphonse. 'We have all heard this stuff about right and God and that is all well and good but it appears that the Marcovians are building up a huge army.'

'They sense victory, Your Majesty,' said Rincin.

'How are our magic users doing?' asked Alphonse.

'They are all doing well, Your Majesty,' said Cender. 'The replenished jains are a great boon. I doubt we'll have our half hour problem again.'

'Just the lack of numbers problem,' said Rincin.

'Indeed,' agreed Alphonse. 'Anyone got any ideas?'

'Well,' said a new Lord called Queros. 'It would appear the battle will lack all guile and cunning, Your Majesty. They are going to hit us with everything they've got and we will do well to resist.'

'We do have the fire mage,' said Cender. 'I have seen him in action, he's quite something and with his catalyst nearby in no man's land, he's going to be quite a handful.'

'His mother?' asked Rincin.

'Yep, his mother. She's his catalyst.'

'So we can look forward to him being even more powerful than in the Battle of the Failing Shields?' asked Alphonse.

'Indeed, Your Majesty,' confirmed Cender.

'It would appear,' continued Alphonse, 'that the battle plan is simple. We just try to survive their three hour magical bombardment. We use Morovius to hit them as hard as we can to try to even up the odds. Then it's conventional. I recommend we go defensive.'

'I agree, Your Majesty,' said Rincin. 'A charge is not a good idea. They have experienced knights. A lot of our guys are new, despite all their enthusiasm and talk of God. We can't hope to win a charge.'

'We get our knights to dismount, Your Majesty,' said Lord Queros. 'Pikemen all around them to protect them, kill their uprushing horses and have done with their dismounted knights.'

'The Marcovians know that tactic well and even used it themselves recently,' said Alphonse. 'If they see us dismounted, their knights will advance on foot, protected by pikemen and it'll be a case of archers and crossbowmen attempting to shoot down the foe from the flanks.'

'I'll take that Your Majesty,' said Rincin. 'Sounds like a recipe for a stalemate.'

'Yeah and then hopefully a hiatus in this war. The enemy are so convinced of victory, a stalemate will seem like a defeat for them and a victory for us.'

'The Marcovians should back off, Your Majesty,' said Rincin. 'That is until the next battle.'

'By which time we'll have replenished our magic users, Your Majesty,' said Cender. 'We have some good kids coming through.'

'So, we're agreed. We aim for a stalemate,' said King Alphonse.

'It's the best we can hope for,' said Rincin.

There was a general nodding of heads in agreement.

CHAPTER 27

The excitement built up throughout Eldara. All talk was of war and many attempts at amateur

psychology were made. The overwhelming power of positive thinking was analysed in detail. The

Churches had never seen so much business as relatives, friends and the soldiers themselves lit

candles and made donations. Prayers were offered and God was constantly reminded that He was

on their side as they were in the right. Some even suggested that the soldiers should undergo a

period of celibacy, but luckily for the prostitutes who had descended upon the camps, most thought

this unnecessary and taking things a bit too far.

The tension built up, particularly amongst the magic users, who however convinced they were of

the moral correctness of their campaign, could not avoid the fact that they were vastly outnumbered.

They practised hard, spurred on by the newly invigorated jains. Morovius even tried to read a book

when he heard what a great scholar he was. He managed fifty pages before giving up and asking

Necarius to explain it to him.

Magins looked strained. He knew from the last battle the importance of shielding. When shields

failed, the battle was basically over. It didn't matter how potent Morovius would be with his mother

nearby, without shields, the Eldarans would be sitting ducks. The responsibility lay heavy on his

shoulders. He wondered if other defence mages were feeling similar pressure.

The mood became sombre, even with the clerics moving amongst the troops, encouraging them,

affirming the rightness of their cause, the aid that God would undoubtedly provide them. King

Alphonse was even thinking of commencing battle before demoralisation set in when the news arrived.

The Marcovians were beginning to move towards no man's land. This was it, time to respond. Whatever practice they had performed, however far their training had taken them, it had to be enough, the day of reckoning was at hand. It was time for battle to commence.

The magic users emerged from their barracks on their horses, apart from the magic warriors who had to walk to the city gates. The mages wore their long flowing robes, the green circle of Eldara prominently displayed. Crowds thronged the streets shouting encouragement, offering up prayers, young women presenting some of the magic users with flowers.

The magic users and Lords made their way out of the city gates and up to the encampment where the bulk of the conventional army was stationed. Magic users would lead the way as they would be the first to engage the enemy. Behind them was the ranged power of archers and the mercenary crossbowmen who would also be involved in attacking the enemy's magic shield. To the rear, led by the Lords, were the knights and peasant rabble, to be held in reserve until the three hour mark in the battle. Three hours! Could this depleted force of magic users last three hours? Many hopeful glances were cast at Morovius who just stared steadfastly ahead.

Finally, bringing up the rear were King Alphonse, Chief Exchequer Rincin, Archmage Cender, their messengers and to many's surprise, the fire mage's mother, Belinda. What was she doing here? Maybe it was a mark of respect to the great fire mage that his mother be allowed to witness the battle.

483

There was silence from the troops as they left the cheering mobs in the city and set off down the thoroughfare to no man's land. Everyone had already discussed in detail what they were going to do, pods had long been formed. There were the sounds of horses clopping on the road, the heavy thumping of Anracs, the creaking of carts filled with supplies like arrows and bolts. The Lords, knights and magic warriors made clinking sounds in their chain mail armour.

At last they could see the Marcovians, who were similarly amassing on their section of no man's land. The plentiful jains glistened brilliantly in the morning sunlight, beckoning the magic users on with their promise of enhanced power.

Morovius and his pod took up their position in the centre from where Morovius could cause the most damage. As he stood there with Magins, Necarius, Candera and Banshin on his Anrac, booing and jeering arose from the Marcovians. They had been recognised.

'Traitor, Traitor, Traitor,' went up the chant.

Warriors clanged on their shields. The Eldarans started to shout back various expletives and that might was right and the Marcovians would soon see who was mighty. The build up was commencing.

Belinda sat on her horse alongside Alphonse, Rincin and Cender. She was quiet as she had been instructed. Apparently, her presence made Morovius more powerful. She noted with concern the huge number of Marcovians. She began to hope that all this talk of Morovius was correct and he was indeed a mage of unsurpassed power. She hoped that Candera would be calm and not become stuck again. Her son would probably be needing his services.

A single arrow shot over from the Marcovian side. It sailed gracefully through the air, arcing its way toward the Eldarans. Whoosh! The magical permeable shields went up as all around the battlefield magic users began to call upon the magic of the jains.

There were plopping sounds as daemons came into existence on this plane. The nimble and deadly imps, the damage absorbing Flanteins, the Cathren seductresses and the huge Bedines. The magic warriors and melee daemons started their charge, imps perched on their shoulders. The battle had begun.

Arrows and bolts filled the air, Cathrens shooting off their magic arrows in quick succession. There was a gasp. A huge fireball of unimaginable magnitude shot across the battlefield, lighting up the melee fighters beneath hurling itself into the Marcovian shield, breaking up into a myriad colours. Morovius was in action. Alphonse let out a whoop of delight and Belinda felt a stirring of power within her. So that's what it feels like to be a catalyst.

Banshin continued his charge, yelling out his war cry, Enraefem peering forward on his shoulder. He saw a single young warrior and charged, Enraefem jumping off at the last moment as Banshin shield bashed his young opponent. A Bedine leapt into view clawing and biting at Banshin's magic shield.

'Get him 'Raef.' Banshin shouted and Enraefem proceeded to attack the Bedine's face, trying to inflict damage through the permeable shield.

Candera arched in readiness, waiting to get off a heal. His nerve couldn't fail him now, the past was the past, no one's perfect, get it right this time. Necarius kept up his mind meld with Enraefem, urging his imp on while letting off his blue bolts of magic.

A stray Marcovian fireball hit Banshin, his magical shield absorbing most of the damage, Candera easily healing Banshin's lesser burns. Morovius decided to unleash fire arrows. He managed to everyone's astonishment seven, all of great potency and they raced across the battlefield one at Banshin's foe. Enough of it penetrated to open a nasty gash on the young warrior's leg and his healer immediately cast blue soothing magic in his direction.

Alphonse could barely contain himself. 'That fire mage sure is something. I couldn't have hoped for better.'

'Let's just hope Magins's shield holds,' said Cender. 'Without Morovius we don't stand much of a chance.'

Belinda sat on her horse, concentrating on Morovius, strange stirrings within her, hoping that whatever she had to offer her son would be enough.

Banshin feinted a shield bash and his young opponent raised his shield in anticipation exposing his midriff. Banshin used all his might to try to slice his broadsword through the permeable shield and

486

managed a glancing blow against the young warrior's stomach. The warrior slumped as yet more healing magic came his way.

Morovius sent off another huge fireball, at what he hoped was the pod attached to the young warrior Banshin was fighting. The fireball cascaded through the air, smoke trailing in its trajectory. It hit the shield with a huge explosion, the greenish permeable shield shuddered, wavered and disintegrated.

This was the chance everyone waits for in battle. The mages stood exposed as Necarius, the Cathrens, archers and crossbowmen shot their projectiles at the exposed mages and a single Cathren. They could see the defence mage desperately attempting to invoke a new shield but it was too late, he was killed by the unerring accuracy of a Cathren's arrow. Necarius's blue bolt took out what he thought was a healer and the arrows and bolts killed the fire mage.

Alphonse stood up in his stirrups. This was going as well as he could possibly have hoped. That's it Morovius, show them what you've got.

Banshin's foe was unaffected by the death of the pod but the Bedine was dispelled. Banshin really felt that he had the better of the young warrior. He kept up his relentless attacks, shield bashing and slashing with his broadsword.

Cender turned to Alphonse. 'Your Majesty, don't just look at Morovius. The others are struggling.'

Alphonse surveyed the battlefield. Sure enough the Marcovian numbers were beginning to tell. Across the Eldaran lines, the green permeable shields were shuddering under the weight of the

Marcovian bombardment. He noticed a young shield mage who was sweating profusely, desperately trying to keep his wall intact. The sheer weight of fireballs coming in was taking their toll, enough getting through to cause real damage, causing the healers to work furiously.

Everything seemed to depend on the rest of the magic users just hanging in there while Morovius did his magic.

Banshin kept slashing and now Enraefem was free to attack the warrior as well. Enraefem went for the face, unable to cause any real damage through the permeable shield, but disorientating the young warrior enough to give Banshin a real chance.

Banshin kept slashing and then saw an opening, there was a tear in the permeable shield wall encasing the warrior, his defence mage must have lost concentration, had Morovius caused this? Banshin immediately used all his might to slash through the opening with his broadsword. There was no resistance until the broadsword connected with the warrior's ribs, slicing into him. The warrior fell from his Anrac, dead.

'That's it 'Raef. On to the next one.'

The Marcovians started to concentrate more of their fire power onto Morovius's pod, realising that he was the key to winning this battle. A nearby defence mage started to give some aid to the hard-pressed Magins, while attempting to maintain his own defensive wall. Fireballs, blue bolts of magic, arrows and bolts began to rain down on Morovius's pod.

Morovius started to go on the defensive. He was sending off seven fire arrows to intercept the incoming magic bolts. All around them fireballs and blue bolts of magic exploded as Morovius's arrows hit them, throwing them off course, dissipating their magical force.

Alphonse started to become agitated. 'If Morovius is just defending his pod, what chance do we have? We need an offence.'

'Maybe Andrin's God will help us, Your Majesty,' said Rincin.

'This is the defensive part of the battle,' said Cender. 'Your Majesty, we always knew the best we could hope for was a stalemate.'

Belinda became increasingly worried. She was no military tactician, but it was obvious this was a turn for the worse. She had no idea how this whole catalyst thing worked, so she just tried to concentrate on her son, maybe that would help. It seemed to be working. She could feel a strange surge of power within her.

Across the battlefield, the Eldarans took advantage of the relief they were experiencing as the Marcovians concentrated on Morovius. They launched as many fireballs and blue bolts as they could manage. Fire and blue bolts rained in on the Marcovians but their shields held firm, the other Eldaran fire mages just did not have Morovius's power.

Banshin raced across the melee front to fight another warrior. On his own he was exposed to magical bolts, ironically up front close to an enemy he was protected as the mages could not see him clearly. Banshin needn't have been concerned.

A huge experienced warrior came rushing up screaming, in his high pitched voice, 'Traitor!'

It was Turinus.

Banshin gulped. This would be a test indeed. He just hoped that Magins could keep his permeable shield intact and charged. The two warriors, teacher and pupil shield bashed each other, attempting to penetrate the others' shuddering magical shields. Turinus had a Flantein alongside him. Enraefem ignored the daemon and tried his usual tactic of going for Turinus's face to distract him.

'You tried to kill us,' shouted Banshin.

'Liar,' screamed Turinus.

Banshin couldn't be bothered to answer, this fight would take all his concentration. He tried a shield bash feint, but Turinus did not fall for the tactic. How could he? He had been the one to teach Banshin. Instead, Turinus thrusted with his broadsword while Banshin swerved out of the way.

Morovius saw an opening in the Marcovian attack and launched one of his huge fireballs. It sped over Banshin and Turinus and smashed into a Marcovian shield wall, enough penetrating to immolate a fire mage. His healer immediately went to work to save the screaming mage, it was unfortunate, Morovius had not dealt a killing blow. He looked up and saw more incoming fire and blue bolts, it was time to go back to defensive tactics.

Magins and the adjoining defence mage were really beginning to struggle. Morovius was intercepting a large number of the attacks but even he couldn't stop all, or even a majority, of them. It was as if the entire Marcovian army was firing at them, not caring about the rest of the Eldaran magical forces. Why should they? Once they had eliminated Morovius, their superior numbers would ensure victory.

Alphonse was becoming desperate.

'Any ideas? We have another two hours of this.'

'Your Majesty,' said Rincin, 'we just have to hang in there. What else can we do?'

'Move another healer to Morovius's pod. He's not needed elsewhere. All the attacks are concentrated on Morovius, Your Majesty,' said Cender.

Alphonse ordered a messenger to carry out the order. A healer from an adjoining pod, called Aslin, moved alongside Morovius.

Belinda looked on worriedly but there was nothing else she could do but concentrate on her son and feel the power within her.

Turinus heaved a mighty blow at Banshin, which Banshin blocked partly with his physical shield and the permeable shield surrounding him. Enraefem seemed to be having little effect, Turinus fighting almost by instinct. In contrast, the Flantein was moving quickly to absorb Banshin's blows. Banshin did manage one thrust at Turinus's thigh but Turinus easily swerved to avoid him.

Magins turned to Morovius.

'I'm struggling, I'm really struggling.'

'Leave Enraefem unshielded,' ordered Necarius. 'He needs a shield least of all of us.'

Magins did as ordered but was still feeling great strain. Morovius kept trying to intercept incoming bolts, but he could only cast seven arrows at a time and as impressive as that was, it wasn't enough to deal with the huge firepower coming in.

'I'm going non-permeable,' shouted Magins.

It made little sense. How could Magins and his comrades keep up an impermeable shield for two hours? Now, they lacked all offensive abilities, but what option did Magins have? Candera had already healed Morovius twice, what would happen if Morovius received a death blow? All around them bolts exploded against the non-permeable shield. The friends looked at one another. What were they going to do?

Magins just concentrated on trying to keep up the shields. In particular, he could feel his grip on Banshin's shield slipping, as Banshin was the furthest away.

Banshin just sat on his Anrac, attack impossible due to the impermeable shield, and listened to Turinus's taunts of 'Coward.' Should he retreat? There was just no point sitting astride his Anrac doing nothing in the middle of the battlefield. He used his mind meld with his Anrac to turn away.

Around him, the Eldaran magic users were furiously casting every bolt they could at the Marcovians. The Eldarans were achieving some success, but not enough to compensate for the Marcovian large numbers. Yet, try they must, the Eldaran ranged attack had to attempt to gain some respite for Morovius. They knew what he was capable of. If they could just draw some of the Marcovian firepower away from Morovius.

Banshin started to turn away and noticed a shimmering in his wall, a weakness, what chance would he have against a shielded Turinus? His Anrac started to gallop but it was too late. Turinus came charging and could just see through Enraefem's infuriating biting a gap in Banshin's shield. He raised his broadsword and brought it slashing down, expertly slicing through the gap in the magical shield and into Banshin's chest, the chain mail offering little protection against the deadly blow. The blade went into Banshin's ribcage, ramming chain mail into the wound, thrusting through towards his heart, blood pouring from the wound.

Candera was ready to heal anticipating Banshin's predicament by jumping into the next pod with its permeable shield. He cast his healing magic. It was to no avail. Magic can only cure the living.

Morovius yelled out a huge cry, 'NO! Make the shield permeable.'

'I can't,' said Magins tearfully, 'we'll all die.'

'Do it,' shouted Morovius. 'I have a clear shot.'

Magins did as commanded and Morovius started to invoke the largest fireball he had cast so far, anger and grief mobilising his emotions. The fireball shot off and sped towards the solitary Turinus.

Turinus's shield was still permeable and he didn't have a chance. Enough of the fireball penetrated to completely immolate Turinus. He raised his broadsword in defiance as he cooked inside his chain mail armour, his silhouette brilliantly outlined in the flaming fireball.

It was the chance the Marcovians needed. They could all see the greenish tinge to Magins's shield inviting them to attack. Magins made the shield as impermeable as soon as he could but not before enough of a fireball got through hitting Morovius squarely in the chest. Morovius dropped to the ground screaming as Candera, running back, and Aslin immediately sent healing magic towards him.

Morovius wasn't dead, but he was down, it would take some time for Candera and Aslin to heal him. Morovius continued to moan. 'I'm sorry,' he said.

'Don't worry,' said Candera. 'It was only a matter of time.'

'What are we going to do?' asked Morovius.

'We're going to go down fighting,' said Magins.

A screaming started to fill the air, piercing, agony ridden, ripping through everyone's ears to their very souls. The inequity of it all, a war without end, all this death and destruction, for what, to build one Kingdom, to build one Kingdom that everyone wanted, to achieve what, for Lords and Ladies to live in luxury and debauchery while peasants slaved away, babies taken from their mothers, talking of right and God while all they were interested in was their own slothful pride and luxury.

Men held their hands over their ears in a vain attempt to block out the screaming and looked up. There she was, red fire filled eyes, black hair chaotically swirling, turning in circles, twenty foot in the air, screaming the agony of the lands, anger and pain filled the air.

The whispers started.

'Banshee.'

'Banshee.'

'Banshee.'

The Banshee's screeching became comprehensible, her screams rebounding across the battlefield.

'YOU WILL LEAVE MY SON ALONE.'

The deep blackness of Banshee magic surrounded her, swirling, intermingling with her jet black hair. Wisps of blackness arose from her, congealing around her hands. Troops stood horrified, staring at the apparition which rose above them, fearing the legendary destruction of the Banshee.

The Banshee amassed a huge ball of black magic and her body went into a spasm, shooting the ball off at a Marcovian pod. The black magic demolished the permeable shield and disintegrated the men in the pod. The Banshee screamed her pain again, drawing once more the surrounding black magic into her hands.

The paralysis that had afflicted the Marcovians ended. All thought of attacking Morovius was gone, this time they had to kill the Banshee, the abomination. Every Marcovian shot at her, their blue bolts and fireballs heading straight for her. Arrows and crossbow bolts followed. In the confusion, even some Eldaran mages shot bolts at her.

Magins jerked his body and put a permeable shield around her.

Morovius looked up from his prone position. 'Mum?' he asked in amazement.

Candera assessed that Morovius had enough healing to recover and shot up healing energy towards the Banshee as she was blasted by bolts and arrows.

'Heal her,' he shouted at Aslin alongside him.

'I can't. She is Banshee.'

496

'Necarius, sort him out.'

Necarius stepped behind the healing mage and placed his dagger at his throat. 'Heal the Banshee or I'll slice your jugular.' Aslin decided to overcome his prejudice and heal the Banshee.

The Banshee reeled in agony as the bolts hit her. She amassed more of her black magic and shot it at another Marcovian pod, completely obliterating it. The Eldarans started to hesitate, maybe the Banshee was on their side.

Alphonse quickly appraised the situation. 'We can't piss her off. Tell our troops to attack the Marcovians only.'

Messengers sped along the lines. 'Leave the Banshee alone, she is on our side.' The Eldarans returned to attacking the Marcovian lines.

The Banshee was being hit with everything at the Marcovian's disposal and up in the air she was an easy target. Magins's permeable shield could only help so much and even with two healers it was not enough to save her. She kept on shooting off huge bolts of black magic, destroying pods, but she was taking massive damage, she had lost a leg, burnt through.

Morovius staggered to his feet, determined to try to intercept some of the incoming bolts, to save his mother, allow her the time she needed to obliterate her attackers. He brought her some respite, as she destroyed another Marcovian pod, screaming her agony, gathering her black Banshee magic, using all the pain she felt to power her on.

Necarius suddenly gripped Morovius by the shoulders.

'She's not a catalyst, she's not even a conduit. Sure, you have a connection but she's a Banshee. You're the conduit, fill her with your magic.'

'What, fireball my mother?'

'No, fill her with unformed blue magic.'

Morovius started to invoke as much unformed blue magic as he could and shot it off into the Banshee. She swirled, absorbing the magic, twisting in the air, screaming all the while, moving her hands, bringing together the blue magic of a mage and the black magic of a Banshee. Meanwhile, Candera and Aslin kept sending up as much healing as they could muster.

The Banshee blasted again, corrosive black and raw blue magic careering through the battlefield, a ball of magic large enough to destroy two Marcovian pods.

The Eldaran magic users gained heart, perhaps this Banshee could be trusted, what choice did they have but to redouble their attacks on the Marcovian lines?

The Banshee kept twirling, the dance of the dervish, uncontrolled, untamed, just raw black and blue magic, the heart of destruction. She swirled for longer, taking damage, drawing upon Candera and Aslin's healing and she swirled a protective black bubble around her to augment Magins's permeable shield.

Now fireballs and blue bolts of magic, arrows and bolts just disintegrated as they hit the Banshee's protective black shield. She appeared to grow larger, black magic swirling around her, black hair chaotically caressing her face. Still Morovius pumped her with his raw blue magic, the Banshee greedily absorbing every last drop.

The Marcovians sensed that things were very wrong, an unnatural abomination was in their midsts. They stopped casting and their shields were made impermeable. The battlefield resounded with Eldaran bolts slamming against the Marcovian impermeable shields and the wailing of the Banshee.

The Banshee was barely visible, black and blue magic encased her and still she twirled in the air, adsorbing the magic of the land and her son as conduit until she felt ready to explode.

And explode she did. The black and blue bolt shot out from her at the left flank of the Marcovian army. Their shields were of no avail, the blue and black magic destroying them with ease. The pods disintegrated leaving corpses in their midst. Still the magic attacks kept going, destruction beyond belief, obliterating the troops behind, the Lords and the knights, the swordsmen, the archers and the rabble.

The Banshee kept going, moving rightwards, her destructive magic destroying all in its path, pods, knights, everyone until it reached the command centre. King Almein, Amran and Marinus looked on aghast. All they had hoped for was lying in ruins in front of them.

'Sod this for a game of soldiers,' said Amran. 'I'm off.'

'Good idea,' said Marinus as he turned his horse.

Almein, Amran and Marinus prepared to ride to safety as the enraged Banshee continued moving rightwards. Once more, the screaming became comprehensible.

'YOU WILL NOT ESCAPE MY WRATH.'

A bolt of blue and black magic sped across the battlefield, tailor made for the men who had planned her son's death. Onwards it went, straight at the three fleeing for their lives. The blue and black ball of destructive magic continued to shoot across the battlefield towards its goal. It engulfed the Marcovian leaders, their momentary screams stifled by death, their misshapen bodies adorning the edge of the battlefield.

The Banshee continued, moving rightwards. Some men started running, others remained rooted by panic to the spot. It did not matter. Nothing could help against the enraged power of the Banshee augmented by her powerful conduit.

The Eldarans stopped casting and just watched as the Banshee vanquished their enemy, magic users, nobility, daemon, swordsmen, archers, rabble, crossbowmen, she made no distinctions, all were disintegrated as she gradually moved rightwards, a destructive power that surpassed everything they had heard of in legends.

Eventually, she stopped. She had reached the far right flank of the Marcovian army, it had been entirely obliterated. There was a pause. Would the Banshee show restraint? Would she now expel her anger on the Eldarans? They waited with bated breath.

The Banshee stopped swirling, the black cloak enveloping her began to fade. She gradually came back down to earth and stood next to King Alphonse.

Morovius walked up to her. 'Mum, what the fuck?'

'I'll have no language like that off you, young man.'

There was silence. The Eldarans looked across the battlefield at the charred remains of their opponents. Nothing, but nothing was left of the Marcovian army. Who would have thought? Was this what victory felt like? It must be.

It started slowly, a cheering amongst the troops, magic users who only a short time ago had been looking at certain defeat looked at one another in disbelief. It was over. It had to be over, only one army was left. This had to be it. The cheering grew louder. Some men even began to cry.

Belinda walked up to Banshin's Anrac who had continued her gallop back to Eldaran lines. She jumped onto the back of the uncomplaining Anrac.

'Mum,' said Morovius, 'you're on the back of an Anrac.'

'I'm not blind. I know exactly where I am.'

'Yes, but only magic warriors can ride Anracs.'

'Look, I'm a bloody Banshee and this wee beastie will do exactly what I want it to do. Isn't that right, Melissa?'

Belinda tapped the uncomplaining Anrac on the shoulder. People looked at one another and all had the same unsaid thought – in future, a lot of things were going to do exactly what the Banshee wanted.

Belinda turned to King Alphonse. 'Look here King, you've won the war, but remember this. Your troops had better behave themselves. No raping and pillaging. If there's any shit from your troops, they'll have to answer to a bloody Banshee. They shall behave as gentlemen towards the peasantry. Just remember, the Banshee is peasant.'

'Ma'am, I shall ensure that everyone is on their best behaviour,' said Alphonse.

Belinda rode off, her black hair waving in the wind.

Morovius walked up to King Alphonse.

'Your Majesty,' he said.

'Yes.'

'I have always found it wise to obey my mother.'

'Good advice, but I don't think any of us need it. The chances of anyone disobeying her are quite remote.'

Meanwhile, enough of the surrounding troops had heard Belinda's words and the whispering started. A whispering that would be repeated across Marcovia and Eldara.

'The Banshee is peasant.'
'The Banshee is peasant.'
'The Banshee is peasant.'

CHAPTER 28

Morovius, Candera, Magins and Necarius walked across the battlefield. Necarius led the way, using his mind meld with Enraefem to direct the friends towards Banshin's body. They knew they were close when they came across the charred remains of Turinus and his Anrac, his broadsword still held aloft by his burnt corpse. Smoke swirled off his dead remains.

'There he is,' said Necarius, pointing.

A large young man lay on the ground, proud of bearing, a huge gaping wound exposing his ribcage. Enraefem sat on the body, a tear in his eye. He looked up at the friends.

'He was awesome,' he said.

Magins's body started to shake. 'I couldn't maintain his shield.'

'I know,' said Candera. 'War is shit. There are no easy answers.'

Magins walked up to his dear friend, the first and best he had made. He sat down on the ground and cradled Banshin's head in his lap. Tears coursed silently down his face.

'Good Bye dear friend. Thank you for putting up with me for all those years. Thank you for your courage and showing us the way forward. You will always be in my thoughts.'

Morovius's mind went back to that time, all those years ago when a young, well made handsome boy came rushing to his defence, fists flying. He put a hand on Magins's shoulder.

'He was the best.'

Necarius stroked his daemon. 'He was indeed awesome. He was even more awesome than you.'

The daemon smiled. 'I have known many warriors. He was my favourite even if he did like crappy novels.'

They all smiled. Banshin. Head filled with chivalric ideals, a seemingly unstoppable force, a man who was ready, who would fight to overcome insurmountable odds. A man who would breath no more.

They looked out over the corpse ridden battlefield. Blood was in patches all over the ground, intermingling with the jain soaked earth. They looked up at the Marcovian lines, their erstwhile allies lay strewn about in grotesque, twisted caricatures of humanity. A smell filled the air, beckoning the circling crows to feast.

'So, this is what victory looks like,' said Morovius.

'Not so sweet, is it?' said Candera.

'It's bloody shit,' said Magins. 'What was it all for?'

'I'm not sure,' said Morovius. 'Maybe now that there is only one Kingdom, future generations will know peace.'

'I'm not sure,' said Candera. 'Knights, Lords and Kings are good at finding people to fight.'

'They could start fighting each other over the spoils,' said Magins. 'Remember Lady Rosemary and Dinran.'

'Well, I'll have no part in it,' said Morovius. 'We'll have to make it clear. There is enough land for everyone.'

'Isn't that a fact,' said Magins. 'Nothing is left of the Marcovian nobility. Surely, the Eldarans will be happy with that. There is more than enough land to go around.'

'The spoils of war,' said Candera.

'The peace dividend,' said Morovius. 'At least let us look on the bright side. Mum was clear, there will be no pillaging.'

'Awesome woman, that,' said Enraefem. 'Did you see her go, bang, bang, bang, never thought I'd see a Banshee in action again, quite astounding really, they didn't have a chance. A Banshee with a powerful conduit, not to be messed with.'

They all looked at the daemon as he sat atop Banshin, wide eyed, apparently innocent.

'How much did you know?' asked Necarius.

'Rules are rules,' came the inevitable answer.

'What I don't get,' said Candera, 'and please remember, I have the utmost respect for your mother, is how did she know how to mobilise all that magic spontaneously. We have had years of practice.'

'She was surrounded by magic users for all her adult life,' said Magins.

'Did we teach her that much?' asked Candera.

There was a pause.

'Berin,' said Morovius.

'Berin?' asked Candera.

'Yeah, Berin. For four years before I went to school Berin taught me the basics of magic through my mother. My earliest memories are of Berin talking to my mother and her telling me about magic, how it worked, how to use it, how to fireball.'

'She'd have been a fool not to have learnt a lot,' said Candera, 'and your mother is no fool.'

'Yeah,' laughed Morovius. 'He taught me but he also taught a Banshee.'

They looked down at Enraefem and Banshin's prone form.

'Let's get Banshin out of here. We have a burial to arrange,' said Morovius.

'They'll want his armour,' said Magins. 'Some new young warrior will need it.'

'The cycle of life,' said Necarius.

They all took one of Banshin's limbs and carried him away, Enraefem perched upon him. Occasionally, a tear would roll down a face. Their friend was gone, never to return. When they reached the Eldaran lines, they put his slumped body over Magins's horse. Due to his impressive size, no one else could ride the horse, so Magins sat with Morovius on his steed. The party made their way back to Bleddin.

They reached their barracks and striped their friend's corpse, working the damaged chain mail out of his wound and leaving it on the floor. They dressed him in his usual civilian attire and finally put his tunic with the green circle of Eldara on him.

Enraefem began to fade. He appeared to be clinging to this plane, reluctant to leave Banshin behind, but go he must. 'Don't forget to evoke me for the funeral,' he told Necarius 'or I'll have your gonads.'

The friends grinned. 'Bye 'Raef,' they said.

They buried Banshin the next day. The authorities wanted a grand funeral, to say goodbye to the member of the heroic pod who had saved Eldara. The friends weren't sure, after all, they hardly knew the Eldarans, none could call him a friend. All those who did know him well, apart from his pod, had been killed by the Banshee. They went to Belinda for advice.

'I hate to be harsh,' she said, 'but it's not going to make much difference to Banshin. He really doesn't need some grand heroic funeral and I don't think you need to see crowds gawking at your grief. Let's keep it simple.'

'Mum, I don't think they'll allow it. They seem quite determined to have a great event.'

'Well, if we just go and bury him they can't do shit. Tell them to build a big statue or something.'

So, they agreed to take Banshin's corpse out of the city that night and bury him in no man's land. It was where he belonged. He was not really a Marcovian or an Eldaran, none of them were. No man's land, that is where his body belonged. No stone would mark his grave, if the Eldarans wanted a memorial, so be it, they could commission a statue.

Necarius evoked Enraefem and the young men began digging Banshin's final resting place. They placed Banshin in the hole and looked down upon the well built, comely young man. A dreamer, a man who knew nothing about quitting, who didn't care about the odds – a friend.

'Should we say anything?' asked Morovius, when they had filled the hole.

There was a pause. Everyone looked at Enraefem. Surely, he could think of something.

'You were awesome. You were my friend. I shall never forget you,' said the daemon.

That would do, it would have to. You just have to accept that at events like this you always think of the best thing to say later. Each of them, one by one, repeated the daemon's words.

And so it was, that Enraefem, Magins, Necarius, Morovius, Candera and Belinda said goodbye to their friend.

The next morning two guards came for Banshin's corpse for the arranged state funeral.

'Go and build him a statue,' Morovius told the guard. 'We've already buried him. Here's his armour.'

Morovius handed over Banshin's chain mail armour. The guards felt that it was best to be diplomatic and left. That is why there is to this day, a statue in Bleddin to a tall, well built magic warrior in the main park, his chain mail unrepaired, the damage to his left side untouched, a sign to all of how this great warrior had died. Flowers and written prayers are put in the gap, the prayers sure to be answered by God as this saintly knight intercedes on the petitioner's behalf. Legends are told, novels are written about chivalry and gallantry and the willingness of this, the greatest of warriors, to sacrifice all for God and the right cause.

Preparations were being made for the march on Bogloris. Supplies were amassed to prepare for a possible siege. Messengers were sent abroad promising that King Alphonse merely wanted a peaceful reunification of the lands, there would be no pillaging. Yes, there would be new Lords and knights, most of them Eldaran, but how could it be otherwise? The Marcovian nobility had been wiped out.

Rumours and speculation abounded in Marcovia. What would happen now? They had always been told that the Eldarans were savages. How could they possibly hope for a fair deal? Bogloris prepared for a siege. Supplies were brought in from the surrounding countryside. Tradesmen did a roaring trade and everyone equipped themselves for the inevitable Eldaran invasion.

Across the countryside there was consternation. If the Marcovian Lords and knights had been so vicious, what could they expect from the Eldarans, foreigners with an unsurpassed reputation for committing atrocities? If life had been hard under the Marcovian nobility, how much harder would it be under the Eldarans, who cared little for Marcovian traditions and customs?

Under these conditions, the refrain was whispered across the countryside.

'The Banshee is peasant.'

'The Banshee is peasant.'

'The Banshee is peasant.'

The speculation continued. If the Banshee was peasant, would she stand up for them, would she ensure that the Eldarans behaved or would she be their new oppressor? Was it a lie? Was there hope?

The Eldaran army began its march out of Bleddin and across no man's land. No man's land had been cleaned up. All armour had been stripped from corpses, needed for the next generation of soldiers. The crows had taken care of the meat from the dead soldiers, leaving only clean, pristine bone to ornament the scenery.

King Alphonse, Rincin, Cender and Belinda atop her Anrac led the army. Behind them were the magic users, the magic warriors in the lead, some holding up pennants with Banshin's name written in bold letters. Following behind were the ten Lords, each leading their division of knights and soldiers. Most of the rabble were missing as they were needed to cultivate the Lords' lands.

They continued their march down through the main thoroughfare towards Bogloris. The surrounding countryside was utterly deserted, the local population terrified of the invading army. An eerie silence surrounded the land broken only by the odd songbird proclaiming his territory and the clanking of troops.

The marching army approached Bogloris, its drawbridge raised, the odd head of a guard visible over the ramparts. The Eldaran army took its position as Alphonse raised an arm to call a halt. They waited. What were they going to do? Sieges were long drawn out affairs, they would have to blockade the city, stopping all goods from entering, fire mages would begin a three hour daily bombardment of its thick walls whilst sappers tried to undermine the foundations from beneath. Deceased animals would be catapulted into the city, ultimately disease and starvation would bring the city to its knees and force it to agree to terms of surrender.

'Ma'am,' Alphonse turned to Belinda, 'what can we do? We have no option but to lay siege. We will have to burn the local countryside to ensure no supplies enter the city. I know you want me to act like a gentleman and you know I want a smooth reunification of the lands, but we have no option but to lay siege.'

Belinda said nothing. She just nodded. She stood up upon Melissa's back and started to invoke her black magic. There was a sharp intake of breath, here was a Banshee in action. Black smoke swirled around her and she began to rise, jet black hair flowing amongst the black magic smoke. She continued upwards, above all the men until she was level with the top of the castle wall.

''Lil Tommy Hutchins, don't think I can't see you behind that helm. You always were a stubborn git but I swear if you don't open that drawbridge straight away, I'm going to tell your mother.'

By the time Belinda floated back onto Melissa's back, the drawbridge was beginning to be lowered.

'Thank you, Ma'am,' said Alphonse.

'You're welcome.'

The Eldaran army began its triumphant march into Bogloris. Around them people stood silently, staring at them, worried looks on their faces. Alphonse made straight towards the central park. The magic warriors accompanied him, the rest of the troops stayed outside to allow the population to assemble within.

People crammed into the park, curious to see what would happen, but also to see the famed Banshee, she who only a short while ago had been a peasant Auntie. Flanked by Belinda, Rincin and Cender, Alphonse began his speech.

'I have no doubt you have heard tales of the great barbarity of the Eldarans. Let me tell you, similar tales were told in Eldara of the atrocious Marcovians. But, I ask you this, what evidence do you have? We have invaded today, I ask you, what atrocities have we committed? My men stand patiently by, gentlemanly, well behaved behind me and outside the park.

'Do you see monsters bent on rape and pillage? Look at them. Don't you see men who look familiar? Troops like the troops you normally see in Bogloris, don't you see the same type of magic users you have always seen in these streets, don't you see Lords and knights, exactly the same as you have always seen?

'We are no different to you. We are one. We have always been one until that day when war broke out and our great Kingdom was split asunder.

'Today, that Kingdom has been reunited. We are not conquerors, we are uniters. We are here to make one glorious kingdom for all its inhabitants. Rejoice for peace has descended upon our lands, no man's land will no longer be a battleground, it will be a play area for those with magical abilities. It will be an area where healers can cure the worst afflicted amongst us.

'I ask you to forget the past, it has gone. Let us look forward to the future. In the spirit of goodwill and to show our true intentions, we are not going to call this new Kingdom Eldara. No, for we are not conquerors, we are unifiers. The new Kingdom will be called Eldovia. It will have two huge provinces, Eldara and Marcovia.

'This is a new beginning, a peaceful beginning, a new start for a bright future.

'Thank you for listening to me.'

There was quiet applause and then it grew louder. The war was over. The Eldaran troops did indeed look no different to the Marcovians. Eldovia – it had a nice ring to it. Things would continue as normal, just without war. Maybe, just maybe, this could be the resolution all had hoped for.

But if the townsfolk were relatively, if somewhat cautiously happy, the peasants were not.
'The Banshee is peasant.'
'The Banshee is peasant.'
'The Banshee is peasant.'
But what is our life, the burden of endless toil, the rich taking our produce, the onerous laws which always seem to find against the peasant? How can we live with vassalage, tieing us to one Lord or knight's land for our entire lives?

It started in Rufus's old estate. There was a rabble rouser called Mortuus. He kept arguing and peasants listened.

'Look, the best we can hope for is that nothing changes. But, is that enough? We will still be exploited, working endlessly while the Lords and Ladies play. They say the Banshee is peasant. Let her prove it. Let us show them we will not tolerate the old ways. Rufus is dead, King Almein is dead, the Marcovian magic users are dead. The Eldarans say they want peace. Let us show them the peace we want. Let us show them that the old ways cannot continue.'

The peasants followed Mortuus up to the Manor House where servants and Rufus's widow resided. The servants fled leaving a timid Lady waiting for the horde which assailed her. And assail her they did. They found her huddled in a cupboard and began to beat her, raining blow upon blow, all the class hatred which had built up over the centuries being meted out upon her prone form. At some point she died and they did not stop.

They went for the records, ransacking the mansion, destroying any they could find. The records which recorded all the laws of the land, the laws which lay down in stone how they should be exploited, how much produce they should give the landowner, their names, all written down, condemning them to a lifetime's servitude on this estate.

News spread of Mortuus's rebellion and others began to rise up. It was sporadic and unpredictable, but always the same. Destroy the records, the writings of lawyers and accountants was devil's work, proof of the binds that bound them. The first step to freedom lay in destroying the records.

The unrest began to spill over into Eldara. Some of the Lords left the victory celebrations in Bogloris to return to their lands to try to restore order, but it was usually too late. The records were destroyed, some disgruntled peasants even left their lands to find a better future elsewhere, all proof of their vassalage to a particular land destroyed.

Alphonse called an emergency meeting of the few Lords and knights left in Bogloris, Cender, Rincin and Belinda. 'What are we going to do?' he asked. 'Anarchy stalks the land. This should be a time of peace, but only chaos beckons. Particularly in Marcovia, virtually the entire landed gentry has been wiped out. All we have fought for could be lost.'

'What do you expect?' asked Belinda. 'You have treated the peasants worse than dogs. You need to offer hope, all you have offered is more of the same.'

'But, how can things change?' asked Rincin. 'The peasants must work the land. Without food we are all finished.'

There was a pause.

Eventually, Cender said, 'Everyone needs a stake in the system, Your Majesty.'

'A say,' said Belinda.

'Peasants have something to say?' asked Alphonse incredulously.

'Yes,' said Belinda.

'How can we listen?' asked Rincin. 'How can we gauge their feelings? What do they really want?'

'It would take a genius to work this one out,' said Cender. 'Seems to me that war and fear of the foreigner has kept everyone in check. Now that the war is over, the main method of control is gone. With the end of the Marcovian nobility, all control is gone.'

Alphonse looked at Belinda. 'I know you are peasant, but we are going to have to resort to repression, we have to put this revolt down. We need order, we cannot have this state of anarchy.'

'A genius,' said Belinda.

'What?' asked Alphonse.

'Cender said we need a genius. There is a man who has worked with the peasantry, who has moved through the corridors of power, who knows how things work. I know such a man. He can write a new Constitution for a new world, a world where all can have hope.'

'Who can such a man be?' asked Alphonse.

Belinda smiled. Cender and Rincin knew what she would say.

'The Assessor.'

'Where is he?' asked Alphonse.

'Funny really, he has retired,' said Belinda. 'Said he wanted a rest. He's retired to my old village of Ander. I shall go and see him. Meanwhile, send your messengers out, give the peasantry hope. Say there will be a new Constitution, a new way forward. Tell them the Banshee is going to see the Assessor.'

Belinda walked out of the room and made her way to her Anrac.

The Banshee began her journey to see the Assessor.

CHAPTER 29

Candera looked at his friends. Necarius was beginning to develop the humped back typical of necromancers due to his contact with the Netherworld.

'Necarius, can you evoke Enraefem? I have something I want to tell you all.'

Necarius did as requested and was greeted with the inevitable, 'Hiya.'

'Guys, I've been thinking,' said Candera. 'All this talk of a new world and the peasants saying they will not be ruled in the old way has made me think about my position.

'The thing is I never asked to be a soldier. I'm a healer, I have a great gift, why should it be used for war? All sorts of people need healing all over the land. Even King Alphonse said that healers should be helping others in no man's land.

'So, I've decided I'm going to become a hermit.'

'A bloody hermit!' said Magins. 'Why that's ludicrous, you'll be all alone.'

'I'll see the people I heal.'

'Still, you'll get lonely,' said Morovius.

'Well, I might eventually get married and have some kids.'

'So, you're going to be a hermit, who sees loads of people and has a wife and kids,' said Magins. 'Not much of a bloody hermit.'

'I'll live in a hut.'

'What, a small hut with a wife and kids?' asked Magins.

'I'll build extensions.'

'You really haven't thought this through,' said Morovius. 'You'll be the most sociable hermit ever, living in a large hut.'

'OK, OK, maybe I haven't quite worked out all the complexities of being a hermit, but I have decided to leave the army. It's not for me, it's not what I'm built for. I just want to be a healer.'

'This isn't about the whole Orken thing, is it?' asked Magins. 'These things happen. Besides, he would eventually have tried to kill us with Flavin.'

'That's a factor, but it's the whole war thing. I'm just not cut out for it. The whole army, 'Yes, Sir', 'No, Sir,' nonsense. It's not for me.'

'How will you survive?' asked Morovius.

'I'll charge for healing. The richer you are, the more you pay.'

They looked at Candera, straining to think of any argument that would make him stay but they knew him too well. He was the least warlike amongst them. They could see him in his hut, with suitable extensions, a family around him, helping the sick and wounded. It made sense.

'I'm going to miss you, terribly,' said Enraefem.

'You can visit. I'm only going to build a hut in no man's land.'

'It won't be the same,' said Morovius.

The pod was breaking up. Banshin was dead and now Candera was leaving. The other three considered their options.

'I'm staying,' said Morovius. 'Army life is all I know.'

'You are one helluva fire mage,' said Magins.

'I'm not so sure about that. What with Mum cavorting about the countryside, I am reduced to being a normal fire mage.'

'That's true,' said Candera, 'but you are still needed in the army. All the Marcovian magic users are dead and the Eldarans were severely depleted in the Battle of the Failing Shields.'

'There are just the youngsters coming through,' said Magins.

They looked at one another. There was one last matter to sort out before Candera left. They agreed on a plan of action and made their way to the magic school in Bogloris. They knocked on Novus's door and were asked to enter.

'Oh,' said Novus when they entered. 'I thought I might see you lot.'

'Yes, Novus,' said Morovius. 'It's us. We've come to discuss all those wonderful childhood memories that you've left us.'

'What do you mean?'

'What we mean,' said Magins, 'is that you are a cowardly sadistic piece of shit. There is something wrong with you. What sort of man gets his kicks out of hitting little boys?'

'I prepared you to become warriors.'

'Not good enough,' said Necarius. 'You are a sadist and we are here to stop you.'

'Make it quick,' Novus said.

'No, Novus,' said Candera. 'We just want you to retire and have nothing to do with children ever again. Just leave all the kids alone.'

'Is that it?' asked Novus.

'Yes,' said Morovius.

'Not a problem. Never liked the little gits anyway. Any reason to retire is good news as far as I'm concerned. Now, you can leave.'

'I'm serious, Novus,' said Morovius. 'If we find you anywhere near children, we'll kill you.'

'I'm sure you would,' agreed Novus. 'Now, you can leave.'

They walked out of Novus's office. They came to a fork in the main road. To the left, lay the barracks and to the right, the main thoroughfare to no man's land.

'So, this is it,' said Magins.

'I'm afraid so,' said Candera. 'I'm sorry guys, army life just isn't for me.'

'All right,' said Morovius. 'I accept that, we'll call around.'

'Many missings for you,' said Enraefem.

'You look after yourself,' said Magins.

'You're awesome,' said Enraefem.

They each in turn gave Candera a hug, Enraefem hanging onto his leg. The time of parting had come. Candera walked down the right hand side of the fork. His friends watched him go until they could see him no more. Slowly, Morovius, Magins, Necarius and Enraefem made their way back to the Barracks to await what army life had in store. For once, even Magins and Enraefem were quiet.

It was an ending.

The peasants kept on revolting. It was not uniform, but there was a general desire to destroy all records. Most estates experienced little bloodshed, just a demand for all the records which were then promptly burned.

The knight Bentham, the sole remaining representative of the old Marcovian nobility was no exception. His peasants got together and approached him. Bentham was quietly shitting himself and looked anxiously at Ledine.

'I don't like this,' he said.

'It doesn't look good.'

'I've only got thirty peasants but that's enough to cause serious injury.'

'What are you going to do?'

'I shall beg for mercy.'

Bentham stood ready to do some begging as his peasants approached.

'Bentham,' said the small peasant whose eyeballs Bentham had previously threatened, 'we want all the records.'

'The what?' asked Bentham.

'The records, all the records. Our names, the lists which keep us in perpetual servitude. The laws which govern our oppression.'

'That might prove difficult,' said Bentham.

'Why? Don't you go stalling us. We are in no mood for your games.'

'I haven't got any.'

'What?'

'Records. Never actually got around to keeping any.'

There was a momentary silence.

'Bentham, you're a shit knight.'

'Well, if record keeping is a sign of a good knight, I'm not that good.'

'He can ride a horse,' said Ledine.

'There is that,' agreed Bentham.

'Well, we don't want any more crap and oppression,' said the small peasant.

'Fair enough,' agreed Bentham, wondering what he had done now. 'What exactly do you want?'

'To be treated well.'

'Come on guys,' said Ledine. 'Bentham isn't a bad Boss. He even works alongside us in the fields.'

There were some nods of agreement.

'He said he was going to put a sharp stick in my eyeball.'

'Ah, that old chestnut,' said Bentham. 'I thought that might come up. I'm very sorry, I beg forgiveness, I shall never threaten to poke anyone's eye with a sharp stick again.'

There was some murmuring and nods of assent.

'Right,' said Bentham. 'Anything else you want?'

They could think of nothing, just warned Bentham to continue being a good Boss, stop threatening people with sticks and walked away.

'That went rather well,' said Ledine.

'Bloody brilliantly, if you ask me,' said Bentham. 'Ledine, feel like an ale?'

'Sure.'

'I need one. My nerves are shot.'

Belinda continued her journey to the Assessor. Peasants lined the way, cheering her on. Questions were shouted at her.

'What should we do?'

'What will happen?'

'What can the Assessor do to help?'

Eventually, she reached a large clearing and stopped. She dismounted from her Anrac and said she would make a statement. She waited for one hour while the peasants amassed in front of her. The grass had the bright green vitality of Spring and the trees were crowned with green buds ready to burst into life. Songbirds sang loudly, trying to attract a mate to their territory.

'Peasants,' she started, 'you ask many questions and I have but few answers. Firstly, I am peasant, always have been, always will be. I want what is best for our class.'

There was cheering.

'But, I am not a politician, nor am I a great thinker. As you know, I am on my way to the Assessor. He is a great thinker, if anyone can devise a new Constitution where all have their rightful place in peace and dignity, it is him.

'Now, far be it to tell you what to do. I can understand and feel your anger. But, I think we need to show some restraint. Yes, destroy all records, this is essential, destroy the old ropes that bind us, but watch the violence. The Lords and knights who oppressed you are dead. What do you gain by destruction, by killing, by attacking Manor Houses? How can this help our cause?

'Maybe I am wrong, but I cannot see how this can help us. Just make sure that all records are destroyed. Now, are there any demands you want me to make of the Assessor?'

'End vassalage,' someone cried out. 'We should be able to live wherever we want.'

'Yeah,' cried another.

'But, who will work the land?' asked Belinda.

Mortuus walked up. 'Oh, we'll still work the land, but as free men and women. Let our produce be our own.'

'Then how shall the Lords and knights live?' asked Belinda.

'Rent,' replied Mortuus. 'Already some exist and exist very well by charging rent for the land they own. They rent out the land at reasonable rates, we sell our produce and pay the rent. Already, there are a few Lords who do that. They can help us to develop the land but ultimately we want to be free.'

'Another thing,' said another peasant. 'Why should we have to harvest the Lord's demesne for free when our crops need the most care? If a Lord needs a demesne, let him hire labour. There are plenty of landless poor who need the work. He can hire them. End vassalage.'

'This seems fair,' said Belinda. 'I shall discuss it with the Assessor. Until then please show restraint. Just make sure you destroy all the records.'

'We want a say in what goes on,' shouted another peasant.

'Yes, yes,' went up the cry.

'Why is it only Lords and Ladies are listened to? Why won't the King listen to us?'

'A say,' repeated Belinda. 'Yes. I'll have to ask the Assessor about that. Let us build a new world.'

The peasants started chanting, 'A new world.'

'A new world.'

'A new world.'

Belinda climbed back onto Melissa and went on her way. Talk of what she had said rebounded across the whole of Eldovia. Violence diminished as long as all records were handed over. Bonfires of the hated paperwork, littered the countryside, lighting up the Spring nights.

Eventually, Belinda made her way to Ander, the village she had left so long ago as a timid young single mother. The Assessor and Markus had seen her coming and were waiting for her outside the Inn. Belinda approached them along the dirt track which constituted Ander's only road.

'So, you've retired,' she said.

'That's what I hoped, but I've heard that you have a job for me.'

'Rather an important job. We need a Constitution, a new way forward, a fair deal for all.'

'You do realise I cannot create Heaven. I'm not God.'

'You can ban the worst aspects of vassalage. You have heard the peasant's demands.'

'I have. No one living in the countryside can be ignorant of their grievances.'

'Vassalage, vassalage, it has to end. Why, it is hardly better than slavery.'

'They want to pay rent,' said the Assessor.

'Exactly, let the Lords live on rents. Some already do. Why should anyone be confined to an estate just because he was born there? If the Lords want their land cultivated let them pay decent wages or charge reasonable rents.'

'This could be arranged. After all, as you said, there are already one or two Lords who live on rents. I think I can work something out. Now, what is this talk about giving the peasantry a say?'

'We want a say. We want a system where the peasants aren't just ignored but can express their desires and wants to the King.'

'Now, that is going to be difficult.'

'You're the Assessor. Think of something.'

'There'll have to be top peasants or representatives. Peasants appointed to gauge the mood of the countryside.'

'Look, peasants work the land. We all want the land to be productive, all of us for the good of all Eldovia. Write your Constitution, convince the Lords that listening to the peasants occasionally is no bad thing. It could even improve productivity.'

'I can manage that.'

'So, it's settled.'

'Not quite, what about the old records preserving the old ways.'

'They are being destroyed.'

'Make sure they all are. It is far easier to bring about the new when the old has been destroyed.'

'So, we are agreed?'

'Not quite. Payment.'

'I have gold.'

'One last thing. I do all this work, get you your Constitution. How do I know I'm not wasting my time? How do I know it will be implemented?'

'The peasants have risen up, the nobility will listen to them and I swear to you, if they do not, they'll damn well listen to me.'

The Assessor looked thoughtful as he took the gold. 'Your terms are acceptable,' he said.

Belinda was about to go, but there was one last thing she needed to ask.

'Assessor?'

'Yes.'

'All those years ago, when you threatened to hurt my baby. If I hadn't cooperated, would you have done so?'

The Assessor took one step forward and stared deeply into the Banshee's dark brown eyes.

'Of course. I am not used to failure and I don't intend starting now.'

The Banshee felt a deep anger surge within her. Swirls of black magic began to form around her body. Her hands began to move. She looked across as Marcus stepped forward, hand on the hilt of his sword, ready to defend his Boss whatever the odds might be.

Belinda smiled, the black magic dissipated.

'Just make sure it's in the Constitution that magical babies can stay with their mothers.'

She nodded her head and using her mind meld with her Anrac, turned and rode away.

The Assessor and Markus watched her ride into the distance, her jet black hair flowing behind her.

'So, that's a Banshee,' the Assessor said.

'Indeed so, Sir,' said Markus.

'Impressive woman.'

'I thought so, Sir.'

'There she was, under our noses, all those years.'

'Indeed, Sir.'

'Ha, funny that, they never suspected.'

'Neither did you, Sir.'

'Oh, I didn't fail. I did my job. My job was to assess babies and infants, not grown women. It was their job to spot her.'

'Of course, Sir.'

They stood there watching as the Banshee disappeared into the distance.

'You know, Marcus.'

'Yes Sir?'

'I expected the Banshee to be, well, how can I put this, a bit more intimidating.'

'Sir, if she had been any more intimidating, I'd have pissed myself.'

The Assessor looked at Marcus.

'Bladder control, Marcus, bladder control. It's all about bladder control.'

CHAPTER 30

The Assessor sat looking at a blank piece of paper.

'Ah, well, all great works start with nothing,' he said to Markus.

'Yes, Sir.'

'Let me see.' The Assessor dipped his quill into a bottle of ink. 'You need a grand opening. All Constitutions have that. Means nothing, but what the hell, it's what people expect.' He started to write.

'In all great Kingdoms and none come greater than our newly formed Eldovia, each must have his place and a stake in society. Outmoded forms of oppression must be abandoned, each must have a say and each should know his place, working hard for the greater good of all.'

The Assessor paused. The Lords might not like that too much, but there is the bit about each having his place, that should keep them happy. If not, the Banshee can deal with it.

'A well functioning society is like a good watch. The parts are different, but they all work in harmony with one another, each fulfilling his role, each an expert in his own right, all working towards a common goal. In our great Kingdom of Eldovia, we all work towards that common good, towards a new found harmony and peace, towards a well functioning society.'

The Assessor looked around. Well, that was easy enough. Now for the nitty gritty, the stuff about rents and so on. Then there was the headache of giving the peasants a say, that wasn't going to be easy. The Assessor stared out of the window.

'Everything all right, Sir?' asked Marcus.

'Yeah, we have a start. Tell me Marcus, why did you retire here with me? I am no longer in authority, I am no longer the Assessor. You could have gone anywhere.'

'My place is by your side, Sir.'

'Thank you, Marcus.'

Marcus nodded.

'Marcus, you are the closest thing I have ever had to a friend.'

Marcus started. 'Why, thank you Sir.'

'I have a name Marcus. I would be grateful if you would call me by it from now on. My name is Andrew.'

'Of course, Sir.'

'Markus.'

'I mean, of course, Andrew.'

'Now Marcus, we need some alcohol. What do they have at the Inn?'

'Mead, Andrew.'

'Of course.'

'Actually two types of mead.'

'Really, two types?'

'Yes, regular and superior.'

'What is it about the one that makes it superior?'

'Not really sure. It does come in a fancy bottle.'

'Of course it does. Would you be so kind as to get four bottles of superior mead.'

'Of course, Andrew.'

Markus started to walk off but Andrew stopped him.

'I say Marcus, I envisage a problem. Perhaps you can help.'

'Yes, what is it?'

'We have a lot of work to do. Now let us say we drink two bottles of mead each and need some more. I am concerned that you might get lost on the way to the Inn as it will be dark and you will be slightly addled.'

'Sir, I mean Andrew, there is only one street in Ander and the Inn is the only significant building but after two bottles of superior mead, the chances of me losing my bearings are rather good.'

'Can you think of a solution?'

'Shall I get six bottles?'

'Make it eight.'

Marcus set off to obtain the mead, the superior kind. His friend looked around his hut and smiled. So, it had come to this.

Andrew sat in the peasant hut, tapping his delicately manicured fingers on his knee.

EPILOGUE

The Lord Bentham and his knight, Ledine, sat in his well tended Estate. Topiaries surrounded them, each expertly pruned into the shape of a beast. The Anrac was the Lord Bentham's favourite. He took another gulp of ale. Bentham and Ledine were quietly getting sozzled.

'You know,' said Ledine, 'I get that you're a Lord now and I'm a knight and you're my liege Lord and all.'

'Great, isn't it?'

'Marvellous, absolutely marvellous. You now control all of Dinran's lands, living in Manning's castle and well, I reside in Cedric's mansion. All rather good.'

'Positively spiffing. Couldn't have asked for more.'

'Right, well, I get all that, but this is the thing I don't get.'

'What's that?'

'Did we lose the war, or what?'

'Oh, we lost. Got absolutely hammered. The Banshee took care of that.'

'So, how did we get promoted?'

'Well, there was a kind of a shortage. The Banshee killed all the Marcovian Lords and knights apart from yours truly. The old Eldaran ranks were a bit depleted anyway. They needed a Lord and a knight and we were there.'

'So, they were desperate.'

'In a manner of speaking, yes. By the way, how's the horse riding coming on?'

'Not great.'

'Been practising?'

'A little, well a bit, you know how it is.'

'Yep, you should try to get the hang of it. Kinda important to being a knight, that whole horse riding lark.'

'Yeah, I'll give it another go tomorrow. How's the record keeping going? Got new records in place?'

'Not as such. Been a bit lax there. Way I see it, the ol' peasantry aren't too keen on records. Why upset them?'

'Why indeed? Thing is, I still find it odd. You a Lord and me a knight.'

'Well, we observed the most important rule in warfare.'

'Really? What is that?'

'Stay alive. We stayed alive.'

The two friends laughed, clinked mugs and continued drinking ale, lots of ale.

Printed in Great Britain
by Amazon

17571225R00312